AFTER

the

RAINS

AFTER

— *the* —

RAINS

EMILY BARROSO

Matador
5 Weir Road
Kibworth Beauchamp
Leicester LE8 0LQ, UK
Tel: (+44) 116 279 2299
Fax: (+44) 116 279 2277
Email: books@troubador.co.uk
Web: www.troubador.co.uk/matador

ISBN 978 1848766 846

British Library Cataloguing in Publication Data.
A catalogue record for this book is available from the British Library.

Typeset in 11pt Aldine401 BT Roman by Troubador Publishing Ltd, Leicester, UK
Printed and bound in the UK by TJ International, Padstow, Cornwall

Matador is an imprint of Troubador Publishing Ltd

This book is dedicated to my son Luca

1976

Rhodesia,
Eastern Highlands

1.

Time floats on hot afternoons like this. Birds are silent, their claws melded to branches like twigs, and the dogs nap in the shade. Up here, our white-washed, tin-roofed house sits splat on the side of the purple mountains that stretch all the way through the Eastern highlands of Rhodesia to Mozambique. Underneath the avocado tree, us Camerons climb into the Simca. Dad tries to start the choky engine.

'Shit man,' Dad wipes the sweat from his forehead and tries again. The engine splutters at us, but then goes back to sleep.

'Everyone out,' sighs Dad.

'Ag, no man, Dad,' us three kids say.

'Out,' Dad says again.

Mom puts her uzi on the floor of the passenger seat as she gets out of the car.

'I hope the safety's on,' Dad says to her back as he tries to start the engine again.

'I said out man! Chop-chop!'

Us kids get out and arrange ourselves along the back of the car in our usual way. The sun slaps us on our backs. We place our hands on the back of the car and start pushing. John falls over and says 'shit' and soon we are laughing more than pushing. Soon Dad is yelling. This makes us hose ourselves even more. Mom laughs too.

'For pity's sake,' Irene, I'm trying to get us to the farm and you're behaving like the bloody kids.' Dad half gets out of the car and glares at Mom.

'Pity's sake,' John says.

Mom starts up again, bending over the back of the car 'til her forehead hits the bodywork. When she raises her head, her forehead is smeared with red soil. None of us can stop laughing. Sometimes laughing just grabs you and whips you away, like the wind, and doesn't put you down again for a while, not until the laughter has become a painful, quiet clutching at your throat and an aching in your chest.

'We're going to miss the convoy.' Dad shouts. Not laughing or smiling.

We stop the laughing and give the car the biggest push it's ever known. The car splutters and jumps a little and then makes its way down the dirt track, leaving us behind in a cloud of red dust. It stops at the gate and waits for us, chugging, like a dog wagging its tail, for one of us to open the cattle gate. Mom ends up doing it, us kids are already fighting for space on the back seat. Carla pinches John's leg to make him move up and John gives me a Chinese burn.

'What did I do?' I ask, 'It was Carla.'

Carla laughs and John gives her a lamie on the top of her arm. Carla digs her freshly painted orange nails into John's thigh. He screams.

'It wasn't that sore,' Carla laughs.

'It bloody, was. Mum!' John wails as Mom gets into the car. Mom sits down on the gun.

'For crying in a bucket, Irene, do you want to blow your arse off?' says Dad. 'Look where you're sitting man.'

Us kids laugh so much that John pisses himself for all of us.

Dad is fiddling with the radio. A minute passes. 'Dave, are we going? I thought we were in a hurry?' says Mom.

'Ja, when are we going Dad?' says Carla.

'Turn it up Dad,' I shout, as *Money, Money, Money* starts up on Radio Jacaranda. I imagine Agnetha and Frieda in their hot-pants: blue satin for Agnetha (my favourite), green satin for Frieda. In my head, they stand on stage, back to back, towering above millions of hysterical fans, in their platform boots. The lights flash and whizz round. Bjorn is playing the guitar like a lunatic. Benny is pounding the piano. Agnetha is wiggling her bum. Frieda smiles but still manages to look pissed off because she's not as sexy as Agnetha. Carla, Mom and I all start singing, 'Ain't it sad, Dad?' I yell.

Dad laughs and joins in, singing in a baritone comedy voice.

We stop singing one by one, Dad first, then Mom, then Carla and then, reluctantly, me. Outside my window, the msasa tree leaves are red and yellow and orange and look like fire on the sides of the hills.

We are approaching the fork in the road where we are going to meet up with the others in the convoy. The Gaylards and the Mackintoshes from local farms are already at the meeting point, a turn off with a toilet block and braai area, along with various neighbours in various cars. Mike Mackintosh leans against his bakkie, one foot behind him on the tyre. He is talking to Pete Gaylard who is smoking. Pete and Mike are both wearing shorts with checked short-sleeved shirts and veldskoens with socks up to their knees. His Kingsgate cigarettes stick out of the pocket over his chest. Their wives sit in their bakkies with their kids, lying around in the covered back section. Pete's girls look like boys, all with short hair. They jump out the back of the bakkie to go to the toilet block. All three are wearing shorts. 'I think they wanted sons,' Mom says, lighting a cigarette and waving at Mrs Gaylard.

'About bloody time, Cameron.' Mike flicks his cigarette into the road.

'Bloody car trouble,' Dad says, getting out of the car.

'Bring your bakkie man, no trouble.' Jan smiles at Dad and slaps his bakkie as if it were a prize mombie.

'Leave the cars for the women, what's the matter with you man?' Pete is laughing. Dad laughs back, even though it's not funny. Adults always do this. Their laughing sounds painful, like spoons scraping on metal bowls. Mom waves at fat Mary Gaylard, who is getting something out of the bakkie parked in front of us. Mary Gaylard looks just like her husband: brown hair, round brown eyes, blobby nose, but with a big bum.

'Are we going gentlemen?' Mom smiles at the two men even though she can't stand them.

Carla looks at me and rolls her eyes. Pete and Mike start looking around for gentlemen.

'Sorry can't see any,' Pete says. Mike cracks up. Dad doesn't. Mom sighs and runs a hand through her short hair. She catches my eye in the side mirror and winks.

Outside my window a concreted-in braaivleis has a piece of dried up old boerewors stuck to it that looks like a poo.

'When are we going?' John asks.

Carla sighs and raises a hand to admire her nail varnish. I make a clicking sound in the front of my mouth and fold my arms.

Dad starts up the engine as the other cars line up behind each other. As they do so, guns begin to poke out of the passenger side windows, a sign to the terrs that we are armed and dangerous, so they better not attack us. We drive for hundreds of k's. The bush looks dry and sharp, even the leaves, with everything tangling into each other. The trunks of the thorn trees are crispy grey, with thorns that are white as bones and can poke right through your foot. After a few hours, we slow down behind a bus loaded with Africans, their luggage tied to the roof. It's farting out clouds of smoke. We overtake and us kids stare up at the bus. The Africans are stuffed in. Some are standing. A woman with a baby on her lap stares at me in an unhappy way, so I smile at her but she does not smile back. Maybe she thinks I'm laughing at her, a thought that makes me uncomfortable. Not many Africans can afford cars, which doesn't seem fair. *That's just the way it is*, Bantam, Dad says. But why is that the way it is? We drive a bit further and slow down again. Footprints are stamped in the dust on the side of the road. Some look like tackie prints, others are large, bare-foot prints. I wonder who they belong to. Is the owner of those feet in the bush, watching us, tracking us? The Christmas beetles are screaming so loudly it is like a hum in the back of your head. After a while, a loud rumbling sound can be heard behind us.

'Check! Check! It's a Crocodile!' John shouts, waving out the back window at the armoured troop carrier.

Carla and I look out the back window. Soldiers' arms, some with FN rifles, angle out from the little windows on the side of the covered heavy-armoured vehicle.

'Check their guns man!' John says. 'It's like a robot box on a lorry. With bars over the top.'

'Honey-comb shaped in the front,' Carla says.

'A long, hexagonal shape,' I say.

'Ja. It's brilliant,' Dad says. 'Rhodesian ingenuity. We have come up with some brilliant vehicles man and we've stuffed sanctions up the…'

'Leave the description out in front of the kids Dave,' Mom says.

'Up the nostrils of the Poms, the Yanks and the rest of the – what rhymes with Yanks Irene? World?'

'World does not rhyme with Yanks, Dad,' John says.

'Well how about Yankers,' Dad says winking at Mom.

'Ja, John says. Stuff the Yankers up.'

'They won't Yank our country from us,' I say, biting the skin around my right thumb nail.

'Sis man, don't eat yourself Jayne,' Carla says.

'Ja. You not a cannibal,' John says.

'Might be. This might be the first stage,' I tell John and start on the skin around my pinkie.

Carla sighs and lifts her ballet-supple leg up to the roof of the car and points her toe. If she could, she would write the word 'boredom' on the ripped ceiling of the car.

'That's enough John,' Mom sighs. She takes a drag of her cigarette, then she holds it up in her right hand like a model posing in a magazine, which is quite funny because she has a gun in her other hand. The Crocodile overtakes us, followed by other army vehicles. Carla stops stretching her legs, flicks her hair, arches her back, smiles and waves out the window. It's quite a show, I tell you. John leans over her legs to wave and she pushes his head down, but he keeps wriggling free and popping back up like a jack-in-the-box. It's quite a comedy. The convoy slows down and the Rhodesian soldiers wave and whistle.

Up ahead guns are being raised out of the windows of our convoy in salute to the army guys.

'The one in the shades was good-looking,' Carla says, settling back into her seat. Did you see Mom?'

'Nah. She only has eyes for me,' Dad says, giving the thumbs up to the final truck in the passing convoy. 'Hey Irene?'

Mom rolls her eyes at Dad and squeezes his leg.

After the excitement of the army vehicles, us kids sleep for a while and when I wake up the landscape has changed into grassy veld. Grasses rise higher and greener and umbrella-thorn trees crop their flattened green tops here and there on the plain. Gigantic, prehistoric balancing rocks, some with lichen stains like poured icing, blob up here and there. We pass the thick black heavy shape of a baobab tree, like some monster's head, sitting on the earth, but looking as if it's just risen out of the sea, its stubby branches sticking upwards like shocked dreadlocks. In the crevices of the huge trunk, I see darker shapes, grooves that could be eyes, knobbly parts that could be noses, ears, anything: like watching the puffy shapes of clouds, only darker, scarier. This is not a tree I would like to climb. There are no clouds in this bright blue sky. For a while the cars are spread out a bit and the Du Plessis' green Renault station wagon in front of us seems far off, but then we come in close enough to see the sun glinting off the back fender. I can see the rifle that Mrs Du Plessis' unseen hands are holding poking out of the passenger window up ahead. I'd like to have a go on it. I've only ever shot an uzi apart from revolvers and stuff. Automatics are much more fun. No one is speaking. Dad is concentrating on the road. Mom is holding the gun up out of the window as if there is someone there and she has just said "stick-em-up!" She looks as though she should have another gun in her other hand. She rests the gun on the outside of the car, just in front of her window, near to the roof of the car. I can see it juddering out of the corner of my left eye. Mom's face is sleepy in her side mirror. Dad is concentrating on the road. Next to me, Carla has her eyes shut. John is staring out the window, into the bush on the right hand side of the road, where he sits behind Dad. As I watch his eyes go half mast, roll a bit and then the lids shut down and he's out. The back of Dad's neck is sunburnt a deep reddish brown from where his neck sticks up from his t-shirt. He is very still, his neck looks stiff. The world rolls slowly by outside the window, like a khaki-coloured film. A mozzie has managed to get into the car. It hovers above us kids in the back, and then it moves near Mom and Dad in the front. Dad becomes aware of its slow whine. Suddenly Dad slaps his leg, at the same time there is a loud crack as Mom fires a shot into the air. The Du Plessis in front of us slam on their brakes. So does Dad. We all jolt forward. My senses scatter like spilt pins.

Dad is leaning out of the car. 'Irene's gun! An accident,' he shouts out the window to the Du Plessis' car up ahead. 'It's okay!'

He gets back in. Mom is saying, 'I'm sorry, Dave.'

Us kids are in shock.

Still sleepy, John is asking, 'Was that the terrs, Mom?'

'How could you be so bloody stupid Irene?' Dad yells. 'If there are any terrs in that bush, they know all about us now.'

Imagine them, hiding in the bush, laughing at us. I look down at my hands. They are jumping up and down on my legs, and are wet with sweat.

'Can we just go, quickly,' Carla looks pale, her thin fingers press into Dad's seat.

John urges: 'Yes, let's go, now Dad.'

Mom reaches behind to touch John's leg. 'It's all right love. Go back to sleep,' she says.

Just go back to sleep hey? For sure ek se. Dad is looking at Mom, like he expects some kind of explanation.

'They've moved off again Dave, please,' Mom looks at Dad.

I cannot see her face, only the side of it, the white skin of her cheek, the black hair curling under her ear. Imagine breaking down here, on the road, the convoy not noticing, just driving off and leaving us, the cars getting smaller and smaller, till they vanish. Leaving us Camerons, in our Simca, with our small gun, that goes off when Dad slaps his leg to kill a mozzie.

We drive off. I look down at the grey tarmac of the road. No footprints here. Carla and John are staring ahead like they are trying to make the car go faster. No one says anything until we get to the turn off to the farm road, where we wave goodbye to the rest of the convoy; and then we all start at once, like birds in a cage.

'Jeez, that was scary,' says John.

'Ja, Mom, you should go for lessons,' says Carla.

Everyone laughs as we approach the huge metal gates with their razor wire bending outwards. The bush presses up against the electric fence that surrounds the hundred-and-fifty-acre tobacco farm where Dad grew up. Dad calls this farm 'our farm' even though his brother, Uncle Pat owns it now and we live on great Granny Rose's farm, which to me is 'our farm,' because it was the land our family first settled soon after Southern Rhodesia was founded. Auntie Nessie says the Africans didn't know their land was lost until the Europeans found it. But Dad just laughs and calls her a bloody communist. Now there is a war over this land. I don't see why we can't share it all out equally, but Mom says it's more complicated than that when there is an economy to run and this economy runs mostly on tobacco and tea I think. Dad hoots and Solomon comes running in his bare feet, his white work clothes all crisply ironed by Josephina.

As we drive through the gates, Dad shouts, 'Howzit Solomon!' out of the window as he drives past. Us kids shout 'Howzit Solomon!' out the window. Solomon smiles and waves a hand in the air before locking the gates. As we drive up the long driveway, everyone is laughing. Josephina, Uncle Pat and Auntie Gail's house girl, is peeling potatoes onto newspaper on the polished red cement steps in front of the kitchen door.

'Hello Medem, Baas,' she says to Mom and Dad, as we walk to the front of the L shaped house. When she looks back down at the potato in her hand she pulls her lip up at the side and raises one eyebrow, which my Auntie Aldie would say is cheeky.

'Hi Josephina!' I yell, slamming the car door.

'Yesie Jayne,' she says and waves her peeler in the air and smiles at me.

Family and friends from neighbouring farms are sitting and smoking and drinking on the long front veranda that runs the length of the front of the house. A kidney-shaped pool is positioned in front of a patio that curves around the right-angle of the house. A group of mostly men stand on the patio with bottles of Castle or Lion lager. The women sit on the veranda in their cotton print dresses, their faces brown and creased from the sun. Some of them have rifles propped against their chairs. The meshed security gates around the low walls of the veranda make it look like a metal cage. They have been left open for the day despite the recent terrorist attacks in this area.

Uncle Pat gets up from the veranda and comes to greet us. The pool is soon occupied by my cousins, sixteen-year-old Neil and thirteen-year-old Anthony and a girl around my age who is shrieking loudly as they splash her. Anthony gets out of the pool and then runs back into it, holding his legs up to his chest as he bombs into it again, sending the water sky high. A little boy wearing orange water wings is playing on the wide, shallow pool steps. He stamps in the water and blinks in surprise when the water hits him in the face. A woman wearing shorts and a green flower-patterned halter-neck top sits on the edge of the pool, with her feet in the water. She takes a swig from a brown beer bottle and then goes back to looking bored and staring straight ahead of her. Maybe she's having an affair and thinking of the guy. Mom says in wars everyone has affairs. *Except you,* Dad says. Uncle Pat is handing Mom and Dad beers on the veranda. Deciding to avoid the adults for a while, before they start droning on about the war and which farm got hit this time, I walk off down the sloping lawn away from the house. At the bottom of the vast expanse of lime-green lawn, Auntie Gail is playing tennis with friends from the neighbouring farm, and a man I do not recognise who is wearing blue-belted shorts and no shirt. He must be from England. Auntie Gail is wearing a very short, very white tennis skirt, her muscular brown legs scissor on the tennis court as she runs from one side to the other, thwacking the ball across the net; as she does so, she lets out a sound that would make you think she, and not the ball is being hit. On the left side of the tennis court is a moonflower tree. The fragrance of the big ivory flowers wafts over to me on the heat. Suddenly I have a headache. I feel overloaded with perfume and heat. Thwack, goes the ball, hit by the man in the blue shorts. I feel the sound in the front of my head. I flick off my yellow and red Bata slops and sit down on the lawn, looking beyond the tennis court, to where the lawn gives way to scrubby yellow grass, interspersed with longer grass, as if it has given up trying to be green or tamed. There are black mambas in that grass, which sometimes take the chickens. Beyond this wilder grassy area the electric fence looms as a warning, and beyond that the acres of tobacco stretch away from the farmhouse as far as the eye can see.

'Howzit Jay. Wanna come swimming? Come and get a drink,' Anthony says. He is dripping from the pool, his blonde hair water-dark. I try not to look at the little point in the centre of his slick-black speedo.

'Can you get me a Coke?' I ask. 'I'll wait by the pool.'

'Ja. Okay.'

I get up and walk over to the pool, pulling my t-shirt and shorts off as I go. I've already got my dark-green cozzie on.

Anthony eyes my chest which is no different to his. 'How old you now?'

'Eleven.' Pervo.

I sit down on the cold, greenish-grey dolphin at the far side of the pool and put my hand out in front of its mouth where the water gushes into the pool, enjoying the pressure of the jet of water in my open palm.

Solomon is pouring coal onto the braai, which is really a sliced-in-half petrol drum propped up on makeshift metal legs. On the table next to the braai, he has placed platters of steak and wors ready to braai. Josephina is bringing out a huge bowl of potato salad with slices of egg on top. She is wearing a blue tunic over her dress, on her feet she wears worn white tackies, trodden down on the heel parts. The men are beginning to gather round the braai. Solomon, who has been trying to light the braai, pours some petrol on it. Suddenly huge flames leap up at him, he jumps back laughing, 'Eweh!'

'Are you penga Solomon?' Uncle Pat is walking towards the braai with a big smile on his face. He is with Mannie the mechanic.

'Trying to braai your face Solomon?' Mannie laughs, pouring beer from his bottle onto the steaks. I hope he doesn't backwash.

'Aikona, boss, aikona,' Solomon wipes his eyes with the back of his hand then shakes his head and carries on laughing.

'We'll take over now, Solomon. Get us some more Castles please,' says Uncle Pat, waving his beer bottle at him.

Anthony comes over to the dolphin and hands me a Coke. 'You're not supposed to ride that you know,' he says. Ignoring him

I tip the Coke bottle back to swig and see the base of the bottle scrape the sky, feeling the fizz in the back of my throat.

In the pool John and some other kid are floating on red lilos in the turquoise water. The braai smells nice, steak with beer poured over it, sizzling nicely. Coils of wors, their skins splitting, spit their juices onto the coal below. Lekker, I can't wait.

I'm pushed quickly from behind. I manage a half-dive as I fall into the pool. I can't believe I've fallen for this again. Neil always does this to me. I surface just as Neil and Anthony are bombing into the pool. A teenage girl stands near the pool looking worried.

'Jump in before they push you,' I say trying to be helpful.

At that moment there is a loud, eerie siren wail. Us lot in the pool look confused. Neil pulls at his nose and mouth, checking for snot. Anthony shakes his head like a dog, trying to unblock his ears.

'Shit,' he says. For a second everyone is in freeze-frame.

Suddenly there is chaos.

'Everyone inside!' Uncle Pat starts running, beer bottle in hand.

'Out of the pool! Inside!' he shouts, as he runs towards the veranda. He begins slamming the wire security windows shut and padlocking them.

Mom runs towards us. 'Get out!' she shrieks at us as she splashes down the steps, fully-clothed. She hauls John out of the pool by his arm. We all get out of the pool and run inside. As we run onto the veranda, Uncle Pat is already holding the heavy chain, ready to lock the gates. I feel sick, like before a race, only worse. Some of the guests lie down under the huge carved dining-room table opposite the lounge. We follow Dad and Uncle Pat into the lounge. In the dark interior, chunky leather furniture from Barlow's fills the room. There is a huge yellow-wood coffee-table and a redbrick fireplace. Above it a copper-faced clock chimes the hour, on its surface, grazing elephants, inked in black. In the right hand corner, on a huge leather pouffe, is a television, its aerial forms a 'v' sign. We stand in the lounge in a clump, us Camerons and the neighbouring farmers and their wives, Mannie the mechanic and the guy in the blue shorts, still with no shirt on.

'Get on the floor, you know the drill!' Dad shouts as he walks through the lounge to the annexe where Uncle Pat is already shouting into the radio, trying to alert the security forces. I can't see Mom, and then I realise she is already lying on the floor on her front, one arm around John and one around the other kid who was in the pool with him. Auntie Gail sits down on the couch and puts her arm around her tennis partner who is going, 'Oh my God.'

Carla and I lie down on our fronts. Carla puts her arm around me.

'Do you think we're going to die? Shall we pray?' I whisper to her.

'Ja, but do it in your head,' Carla whispers back.

'Do what in my head?'

There is a pounding in my head. My hands are slippery, my mouth is dry. I think of the stories people have told of angels surrounding mission bases in the bush during terrorist attacks. I wonder if there really are angels and if there really is a heaven and wish I hadn't joked around so much in Sunday school. And then I know there is. When I shut my eyes I can see a big handsome golden angel, about seven feet tall, with huge, bright-white wings. The slow steady drone of a plane flying overhead cuts through my thoughts and the vision of the angel disappears. I wonder if it's going to drop a bomb on us. And then I remember. The terrs are finally here. We're going to get shot. We're all going to die. It will be our farm on the front pages this time. At least we'll all die together.

Mannie and Neil are checking that all the doors and windows are bolted. We can hear Uncle Pat on the radio. 'Alpha bravo? This is red seven...we're under attack...shit.'

'I don't know if they heard, it's just crackling,' Uncle Pat says to Dad.

Suddenly Gail shouts, 'Solomon and Josephina! Pat! Solomon and Josephina!'

'You're thinking about the Afs at a time like this?' A plump woman I don't recognize says in an English accent. She is squeezed into a sundress with huge blue flowers on it. 'They probably tipped them off.'

'For goodness sake,' says Mom. Her voice sounds funny.

The Poms are always the worst racialists.

'Get down on the floor Gail,' Uncle Pat shouts at his wife on the couch.

'I'm not getting down on the floor like a dog. If they're going to get me, I'm going to be sitting right here, on the couch,' says Gail, running a hand through her wavy iron-grey hair.

'For goodness sake, Gail, you're scaring the children,' Mom says.

'Shut-up Gail, if you wanna sit on the couch, sit on the couch, just keep it down man,' Uncle Pat shouts again. 'It's not a bloody cocktail party.'

On the other side of the room leaning against the wall by the edge of the window, his gun raised like a cop from some American film, is the man who was playing tennis with Auntie Gail.

'The dogs. Where are the dogs? Why aren't they barking?' Auntie Gail asks the air in front of her.

'They've probably poisoned them,' says the plump woman.

'If you don't shut up I'll shoot you,' says Dad as he walks past with his FN rifle. A man who is also holding a gun says, 'Yes. Shut it Barbara.' He must be her husband.

The woman sits up. 'Where did you get that gun Bob?'

'Lie down woman. Or you might have your bloody head blown off.'

The woman lies down and starts to wail.

I start to laugh. Then I laugh so much I think I'm going to piss myself. Carla slaps me.

'Don't get hysterical, Jay.'

'You deserved that. It's not bloody funny,' says Neil who is crouching behind us with a rifle.

I don't mind about the slap. People get weird. Time goes funny.

Suddenly the clock in the hallway chimes the hour. Everyone jumps and the plump woman screams. Dad, Uncle Pat, and Mannie the mechanic, plus the man who must be the plump woman's wife rush into the room followed by Josephina.

'What the bloody hell's going on in here?' Uncle Pat and Dad shout at us, both at the same time. Again this makes me laugh. This time I can't stop. My body is shuddering. Carla slaps me again, this time on the arm, which makes me laugh more.

'We're going to go out and have a look,' says Dad.

'Please don't, Dad.' Carla begins to cry.

'Don't go with them Bob!' the plump woman says to her husband who is standing next to Dad. He has a red face.

'Shut up Barbara,' the man says, then looks at Dad, which makes me want to laugh again.

'Neil, Mannie and Frank (so that's the name of the man in the blue shorts) will stay with you.'

Frank still has the revolver raised like he's a cut-out of Clint Eastwood, he's not moving. I wonder if he will move if he has to.

'Irene, where's the revolver?' Dad asks Mom.

'I don't know. With my handbag.'

'Where's your bloody handbag? Get the gun Irene,' says Dad.

'You get it,' Mom screams, gesturing towards an armchair with her handbag on it. Her gun lies between the loops of her bag. John is quiet. Dad hands Mom the gun. Mom doesn't take it. He shoves it across the floor at her, it spins and hits John's arm just as the plump lady, Barbara, jumps up onto her knees and begins to make a kind of screamy crying noise and pulls at her yellow hair that looks like short doll's hair. She looks crazy. We all stare at her.

'Pull yourself together,' Mom says. 'Just get your head down for goodness sake.'

'We are armed, and there are plenty of us,' Uncle Pat says calmly while Barbara rolls around on the floor. He looks from Mom to Auntie Gail, who is still sitting on the couch with her arm round her tennis partner. Josephina is sitting down on the far end of the couch, away from Auntie Gail. It's quite funny, Josephina would never usually sit next to Gail on the couch.

Josephina turns to look at Auntie Gail: 'Hondo, hondo,' she says. And then she begins turning her head from side to side. Sweat gleams on her skin beneath the red scarf.

'Yes, Josephina. Hondo,' Auntie Gail replies. 'Bloody war.'

Josephina keeps turning her head from side to side, clucking with her tongue.

'Where are the dogs? Why aren't they barking?' Auntie Gail asks.

Everyone knows that terrs poison dogs before they attack. My ears are ringing from listening for the sounds of the attack and I wonder if we have died and gone to hell. Maybe we will stay like this forever, trapped, on the floor, waiting for Dad to come back. I close my eyes and try to make the angel come back. Carla's nails are digging into my hand. And then Carla and I scream. A dark face has appeared at the window, where the man in the blue shorts is sitting. Holding his revolver with both hands, Frank shoots at him, shattering the glass of the window. The face disappears from view.

'Ai, ai, ai, aiee!' Josephina wails, 'Solomon! Solomon!'

'I think you just shot Solomon,' Auntie Gail says.

'Well, if I have, he's a bloody fool to appear at the window like that,' Frank says. The end of his gun is smoking. A thin trickle of blood runs down his left cheek. Auntie Gail leaps up to help him. She dabs at his cheek with a pink tissue from her pocket.

'It's only glass cuts,' she says and then she starts to laugh.

'Shut up Mom,' says Neil, from behind us.

Auntie Gail continues to laugh. Her shoulders are shaking and her make-up is streaked across her face.

'The dogs are at the vets,' she says. She turns to her tennis friend. 'The dogs are at the vets,' she says again. 'Getting their shots. How could I forget?'

'Oh, yes,' says Neil. 'How did we forget?'

And then we jump again, as Dad, Uncle Pat and Mannie walk into the room. Uncle Pat holds up a small, grey vervet monkey. Its pink tongue pokes out of its blackened mouth, baring its useless teeth. Its hair looks stiff and bristled from the electric shock that killed it.

'Here's our terrorist,' says Uncle Pat.

'You shot Solomon,' Dad says to Frank. 'Just a graze. I'm taking him to the clinic.' Get Irene and Gail and the ladies a stiff one. And the girls too.' Dad smiles at us.

I jump up. 'I'm coming with you Dad!'

'Not this time, Bantam,' Dad says.

Auntie Gail collapses onto the couch still smiling and shaking her head. Josephina runs out of the room. The rest of us sit up. We look blankly at each other, and think of the monkey, climbing the fence and getting the shock of its death.

2.

Back home, at Angel's Peak, Enoch and I send lucky beans flying into space far above the valley from a rocky overhang beyond the workers compound. Heat ripples above the valley. The bush covering the hills looks like green peppercorns on a canvas tablecloth over a giant's knees. Enoch's wearing a vest that hasn't seen the Omo for a while and a pair of blue shorts that have seen the rounds. He stands up and throws a bean wider than I could, even if my arm was made of Dunlop rubber. He laughs when he clocks my wow face, spits on his palms, rubs them together and flings another. It spins in a high arc above the mountains. Happy with himself, he sits down and puts a handful of lucky beans on the smooth rock, his long fingers spacing them out.

'These ones have muti inside that can kill you.' He holds up a lucky bean between his thumb and forefinger as if it's a diamond

'Oh ja? How?' The red bean with its black eye does look magical.

'First you must break, boil and then if you drink –' He clutches his neck with both hands. 'You can die.'

'Okay. I'll just make necklaces out of them then.'

Enoch laughs, tipping his head back and opening his mouth wide. Then he points his forefinger up and taps it on his temple. 'But also, they can make muti for healing. The bark can be make for the old people to walk better.' He hunches over like an old madala, one hand on his back, his short forehead wrinkling up.

'Oh,' I laugh, 'for joint pain. So the bark is better than the bite of the seeds,' I smile, happy with my joke.

'Yes and the leaf – this one can be good for tooth pain,' he says ignoring my joke and tapping on his jaw.

'Wow, that's good,' I say. 'A tree that can kill or heal.'

'For sure. You can burn the bark and put in the wound to make better.' He sits down and leans back on his elbows, his big toe skimming the sky as he bounces his leg up and down.

Two goats are pulling at the tufts of long grass under a thorn tree. One stares at Enoch with yellow eyes, its jaws moving sideways.

'They don't believe you,' I say.

'Ah, this one, these are my dead uncles.'

'What?' I sit up straight.

'For sure, my mother, she curse them and now they are goats.'

'Ja. For sure,' I laugh, pulling my legs up so my bare heels are on the hot bum polished rock. 'She may be a witchdoctor but she's not God. She can't turn people into animals.'

He widens his eyes and leans his head closer to mine as he speaks so I can see my tiny head reflected in his black eyes. 'For sure, she is nganga. She can do it.' He jabs his thumb in the direction of his mother's medicine hut, halfway across the dusty compound behind us. He doesn't laugh which is a bit freaky, so I look down at my toes, and then lift up a foot towards a fat cloud floating over the valley that looks like a sheep, legs and all.

'Let's play 'kick the sheep,' I say, kicking my legs up at the clouds.

He looks at me and shakes his head very seriously and says, 'This is too much stupid.' Then he bursts out laughing. I laugh too, but I feel too much stupid.

A story will impress him.

'Enoch? D'you know the one about the tortoise and the hare?' I watch the pulse on the dip of his temple where his frizzy hair straightens out a bit.

'This tortoise, he can be faster than the hare?' he says, sitting up. 'I know, but you tell me.' He settles back onto the rock raising his heels so his knees stick up on either side of his ears. When I finish telling him the story, he says,

'You are the hare, I am the tortoise.'

'Why?'

'Because you think you are clever, because you can throw thing at me, but then, you fall out of tree, so you are not so clever.' He laughs and shakes his head. 'You can be dead on the ground!' he raises his eyebrows at me. 'And now you can be slow.' He slaps his leg, he thinks it's such a hose.

'Ha! Ha! Ja, Enoch, that was an accident,' I say remembering how I fell out of the lucky bean tree after surprising him with a missile attack.

'Aikona, nothing is an accident.' Enoch laughs, his smile strapped on from ear to ear, across his big even teeth. Africans always have nice teeth. John says it's because they drink milk and blood mixed together. *Sis man, it makes me feel sick.* I don't believe him anyway and I don't want to ask Enoch if it's true. I look at Enoch a bit longer than I normally would. Any further and his wide apart eyes would be like a chameleon's, but they are still this side of pretty. His long lashes are just like a zebra's, but his chin is like an action man doll's. He doesn't look like his mom, with her freaky tribal face scars and her hard narrow eyes. I don't remember if he looks like his father, he left ages ago to work on my uncle's farm. That was before my Auntie Penny died in the shooting accident. Anyway, criminals are supposed to have mean faces, not pretty eyes and round cheekbones like little hills. I get up. 'I've got to get back before dark.'

Above the valley, something catches my eye.

'Check! Enoch! An eagle!'

The eagle swoops and then hovers, his dark wings slicing through the air.

'Look! There it is!' I say as the eagle swoops down again, the air rippling through the feathers at the edges of its wings.

This time he sees it.

'I am born under this one. This eagle can protect me.' He pulls his long legs up, coiling his thin arms around them, his huge feet flapping over the valley.

'I don't need an eagle to protect me. I can look after myself,' I say, beginning to walk away.

He raises an eyebrow at me, then the left side of his mouth as if the eyebrow is pulling up the mouth.

'You are a girl. You need a boy or a man to protect you,' he says through his laughter.

'Ja, for sure,' I shout sarcastically over my shoulder.

'You come later. I show you something!' he shouts back at me.

On the way back over the compound I circle round the goats and avoid the medicine hut. Enoch's laughter follows me. When I get to the far edge of the compound I stop near the lucky bean tree that I fell out of yesterday and turn to look behind me. The nganga is walking through the bush across the dirt road that winds up from the base of the valley. She has a cardboard box on her head with Surf printed on it. Maybe there's freaky stuff in there. I hear her shout something to Enoch and he stands up quick. In the cool shade of the wattle trees that divide our property from the compound I'm imagining Enoch in his little two-roomed house with his scary mother. Our big white house surrounded by rose bushes appears between the trees. The only similarity between our houses is that we both sleep under tin roofs that creak like madala's knees.

In a back bend, I scope the trees beyond the lawn out back. I can't see him, so I come out of my bridge and head over the back lawn towards the trees. A shot almost clips my left ear and then Enoch's long brown leg appears from behind a wattle tree, followed by the rest of him laughing. Digging another stone from his pocket, he puts it into the sling and aims another shot only slightly above my head. When I duck he laughs.

'Huh I scare you,' he jabs a finger at me.

'You'd be scared if I did it to you,' I say hands on hips. Then I get embarrassed because my dress is still tucked into my pants from the back bends and he's looking.

'Never. I can never be scare of one girl.'

'Oh ja? Give me the sling.' I grab at it.

He holds it above his head. I lunge at it.

'You have legs like a giraffe,' he says laughing, 'so you catch.' He jumps, flinging the slingshot in the air.

'Shut up man,' I say, catching it. 'Go stand by that tree,' I say, bending to look for ammo.

He half cartwheels, half jumps over to the spot I indicate with my head. Enoch likes showing off like this, especially because I can only do straight cartwheels. *Thwuck, thwuck, thwuck* the slingshot sings through the air above my head. He closes his eyes.

'Keep your eyes open man.'

I try again. Again he closes his eyes, only this time he dances his torso from side to side, his arms waving around like an Indian dancer.

'If you don't keep your eyes open how can we check whether you're going to duck?'

'Still I may duck with my eyes close. Still I know the stone must come,' he says lifting one leg out sideways as he continues his dance.

'That's cheating man Enoch,' I say trying not to laugh.

'No it's clever,' he laughs, opening one eye and still dancing his arms around.

'Very funny.' I swing and let go, aiming the stone about a foot above his head. He keeps his eyes closed and doesn't jump. He carries on laughing too.

'You can laugh but I'll get you another time.'

'Aikona,' he laughs, shaking his head. Then he stands up and with a serious face, he says, 'You scare?'

'No. I'm not scared of anything,' I lie.

'Oh yes?' he leans his face close to mine so I can smell his baked bread breath smell. 'Come.' He pulls me by the wrist.

I follow him through the trees and down the sun-hot path to the compound yard.

'You can let go you know man.'

'No if I let go you can run.'

'I won't I'm not a chicken.'

'Yes, but after. You can be chicken.'

'Where are you taking me? Oh no ways man, I'm not going into that freaky medicine hut.'

I try to pull my wrist away but Enoch just laughs and drags me past several thatched huts, the heels of my tackies skidding in the dust as I try and use them as brakes. He doesn't let go of my wrist until we are outside the grass door of the nganga's medicine hut. Last year John ran in here, but ran out screaming just as quickly.

No bloody wonder. He said he saw a baboon in there. *True's fact, the nganga was talking to a baboon, me and Nakai ran out of there so fast our legs went round like in the cartoons.* Enoch twists my arm till it burns. A little kid in a long t-shirt and zero pants stares at me, holding a half-chewed mealie cob and then runs inside one of the huts.

'Owie! Let go man.'

Enoch laughs and grips even tighter, pulling me inside the hut. The grass door flaps behind us. Inside it's dark and smells of stale cooking fire smoke, and the vomity aroma of Chibuku beer. Light slices through the thatch roof, animal and bird bones sway slowly from the rafters. In the space between the top of the hut wall and the rafters holding up the thatch, a lizard appears for an instant and then is gone in the flick of a tail. Something is crouching in the corner of the hut. For a moment I think it's a leopard and leap back towards the door, making Enoch laugh a laugh that hangs above us in the dusty thatch. Then the crouching figure gets up onto her haunches and I realise it's the nganga. She's wearing leopard skin over a black and red African print wrap. She barks out a command which makes me jump. I feel really scared of this witchdoctor who makes muti for ladies to have babies, or to get revenge on their neighbour for a mombie dying.

'My mother says sit down. Now!' He pulls me by the hand onto a plastic mat. It feels scratchy and hard against my bare legs.

She shuffles closer, still on her haunches. I can't stop looking at her, I've never seen her this close. She has a wide face and jaw, with rounded cheekbones and long narrow-shaped eyes. Her skin has a bluish-grey tint to it, and deep tribal slashes scar either side of her face, above and below her cheekbones. Her hair is twisted into long dreadlocks and bits of white and grey fuzz grow like roadside grass at her temples. I stop looking when I realise she is looking at me too. It feels like she can see all the way through my eyes, past my brain and through my skull straight out the door to where the chickens are pecking around in the dust and the kids are playing. Some of the Africans say that the nganga can hypnotise them. Maybe she hypnotised the leopard's coat right off its back.

The nganga throws the bones on to a piece of dirty cloth in front of her, rocking backwards and forwards, making guttural noises, her voice travelling up and down, up and down like it's going through rusty pipes. Suddenly she claps and shouts something at Enoch. Enoch laughs, tipping backwards, his legs in the air, but she shouts again and says something that cuts him laughing and makes him sit up straight. His mother points at the bones and carries on speaking.

'What's she doing?' I whisper to him.

'She's make muti,' he leans over so that I feel the spongy fuzz of his hair against my temple and smell its smoky smell.

'Who for?'

'For one man,' he whispers loudly, his neck extending towards me.

'Which man?'

'A man who wants to have many, many children,' he widens his eyes so the whites glow in the dark like slivers of moon.

'So? Why does he need muti?'

'For have children.'

The end of the animal-tail whip touches my knee when she swipes it over the bits on the mat. I wish it hadn't. It makes me feel as though I'm part of the spell. She says something quickly to me, her eyes look like they could cut their shapes out in my face. I ask Enoch what she's saying.

'She says, why do I play with the white girls? They will bring me trouble.'

'What else?'

'She says you won't camp here anymore.'

'What do you mean camp? I live here. I was born here. What else?'

The nganga yells out a load of other stuff.

'She says your father should pay tax for living on her land.'

'What? This is our land. My great Granny Rose bought it when she married Grandpa Patrick. Ask her, she's probably on the veranda painting right now.'

Enoch says something to his mother. He laughs.

'She says you cannot buy the land. This land cannot be bought.'

'Well we bought it.'

Enoch laughs, 'You ask, now you must receive,' he says leaping onto his feet and dusting off his shorts.

The nganga shouts something and I leap to my feet and shoot the hell out of there, like a baboon having stones thrown at his backside.

Outside the hut I stand blinking in the sunshine. Enoch's doubled over, hands clutching at himself, killing himself laughing.

3.

At school, during break time, Courtney's crocodile eyes creep around my face. I realise she didn't call me down here to the rugby pitch to be friendly. Jeez I'm slow.

'What?' I say, all Brando.

'Kaffir lover,' she says.

'I thought you had something to show me? One of your brother's snakes?'

She moves her face about two inches away from mine, her hot breath smells of old cabbage. I bet her spit is green.

'Who your friends?' Courtney asks.

The words come out all snotty. Her slit mouth is the size of a mean red eye, freckles cover her nose like splattered mud, and her nostrils are all crusty.

'Ja, who your friends?'

'Well, not these monkeys here.' I thumb Courtney's friends from 4C.

'Who are they?' I ask. 'Hear no evil, see no evil, speak no evil?'

My words scare me. Now I'm in for it.

She kicks me hard in the shin and my breath traps in my throat.

'I SAID! WHOOO YOUR FRIENDS!' Courtney yells, her face screwed up like a red cricket ball with dirt streaks. My kicked leg jumps like a puppet's. Far away the giant grumbly-belly echoes from the frowny sky. Maybe if it rains again now, the teachers will come out and ring the bell early.

'Oh,' I say, 'You mean, "Who are my friends?"'

'Ja, domkop, who your friends.'

'Well, if you'd told me you wanted to meet them, I'd have brought them with. There's Felicity and Samuel in my class –'

'I don't wanna know that! WHO YOUR FRIENDS?'

'Jeez, stop shouting man. Need some more? For your troop?' I look at her three friends who whisper to the side of us.

'Ja, she's got no frie-ends,' says the one with the blonde plaits. The other two giggle.

'You think you clever? Using a word like that – troop? Hey?'

'Troop is a common word, Courtney. You can look it up in the dictionary at home.' No wonder they're in C class. Thickos.

She kicks me again.

'Ja! Get her Courtney! Get her man!' the monkey-girls shout.

'Ja, but you got friends at home, hey? My friend told me.'

'Oh, you mean *Enoch*. Ja, Enoch's my friend. You wanna know about Enoch? You jealous?' My kicked leg shakes, the other one starts up too, like I'm in some kind of cartoon. The girls explode with laughter and a jagged streak of lightning flashes white into the inky sky.

'It's gonna rain,' I say.

'Who you, the witch doctor?' Monkey B shouts.

'You mean the rainmaker – the swikiro?' I bat back.

'You play with kaffirs, you speak kaffir.' Courtney spits, 'Kaffir lover.'

'Ja, you play with kaffirs, kaffir lover,' the girls chant.

'What's a "'kaffir?"' I ask them.

'Diiiir, a blek person, domkop,' says Monkey C.

'Er no, a 'kaffir' is an unbeliever. An unbeliever in God,' I say.

'Ja? Who you? A teacher? Kaffir lover!' Courtney yells in my face. Tiny speckles of spit fall on my left cheek. I wipe them off.

The bell rings. For once I'm glad.

'You love kaffirs! You love kaffirs!' The monkeys sing over their shoulders as they run towards the school buildings.

'Ja. And you've got kaffir lips!' Courtney shouts.

'Kaffir means 'unbeliever'!' I shout after them. Then I touch my too fat lips.

At home time, Auntie Nessie is waiting for me in the farm bakkie, which is a surprise because I didn't know she was coming down from Salisbury for the weekend. She waves at me from the other side of the road as I walk through the school gate. Nessie's a stare-at-me, raven-haired beauty queen in a man's shirt and jeans. I wrote that in a poem about her in school. In the dirt underneath the trees outside the school walls, John aims at a pile of marbles. Hooking my thumb and forefinger in my mouth, I whistle loudly. He waves at me to wait, turning back to his aim, and then he leaps up in a victory whoop, as the marbles scatter in the dirt. Grabbing his satchel, he comes running over, his black hair sticking up in front like toothbrush tufts.

'Did you check! Did you check? I got the goon! I got the goon!' his pond-green eyes swim wide.

He holds up the metal orb between his thumb and forefinger.

'Ja,' I say, 'nice one, hop in.'

He chucks his satchel in the back and gripping the side with his right hand, bolts into the back of the bakkie, yelling, 'Hi, Nessie!'

'Where's Mom?' I ask throwing my bag on the floor in front of the passenger seat.

'Mom's working late at the surgery this arvie, afternoon receptionist's got compassionate leave,' Nessie says. 'Her husband's been sacrificed to the Gods of War. Carla's got ballet, Dad's in the nurseries loving the tea-plants. Two days back from call-up and he's gone straight from shooting to planting.'

An image of Dad comes to mind, crouching in the bush, his FN firing at terrs. It seems unreal. I switch to thinking of him at home, being a farmer like he's supposed to.

'So how was school?'

'Thank God it's the holidays. I hate school. It's a school for fools.'

Auntie Nessie laughs and puts a bare tanned foot on the accelerator. She hardly ever wears shoes, unless she has to, putting them on to go to the bank and taking them off again straight after. Once, in Salisbury she was walking without her shoes on. Cars were hooting, and an old lady stopped a policeman to complain. *There's no law, surprisingly, that stipulates the wearing of shoes in this city*, she said.

Perhaps this woman would like to provide shoes for all these people round here to wear, and she pointed at the beggars sitting around outside the bank. True some of the beggars there don't even have legs, but some do. She's been asked by the principal of University College, where she teaches Sociology, to wear shoes when she's lecturing in class. *My ability to wear shoes, on occasion, has no bearing on my ability to teach this class.* Nessie hardly ever walks, she runs, from the car to the OK bazaars in Umtali, from her jeep when she pulls in to visit us at the farm, into the college buildings, or into the Standard Bank.

We're heading for the main road into town. Nessie drives fast around bends fringed with pine trees, planted by the Scottish settlers to remind them of home. The tips of the trees spike the clouds that are hanging as low as full nappies, and sunlight ripples like music through trees that seem to move in and out like they're part of a giant accordion.

'Ja. Penga school for penga people,' I say.

Nessie takes another sharp one. We laugh as our bodies are hauled to the left, then we swing back to the right. John whoops it up in the back.

'Already?' Nessie asks, 'Well, Jay-bird, you're gonna be institutionalised for a lot longer, so you better get used to it.'

'Ja, well, there's kids in my school that need to be institutionalised at Ingutsheni.'

Nessie smiles and shifts into second gear. John bashes on the roof from behind, revving up Nessie to take the bends sharper. He's taken off his blue and white striped tie and is lassoing it around like a cowboy in khaki shorts. I knock on the back window and his face appears upside down, forefingers hooked into the sides of his mouth. It's quite a hose. Nessie clocks him in the rear-view and laughs, her smile as wide as blue sky, her lips like the curved petals of flame-lilies.

'I know what you mean Jay,' she presses her foot on the brake, just as a lorry comes fast around the bend towards us. About ten African forestry workers in green overalls shout, whistle and wave. Nessie laughs and hoots at them.

'Half the government of this country should be institutionalised, or at least locked up till they see sense,' Nessie says. 'And the descent into madness starts at school.'

We laugh, but Nessie's comments make me jiggly inside.

'I'm starving,' I say. 'Can we stop in town for hot chips and ice-cream? From Dairy Den?'

'You're on,' Nessie winks an emerald eye at me and the sun chucks light spears off the bumper.

In the car outside Dairy Den, I lick quickly round the rim of my melting cone. Nessie smiles and lights up one of her stinky hand-rolled cigarettes that she doesn't smoke in front of Mom and Dad.

'Now we can all be happy,' she winks, exhaling, smiling and changing gear all at the same time.

We drive down grey tarmac shaded by jacaranda and flamboyant trees, past the park towards the mountain road. I imagine the hand of God, scooping up the town and spilling it into the valley where we are now. The first settler-town of Umtali died a death when the railway Cecil John Rhodes was building from Mozambique couldn't get through the mountains. Rhodes, roads, good name for an explorer.

The air in the car is hot and herbal. I wind my window down completely and the air cools and sweetens as we wind further and further up the mountains. Granite peaks rise up like prehistoric rhino rumps.

'So what happened today Jay? You gonna tell your favourite aunt?'

I watch the side of her face and listen to my voice as the words come out. Her long fingers flutter up to her mouth and the silvery ash floats down onto her jeans.

'They are the stupid ones, Jay. Anyone who uses words like 'kaffir' should have a lobotomy.'

'What's that?'

'When you have the rotten part of your brain cut out, like cutting away the bruised part of an apple. Three-quarters of the white population of this country need lobotomies. Don't worry Jay, you won't grow up like them hey? You can think for yourself. Just don't let the buggers get you down. It's easy to become,' she takes a hit of her rolled cigarette, 'conditioned.'

'But what do you mean, conditioned? Like brainwashed? And who are the buggers?'

'Those kids you go to school with. And their fathers,' she says taking a drag of her roll-up. 'And their fathers' fathers,' she says exhaling.

I look out the window thinking of Courtney's ugly father's father. As we drive through the granite mountains, I can see the stacked, purple-grey peaks of the mountains that we look out over from our veranda. Puffs of creamy cloud float above the mountains like fluffy hats. The sky is a lavender-blue. We drive higher past gnarled trees that stretch out of the rock like withered hands and pines that stand straight up from the rock like lookout soldiers, their green-gold tassels softly falling through the thin air.

Samantha and Brandy come skidding off the veranda as soon as we drive through the hibiscus hedge at the top of the twisty driveway. We pull up by the avocado tree near the back door. Samantha covers my uniform in cream and grey collie fur as she licks my face. John pats his thighs and Brandy jumps into his arms like a circus chimp, caramel-coloured ears flapping outwards like wings. John lets him lick his whole face like it's a dinner plate. The raincoats hanging and shotguns stacked just inside the backdoor look like sentries standing guard. Nessie flings the bakkie keys and her fringed leather handbag on the big wooden table.

'Let's see what the The Rhodesia Herald has ordered for us today,' she says, picking up the newspaper from the table. 'Another farm attack. What will it take hey?'

'For what?' I ask, looking at the newspaper over her shoulder. The terrorist leader, Joshua Nkomo stares up at me in black and white. He looks like an overfed baby. His smiling eyes have disappeared into his fat face. *He's as lethal as an unpinned grenade,* Dad says.

'For people to wake up,' Nessie says.

'To what?'

Down the page is a photo of a farmhouse sprayed with bullets and grenades. A bullet-hole has formed a large glass spider-web in a French door.

'To the fact that the war is not going to go away,' Nessie says reading.

A chair lies on its side a little distance from the house, like the wind's blown it there. The family smile out at me from the photograph. *Dead in their Beds*. Only one son survived because he was staying the night at a friend's.

Nessie looks further down the page. 'Hmm, Nkomo and Smith are still going round in circles.'

A tin bucket of fresh milk stands in the corner, little miggies floating on the top. *Extra protein*, Grandpa Patrick used to say to me when I was little. *Put hairs on your chest*. I never wanted hairs on my chest. Just no flies in my milk. I get ice out the chest-freezer in the pantry for cold cocoa.

'About what?' I ask, mixing cocoa and sugar.

'Oh, the little matter of black majority rule. Joshua Nkomo wants it, obviously, and he'll stop at nothing to get it. But our unfortunate PM is chasing his tail.'

'What do you mean?' I put ice in the glass, then grabbing a cup from a hook under the dresser, I dunk it in the milk and ladle it into the glass.

'Well, he knows it's going to happen eventually, but he's just trying to stave it off for as long as he can, and trying to kid us all in the process.'

'How can you say that Nessie?' I ask, running my finger over the condensation of my glass. The cold seeps into my fingers. I put the glass down and leave it there, with its little bubbles of milk popping and dying.

'Jayne,' she puts her hand on my arm as I turn to go out the back door, 'there are two sides to this story. There's a back story too. Don't be like the girls at school. If you don't keep an open mind, you could end up like them.'

Ja really. I wasn't born with kak for brains.

The corrugated iron roof of the tea-planting nursery is lit up gold on silver, flashing through the tea plantations that snuggle into the upper slopes of the mountains. Tea bushes are laid out like emerald green blankets and the air smells of soaked tea leaves. Green slopes blend into royal blue as they are swept up into the mountain peaks. From the slope on the dirt road, I can see the workers moving slowly through the waist high tea-trees. They look like tortoises standing on hind legs as they hold out their levelling rods to pick the top leaves from the bushes and fling them into baskets hanging from their backs. Moses stands head and shoulders above the rest of the workers. His voice is as deep as an African drum and his laugh sounds like distant thunder. Moses has been Dad's tea manager for over ten years now. He now has his own little tea plantation on land close to the compound, given to him by Dad when he married. He sells to the local tea factory for export, which Nessie says is progress.

'Hi Moses!' I shout.

Moses tips his hat at me, then turns and laughs and tips his head back at something a worker says, then he continues to walk up and down between the tea bushes, every now and again reaching out a hand to touch a leaf or a bud with his fingers.

In the nursery, Dad is planting out the clones that he cut from the mother bushes with Moses this morning. Radio Jacaranda is playing my favourite song about a man who's not afraid of being in love with a fat lady. Dad looks up at me from above a muddle of plastic pots.

'Howzit Bantam, come to help your old Dad? It's bloody hot hey?' He wipes his forehead with the back of his hand smearing his tanned face. With his dark hair and eyes, he looks like a Cherokee Indian with soil war paint.

'For sure, what do I do?'

He shows me how to gently lift the little cloned plant, harvested from the mother plant, from the plastic bag filled with soil. Its roots coil delicately.

'Look at those,' he says. 'They're fine, but determined. They'll suck the life out of this soil. Greedy little buggers.' The soil trickles through his splayed fingers. They'll be here for at least a year and then it'll be another two years till we get a yield.

'The best. Good mature soil. Seen a lot of life already.' He finishes sprinkling and patting in the upper layer.

'There. Do you think you can do that? Plant out eight and I'll call them Jayne's tea-bushes. Hell you might turn into an excellent-tasting brand all of your own.'

He stands up, and takes a sip of tea from the pottery mug I made him in art class.

'Well this beats running around with guns, hey Jayne?' he says.

'Or going to school,' I say.

'Well anything beats going to school, hey Bantam.'

'Especially since I have to go to school with domkops.'

'Not keen on domkops myself. Something happen today?'

Standing next to Dad at the trestle table, I tell him about Courtney, digging my fingers into the cool dark soil.

'Next time Courtney gives you hassle I reckon you paste her.'

'What do you mean paste her?'

'Thump her. Really hard right there, so she's winded. Like this.' He gives me a pretend upward hook under my ribcage.

'Why there?'

'No marks. If you deck her on the chin, you give her a trophy. If you thump her, and wind her, she'll never do it again.'

'Okay Dad, I'll try that next time.' I enjoy imagining her horror at my pasting her.

'She play hockey?' Dad asks.

'Ja.'

'Well next time you're burning it down the field, chasing the ball, trip her up. And make sure you bash her hard in the shin first.'

'And at half time I'll make sure I shove her orange quarter as far as possible into her mouth when she mouth-guards it in.'

'Show her how to wear it as a brace.'

We laugh.

'That'll probably help with her looks.' Dad laughs some more. 'Poor girl's been cloned from poor stock, she could use your help.'

We're totally hosing ourselves.

'Hey, Jay. Don't tell Mom. You know how she likes all that turning the other cheek stuff.'

'Ja, sugar stuff!'

Dad puts his arm round my shoulders as we walk out of the nursery. The sun is rubbing itself out against the sky, turning it shades of red.

4.

From the back step, I can hear sounds like a baboon barking mixed with boys laughing. I run over the back lawn and down to the wattle trees chop-chop. The baboon bark comes again, followed by something like the hiccupping sound of a hyena's laugh, and then I hear the chattering of a monkey. The tree I'm passing shakes and I look up to see John, the monkey, his bare feet curled round the branch he's standing on just like a monkey's hands, his face edged with a mane of leaves. He presses a finger to his lips. The hyena laugh comes again and I see Nakai stick his woolly head out from behind a tree trunk. He widens his eyes at me and then ducks out of sight again, the bush behind him thrashing then quivering.

'Can I play?' I whisper up at John.

'No. Shush.' He climbs higher up the tree.

The baboon bark comes again. John and Nakai reply with their monkey and hyena sounds. I laugh. Nakai sounds like a donkey being strangled.

'Shush', John says again. 'You'll ruin the game man.'

The ground vibrates. I duck behind John's tree.

Enoch comes along, kicking at bush, and poking his long stick at the trees.

I skirt round him, darting behind tree trunks, ducking under bush, trying to get behind him. He barks his baboon bark and Nakai and John reply with their animal sounds. Enoch heads in Nakai's direction. I decide to fool him by doing monkey sounds too, which makes him turn round for a moment.

The hyena sounds become giggling human sounds. Nakai can never keep a straight face and he's easily found.

'Ndeipi,' Enoch says to Nakai slapping his raised hand.

'Hapana sha,' Nakai replies shaking his head and laughing.

Enoch leads him still giggling from his hiding place. 'Hey, that's not fair.' Speak English!' John yells. 'Oh no man,' he adds, realising he's blown his cover.

'Domkop,' I say as he swings upside down from his branch. 'You're supposed to chatter not speak.'

'Shut up,' he says.

'Why not you speak our language? We always speak yours,' Enoch says, coming up underneath the tree and poking at John's bum with a stick. 'You are a monkey that speaks English.'

'All they said was what's up and nothing, John,' I say.

'So what? Kiss the kettle while it's hot,' John says.

Nakai taps his head to show he thinks we're penga. 'And now we can be tired, too many words to say nothing,' he laughs, putting his arm round Enoch's shoulder.

'You are a better monkey, Jayne. But so. I knew it was you,' Enoch says.

'Oh ja how? I followed you for ages.' I fold my arms.

'But who else makes a girl monkey sound?' he laughs.

'You are a girl monkey for sure!' Nakai laughs. But when I look at him he looks at the ground. His dimples are like two studs pinning up his smile.

'Come!' Enoch pokes me in the side with the stick. 'I will race you to the giant's face! And you monkey!' he waves the stick in John's direction. 'How fast can you climb the face on the mountain?' he says to John.

We race through the trees and out through the tall elephant grass, over the dirt road and through the bush till we reach the balancing rocks at the base of the Giant's Face. Enoch disappears along his secret way. He'll get there in two minutes flat. John's feet move quickly above and away from me, disturbing bits of stone and dust which get into my eyes, and I wish I was faster. As I near the top I look down. Nakai has already given up and is on the way home, slipping and sliding down between the rocks on his bum, grabbing at tufts of grass. The first time we saw him do this we nearly fell off the rock from hosing ourselves so much. John and Enoch have to pull me over the last bit, my legs dangling in the air while they haul me over the orange-oxidised rock, my tackies jabbed into footholds only centimetres wide, my hands all sweaty, partly because I'm scared of heights and partly because I'm scared Enoch'll find out I'm scared of heights.

We stand on the Giant's Head checking the view. No clouds in the purple sky. The workers in the tea-fields look like Lilliputians moving slowly through the bright green tea bushes growing out of the dark chocolate earth of the valley. In the east the mountains are lilac and hazy. Pine forests grow up the planes of the stacked mountains in the west, giving them jagged edges. Granite peaks rise up behind us. We lie down on the warm rocky slabs. The rain that fell like bath water this morning has soaked into the thirsty ground and the heat is no longer wet but dry and satisfying like the warmth of a fire. For a while we drift, the air on our faces smelling of plants. John and Enoch stand on the Giant's brow that juts out over the valley, their arms folded like little emperors.

'Now we are one with the mountain,' Enoch says.

John doesn't reply. He doesn't understand language like that.

'You know, eagles can look directly at the sun,' John says picking at the long grass that rises above his knees. 'They've got special eyes,' he says chewing the sweet green base of a grass stem.

'Ja. They specialize in looking at the sun,' I say leaning back on my elbows and glancing at the sun's burning eye.

Out of the corner of my eye I see a dassie dart behind a rock.

'Check!' John says getting his catty out of his pocket. 'See you guys later!'

I watch him crash through sun-dried fern, placing a stone in the leather cup hanging from the y-shaped catty, ready to make a dassie kill.

Enoch goes and sits on the edge of the precipice, dangling his legs. He might as well be sitting down for dinner.

'Here we can see all over Africa,' he crosses his legs and leans back on his arms. 'It belongs to us. We can be like kings,' he says, tipping his head back to catch my eye. 'We don't need to think anymore. Even you Jayne. You can be a king. But not over there.'

He gets up and opens his arms wide, just as a sharp gust of wind buffets our exposed part of the mountain. He laughs and swoops his body around as if he's flying.

'Come! Come and fly!' he shouts, standing on one leg, and raising the other forty five degrees towards the sun, arms flapping, white vest billowing in the wind. He looks like he should be attached to the bumper of a super-car.

I get up and stand slightly behind him, electric currents prickling down the backs of my legs, like chongololos are crawling around inside them.

'You are not afraid Jayne,' he tells me.

'No I'm not,' I say, believing him.

'Come,' he holds out his hand.

I take it and for a moment his fingers curl around my damp ones and I feel his strong, dry hand. Then he takes it away and laughing, stretches his arms out like wings. I edge towards him, my hands sweating, trying not to look down.

'Like this!' he shouts into the wind, bending his knees and stretching out his arms, he swoops again.

I move closer till my wobbly legs are in line with his, stretching out my arms till the fingertips reach like spread wings. I close my eyes as the wind travels over my face and whips my ponytail.

'We are flying! We are eagles!' Enoch whoops and yells into the wind and I join in, swooping and bending like an eagle searching for prey.

Mom and Dad, sun-downers in hand, sit on the veranda reading the *Rhodesia Herald*. From the swing chair, I watch the shadow of the flamboyant tree stretch monstrously across the front lawn and hear again my teacher explaining the meaning of fate. *It is the zebra's fate to be eaten by a lion. It was your fate to be born Jewish, or Catholic, African or European.*

'Mom? Do you believe in fate?' I say rubbing the lump on my shin.

'No, I believe in God.' Mom fixes her denim-blue eyes on me in a hazy way.

'That is her fate,' Dad laughs from behind the newspaper.

'So do you believe God makes accidents happen?' I ask, eyeing the rockery where the aloes point at the sky like red bottle-brushes.

'Well, I believe there are consequences for people's actions.'

'But what if something accidental made them do an action, something happened to them that made them do something? That wouldn't be fair would it?'

Mom sighs and takes a Berkeley from the blue box of thirties on the table, then she picks up Dad's Kingsgates and waves them at him. Dad shakes his head. Lighting her cigarette, she takes a drag with her right hand and runs the fingers of her left hand through her short black hair. I inhale the lekker vanilla-smell of just-burned tobacco.

'Life's not fair, Jay,' says Mom, exhaling. 'Sometimes we just have to accept things, and just trust God for the outcome.'

'Life's not fair? Why? We didn't ask to be born. Why does God make us suffer?'

A flock of birds rise and hover for a moment above the tree canopy in the valley, and then they glide across the sky disappearing over the mountains crouching in the darkness.

Dad looks up from his newspaper. 'Ja, Reen, why does God make us suffer? I'm sick of this bloody war.' Dad winks at me.

Mom takes a sip from her frosty brown bottle of Castle. 'We have to turn to God. He puts us through tests.'

'Tests? What do you mean? He does cruel things to test us? For what?' I ask, putting my bare feet on the veranda wall.

'Ja. Why Reen?' Dad asks. 'For marks outa ten hey?'

'Oh, Jay,' Mom says. 'He gave us a choice, and we chose to sin, so now we suffer the consequences.' She smiles at me, her small, lower lip curving at the edges, her larger, fleshier upper lip closed tight over the crooked greyish teeth that she hates, but Dad loves. He thinks they're cute.

'But I didn't. I didn't choose to sin. So why do I have to suffer? And the war? Why does Dad and everyone else have to suffer the consequences.'

'Ja, I'm suffering the communists, this whole bloody country's suffering the communists,' Dad laughs.

'I said consequences, Dad,' I laugh.

'Consequences. Communists. Same thing. Let's shoot them.' Dad wiggles an eyebrow at me, and then looks back at the paper.

'Don't fill her head with that nonsense Dave.' Mom exhales.

'Well you fill her head with all your Catholic kak.'

'It's not kak, Dave,' Mom says as she flicks one of her gold Bata slops off and puts her feet on his lap. 'Blasphemer.'

'Bead twiddler,' he says squeezing her big toe. Mom sticks her big toe near Dad's face so it almost brushes his beard. He rounds his marmite-coloured eyes at her and squeezes her thigh, his eyebrows moving up and down like a pair of runaway moustaches. Mom looks like a pretty lady version of Elvis, with her short black hair and her dark blue eyes. She hardly ever wears make-up, just jeans and t-shirts or a wraparound skirt, sometimes with a rifle slung over her shoulder and a black-leather handbag that's ripped all down the one side, but she won't get rid of it, *because it's just the right size.* She even fits her ammo in the front pockets. Most people say she still looks pretty hot, even though she's thirty-two and been freaking out about that for the last two years. *I'm in my thirties!* Like she'd been sleeping beauty for the last ten years and Dad had just woken her up, and my sister Carla had just leapt out of a Christmas box. *I can't bloody believe it! I can't believe I've got a fifteen-year old daughter!*

'So what have you been doing this afternoon?' Mom asks.

'Playing with Enoch.'

Mom sighs.

'What?' I ask, swishing my feet on the veranda floor.

'Well, darling, some people would find it a little odd. You do seem to prefer playing with him to girls your own age.'

'Who are some people? I've played with him since I was little.'

'Well I played with dolls, but I grew out of them.'

'Oh ja Mom. That's a dof comparison. Enoch is a person.'

'Ja Reen. He's a person. Not a golliwog.' Dad laughs from behind the newspaper.

'That's racialist Dad.'

'You been brainwashed by your red Auntie?' he says. 'Ja, my little tomboy, you may have to stop playing with him.' Dad puts the paper down. 'You'll be twelve soon, growing up. He's older than you, what is it two, three years? The playing will have to stop Bantam,' he says going back to reading the newspaper.

'What? Are you joking me? He's my friend.'

Mom and Dad laugh. 'He's not your friend Jay,' Mom says.

The air cools and a baboon barks somewhere to the east.

'What is he then?' I say, watching the globe of the moon rise up above the dark mountains.

'Well, Prospect's son. Wilson's grandson,' she says.

You mean an African. Up in the sky the stars are coming up cold and spiky.

'Is it because he's Prospect's son, that he can't be my friend?' I get up. The swing-couch clatters against the wall.

'Jay!' Dad shouts. 'He's getting too old for you, that's all.'

In the lounge, I hide behind the thick cream curtains near the open veranda doors to listen.

'And his mother gives me the creeps,' Mom says exhaling the words with her smoke.

Too old? How can someone be too old for you? Or too fat – too thin – too short? Maybe too stupid or nasty or thick. The bobbles on the curtains feel good against my fingertips.

The hurricane lamp in the kitchen makes a halo over the half-full ashtray and the pocked paw paw in the fruit bowl. Moths and mozzies circle the lamp, drunk on the light. From the side board where I sit on the chipped Formica surface near the sink, I lift my leg over to the table in the middle of the room and push my toes against the edge of the lamp, making it swing gently. The moths flutter in surprise then circle madly. It's like a death dance. My bare heels clunk, clunk against the wooden cupboards, beating out their own tune.

'You are make too much noise,' Wilson clicks his tongue at me, 'All the time you make too much noise.'

'Gissa break Wilson, I'm a kid.'

Wilson's quick hands chop the carrots as evenly as a machine. I stretch my hand out to scale a piece from Wilson's chopping board.

He waves the knife at me. 'I'm break –' he brings the knife down to within an inch of my hand, – 'I'm break your finger.'

'Jeez Wilson. Wanna get blood in the veggies? Cannibal.'

His shaved head gleams in the lamplight, smooth as milk chocolate. His face is lined, two deep furrows form a 'y' shape above the bump on the bridge of his nose, as if his whole face is asking 'y.' He wheezes and begins to cough, and I remember he is old, even though he seems ageless. Catching sight of his feet turned outwards slightly as if they're in first position in the grey, laceless tackies, turned into slippers by years of treading, I hose myself at the picture of Wilson in his khaki shorts, delicately holding his apron with his fingertips as he partners my sister Carla in one of her dance routines.

'Why you laugh?'

'Nothing. Much.' I make a leg bridge by putting my heels up on the back of one of the ancient wooden chairs in front of me.

I sigh out the last of the laugh, shaking my head slightly. Wilson mimics me, plus sarcasm.

'Jah, jah, too much funny.' He moves his hips from side to side as if spinning a hula-hoop really slowly.

'Jeez, you're a hose Wilson,' I say grabbing a carrot and sticking it in my mouth.

It's hard to think of Wilson young, falling in love with Charity and luring her away from the abbey to marry him. I'd like to ask him how he felt when Charity died giving birth to his son Prospect, but I'm too scared. Hard to imagine too that Wilson is Enoch's grandfather. They seem so separate. He seems more ours than Enoch's. That makes me feel really bad. Wilson never goes down to the compound because the nganga doesn't like him. He lives up here in the kaya under the gum trees next door to his other son Righteous and his family. Poor Enoch, imagine what it's like to have a mom who hates your dad? Jeez life's a mess sometimes. It must be like trying to tear yourself in half. I grab another carrot and Wilson's knife comes down a mosquito's breath from my fingers.

5.

The morning mist puffs up through the valley and swirls around the mountains. The heat of the sun will frighten away the mist before long, but now it hangs around the avocado tree that drapes cartoony shadows over the back yard, and reaches above Carla's ballerina legs. Carla's warming up, she flicks her tutu from out of her bum cheek, then bends her torso towards her leg, sticking her arched foot between a branch of the avo tree at her shoulder level; it's the kind of thing you can make a Barbie doll do just before you snap its leg off and twist it into a gun. Turning her back to me, she stretches the other leg above her head, it all looks pretty painful if you ask me; then she takes a hairpin out of her bun, and stabs a stray piece of hair. She looks like she could use a steak; she's so white, she also looks a bit out of place here in the Rhodesian mountains, but what the hell.

In the kitchen behind me, Wilson clatters around with the breakfast dishes. His radio plays the krinky-chinky sound of African guitar with the *aih, aih, aih, aih, aih* of an African singer over the top.

'Is someone torturing him Wilson?' I yell over my shoulder, shifting my bum from the painful ridges of the back doorstep.

Wilson turns the music up just as a baboon barks from the direction of the gum trees out back.

'What a racket man!' I laugh, 'wait till we start.'

'Why 'you standing over there domkop?' I shout, 'you gonna slip on an avo, and then you won't be able to dance at all.'

Carla looks up.

44

'I don't want the sun on my skin,' she says.

'Are you penga? It's still shady over here.'

'Er no, look.' She points at the sun on my legs, falling a little way out in front of me.

'Better go live in England with Granny and Grandpa if you don't want sun. It's greyer than a tin bucket over there.' I say.

'I intend to.'

'Better not, you bloody traitor, the British are trying to hand our country over to the terrs! They've screwed our family too.'

Carla rolls her eyes at me and then walks slowly towards the centre of the yard, her feet, stuck forever in the first position, pointing east and west.

'They haven't done anything to our family Jay,' she says.

'Oh ja? What about sanctions? What about Dad not being able to sell any of our tea crop overseas?'

Carla sighs, 'Jay, there's only so far I can go with my dancing in Rhodesia, with this bloody war on. And Mum's British.'

'She's not anymore. And there's only so far you can go without getting sun on your face. You gonna dance in circles round the avo tree? Ready?' I ask, my finger pressing down on the pause button of the portable cassette recorder.

She moves forward and lifts her arms and tilts her face perched on its curved veiny neck. Her hands flutter down, soft as wings. She holds them in front of her waiting, head down, like a flower preparing to open.

'Ja,' says the flower, without raising her head.

The music from Swan Lake belts up to the sky, just as the louries take off from the trees. Maybe they're getting involved, they've got the fancy head feathers for it, especially the purple-crested ones. I hoik my heels up to the edge of the step and wrapping my arms around my legs I settle in to watch her. Her feet en pointe, she pushes her chest forward, pulling her arms upwards, her body curved like a question mark. Her arms sweep down, then up, out, and behind. She takes her wings and folding them in, crouches to the ground, repeating the movement several times, until her movements seem to chase each other as the music builds. She raises her right leg in front of her, then sweeping it down, stretches it out backwards, her arms moving forward, reaching towards me. Then, she snatches her arms back, pulls her elbows into her waist, and knees bent, crouches inwards. Then she is up again. I laugh. She's good man. Her back leg comes down again and she arches her back, her fingertips grazing the ground before they are swept up again. She bends her torso right over to the left and then to the right. With her leg out behind her, she flicks it around, using it to force her body in circles that become faster and faster. The music climbs again and she widens her leg out sideways, then points it in to the knee of her standing leg, arms raised up high with the fingertips of both hands touching, like the ballerina that dances when I open the lid of my jewellery-box. When the music dips, she crouches down and then, as it builds again, she's off, spinning like penga, her left foot beating at the ground. Now she's darting to the north, to the south, to the east and to the west, arms flung up and then down, like she's trying to escape from something. The music fades and I press the pause button.

'You look like a frekked swan,' I say.

She laughs and gets up from the ground and comes and sits on the wide step next to me, all sweaty where her dark hair is pulled tight into a bun.

'That was really good Carls.'

'Thanks. I need to keep practising though. Come watch me tomorrow, at class?'

'Maybe.'

Carla's really good, but I can see why not many people like it around here. Carls says there's only one ballet boy in her class and he's very 'effete.' *Effing what?* Dad said when she said that. *A poof you mean?* My brother John nearly wet himself.

Carla looks up at the sky, with her pretty, antelope-like eyes.

'It's gonna rain,' she says.

Puffs of silver-laced clouds pile up in the east above the mountains.

'No jokes hey?' I say looking up.

Wind shivers across my upper arms. Maybe what I feel are the spirits of the dead and the dying, as one more troopie falls in the bush. My eyes scan the purple mountains that stretch into

Mozambique where our enemies hide like mambas in the grass. Enoch says the dead haunt the mountains. Thunder like distant bombs echoes through the valley and a fat drop of warm rain explodes on my arm, followed by several more. Carla puts her arm on my leg; it's thinner and whiter against my own tanned skin. Blue veins river just beneath the surface.

'Your legs are longer than mine,' she says, wiggling her hips up close to me on the step.

'So?'

'But not thinner,' she says, staring straight ahead. 'You're as brown as a coloured, Jay.'

Raindrops splatter on the dust of the backyard. Jeez, I love the spicy smell of the earth when it rains, it almost makes me feel like dancing. Carla taps the tops of her feet to the rhythm of the rain. An electric shock of lightning rips through the sky floodlighting the yard. 'Let's dance in the rain while we still can.' She says grabbing my arms.

'No man!' I laugh.

Springboking it across the yard, she rips her hair out from the bun, flinging her hairpins up at the sky, laughing as she spins round, head back, arms open wide. Samantha comes round the house and begins to bark, her grey and cream collie coat rippling behind her in the wind. We're soaked and I feel myself getting up and grabbing her outstretched hands and spinning with her till the farmhouse, mountains and hibiscus hedge out front, the gum trees by the kaya, and the yellow fuzz of the wattle trees beyond the back lawn blend into a kaleidoscope with us in the middle. We let go of each others' hands and I stagger backwards landing heavily on my bum in the dirt, legs in the air, laughing. Carla's tutu droops and the water runs down her face, her legs all orangey with the rain and the mud. On the wide, warm step, I spread my arms palms upward so that the rain can crucify me with warm nails of water. Samantha stops barking and jumps up the step behind me to take shelter near the kitchen door.

'You stink man Sam,' I tell her. 'Of wet dog.'

She wags her tail in my face.

In the afternoon, I lie on the back lawn reading a Wilbur Smith book that is quite rude, which is why I'm not supposed to read it, but Mom left it on the veranda and I started, and now I can't stop. I am wearing a boob-tube even though I don't have boobs, with shorts and Carla's big red sunglasses, drinking iced Mazoe with the book on a towel so I can shove it and the sunglasses under it if I hear a car pull up and just pretend I'm catching a tan.

'You look like a fly,' Granny Rose calls out. She's pruning the rose bushes beneath the kitchen windows. She jabs her secateurs in the air towards me.

And I thought I looked grown-up, like the lady in the book. In the morning light, Granny Rose reminds me of her portrait above the fireplace in the lounge, only she has swapped the riding habit and crop in the painting for the secateurs and one of dead Grandpa Patrick's old shirts and a pair of his suit trousers. Her hair is piled up in a loose bun like an onion, with curly bits hanging down.

'Granny Rose? The nganga says you didn't buy this land. Is that true?'

She turns round and looks beyond me, in the direction of the compound.

'I never wanted to grow tea you know, but Patrick insisted,' Granny Rose says. 'I wanted to stick to wattle. People will always need paper; one always wants to read, to write letters. Silly man, I think he thought I was fanciful.'

I prop myself up on my elbows.

'It took six weeks you know, the crossing, from the Cape,' Granny Rose says. 'Bloody boring it was, night after night, fending off sweaty men who wanted to dance with you.' She looks at me. 'And you couldn't get away from them you know – no fear; they knew where your cabin was.'

She stares at me, her grey eyes frozen for a few seconds, and then looks at the secateurs. Then, like she's suddenly remembered what she's doing here in the first place, she turns to the roses and begins to snip, snip, snip.

'Tell me how you fell in love with Grandpa Patrick,' I ask, thinking of the love scene in the book.

'Well, it was over the Baxter's soup. I had to feed him you see.' She stops for a second, the secateurs suspended in mid-air, framing a lourie flitting above the avocado tree. What are the chances of seeing that?

'It was his helplessness.'

'His helplessness?' It's hard to imagine Grandpa Patrick with his tractor-engine voice and his big tea-planting hands as helpless. Even though he's been stone dead as Fred for the last three years.

'Granny Rose?'

'Blinking louries, they must call, call, call, so rude,' says Granny Rose, snipping at the pink rose bush, maybe wishing it was a lourie.

'Do they blink, Granny Rose?'

'No they blinking don't. Don't ask stupid questions. Where's the tea?'

'I don't know.'

'Well, ask Wilson, then. He should have brought it by now.' She snips at the air in front of me with the secateurs. Tipping my head back, I spot Wilson coming down the red cement steps outside the back door with the tea-tray, his white apron hanging way past his khaki shorts to his knees.

'About time, Wilson, it's a quarter past three.' She looks at him over her half-rimmed glasses. Her face gets softer. 'A quarter past tea time.'

She used to look at Grandpa Patrick like that too, when he read out bits of the newspaper to her as she painted. She was interested but never said anything, just looked at him like he was the radio or something.

'Yes Madam,' says Wilson. He smiles a bit as he says it.

Wilson crouches down to pour the tea out of the silver pot. He takes Granny Rose's cup and places it on the wire table in front of her, then he sits down on a rock near me, one leg crossed over the other, one foot moving up and down, lawn to sky, lawn to sky as he takes a bit of newspaper out of his pocket and rolls some tobacco in it. Granny Rose likes him to stick around till she's finished her tea.

'Of course, you really should marry a tobacco farmer,' Granny Rose says, as if we'd been talking about marrying in the first place. 'Only make sure you find the right sort of farmer.' She turns and points the secateurs at me. 'But don't delay, by no means delay.' She waves the secateurs at me as if I'm a mombie that needs moving. 'There are too many women for too few men in this country.'

'What about me Wilson?' I ask. 'No tea?'

Wilson lifts his arms up and waves his hands. 'Make like this.' I mimic him.

'For sure, your hands, they work,' he says.

'Ha, ha, very sarcastic Wilson. I just wanted you to pass me some.'

I plop two teaspoons of sugar into the cup. An ant crawls up the climbing rose pattern on the side of the sugar basin. Deciding to let it live, I flick it off sending it into orbit over the kikuyu lawn.

'One cannot sit around hoping for an invitation,' says Granny Rose. 'You must get out there, present yourself, dance with the right men at the right parties. Is that not the case Wilson? Wilson?'

'Yes, Madam, sure, Madam.' Wilson folds his arms and nods bringing the hand-rolled cigarette to his lips. The foot goes slowly up and down, up and down, with the rhythm of Granny Rose's words. She sounds like BBC World Service coming out through a gramophone.

'Yes indeed,' she says, waving her secateurs again in my general direction.

'And do make sure to get married, can't be having any little heathens.'

Wilson only ever smiles at the things that Granny Rose says, shaking his head and going, 'Eh he Madam,' and then hacking away on his rusty cough. I can never make him laugh.

'Don't look to my May as an example. She married a fool, and gave birth to fools, your father included. Stupid man.'

'Granny Rose, I'm too young to get married, and Dad's not stupid.'

'He married your mother didn't he? She's a Catholic isn't she? Bead twiddler. Kissing the Pope's hand, bloody ridiculous. Head of the church? Where does that leave God? Left field, that's where. Like playing cricket without a bat. Bloody Italians. Mind you, the Anglican church is not much better, silly arses, silly dresses.'

My throat hurts with the laughter. Wilson's leg goes up and

down as he wheezes, his shoulders shaking.

'And steer clear of all politicians. Especially RF ones. And never, ever go back to England. Cold, dreadful place. Full of do gooders,' she snips quickly twice as she says 'do gooders,' as if she's decapitating them. 'They have no idea about anything.'

'Stupid of your father to marry an English girl.' Granny Rose throws her secateurs on the ground, picks up her big black enamel watering can and tries to water the roses. Only there's no water in the watering can, but she just keeps watering air. Wilson goes over and takes the watering can gently from her hands. She lets him take it. She is penga, but such a hose. Auntie Nessie says we'll never put her in a home even if she has a brain-rotting disease that John calls 'ants-in-your-trousers.'

6.

From the kopje overlooking the river up here, they are as small as lego, their ankles sploshing in the water look like matchsticks. Enoch moves towards the middle of the river stepping on the stones that lie under the water like slippery toads. He stops to pull a stone from his shorts for his slingshot. John shoves Nakai and he grabs John's ankle. John falls in too. Enoch runs off, his long legs flying over the river's edge, the water spraying around his ankles like jewels. Before you can say chongalolo, I too am at the edge of the river, my t-shirt covered in blackjack needles.

'Jaaaay. What are you doing here? You don't have a catty,' John says.

Light sparks off the river like tiny camera flashes.

'I wanna swim,' I say, panting, my eyes following Enoch's back. He's not wearing a t-shirt and his back muscles ripple like fish under his dark skin. 'I can use yours anyway.'

'No you can't.' He flicks water at me with his foot.

'I can. I'm a better shot than you.' I flick water back, aiming for his face.

'Oh ja. Prove it.' He drenches me and Nakai laughs. I couldn't care less, my eyes are following Enoch and the water cools my baking neck. Grabbing John's catty from his back pocket I run after him. Nakai kicks water up at John, distracting him from stopping me.

'Nock!' I yell at his back.

'Leave him alone,' John says. 'He's gone hunting. And he's in a bad mood. He doesn't want to be followed by a girl.' Nakai laughs too. He laughs at everything John says. For a moment Enoch disappears behind rocks and bush. I follow him along the wet mud of the riverbank at a distance, till the river widens into a pool. Christmas beetles scream in the bush and the water gushes down the mountain and falls into rapids further down the river. Enoch hasn't seen me but I know he knows I'm here. I don't know if he's annoyed or not that I've come, but he hasn't turned round to wave me away. He stops and puts a stone in the cup of his slingshot and takes aim. There's a flutter from the bush, but no thud.

'Check! Check! A bronze sunbird!' I say, pointing as the bronzy bird flitters over the rock near us and then disappears into a msasa tree.

'You have scared the bird away. Why you follow me Jayne? Why you not mind your business?' He chops the air with his arms in frustration as if he's trying to get the animals in the bush to lie down so that he can shoot them.

Oh ja. Nothing to do with your aim.

'What? Come on man it wasn't my fault. I wanted to have a go – there's plenty more birds on this farm,' I say.

Enoch says nothing. Birds call and flutter from tree to tree. He stops and takes aim again. A flap disturbs the branches above us and a few grey feathers flutter down. We wait for a thud that doesn't come.

'I shot him,' Enoch says, arm raised against the sun as he scans the tree.

'Well where is he then?' I ask, bending to find a stone for John's catty.

Catching sight of a bird above us in a mopani tree we take aim. It almost lands on our heads. I laugh and run towards it, but Enoch gets there first; snatching it up, he holds it by its legs. Its bluish grey head hangs down limply and a gentle pulse flickers in its neck. A tiny round jewel eye stares.

'Look at its bluey spots.' I feel bad for killing it. 'You can have it,' I say.

'It is mine. I hit first.'

'Ja. But I brought it down. So it's ours.'

He walks away with the bird hanging upside down in his left hand, its wings splayed like a stiff Christmas decoration.

'What's the matter Enoch? Why are you being like this?'

'How?' he says over his shoulder.

'You know, unfriendly,' I say.

He turns round. 'You want to swim?' he says.

Enoch smoothes the bird's wings close to the body, places it in the crook of a msasa tree and covers it up with leaves and branches. Then he puts his slingshot on top. He runs towards some balancing rocks three times his height and scrambles up barefoot, quickly disappearing from view. As I near the top of the first rock, he disappears over the second. My tackies slip over the knobbled surface of the rock. Using an indentation in the rock for a foothold, I graze my ankle, but I hardly feel it. A splosh tells me he's jumped into the river from the diving rock that looks like an elephant-sized brain on a stem. Coming over the top, I see Enoch lying in the river, floating on his back, his toes raised upwards.

'You look like a big fat lazy hippo!' I shout, pulling my tackies off. My feet are pale in the areas covered by my tackies, nut-brown as my legs everywhere else. I consider taking my shorts off too. Maybe not. At the edge I stand in the small basin-like dip, looking out over the red dirt road that cuts through the valley and away from the farm, rocking backwards and forwards on my feet, liking the rough massage on my soles. When I look up, the white circle of sun in the deep blue of the sky burns onto my eyes so that little white circles dance in the line of my vision, over the water and across the bank. The rains have swelled the river and the water swirls where it is sucked by invisible tides. I rise onto my toes, remembering the story Enoch told me about the water nymph that sucked young children into the river by gently whistling to them and then pulled them down to the crocodile cave where they woke up only to be devoured.

'Jump! You scared?' Enoch yells from the water.

The water rises behind him like the earth had just tipped sideways.

'Ja for sure,' I say sarcastically, taking a couple of steps backward. As I jump I catch sight of Nakai and John making their way down towards us. My feet hit the rocky, sandy bottom just as a flash of lightning turns the sky white. Water rises above my ribcage making me shiver. Taking a lungful of air, I dive, mermaiding it up and down, hearing the drowned sound of thunder echoing through the mountains.

'You don't have to make a show for me. This view is good enough,' Enoch shouts as I surface.

He lies back in the water and puts his arms behind his head as if he's watching TV in bed.

'Think I was doing it for you?' I splash him. This turns out to be a mistake because when he splashes me back my face goes surfing.

Water is gushing from the sky too. The lightning comes and makes me jump down deep in the water and then up, like a bullet aimed for the sky. Enoch faces me and jumps too. We get closer and closer to each other, our noses almost touching, our knees knocking now and again under the water. When I surface my middle bumps against his. Our eyes meet for a moment, but the energy has gone and now it seems embarrassing to continue jumping so we stop. The rains clear and the sky smiles.

'Monkey's wedding,' I say.

'What? Monkey?'

'Ja. When the sun comes out and it's still raining, that means it's a monkey's wedding.'

'A monkey cannot be married.'

'Why?'

'Hwai is a sheep,' he smiles.

'What do you mean? Oh you mean in Shona, 'why' is a sheep.'

'For this, you can be clever. But not too clever.' He grabs my shoulders and pretends to drown me instead, leaving me for just a bit too long under the muddy water until I poke him in the ribs to let go.

Later, we lie on our fronts, on the surface of the flat-topped rock, watching the water from our bodies evaporate in the sun, me on the edge, John next to me, then Nakai and Enoch on the far side.

'Look at how the water jiggles around on the surface of your hair!' John raises his head from his hands and laughs at Nakai.

'Look at how yours falls like weeds,' Nakai says.

'These are the best holidays I've ever had,' John says, his chin on his hands.

'You always say that,' I say.

'I never want to go back to school,' John says.

Nakai laughs. 'But if you don't go to school you will remain an idiot.'

John and I laugh. Enoch doesn't, he is sitting up and staring out over the bush.

'What about you Enoch?' John says.

'Oh he likes school, don't you Enoch?' I say. 'He likes books.'

Enoch stares straight ahead, his arms wrapped round his knees.

'I cannot go to school anymore,' he says.

'What? Why?' I sit up.

'My mother says she does not want my brain to be disturbed by the settler priests,' he laughs in a way that is not funny.

'What do you mean settler? I ask.

Nakai says something in Shona to make Enoch laugh, but he doesn't.

'A settler is one who cannot stay.'

'What do you mean?' I ask.

He says nothing. I hate it when he does that. As if I'm too thick to understand or he doesn't feel like answering because my question was too dof.

'Shame man. That's really bad,' I say. 'I wondered what was bugging you earlier.'

'Ja. Shame man,' John says.

'I'll speak to my Dad,' I say.

'No.' Enoch says, glancing at me. 'She say no. It can be no.'

Jeez. Okay Jose.

For a while we are silent, lying on our arms, drifting in the heat. I wonder whether it's better to have no dad at all than to have a dad like Prospect.

'Do you miss your Dad Enoch?' I ask. My voice floats over the river like a kite. We never speak about his dad. John jabs me with his elbow.

'Shut-up!' he hisses. From the corner of my eye I see Enoch still sitting with his arms looped round his knees, feet up and out like flippers.

'I can miss. But I can see him,' he says, staring straight ahead.

'No you can't. He's in jail,' I say

John digs me again. 'Jay!'

'Sometimes. I can see him,' Enoch insists, pulling at an elephant grass stem.

'When?' I ask.

'Oh just shut-up Jay,' John says.

'No you shut-up.'

'My father is bigger than a baobab tree,' Nakai says loudly as he gets up.

We all burst out laughing.

'A baobab tree? Moses?'

'Our father is bigger than that mountain,' John says pointing in the direction of Chimanimani.

We laugh some more. Enoch doesn't. Using a branch of a split tree growing near the rock, he jumps down and runs back to the water. He's moving further up the valley towards the waterfall. A mass of steel-coloured cloud moves over the sun and the air cools.

'Why'd you have to bring up his father Jay? Especially after the school stuff? He was really upset man.' He leans over me so that I can see the hazel flecks in his round green eyes.

'I dunno. It just came out. I just wondered – I wanted to hear how he felt.'

'You can be so stupid sometimes Jay.'

'Shut up. You're nearly two years younger than me you know. You shouldn't tell me off.'

'Well you don't act older sometimes, you know,' he glares his eyes at me.

Nakai gets up. 'Sadza time,' he says.

'Ja all you think about is filling the pot hey,' John pats Nakai's belly which is just like a little round cooking pot.

Nakai laughs and turns to go. John grabs him by the ankle, Nakai laughs and shakes his ankle free.

We watch as he heads home through the bush.

'He's quite fat hey?' John says.

We laugh.

'Ja he jiggles.'

'Check!' John sits up. 'Eagle! Check the size of those wings man!'

His wingspan sweeping the mountain, the eagle circles up and then swoops so far down that I see the feathers of his snowy head.

'I think it's the same one Enoch and I saw the other day,' I say.

'I'm gonna go tell him!' John says getting up. 'Maybe he'll get him.'

Ja maybe not.

I watch John follow Enoch past the pool and further down the valley. When I can no longer see him, or the eagle, I lie back down on my arms and drift on images of letters: Enoch's father pausing to stare out of a grille where the light comes into his cell, as he writes a letter to Enoch; the priests at the missionary school shaking their heads sadly when they receive a letter written in Enoch's mother's writing – maybe in goat's blood – that Enoch will not be returning to be taught by the settler priests. A shivery feeling tickles up the backs of my legs, waking me up. Lifting my head off my drooly arms I see that my watch shows it's almost five. The rain begins again as I slide down the rock and run home.

Rain showers on the roof and trickles down the knobbled glass of the steamed-up bathroom window. Floating my arms up, I close my eyes and imagine what it must be like to drown. Mom says it's supposed to be the nicest way to say goodnight nurse. Enoch never says goodbye, he just vanishes. It makes me wonder whether he likes me at all sometimes. We never arrange to meet up either. We just both know where to find each other. He didn't understand about monkey's weddings and I took a while to get what he meant about 'why' meaning sheep. But even though we don't speak the same language, in our heads we do and we always understand each other in the end. Actually it's when we speak that sometimes we confuse each other. Maybe that's why he doesn't answer me sometimes, and why we don't always speak when we're climbing or tracking or whatever. Why is a sheep. And a sheep can baa. My raised foot has more ridges in it than a geological exhibit from being submerged for so long. I lower my leg and watch my splayed fingers travel over my middle.

'Hurry up! I need to go out!' Carla bangs on the bathroom door, it's like an electric shock tearing me from my mind to my body. I snatch my fingers away from my tummy.

'Use Mom's bathroom,' I shout back, before submerging my head underwater.

After my bath, Dad and I almost bash into each other in the lounge.

'Where's your brother?' he asks. Samantha stands beside Dad looking up at me, wagging her tail like she wants to know too.

'I thought he was with you. He always helps you and Righteous in the dairy.' I sit down on the edge of the armchair.

'Ja well not tonight. Where were you this afternoon?' he asks, going down the hallway calling for John. Samantha follows.

'We went swimming,' I say picking at a stray bit of cotton on the beading of the chair. 'With Nakai and Enoch. Nakai went early!' I shout after him. 'John went off with Enoch!'

Dad comes back into the room. He stands right in front of me.

'You know I've said back before dark. The lot of you? Haven't I?'

'Ja Dad. I thought they'd come back, so I came home about five,' I say, looking out past the veranda and over the lawn where the clouds hang heavily over the valley like ghost zeppelins.

Carla comes in, a pink towel tucked under her boobs, her hair wrapped in another towel.

'Have you borrowed my round hairbrush?'

'As if. Do I look like I'd use a round hairbrush?'

'No. You look like a drowned rat. What's going on?' she says clocking Dad's face.

'And he wasn't here when you came back?' Dad asks, ignoring Carla.

'I just went straight in the bath. I thought he was back.'

'Was Brandy with you?'

'No.'

Dad whistles for the dogs and goes out through the veranda.

'What's the big deal?' Carla says. 'He's been later than this before.'

'I know.'

In the kitchen Wilson's getting the casserole out of the oven.

'Have you seen John, Wilson?' I ask.

'I am not his keeper,' he says stirring the casserole. A rich, sweet smell of oxtail steams into the room.

'I know but have you seen him?' A quicksand feeling bubbles in my stomach.

'I have seen him but not today.'

'You're so annoying sometimes Wilson.' I plonk down on a kitchen chair, tipping my head back to stare at the shadowy ceiling.

It's almost dark outside when Mom arrives home from work.

'Where is everyone?' she says dumping her keys, bag and the Bon Marche packet on the kitchen table. 'Why are you sitting in the dark?'

'Dad's out looking for John.' I don't look at her, I just keep kicking the kitchen chair, staring at the greasy, black indentations on the old oak table.

'What do you mean?'

'He hasn't come home from this afternoon.'

'What?'

Dad comes back, slamming the bottom half of the stable door, which is pointless because it just goes back to where it was before.

'I can't find him,' he says from the shadowy hallway where the raincoats look like dead soldiers. I get up to go to my room.

'Sit down!' He leans his 303, Grandpa's old hunting rifle against the wall. 'When did you last see him?'

I sit back down and tell him again.

Dad leans close over me gripping the edges of the table, so that I can smell his Kingsgate-laced breath. His eyes stare into mine and I stare back at mine in his.

'I told you. No staying out after dark. Bloody Enoch. No more, Jay. No more playing with Enoch.'

'Why you saying it like that?' I say leaning back slightly. 'It's not his fault. We were all together, we were all swimming. What's wrong with that?'

'We told you about playing with Enoch Jay,' Mom sighs from over by the dresser where she's pouring Bols into two glasses.

'They'll be back Dave,' she says putting a glass in front of Dad. She knows Dad's thinking about Michael Roberts, who got blown up opening the gates at Greenways farm only 60k's from ours, his body exploding in the air and falling on the sacred marula tree, while his father watched from the bakkie. Carla comes in all dolled up.

'Why are you looking like the fairy from the Christmas tree?' Dad asks.

'I'm going to Umtali. Madame's birthday dinner in town. Remember?'

'Sit down,' Dad says. 'You're not going anywhere.'

'But Dad. They're waiting for me at the turnoff. We're going by convoy.' She looks at Mom.

'Please? Mom.'

'Just sit down Carla,' Mom says, snatching her cigarette from her mouth, before Dad has a chance to say anything. 'Just for a minute.'

Dad grabs his rifle and goes back outside.

We listen to the grandfather clock, ticking away the minutes from the hallway. The room gets darker and darker but no one switches on the lights. Wilson comes in to stir the casserole and get some matches from the pantry. Our eyes follow him like he's on the TV. He goes out again to smoke his tobacco wrapped in newspaper on the back step, banging the bottom half of the stable door as he goes. Mom's cigarette glows like a firefly. Half an hour later the dogs begin to bark. But it's only Dad.

'Is he back?' Dad's hand slaps the light switch next to the door and his shadow stretches out towards us as he comes into the kitchen. His face expects us to say yes. When we don't he runs his hand through his hair. 'Can't find him. The boys are still out searching.'

A figure appears at the back door, clothes hanging off its body. It makes me jump and my loud breath makes everyone get up. It's John, sopping wet.

'Where've you been?' Dad asks.

John looks down.

'Sorry Dad.'

'That's not an answer.'

Another dark figure stands a little way behind him. Dad catches sight of him.

'Where've you been Enoch?'

'You are not my father,' Enoch says. His eyes tunnel straight into Dad's.

'What?'

'You are not my father,' he says again, then he looks at me, and his face seems hard in the bluish light.

'Bloody cheek!' Dad goes to the kitchen door. 'Hey!'

But Enoch is turning away. As he does, thunder makes the hurricane lamp swing and lightning streaks the room. Jeez it's like Hollywood. I watch out the window. The rains start again but Enoch does not run down the path, he just walks towards the trees, not looking back.

'Get some towels Jay,' Mom says.

When I come back John is telling Mom and Dad all about how he followed Enoch upstream till the water got to neck level.

'I thought Enoch was nearer than he was, I kept trying to catch him up and he just kept going further and further away. And then it was like the river just pulled me. I tried to swim but it just kept pulling me and pulling me towards the waterfall. And then I was over and being pulled along the other side. Then I was with Enoch and he was being pulled too. And then I think he must have grabbed onto some tree roots or something. He held out his arm, but I couldn't get it. I was being pulled further away. So he let go and came after me. He grabbed me again and managed to pull me over to the tree. And then he pulled me out.'

'Oh my God John. You were that far down?' Mom says.

'Ja. Lucky Enoch saved you,' I say.

Dad lights a Kingsgate. Shaking the match he says, 'That's the last time Jay.'

A smell of sulphur hits my nostrils.

'And you too John. No more playing with Enoch.'

'C'mon,' he says to the sulking wooden dolly in the corner, 'Let's get you to the turnoff.'

'Yesss!' Carla says. She goes over to John and hugs his head to her waist.

'Oh great. So he saves John's life and you thank him by taking his friends away from him.' I say.

Dad shoots me a warning look as he picks up his FN rifle off the table.

'Leave it Jay,' Mom says.

From my bedroom I listen to their voices flying up and down the passage from the dining room where they are eating dinner. *Just leave her. She'll come out when she's hungry.* I'll come out when I'm dead. Someone knocks on my door. When I don't answer John comes in with a tray.

'I'm sorry Jay.'

I turn my face to the cold wall.

He leaves the tray by the bed and goes out. Then he tries to come back in. Leaning over the bed, I grab a boerewors coil from between the mashed potatoes and peas on the plate. John tries to exit quickly. I throw the boerewors at the door. It slithers down the ABBA poster and lands on the floor like a big curved poo. It doesn't even make me laugh.

'He saved me Jay!' John shouts from behind the door. I wipe my fingers on the sheets and remember Enoch's face, the way he looked at me, accusing me even though I'd done nothing wrong. *You're not my father.* Jeez he's got guts speaking to my dad like that. And he can't even go to school now. What a kak day he's had.

When I switch my bedside light off, the darkness covers me completely, wrapping me in its cosy blanket. The darkness drifts me back. I see little Enoch, in the days before he began school, following his father Prospect from the compound, climbing the trees out back while Prospect drank strong sweet tea from enamel mugs and smoked newspaper-wrapped tobacco with his old man Wilson on the back step. Me swinging on the tyre and rope swing attached to the avocado tree. *Push me! Push me!* I called to Prospect. He pushed me so high into the flashing sun coming through the leaves that I thought the swing was going to swing right around the branch. I wasn't making a noise, but my face was pushed up to the sky and inside I was wetting myself laughing, scared and happy. Sometimes, I could see Enoch watching me from the trees far over the back lawn. He used to hang upside down by his legs down in the woods and from the branches of the avocado tree. I copied him. Once I fell, but I didn't hurt myself, and I heard him laughing at me through the branches of the wattle trees. The trees between our house and the compound became a meeting place. I don't know how that happened, it just did, or how we became friends, we just did. By copying each other and laughing at each other I suppose.

In my dream Enoch and I ignore the voices of our mothers calling us to come home and instead we walk hand in hand deeper into the jungly forest under the sky-high yellowwoods where we live in a house carved out of a trunk as wide as a hut. Samango monkeys swing in the vines roping the trees, their branches and leaves high enough to tickle a giant's armpit. Below us, poisonous toadstools poke out from beds of brown pine-needles and branch-thick Gaboon vipers lie waiting like terrorists in rotting logs, their pink, purple and brown diamonds pretty deadly. But we don't step on them because we know where to look.

6.

It's the fourteenth of May, my twelfth birthday. At the Dairy Den, in town, I'm just digging my spoon into my knicker-bocker-glory when everyone screams 'Surprise!' and Glen pulls in. He's changed since I last saw him. I suppose it's because of all the time spent fighting terrs out in the bush. He's grown a beard and moustache and is wearing an army-cap, khaki elasticated shorts, a tight camouflage t-shirt, and black baseball tackies with no socks. He also has a revolver poking out a bit above his waistband. He looks pretty mush if you ask me. You can see his torso through his tight t-shirt, like a chocolate bar under foil. He rushes up behind me, and tickles me, digging his hands into my shoulders and squeezing in a love hurts kind of a way.

'How is it out there cousin?' Dad asks, slapping Glen on the back, while Glen pulls a chair over from another table and sits on it back to front.

'Hotter than Zambezi Valley elephant arses,' Glen says, leaning on the back of the chair and smiling all around. He puts a present in front of me on the table. I rip the paper open.

'It'll be your turn again soon,' he says to Dad.

I hold up a little black-painted guinea fowl with white spots and red head markings.

'I looked for a little Bantam, but couldn't find one,' Glen says. 'So you got a guinea-fowl!' He laughs, his green eyes sparking under his dark eyebrows, and we all laugh back. Glen's the kind of person you laugh back at no matter what he says. His eyes make you do it.

He doesn't look like Uncle Joe or Auntie Penny. John comes back from the men's and jumps on Glen's back. He clocks the gun as he hangs over Glen's shoulder. 'Show me your gun, show me your gun!' he shouts.

'Not in here, John,' Mom says.

'Ja, not in here, we don't wanna get our guns out, hey. They might go off and give everyone a skrik, ek se.' Glen stands up and pulls John over his shoulder, then twists him backwards onto the floor. He used to do that to me. I show Dad my present and he ruffles my hair.

'Well I call her my little Bantam, not only because she's my second little bird,' he says, stretching out his arm and placing it on Carla's shoulders.

'Daaad,' Carla says, shrugging Dad's arm off and going back to reading her magazine.

'But because bantams are domestic birds. And my Jay-bird won't fly far from the nest. Will you? Jay? You're a Rhodesian bird aren't you?' he smiles at me.

Cheesy, but if I had wings I'd stretch them in the sunlight of his smile.

He looks at Carla. 'Now this one's my exotic bird, who flies close to the sun.'

Carla continues to read her magazine, her sunglasses on her head and her long lashes sweeping above her cheekbone. Then she jumps and screeches just like a bird when she spots her friend Michelle and her boyfriend Neil pulling in.

'What are you doing here?'

She flings her arms round Michelle's neck as if she's meeting her at the airport after a trip overseas. Man, she's a drama-queen. Michelle throws her arms up, shrieks back and jumps up and down on her messed up ballet toes. Well, ballet dancer's toes are like twigs with knobs on and not where you'd expect them to be.

'Looking good, Carla,' Neil says, his eyes checking Carla's boobs and hips, 'very nice.'

Michelle smiles a freaked out kind of smile and twiddles a pink plastic disc of an earring that pokes out of her nest of permed blonde hair.

Dad gets up. 'I don't think we've met before, I'm Carla's father.' He holds out his hand to Neil.

'Nice work,' Neil says, still looking at Carla. He grasps Dad's hand.

'Ja, well, take your eyes off the goods,' Dad jokes. He introduces Mom, and Glen. Glen eyes him up and down, but doesn't get up.

'Join us?' asks Dad. Neil looks at jellified Michelle, then at Carla who looks like her insides are playing tug of war. John wiggles his eyebrows at me.

'Ja. Why not hey? Just for a smoke.' He reaches across the table for Glen's Madisons. 'May I?' he asks.

'Help yourself,' Glen says, still looking him up and down with his head tilted.

'Nice shirt,' says Glen. 'Paisley, is it? Very psychedelic Derek.'

'Thanks,' says Neil, lighting up with the box of matches, 'I try.'

'Nice purple trousers.'

'Thanks,' says Neil, smiling, but only a bit.

'Nice long hair too,' says Glen. Neil shifts in his seat and Michelle clings to his arm tighter.

'Ja, you look like something out that band, what they called?' Dad laughs.

'Steppenwolf?' Neil says, 'ja everyone says that, hey,' he laughs and flicks his ash on the floor. Glen spins the metal ashtray across the table at him.

'If you flick your ash on the floor, someone else will have to come and clean it up for you,' he says.

Neil smiles, takes a long drag, then flicks in the ashtray.

'Gle-en,' Carla says. Her eyes beg him to stop.

'I think I've seen you around town,' Mom says. 'Are you working at the moment?'

'Ja. I've got a job at the record shop.' He takes a toke on his cigarette. 'I'm into my music,' he smiles. 'But I've just found out I've got a university place overseas, so I'm thinking of leaving.'

Everyone looks at him like he's got a grenade pin clenched between his teeth.

'Oh, I'll come back,' he says quickly, smiling at Michelle.

'Maybe.' He lets out a sharp laugh that looks like it's stabbed her in the chest.

'So you don't believe in fighting for your country then?' says Glen.

'I don't believe in fighting,' says Neil.

'Oh ja?' says Glen. 'So d'you reckon we should've just let Hitler march into England because we don't believe in fighting?'

'I believe in passive resistance,' Neil says, exhaling upwards, the smoke billowing from both sides of his mouth.

'I've heard it all now,' says Glen. 'What's passive resistance? You can't resist something by being passive. You can only resist with force, by applying pressure.'

Carla reaches out over the table. 'Glen? Can we not talk about the war? It's Jay's birthday?'

Neil gets up. 'Shall we get our ice-creams?' he says to Michelle.

Michelle looks like she's been let out of jail free plus received the bank stash. She gets up. Carla stands too.

'Nice meeting you, guys,' he laughs. 'I think.'

Dad stands up to shake his hand. 'Best of luck for your future,' he says.

'Ja. Best of luck for your future, hey,' Glen says.

Neil raises his hand. Carla follows them to the counter, whispering something to Michelle.

'Ja. We'll be there to protect your family when they get attacked!' shouts Glen. 'Don't worry! You carry on! Go overseas, go study. Leave us to it!'

A family on the other side of the room lick their ice-creams and stare. I widen my eyes at them and John laughs, dangling his ice-creamy tongue over his cone.

Mom puts her hand on Glen's arm, 'Leave it Glen,' she says.

Neil does not turn round. He just orders a couple of choc 99's.

'I believe in passive resistance. My arse,' says Glen, 'I believe in doing nothing, but sorting out my own future, you mean. Get on your bloody magic carpet and fly to England.'

On the way home I doze on the back seat. *What's your birthday wish Bantam?* Dad asked this morning. *Enoch to come over and listen to my new ABBA album on Carla's portable record player? He'd like the helicopter on it! That'd be really mush.* Dir Africans don't play with Europeans in their houses.

'Look! Baboons! Mom! Baboons!' John bounces up and down.

Dad slows the car down and John opens the car door. A troop, mother, father, three little ones – no four, a baby clinging on under its mother. The father baboon bares his teeth and rushes at the car.

'Shut the bloody door man!' Dad yells.

John slams the door. Dad hoots and the baboon turns his blue rump and runs back to the troop. Carla and I laugh so much I nearly wee on the seat.

'Look at its bum!'

'Look at its teeth,' says Mom, 'they'd tear your arm off in a second.'

The troop move to the side of the road.

'Mom, throw them a banana!' I say.

Mom throws a banana out the window and a baboon catches it. The other baboons try to snatch it away. The father bares his teeth and rushes at the others. Some of the troop screech at him but don't move. Mom throws another couple of bananas. The mother grabs one and the little ones pounce on the remaining one which breaks and scatters. The bigger of the three snatches the biggest bit and scoots off under a tree to eat it, eyeing his brothers and sisters. Hey, maybe we are descended from monkeys after all. I look at John as he bounces up and down on the seat and figure, true's fact.

'Survival of the fittest,' Dad says.

'Give them the rest Mom,' I say.

'Ja,' says John. 'Let's see a baboon fight.'

Carla raises her eyebrows at him. 'Doos,' she says.

'Bye, bye bananas,' Mom throws the rest out of the window.

'Let's catch the view across the valley,' Dad says.

On the dirt road that leads to the top of the mountain ridge, we move through cloud.

'I can't bloody see a thing.' Dad peers out over the steering wheel.

'They don't call this mountain Mubvumbi, mountains of the mist, for nothing.'

'Who Dad?' I ask.

'The Queen and Prince Charles, who d'you think?' Dad glances at me through the rear-view mirror. 'The Afs.'

'Dave, we're off the road.' Mom's hand clamps the edge of her seat.

Dad turns the wheel and the mist swallows the car. We can see the road. And then we can't. There's a crunch. The car tips slightly to the left.

'Just stop the car, Dave! We're off the road! Just stop the car!'

'Jeez, Mom, don't shout! You're freaking us out!'

'Shut up!' Dad hits the brakes.

Everyone's silent. The mist slides over the car like a mink coat. Then, just like abracadabra, it lifts. Sunlight gleams on the bumper. We all laugh. Carla and Mom look out the window and both scream at once.

'Shit!' says Mom, running fingers from both hands through her hair.

'Just don't open your doors,' Dad says, looking out of Mom's window.

'Ja really, Dad, I think we'll just step outside for a stroll,' Carla says.

Dad jerks the wheel and steps on it. We all scream. Dad brakes.

'Shit, Dave, what you do that for?' Mom's hand grabs at Dad's arm. Us kids release our hands from the front seats.

'Did you wanna end up dead?' He points, 'down there?'

If he hadn't stepped on it and swung, the back wheels would have gone over the edge into the steep valley. Us too.

The high, thin air outside the car is cold and fresh and smells of dried herbs. John stands and I sit on a rock looking down at the valley below. The view is to die for, but not in our case, ha, ha. Trees spread over the piles of purply mountains like moss. I feel like a giant and an ant at the same time. Sloped behind us, giant tree ferns spread themselves over a stream that trickles its way down the valley. Mom stoops, scoops and wets the back of her neck, then she flicks water at Carla, who side steps the arc.

'Look! Look!' John points into the west of the valley.

An eagle hovers, drops, hovers and then swoops, only to return again and climb, this time with something long in its beak.

'What's that?'

'Snake,' says Dad. He points, 'Crown Eagle – see the crown of feathers? Beautiful creature.'

I think of John scampering down the rock to find Enoch, to tell him about the eagle. That's three times now since the Christmas hols that I've seen crown eagles.

'They can look directly into the sun you know.'

Ja we know.

'That's why they're often a symbol of prophesy. Carriers of truth – pointing to the future,' Dad says.

The eagle tilts, his lower wing grazing the tree canopy covering the valley. So eagle, where is Enoch and when will he be back? Not even Wilson can tell me where he's gone. *I am not his keeper,* he says when I ask. How come I can never find him in the usual places? He's not scared of my dad is he? No ways. I saw his face that night after John nearly drowned.

Carla sings as she clambers down the mountain a little way to join Mom.

'What else?' I ask.

'They also symbolise action, men of action have them as their symbol.'

And then, like the mist, the eagle is gone. A sign near Dad reads, *Danger, Cliff Edge, Keep Clear.* The word 'danger' is underlined. Dad stands on the edge of the cliff, with his back to us, his FN rifle hanging from his shoulder like a handbag.

'That's what's causing all the trouble, bloody terrs coming in from over there.' Dad takes a pee in the direction of the mountains of Mozambique.

'The old forts of the Mbiri tribe are down there.' He waves his free hand over the valley.

I'm sure the ancestor spirits of the Mbiri will appreciate Dad weeing in their general direction.

'They used to hide out in those caves.' Dad shakes himself and flicks his shorts up.

I peer across at the green knobbled slopes of the mountains in the foreground.

'I can't see any caves.'

'Ja, but they're there, hideouts, hidden in the clefts of the hills.'

I imagine little warriors with spears, like rock paintings come to life, Mbiri spilling out like ants from anthills to ambush their enemies below.

'This whole valley was the Rozvi kingdom, the hill that we're standing on now is known as Tsayuru, it's the highest point in the kingdom.' Dad shields his eyes with his hand as he looks out over the mountains.

'There's leopard all over these mountains too. They particularly like twelve-year-old-girl-flesh.' He lunges at me, making me scream.

Mom looks up from where she's crouched a little way down the mountain below us beside a silver gum covered in ropey liana. She's found some orchids. Her t-shirt rolled up, Carla lies next to Mom in her red plastic-rimmed sunglasses, her hipbones pointing at the sky.

'Don't scare the kids, Dave – Look! Flower of the Gods – I think,' she smiles and pokes her forefinger into the red and gold-striped cup of the flower. The orchid nods at her, but Dad pays no attention.

'They're not as dangerous as the bloody terrs though, hey –' he nods towards Mozambique. 'Bloody thousands of them,' he laughs, 'and they don't run away if you shout and clap your hands, not like leopards, hey, they just keep bloody coming.'

8.

The workers are leading most of the mombies out through the lower gate of the dairy and down to pasture. There are still four cows in the dairy, their teats being pumped and sucked by the tubes that lead to the big tanks. The floor is muddy and wet and water spills out from the little gutters that run down both sides of the dairy. Righteous smiles at us from behind a black and white Friesian.

I wave at him, 'Hi, Righteous.'

Righteous touches his temple with his hand and smiles, then he slaps the rump of the cow with his blue cap and she follows the sound of the bells down to the paddock.

'We got the dip from the vets in town,' says John. 'Are we too late to feed the calves?'

'No, you not too late, but careful, they are too much hungry!'

Two calves peer through the wooden gate of their enclosure.

'Aaah, they're so sweet man!' I say, patting the backs and sides of the calves. They're black and white like their mother, with long-lashed Bambi eyes. I feel guilty for liking steak. John strokes their noses. Righteous hands a bottle to me, then grabs the first calf's upper jaw and inserts it deep into its mouth. The calf sucks, spit drooling, eyes rolling. I laugh as I'm jerked forward by the sucking pull of the calf.

'Mine's gonna finish first!' John calls.

'It's not a competition, the calf's drinking it, not you.'

The calves are finished in two minutes flat.

'Eh he, this is the way,' says Righteous, smiling.

Righteous calls out and a worker I half recognise appears. Righteous hands him the empty bottles. He takes them and looks at us but doesn't smile. Like Righteous, he's dressed in overalls and gum boots. He walks very slowly, as if he's not happy to be here and keeps looking at me with his narrow eyes. His skin is pocked and around his right eye are lots of little scars. Twists of hair stand up all over his head. He doesn't look like a farm worker.

'Who's that, Righteous?' I ask when he moves to the back of the dairy.

'He is Justice, son of my brother.'

Oh ja. I sometimes forget Enoch has another brother besides Godfrey.

'Isn't he one of Nessie's students now?' He was allowed to finish school, I remember him sitting outside his mother's house reading when I went to find Enoch once a few years ago. He just looked at me, scaring me, which made me circle round the compound and into the bush instead, as if I was planning to go there in the first place. He's been gone for ages now. He went when his father left to work on Uncle Joe's farm.

'Yes, he can be student, and now, he can be farm worker.' Righteous doesn't sound too happy. He wipes sweat from his temple with the back of his arm.

Enoch's other brother, Godfrey has finished school too and has become our gardener. Will Enoch work for us as well? I can't imagine it even though his brother, uncle and grandfather do. I've never met an African doctor but I bet he'd be good at that. He knows everything about bush medicine.

'Is that Justice?' asks Dad, coming up with a cold Castle in his hand.

Justice steps out of the dairy and into the sunlight. 'Yes, Mr Cameron. I am Justice.'

'Mr Cameron is it? Bit familiar aren't you?'

'You call me Justice, this is more familiar.' He folds his arms in a way that dairy workers don't when speaking to their boss.

'Ja, but it looks to me as if you're the one working on my farm.' Dad takes a step towards him.

'This might be your farm, Mr Cameron, but the land belongs

to my ancestors, so I think maybe we are equal, for today.'

'I don't remember hiring you.'

'Ernesta is the one.'

'Ernesta? Now that's familiar. Well Justice, you can stay for now,' he says. 'At least until I've spoken to my sister.' Then he calls out to Righteous, 'Everything alright?'

Justice just stands there with his arms folded, his eyes on Dad.

'Yes boss. It is good,' Righteous says from where he's disconnecting tubes from Caramel's teats.

'Good,' says Dad. He turns and walks quickly back to the house.

Justice moves around the dairy like a shadow. He's taken the top part of his overalls down, the sleeves flap like dead arms where they hang below his waist. He wears a pink t-shirt with the sleeves cut widely off so that I can see the muscle of his chest. A ropey knot of pink scar tissue runs from his left nipple, under his armpit. I try not to look at him but I can't help it. When he catches me looking he stares at me with eyes that could glue mine to the back of my skull.

Granny Rose dabs paint on her canvas and then stops and, holding her paintbrush in the air, leans forwards in her high-backed cane chair to gaze out over the lawn towards the mountains, like she's listening to them telling her something. Carla and I are on the swing-couch in our pyjamas, with Mom and Dad, our bellies warmed by Wilson's bobotie and carrots. John is racing his dinky toys up and down the veranda, crashing them into the walls, spinning them across the red-polished cement and making explosive sounds with his mouth. Carla pops gum at Donny Osmond, David Essex and the rest of the yawns with the latest hair don'ts in Jackie Annual 1976.

'Howzit!' Nessie yells out the window as she pulls up in her car, before running over the lawn barefoot. On the veranda she kisses Granny Rose, who says, 'Oh it's the red brigade arrived.' Then she comes over and begins kissing everyone else on the cheek.

'Why did you hire him, Nessie? After all that's happened?' Dad says looking at his beer bottle, when she gets to him.

'He's one of my students, one of the brightest in fact, and he needs the money.' Nessie dumps her suede fringed bag on the floor.

She hands me a parcel. A huge butterfly in pink and purple neos has been drawn on the brown paper. Around the butterfly, Nessie's created a halo effect with silver glitter. She's added two badges to the front lapels, a Rolling Stones logo of lips and hanging tongue, and a "Ban the Bomb" peace sign.

'I love it! Thanks Nessie.'

Nessie smiles at me. She's as beautiful as any butterfly.

'I know he's one of your students, Nessie. A moderate one no doubt. This'll be a convenient location for him, won't it? He'll be able to nip over to bases in Mozambique whenever he wants to hey?'

'He's a student Dave,' Nessie says sinking low into a veranda chair, with her legs splayed out in front of her. 'He's studying.'

'Ja. I can imagine what he's studying. Don't be so bloody naive little sister. What do you think most black students are?'

'I dunno Dave? Frustrated? Fed up? Oppressed? That's what they are.'

'Well he's not staying. He can work the month out and that's it.'

'Whatever you say Dave,' Nessie gets up. 'I think I'll be needing a beer,' she winks at me.

'Here's to the Frasers, who're taking the gap down south, because they can't stand the heat,' Dad says raising his beer, about his fourth one. 'Up yours Frasers, hope it doesn't get too hot for you in South-Africa. Only a matter of time before the South-Africans bow to international pressure and sell out. Hey Granny Rose?' he calls out. But Granny Rose is lost in her painting.

Mom says, 'C'mon Dave. You can't blame them for wanting to leave, for wanting to sleep at night. They're afraid for their children. The Roberts were friends of theirs. It's a bloody frightening situation.'

'Cue the lecture,' says Carla, peeling bits of red nail polish off her nails and flicking them in my general direction, without raising her eyes from The Bay City Rollers, who look like rejects from planet Agog.

'Gross man.' A bit of Carla's nail-polish lands on Gary Glitter's face. I lift the book and check out the photograph. 'He looks better with a red moustache. Disco dwarf.'

'I saw old Mrs Giles yesterday, Granny Rose,' Nessie says.

Granny Rose peers at Nessie from behind her glasses.

'Really? I never liked her much. She wasn't much of a dancer. Always refused a drink. Only controllers don't drink.'

Mom laughs, 'I think you may have a point there Granny Rose.'

'Well, of course dear, I always have a point, and the point is this, life is enhanced by a drink. If you cannot see that, there surely must be something wrong. One or two mind,' she waves her paintbrush at Dad, 'not six or seven. You drink too much, just like your father, and your grandfather, no wonder you got yourself into such a muddle.'

She looks at Mom, 'Do you Catholics drink? Apart from the cannibalistic blood, of course.'

Mom smiles a stiff smile, 'Yes Granny Rose, we like a drink,' she waves her beer at her, 'though it's a matter of personal conscience.'

'Personal conscience? What's that, you mean personal consumption? Catholic claptrap.' She waves her paintbrush at Da. 'See what you've done, you silly boy?'

Dad laughs. 'Shit I can't believe Mrs Giles is still alive. Didn't her father work with great Grandpa Mellville on the railway?'

'Her mother died of black water fever, along with two of her brothers,' Granny Rose says. 'That blew her chances. She nursed her father instead of marrying. Became a spinster, very silly. No lovers either. Ridiculous.' She dabs paint at the canvas.

Trying not to snort with laughter, I dig Carla in the ribs, but she's more interested in looking at the chinless wonders in her annual.

'My father put his life into that railway,' says Granny Rose, putting down her palette on the low veranda wall. 'He put his life into helping build this country.'

'So did over a thousand black men, Granny Rose. Hundreds of them died of black water fever, malaria, injury, miles away from their wives and children.'

'Yes but they wouldn't have known what to do if we hadn't shown them. Honestly.' Granny Rose pokes her paintbrush at Nessie.

Nessie throws her arms up and laughs.

'Cue the documentary presentation,' says Carla, still reading the Jackie, lying down and stretching her legs over me.

'My father worked with Cecil Rhodes, helped with the laying out of the new Umtali. Said he wasn't all he was cracked up to be, said he was an arrogant bastard. Said some other things too,' Granny Rose says.

'Those black men didn't get their land though, Granny Rose,' says Nessie. 'They were shoved off to the tribal trust lands, they're still there now – well their children are, waiting for their land,' Nessie says.

'Oh do be quiet. You're such an agitation, Ernesta. Why don't you get married? You need a man to occupy you. Get a lover, do something constructive. For pity's sake, don't be so political. It's not attractive dear,' Granny Rose says peering at her painting.

Nessie laughs. 'I do have a lover Granny Rose.'

'He's not an African is he? Or a politician?'

'Well he might be,' Nessie smiles, 'possibly even both.'

'Well, I'm sure we can rely on you to muddy the waters. Your mother was a terrible handful,' says Granny Rose. She takes up her palette again.

Carla yawns loudly. 'Same old bloody record,' she says.

'It's a hose man,' I say, still laughing.

High pitched boy voices travel from the kitchen roof followed by the pinging sounds of small stones as John and Nakai launch an attack on us from above. The adults, too bombed and hot on conversation don't notice.

'I'm going to watch the news.' Mom sighs as she steps through the veranda doors into the lounge.

Carla slaps her annual shut and follows Mom. Stretching out on the swing-chair, I catch sight of a bloody huge baboon-spider making its hairy way down the wall. An electric shiver travels down the backs of my knees. I'd almost rather see anything than one of those. It scuttles across the floor towards Dad.

'Chips out Dad! It's a baboon spider, on the floor, next to your foot man!'

Dad looks down, lifts his foot, then stamps down really hard on the spider.

'Jeez Dad, why d'you kill it?'

Dad looks at me, wriggles his eyebrows, and says, 'Because I'm bigger than it?' He smears what's left of the spider over the front lawn.

'What I try to do Dave, is speak the truth as I see it, and not just follow someone else's ideology,' Nessie is saying.

'Ah, you mean Smith's?' says Dad.

'Not just Smith,' says Nessie. 'Smith's stubborn, misguided, slow even. But I don't think he's a bad bloke. It could be worse, much worse.'

'Ja, well at least he's trying to keep Rhodesia Marxist free,' says Dad.

Nessie snorts. She reminds me of a beautiful black horse.

'My God, Dave, you take a simplistic view. Do you ever waver from the party line?'

'Look at Angola, Nessie, look at the rest of bloody Africa. The African is not ready for power.'

'Oh and we should decide for them when they are ready for power? How bloody patronising. We come in, take over, enslave –'

'Enslave? Don't you ever waver from your party line? They were bloody killing each other when we got here, man.'

'We have taken away their choice, Dave. To live as they see fit. However unfit that may seem to you.'

'Rubbish man, they have the Tribal Trust lands, where they live as they always have. With their chiefs –'

'Ja, we keep them sectioned off, now, in PVs so we can see what they're up to. Protected Villages my foot.'

'Nessie, if they didn't collaborate with the terrs we wouldn't have to –'

'The terrs. Even your terminology is quaint. To some, Dave, these men are freedom fighters.'

'Well, Nessie, I get to see what these freedom fighters do to the people they are trying to liberate. I've seen people, African people, liberated from their noses, their lips, for not being able to give satisfactory information to terrorists.'

Nessie sighs and puts her arched brown feet on the edge of the table; the glasses shiver slightly.

'The writing's on the wall, Dave. Just wish you and the rest would read it.'

Dad jumps up the veranda steps and heads for the doors into the lounge. 'What's a bloke got to do to get another beer around here? – Wilson! – You'll never get married at this rate Nessie.'

She smiles and twists a silver ring with a huge blue stone in it.

'No, I'll just take lovers,' she shouts at his back.

'Ja, black ones,' Dad shouts as he disappears inside.

'Ja!' she shouts. 'I like a bit of contrast in my life!'

'Happy Birthday Jay-Bird,' she smiles at me. 'So how've you been?' she asks, putting her bare feet up on the table.

'Okay. Well not okay.'

'Why?'

'They won't let me see Enoch since John nearly drowned in the river. I haven't seen him for months. And anyway, I think he might be away, he's never in the places we used to go to and Wilson won't say where he is and –' I try not to start crying. 'You know, Dad's so ungrateful. He saved John from drowning.'

'Well, Dad is not always grateful about the same things that we are,' Nessie says sitting down next to me and putting her arm round me. 'He sees things in a different way to us. Hey, I've got a women's co-operative meeting down at the compound tomorrow with Patience, Godfrey's new bride,' she smiles. 'You can meet her, she's lovely.' She presses my head to her shoulder. 'No more tears hey.'

Ja, no more tears.

9.

For the first time this year I'm wearing a jersey over my school uniform. Nessie's blue man's shirt and rolled up jeans match the sky.

'Getting cooler earlier isn't it Jay? The words come from the King James Bible,' Nessie says, referring to the song she has been singing about seasons. 'I'll play that to you next time you come visit me.'

I focus on the thatched points of the huts as they come into view and on the corrugated iron over Enoch's house. Nessie's voice drifts around me.

'Patience works at a mission hospital. You'll like her Jay. She's good for the other women. She wants to do things, you know?' Nessie says.

'Ja. I know. She doesn't just want to be a nanny.'

I watch the ground. If I don't step on any paper thorns then it means I'll see him.

'Of course not. Apparently it was love at first sight for Godfrey when he saw her in the village shop. He made enquiries about her, declared his love and began courting her,' Nessie says. 'So simple!'

Stooping to pick up a lucky bean, I decide that if I find five lucky beans, I'll see him.

'Patience played hard to get for a while. She said she had no intention of marrying a garden boy. She was a career girl and wanted to marry a doctor, or at least a teacher. But Godfrey persuaded her by telling her that he was a 'doctor of the land' and giving her plants and flowers every time he saw her,' says Nessie.

I scan the sky for signs. If I see an eagle, definitely, definitely I'll see him. A white helmet shrike quivers above the bush. Its plump white breast beats quickly.

'He made sure to observe custom with her family too. When he went to visit her parents, he brought mealies, pumpkin and sweet potatoes. He has also had to raise quite a lot of money for the bride price – lobola – enough to buy at least one cow – are you listening Jay?' Nessie laughs.

Patience and Godfrey are arriving from across the compound. Patience carries a large navy-blue suitcase on her head and her arm is raised, obscuring her face, so at first I can't really see what she looks like. People start coming out of the huts clapping and whistling, the women dancing round, flicking up their bottoms. Godfrey wheels his bicycle with several boxes tied to the carrier and various plastic bags and a pot hanging from the handle bar. His smile is a biggie. Patience puts the suitcase down in the dirt and unties the boxes and the plastic bags outside the nganga's house. Everyone is hand clapping and hand clasping as they greet the newly-weds. Patience smiles widely and tips her head back when she laughs. She has teeth like pale mealie corn and a wide smile beams out below her leaf-shaped eyes. Other women begin arriving for the meeting. Godfrey has disappeared into one of the huts, probably to drink chibuku with the men. The women lay out plastic mats on the floor under the mahobohobo tree. Their babies sit staring around or crawl in the dust amongst the fallen tan-yellow fruit. Nessie crosses her legs and begins giving out the white envelopes of money she got from selling the cushions, bedspreads and tablecloths made by the women. One of the women says her husband doesn't want her to be involved in Nessie's co-operative. Another says the swikiro from Mdisa village said that the ancestors wouldn't like it and they'd better stop before their cattle start disappearing. She scratches her head under her beret and then laughs at how he said that if they gave him some of the money, he would get some muti to keep the ancestors happy and the tsotsis away.

'He's an unscrupulous old bastard,' Nessie laughs.

A woman cups her hand with her mouth, her eyes bulging. She

can't believe Nessie would say something like that. Everyone laughs and the women clap their hands against Nessie's.

'Yes. Teach her while her mind is supple. Or it will harden and then it will need to be cracked.' The voice is deep and heavy.

A creeping centipede of fear tickles down my spine.

'Justice!' Nessie says. 'Are you coming to join the women's meeting?'

The women laugh. His footsteps thud on the ground behind me.

'Why not? If I had nothing important to do, I could do this.'

He stoops and picks up a mahobohobo fruit, then stands in front of me, tall as a tree, with arms like branches stretching out from his gaping t-shirt, all gnarled and the colour of rubber inner tubes.

'You white people do not eat the fruit of this tree. You prefer imported fruit. Apples. The fruit of the imported people.' When he brings the fruit to his mouth I can see the edge of the ropey pink scar that runs from his chest to underneath his right arm. He looks at me as he chews slowly. Juice runs down his hand and into his copper bangles. The many scars around his eyes seem more fierce in the sunlight. They look like they've been slashed at with a pen knife. One scar runs from the edge of his left eye in a straight line towards his ear. I can't help looking at them. But when he looks back it feels like he could set me on fire and just wipe me out with one look from those narrow, mean, deep-set eyes above cheekbones that look like they'd carve into you like pangas. He spits a bit of fruit on the ground.

'You don't mind the tea though do you Justice?' Nessie smiles up at him. She looks at him like he's a child that she is afraid of setting off.

'No. The tea is good.' He throws the half-eaten fruit on the ground and wipes his mouth with the back of his hand. Then he turns and walks back very slowly to his mother's house, his bare feet swishing slightly in the dust.

The women laugh a bit more, but not too much.

'I sold some of your cushion-covers to one of the professors at the university. They are in his office,' Nessie says to one of the women.

'Ah so his wife did not like them? Or they can be in his house?'
Everyone laughs.

'Well if she didn't like them she does not have good taste,' Nessie
says.

Patience spreads out her bedspreads and cushion covers on the
plastic matting.

'This is really lovely work, Patience,' Nessie says. 'I definitely
think I'll be able to sell this kind of thing to the medems in the city!'

The women laugh at Nessie's African pronunciation of
'madam.' Patience looks really chuffed.

'So. I'll sell for you, give you eighty percent, and put twenty
percent into the co-operative bank account, so that it grows your
mutual investment. Eventually, you women can build your own
building.'

'For what can we have a building?' a woman asks.

'For anything you like,' Nessie says. 'All of you could vote, come
to an agreement and decide. Maybe a clinic, a library, a school, a
women's factory –'

The women laugh and shake their heads, 'A building?'

'A vote?'

'A factory?'

'Yes,' says Nessie. 'Anything is possible. If you believe.'

And the women laugh some more.

When the women are all standing up, saying their goodbyes and
laughing with Nessie, I slip away to sit on the rock behind Enoch's
house. Maybe I'm hoping he'll turn up too. But he's not there. It's
just me and the view of the gaping valley. I don't want to look, so I
lie down on the rock and close my eyes to the sun melting into my
face, listening to the women walk away, their voices disappearing
down the dirt road into the valley. I drift for a while. Then I hear
voices. Nessie's voice is coming from the window of the nganga's
house.

'You could be kinder to my niece.'

'The truth is always kind Ernesta,' he says.

His voice sounds less mean when he's talking to her.

'Come here, I will be kind to you.'

Nessie laughs.

'You're going to have to leave. My brother's not happy about you being here.'

'Ah. I am not happy about him being here.'

Nessie laughs again.

'It is enough time,' he says.

Nessie laughs some more and then says quietly. 'I love my family very much.'

'We all love our families. And we love freedom for our people, our family,' he says.

Then the voices are silent and soon there is the gentle thud of footsteps moving away, Nessie's I suppose, going back to the house. I close my eyes and wait, all the time getting the creepy feeling that he knows I'm here as I know he's still in there. I sit up quickly, trying to decide what to do. Rounding the side of the house, I almost scream as he appears at the door. His hair twists up around the top of his head like the thorns of Christ. He covers the door frame with the angles of his body. A curve of hip bone pokes out like the handle of a revolver above the overalls that he's rolled down below his hips. He loves himself.

'You are the second daughter,' he says dragging deeply from a rolled cigarette.

I look at the space across the compound and then at my own bare feet in the dust.

'You like my brother? Why? You are not happy, in your big house, on African land? With your European things? You come here to see him but he is not here.'

I want to run, but can't seem to even walk away.

He makes a sound like a laugh and blows smoke through his nose and mouth that floats around the compound yard.

Shut up. I hate the words you're saying. But I can't say anything. His words have trapped mine in my mind.

'Even if you rub your body on my brother's body you will not become African. Even if you mix your blood with his you will not become African,' he says, his black eyes digging into mine. 'Our skin is the colour of the land.'

What? Blonde and green and khaki? Now his words are stupid and I watch my feet walk quickly away from the sound of his voice.

'I was born here!' I yell it over my shoulder from halfway across the compound.

'Go where there is snow,' he shouts. 'That is your white land.'

'My aunt is white!' I shout back.

Well sort of caramel-coloured from the sun. Like me.

At dinner, Nessie pushes her long hair behind her ears, swigs her beer and jokes with Dad. Carla blends her gravy into her mash, turning it all beige.

'Have you met Godfrey's new wife, Patience, yet?' Nessie asks Dad.

'No but we could do with a house girl,' Dad jokes.

'Is that all you think about? How these people can serve you? Maybe there's been a we-dding, a cele-bration, maybe there's gonna be chil-dren, new lives.' Nessie jabs at him with her empty beer bottle, her face pink from the beer, her green eyes blocked out by her big, black pupils.

'Ja. Lekker, more and more wor-kers, we're really short sta-aaffed.' Dad mimics, poking a finger at her side, then he leans back in his chair towards the curtained windows that look out on the darkened slope leading down to the dairy.

'Must you do that Dave? One day you'll just fall backwards,' Mom says.

Dad leans back even more, pulling the curtains over himself.

'You're so childish Dad,' Carla says.

Dad mimes her to me, so I give him a half-baked smile.

'Jay came to the meeting today. She saw how beautiful the work was didn't you Jay?' Nessie says.

I glare at her. But Mom and Dad don't say anything about me being at the compound. Nessie gives me a look that asks me what's wrong, so I look away from her.

'Bloody communist,' says Granny Rose to Nessie, a bit of carrot flying from her mouth and landing on her serviette.

John laughs, but I don't laugh back.

Carla puts down her fork. 'That's it. I can't eat anymore.'

Mom puts down her own fork and gives Carla a 'for goodness sake' look.

'Well I'm sorry Mom, she puts me off my food,' Carla hisses.

'She's ill,' Mom whispers to Carla. 'And old.'

'Ja. She's got ants in her trousers,' John whispers to me.

But I cannot laugh at what he calls Granny Rose's Alzheimer's. The sound of Wilson clattering in the kitchen as he washes pots and pans and dishes becomes very loud in my head.

In the dark passage, sounds make me tiptoe on mouse-feet outside the bathroom door. Vomiting. Other sounds, of the adults arguing about the news on TV, come from the lounge. I knock gently.

'Go away!' Carla shouts. 'Use Mom's bathroom. I'm not feeling very well.'

Carla's white dressing-table is covered with photos of her and her ballet friends in rehearsal and backstage in full make-up, their hair pulled back into buns, their legs hard and thin. They look like nervous racehorses. Old ballet shoes hang from their ribbons around the shuttered parts of the central oval mirror. Pictures of Margot Fonteyn and Baryshnikov, who Carla says she wants to marry, pulled from the pages of *Fair Lady* magazine, paper the walls around the dressing-table. She always pushes her food around on her plate and saves her arguments for dinnertime and leaps up at the slightest excuse. I pick up a pink and white cushion with a picture of an old-fashioned ballerina bowing to an audience. It makes me feel quite sick myself. Pink reminds me of artificially rouged skin to cover up disease, or scars and wrinkles. It reminds me of nipples and giblets and other kinds of male and female things.

Carla jumps when she sees me. She pulls at the turban of her towel and begins rubbing at her hair.

'What are you doing in my room?'

'Why were you kotching in the bathroom?'

She goes over to her dressing-table and sits down. Her yellow towelling dressing gown is part open, showing her long white nightie and the bones of her shoulders.

'I don't know. Stomach bug?'

'Brain bug you mean.'

She looks at me quickly, eyes raised from beneath the towel. 'It's really none of your business, Jay.'

'Ja? I'm your sister. Maybe I'll ask Mom –' I start to get off the bed, but she stops me by coming to sit next to me.

'Look, Jay, it's no big deal. We all do it –'

'No. We don't. Who's we?'

'Us dancers. Lots of girls. Women.'

She clocks my face. 'Really Jay, there's nothing to it, you just –' she sticks her finger down her throat, then pulls her finger out, 'like that. Or use a toothbrush.'

I'm shaking my head slowly. So she stops.

'You're sick Carla. I think you should see a doctor. How long has this been going on? You hardly eat anyway, so if you're hurling what you do eat – where do you find the strength to dance?'

'Look I do eat,' she says. 'Healthy stuff.'

'Ja. Like lettuce,' I say. 'Dipped in vinegar.'

'Look, Jay,' she grabs my shoulders and smiles into my eyes. 'Hey sis, don't tell Mom okay? And I won't tell about your sneaking around looking for Enoch?'

I shake my head at her. 'How did you know? I can't believe you're blackmailing me.'

She smiles, 'Well I can't believe I have a sister that prefers black boys to the white kids at school.'

'I have friends at school. Felicity. Samuel Hillman from my class.'

'Ja. Felicity who runs the Scripture Union? That Christian freak?'

'Ja, well, at least she has beliefs that she's not afraid to stick up for. And she's clever, she's top of Standard Five A.'

'And Samuel? He's a swot. And he's overweight.'

'No he's not. He's big built. He plays rugby. Anyone's overweight to you Twiggy-brain. He's funny as well, he makes me laugh.'

'Ja, well. You seem to prefer Enoch. The other two never come over. Face it Jay,' she smiles, 'you're the weird one.'

I wander out to the veranda, trying to digest Carla's words. Granny Rose sits alone in the dark. It seems the right place for me too.

'Who's that?' She narrows her eyes at me. 'Which one are you?' Granny Rose asks.

'It's me man, Granny Rose, Jayne,' I laugh. The weird one. Jeez Carla's something else. She stage manages everything. Including me.

'Oh, yes, of course, you're a true Cameron aren't you darling,' she says, stroking my hair. 'Your hair is quite golden from the sun.' She takes me by the shoulders and peers at me. 'You're as brown as a coloured, though.' Looking down at my legs, she says, 'Lovely long legs, like a colt's.' She looks at my face, as if seeing me for the first time. 'And your eyes are like your father's, big and brown – no not brown – hazel – just the right amount of yellow – like a cat – yes, that's what you're like.' She taps me on the nose, 'you're a little cat.'

'Why do you wear those denim shorts all the time?' she says as I jump off the veranda on to the lawn, 'you won't marry an African now, will you, or a politician? Marry a nice farmer.'

The lawn prickles damply under my bare feet. I feel like leaping and running and hand standing all over it.

'That's what you need,' she calls out. 'A nice farmer.'

Her words float between the arch made with my body as my feet point to the sky, then touch the earth. The music announcing the roll-call of our dead soldiers floats above the conversation drifting from the lounge, like pink icing on slowly rotting cake.

10.

Months later, I scope the compound again, from the safety of the lucky bean tree, my arm looped around the trunk. It feels wide as the desert. Moses and Godfrey are sitting under the mahobohobo tree near the nganga's house on upturned boxes. When he sees me, Moses raises an enamel mug and calls out, 'It is the young madam!'

'I'm not a madam,' I say. 'I'm just a girl.'

Moses and Godfrey slurp and laugh, their noises blending with the sounds of chickens scratching in the dirt near the thorn tree and the birds being busy in the bush.

'But you are European, so you are a madam,' Godfrey says.

Jeez, he hardly ever speaks to me. It must be the beer.

'No I'm not.'

'What can we do for you?' Moses asks.

'Nothing.'

'Ah it is not for nothing that you have come here. Maybe you have a reason?' Moses raises his palms upwards, flashing his creamy-toothy smile. His breath is enough to kill flying mozzies. I can smell it from here.

'Is Enoch here?'

Moses slaps his hands on his thighs.

'For sure now we see the reason.'

Enoch's mother comes out of the doorway of her house, scratching her head under her doek. She is wearing a blue button-fronted housedress, just like a nanny would wear. She does not look like her nganga self. She's less freaky out here in the sunlight than the last time I saw her in the medicine hut. The tribal slashes on her face are purplish and seem less scary. Her nose is like the head of a swallow flying downwards, the nostrils its curved wings. It seems stuck on from someone else's face, because the rest of her face is so hard and strong, just like Justice's. Enoch's mom ignores me and just pours more doro into Moses' and Godfrey's tin mugs, one hand in the curve of her back, like I'm not standing here like a spare part. Only her scars smile, they're like tiny curved up mouths on the hills of her cheekbones.

'Is Enoch here?' I ask again.

She looks at me for a moment and I can't understand what her eyes are saying. Then she says, 'You go in,' jerking her head in the direction of the doorway. I walk past her, smelling her peppery, smoky smell, and the world slows down. I've known him for years and this is the first time I've been in his house. In the main room, Enoch is sitting at a big wooden table reading a book. Something lights up in his face and then goes out again.

'Your mother let me in,' I say, trying not to stare at him. His shoulders look like bicycle handlebars. His face has sort of got longer.

He continues to look at me, hands resting on the table like it's a piano.

'Can I sit down?' I ask.

He gets up and pulls a chair out. And he's taller. I sit down. Then he goes outside. I don't know what to do, so I stay sitting. Along the wall behind me is a long, polished wood record player unit with a crocheted cloth on it. It looks kind of out of place, an old fashioned 'European' piece of furniture. I wonder if it works. Under the window are piles of boxes, some covered over with blankets, who knows? Maybe containing human body parts used for the nganga's muti. A spider descends from the ceiling on a line of web, hovering above the table. It swings slightly in a galaxy of dust over a shaft of light coming in the window. Enoch comes back holding an enamel mug that he puts on the table in front of me. I thank him and lift the cup to my lips, not knowing what it is. Thank God, the cup contains warm Coke. I gulp some of it down while Enoch watches me.

'You have lost your hair,' Enoch says.

I laugh. 'I didn't lose it, the hairdresser cut it. It's a pageboy.'

He laughs, 'A pageboy? A boy who must turn pages. Like me. I am a boy who must turn pages.'

We laugh together and the spider scoots up its web and disappears into the wooden beams holding up the corrugated iron roof.

'What are you reading?' I ask reaching out.

He snatches the book and turns it over. As he does so I catch sight of a book I read at school a few years ago.

'It is too much stupid. But I must read.' His voice travels up and down rusty-sounding pipes.

'Ja. I thought those books were stupid too.' I smile, then run my fingers over the chipped edges of the table, trying not to look at him. Enoch looks down at the book.

'At your school you have too much books?' He looks up.

I look at him quickly then look down at my hands. 'Ja. We have loads. Most of them boring.'

'You can bring me some books?'

I laugh, 'I dunno. Maybe. Why do you want them?' I look up then down at the table again.

'For read. Why you think?' he asks.

'Okay. Sorry.' Dir. 'Ja, I'll try.' I look round at the walls. They're bare save for some women's clothes hanging in plastic in front of me and a tattered black and white photograph of an old man in tribal clothing in a wooden frame.

'Who's that?' I ask.

'This is my mother's father.'

'Oh,' I say. 'He looks like he's wearing a leopard.'

Enoch smiles. 'He kill that leopard. That leopard can kill him. But he kill that leopard.'

'How?'

'With his hands. With only his hands.' He mimes his grandfather wrestling with the leopard with his long curved hands.

I laugh. 'I don't think I believe you Enoch.'

He laughs. 'I can make you believe.'

'Oh ja. How?'

'I can take you to my mother.' He widens his eyes in mock fear.

'No thanks.'

We laugh remembering me all jumpy in the medicine hut.

'You are too much scared of my mother.'

'Ja well. She is scary.' We both look at the table.

'Do you all sleep together?' I ask about the sleeping area with the mattresses on the floor and the clothes hanging on hooks next door. 'In that room?'

Enoch laughs, 'My mother, she sleep outside.'

'In that hut – the medicine hut?'

He laughs again, 'She sleeps with ghosts.'

'Oh. A ghost sleeper,' I laugh.

The voices of the men outside the window grow louder.

'Where have you been?' I ask. 'It's been months.'

'Away. My family.'

'Ja but where?'

'It does not matter. You cannot go there.'

'You mean your mother's family, in Mozambique?'

He just stares at the table jiggling a knee, so I rec a yes.

'Hey Enoch? Why don't you teach me Shona and I'll teach you about books!'

Words come easier when we are outside, under the sky.

'For why? Can this make us understand each other better? You can hear what I am saying but you cannot understand.' He shakes his head.

'What do you mean?' I watch the sun falling partly on the edge of the wooden table, and on the mud-packed floor between us.

'You see. What do I mean?'

'Oh you mean I can't understand your life.'

Jeez he makes me feel bad. And stupid for asking. His mother walks past the window, but does not look in. Please don't come in.

'You were pretty cheeky to my Dad,' I laugh it out.

'I should have let the water swallow him.' Now his eyes dig into mine, just like his brother's. Outside Godfrey and Moses laugh and it feels like they're laughing at me.

'Why are you being like this? I was just saying – I thought it was – it's brave –'

'You need to be careful for what you say.'

'Why? I thought we were friends.'

He laughs like a whip.

'He didn't mean to tell you off Enoch. He was worried. That Roberts boy – kids are being killed around here you know.'

I watch the side of his face, his temple is delicate, china covered in a thin layer of brown skin.

'Some parents can be worried, but they can do nothing.'

'You mean your father?' I move my hand a little towards him.

'I do not want your sorry.' He shoves his chair back.

'Why do you say that?' I get up. 'What have I done to you? None of this is my fault!' I try to force the stupid lump in my throat back down. 'You've changed. I thought we were friends.' My cheeks are baking. I've never spoken about our friendship before.

He stands up and I see he's wearing grey school trousers a little too small.

'What are friends?' he says.

'I don't know. People that like each other?'

He sits back down and his face softens. 'For sure you are my friend.'

'Shall we go outside?' I ask, trying not to cry. 'My parents will be back from work soon.'

'No,' he says, 'I want to read. I must read.'

If only I hadn't said let's go outside, I could have stayed.

'Okay. I'll try to come tomorrow.'

He doesn't even look up.

In the shape shifting light of late afternoon, I stand on the smooth round rock under the window of Enoch's house. I can see him sitting at the little wooden table.

'Enoch! Hey Enoch, I brought you a book.'

He jumps up.

'Wait! I'm coming.'

He stands beside me.

'I had to wait for my dad to go down to the dairy and my mom to start drinking on the veranda.'

He smiles, and taking the book looks all over the front and back covers.

'Nancy Drew?' He laughs, but he doesn't think it's funny.
'Why you laughing?'
'This book,' he says, 'It look too much stupid.'
'Why?' I ask.
'What is this? This book for girls.' His voice cracks. 'Why you bring me girl's book?' He hands it back and leans against his house, one foot up on the wall.

What's wrong with girls. I know what's wrong with girls. But not all girls. 'So? It's about adventure. She's like a detective.'

'This cannot help,' Enoch says. 'Bring books to help. Many books. Come tonight. There.' He points at the largest thorn tree on the edge of the compound. He takes a step closer to me and looks at my face. 'You scared? Of the dark?' He makes me feel funny inside. Different.

'Ja, sure.' I say it sarcastically, but I feel scared and excited at once.

'See that tree?'
'What? You gonna meet me by that tree – at night?'
'For sure, I meet – at twelve 'o clock.' He steps back and folds his arms and tilts his head. 'But you too much scared,' he smiles.

'I'm not scared of anything, okay?' But Enoch just laughs.
'Bring books!' he shouts at my back. 'Bring books with army, with soldiers!'

The breeze puffs frangipani fragrance in through the grenade mesh and makes my curtains gape. It's half past eleven. I'm in bed fully dressed, waiting for my parents to stop arguing and go to sleep.

'She did put her part of the inheritance from Grandpa Patrick into the farm Reen.'

'So? She shouldn't hire staff behind your back. Especially him. He's like his father.'

Dad laughs. 'Look Reen, he's going soon okay.'
'Did you order the security fence?'
'Not yet. I'll do it tomorrow.'
'You better do it or it won't be ready before you go on call-up.'
'You have the agric-alert, the neighbours –'
'Ja? What good is that? They're bloody miles away.'

'I'll do it Irene. Don't worry okay?'

Unlatching and pushing out the mesh, I jump out of the window, landing in a crouch on the ground. Then I race across the kikuyu grass that glows a luminous lime colour in the safety light. An owl hoots. Up in the avo tree a sliver of yellow eye catches mine. My heartbeat matches my running thuds as I look down at my bare feet racing through the trees and down the moonlit path towards the compound. I skirt around the far side till I get to the thorn tree at the far edge of the compound. Skeletal thorns like witches' fingers claw at the moon, now higher and yellower against the inky sky. The huts of the compound glisten and glow in their moony whiteness. Something rustles in the quivering bush. Then a flick, like a snake whipping in the long grass. Above, the constellations look pricked out and patterned with God's giant compass. Pressing myself against the trunk, I stare into the darkness, trying to imagine funny thoughts. When a thought does come, it's not one I'd have over for fun. There are still leopard in these mountains. Dad says they come down looking for Eland foal. Then, like a stalking leopard, something comes up behind me through the darkness. If it weren't for a dry hand on my mouth, maybe I'd scream. And then laughter, lots and lots of wheezy snorty laughter. I slap Enoch hard on the arm.

'You are scared!' he says.

'Shut up man. I'm not scared. I just got a shock man.'

'Where's the book?' he says. His laughing eyes shine blackly out of white. My hands begin to sweat. Jeez. I left them under my bed. Dad's book on the SAS, John's 1974 Action Adventure Annual and Treasure Island. Now he'll know I just wanted to see him.

'Sorry Enoch. I forgot.'

The light goes out of his eyes, he turns and slaps his hand against the trunk of the tree and I slap the heel of mine against my forehead.

'I'll bring them tomorrow Enoch. What's the big deal man?' I touch his upper arm. 'You'll love them – boys books.'

Looking down, he shifts his bare feet amongst the mound of dirt beneath the tree, his hands in his trouser pockets. His cheeks suck into his mouth. I can't read his face. Then he stoops and picks up a thorn.

'Now I must prick you with this thorn. Then you can remember.'

'No ways man.' I pick up a thorn too. 'If I get it you get it.' I pretend to lunge at him.

He laughs and stabs his thorn at me. The tip grazes my arm. My arm darts out. The long white thorn pricks his forearm. There is blood on the tip when I glance down at it.

'Yikes! Sorry man. I didn't mean it.'

Enoch sucks his arm. His eyes look up at me. They kind of give me the shivers.

'Now you must bring me many books. I want your brother's books. Your father's books. Books about soldiers.'

'Okay,' I say laughing. 'Anything you say man.'

He puts a hand on my arm and a finger to his lips. His luminous eyes stare in the direction of his mother's medicine hut. A tall man stoops and comes out of the woven grass door, something long in his arms. We back up against the tree. The figure walks across the moon-bright yard of the compound, heading for the trees. Enoch calls me with his arm, starting to follow.

'No ways man,' I whisper. 'I'm scared. Let's stay here.'

He pulls me towards the path. The figure walks quickly. Enoch and I follow him at a safe distance through our trees, down to the gums where Wilson and Righteous's cement kaya is lit up all silvery in the moonlight. We tail him to the edge of the bush that slopes down to the side road and wait behind a gum tree. We hear a car, its engine idling. I creep forward a few trees and stand behind a trunk. Peeking out I can see down the slope to the road where the front boot of a small red VW beetle is flung open. The man glances back in our direction, his hair sharply spiked like a crown of thorns. He places the long package that he's been carrying in the boot, then the car drives off and the man heads back up the path. Enoch joins me and we shrink behind a wide gum trunk as he passes about a metre away from us and stops and listens. It feels like he can hear my hair prickling in my skull and then we hear his footsteps going away towards the compound.

'If you say anything you can die.' Enoch's face is very close to mine. 'My mother will curse your family.'

'I won't say anything man.'

We walk back in silence. Ivory roses big as cabbages sway gently in front of the west-facing windows. Near my own window, he whispers,

'Bring books. Your father's books.'

'Now? Are you crazy?'

'When?'

'My Dad's going away on call-up on Saturday. I'll bring them then.'

Or maybe I won't. Bloody books. Enoch gives me a leg up onto the wide windowsill and I am able to climb through my bedroom window easily. In bed I lie looking at the ceiling till it grows whiter and whiter and I feel angry and excited and lots of things about lots of people and then the birds start calling and it seems like it can't have really happened. And then I fall asleep and wake up hot and sweaty in my clothes and get up and go for breakfast as if I've just put them on.

On my way to the compound to find Enoch, I'm picturing his chuffed face when he checks out these books. But then I look down at the painted picture of the black ship and Long John Silver and figure Enoch won't like him, but he might like Jim. I'll take it back anyway in case he gives me the Nancy Drew treatment. Near the lucky-bean tree, I hear shouting, loud and high pitched, and I can see a vehicle through the trees in the buttery morning light. A carpet of coral flowers layers the ground beneath the tree. Screaming and slamming sounds are coming from the walls of the Land Rover. Dad, his FN slung over his shoulder, is talking to an African policeman. Before he can catch sight of me, I put the books in the shelf-like space between the trunk and a crook of a branch and pile some flowers on top of them from under the tree.

'Get back to the house Jay!' Dad says, spotting me.

'No. Why?' I hold onto a branch of the lucky-bean tree and several fleshy-coral flowers fall at my feet like bunches of chilli peppers. When he turns his attention back to the African policeman, I crouch and pile some more flowers on the books.

Dad turns round again. 'Get back to the house. Now!'

As I turn I see a face staring out at me from the back of the police Land Rover. Several loud bangs come from the roof. Enoch's bashing the roof with the heel of his hand. I run forward shouting his name. Dad grabs me round the waist and pushes me back across the compound.

'Get back to the house before I sjambok you!'

Wrestling free from him, I break into a run, ripping at the long grasses with my hands as I tear through it.

'If you do not use your head you will have to use your legs Mr Cameron!' I hear the nganga's deep voice shout before the engine drowns her out and the Land Rover drives away.

On my flat rock at the end of the front garden, a cushion from the couch under my head, I'm drifting between my world and some English one far away in the pages of my book. My gaze keeps pulling from the black letters towards the mountains. I hear Dad's footsteps walking over the lawn but do not turn my head. I put the book over my face.

'Jay?' Dad says, crouching beside me and taking the book off my face.

'Where've they taken him?' I ask, staring at Dad's hairy knees.

'Jay, his father has died.'

I sit up shading my face with my arm. 'What? What happened?'

'It seems there was an accident.'

'I thought he was in prison.'

'It was when they were driving him from one prison to another.'

In the valley, a flock of birds rises above the tree canopy like black question marks. They seem to hover for a moment before flight and then they disappear into orangey-pink cloud smeared across the sky.

'Why did the police take the nganga and Enoch away?'

'They needed her to identify the body.'

'Why? Aren't they sure it's him?'

Dad laughs. 'When someone dies they need to be formally identified.'

I pick at the grass.

'Jay, I'm not sure they'll be back.' Dad picks at the grass too.

'We're not sure it's best for the nganga to be here anymore – or Enoch.'

'Why? What will happen to him?' I watch the fluttering butterflies as they halo around the pink-edged white star flowers of the sabi star tree.

'Well he can't stay here on his own.' Dad's brown eyes smile at me.

'Why not? Wilson's his grandfather, he could look after him.'

'It's more complicated than that.'

'Why? Why does it have to be?'

Why is a sheep. Far below me in the valley the racket of birds has blended into a fuzzy hum.

'They'll be put in a PV? Won't they? Granny May's told me about PVs. They have fences around them and curfews don't they? Nessie says they're like concentration camps and people are taken there against their will.'

Dad laughs. 'Look Jay. Nessie sees everything in red. They're there so that the terrorists can't get at them. Mom – your Granny May drives staff over and keeps an eye on them, she says they're fine. They're just like the villages in the TTLs Jay, they have their huts, and they grow crops –'

'Ja but he won't be free will he?'

'Well, he will inside the PV.'

'Ja well that's not free is it? Is there a school there?'

'No. But Jay, his mother didn't want him to go to school. I offered the fees. If he'd stayed with the Jesuits – well he could have stayed with them. Look Jay. His mother is trouble.'

'Why? What does she do?'

Dad smiles and moves his eyebrows up and down at me, but he doesn't make me smile.

'I'm sorry Jay. I do understand you know.'

Dad stands up and takes his Kingsgates from his top pocket. He smiles, the cigarette hanging from the corner of his mouth as he walks away.

11.

Us kids sit on the low veranda wall waiting for the long goodbye. Dad deals with kisses and hugs in descending order. He presses Carla's dark head, delicate as a bird's, into his chest. She cries into his heart, then he pulls her head away and kisses her on the mouth, then on both cheeks. She throws her arms around him and sobs into his neck. When he lets go of her she runs inside.

'Dance your socks off chicken!' Dad calls after her. She lets out a sob and soon we hear the sad tune of her crying floating out of her bedroom window.

When it's my turn, I try to hug Dad hard enough to make an imprint on his body to carry around in the bush.

'Bye Bantam,' he says to me. 'Look after your mother.'

Then he swings John up and he bracelets his legs around Dad's waist. Dad pretends to drop him a few times and then hugs him hard. Putting him down, he rubs his knuckles on the top of his head. John runs over the lawn and disappears over the rocks and cacti at the end of the lawn and into the side of the mountain. Mom stands waiting her turn. She's wearing red lipstick and green frosty eye shadow and looks pretty wow in her green t-shirt and jeans. Mom believes in making Dad's mental snapshot of her a good one. *Well he'll have to carry it around in his mind for weeks on end, I better be looking good for it.* Dad moves towards her. Mom keeps her eyes level with Dad's camouflage-covered chest. He stops in front of her, his arms in their rolled up uniform sleeves hanging loosely by his sides and allows himself to be inspected. Mom begins by swiping invisible dust from his uniform. She adjusts his beret and repositions his stripes, then she lightly runs the tips of her fingers over his biceps and pulls at his belt buckle. Dad laughs and hugs her.

'Are you gonna be okay with the agric-alert?' Dad asks Mom.

'I'll have to be.'

'They'll be here to put up the fence any day now Reen. They're working as fast as they can. Every farm in this bloody country is after one.'

'Ja, well, we'll survive,' she says, smoothing down his beard and running each of her forefingers over either side of his moustache.

Dad grabs her round the waist and gives her a big squeeze. She lifts the backs of her legs off the ground and he swings her gently by the waist so that her slip slops fall off. She laughs and then the laughter catches in her throat.

In the spaces between the trunks and branches, the sinking sun is like fire, highlighting the leaves gold. John sets up our old tins for target practice with his pellet-gun. We are arguing and laughing so much that we don't notice Mom returning from dropping Carla at the convoy point until she's right next to us.

'Jeez Mom, what's wrong?' I ask clocking her pale face, her wide eyes.

'I heard guns.' Her hands clutch at the brown grocery bag in her arms. The knuckles round her car keys are white.

'It's a pellet gun Mom,' I say.

'No. I'm sure I heard the rattle of machine-gun fire,' Mom says, one hand smoothing the hair away from her forehead.

'We didn't.'

'No. We didn't. And the dogs didn't bark.'

'Mom you're acting really weird,' John says.

'Ja, Mom, gedda grip,' I say, raising the gun to my shoulder.

'Anyway, come inside hey,' Mom says, lowering my gun. 'Let's see if I can find some rock cakes for tea.'

She grabs me and hugs me, then she does the same to John.

'Ah. And it was my turn,' John says, holding his hand up flat in the air so that Brandy jumps up and licks it. Raising it higher, he says, 'C'mon Brandy, c'mon, higher.'

Brandy leaps higher till he looks like he's up in the sky in the last blast of the blazing sun.

I'm lying in bed reading by torch light because we have all the lights out for safety after eleven. Mom's face appears around the door.

'Thought you might be awake, I can't sleep. My sweet tooth's keeping me awake. Wanna come make some toffee?'

She didn't even tell me off for reading late. In the kitchen Mom switches on the hurricane lamp then quickly switches it off and lights a candle. She grabs a milk pan from one of the hooks near the stove.

'Get the sugar out the pantry Jay,' she says.

I find the sugar next to the tin of Milo, so I take that too.

'Can we have Milo too?' I ask.

'Shhh, what was that?' Mom looks up from the stove, her pupil-large eyes wide.

I peer out the windows over the sink into the pitch darkness. 'I didn't hear anything.'

The pointed edges of the poinsettia lick across the edge of the glass plane like red flames shot by the wind.

'Like a shuffling sound,' she says

She grabs Dad's hunting rifle from behind the coats near the back door.

'I didn't hear anything.' The tiles beneath my bare feet are ice cold.

'Well I did.' She lays the hunting rifle down on the table.

The corrugated-iron roof creaks and the hurricane lamp swings slowly as if it knows something we don't.

'It's just the roof Mom.'

We sit at the kitchen table eating hot sticky toffee from the pan off two teaspoons.

'Do you think Carla's off on the razzle-dazzle tonight?' I ask.

'I'll give her a bloody good hiding if she is. She knows it's not safe. I'll feel better when she's home.'

I bet she's thinking about the mortar attacks in town last month where five men died. We hit the terrs back really hard though. Killed hundreds of them at their base in Mozambique. Uncle Bob was involved in the raid. *The floppies were piled up man*, Dad said. But there was more rocket and mortar attack after that.

'I wish we'd been evacuated to the Cecil Hotel.'

'We don't live in town Jay.'

'Ja but still, it would've been fun. Hanging out with my friends, like in the second world war.'

'War's not fun. Let's get some sleep Jay-Jay.'

Halfway through the night I wake to the sound of the mombies stirring, but go back to sleep as rain begins to fall. Then a sharp sound wakes me properly. It sounds like thunder. Then it comes again – a crackling sound. My throat is dry. Dad's not here. My bedside clock reads three-twenty am. I hesitate, trying to decide whether to wake Mom or not, when a shuffling sound, followed by the low moan of cattle, makes me fling my legs over the side of the bed. I look down at my feet, trying to think calmly like Dad would tell me, trying to hear his instructions in my swimmy head. The cattle shuffle sometimes when it's going to rain. I listen for the dogs but can't hear them bark. With wet palms, I sit sideways for a moment, my heart bouncing around my chest like a rubber ball. Then I hear a soaring swishing sound, followed by an explosion. My senses scatter like dropped pins. I leap out of bed and into the passage. Mom's bedroom door is thrown wide open. She comes out in one of Dad's t-shirts and her pants, an FN rifle slung over her shoulders. In her hands is the uzi and a couple of magazines. She hands me a magazine, then pushes the other into the pistol-grip of the uzi and hands it to me.

'Check on John, Jay!' She goes up the passage towards the lounge.

The gun is a dead weight in my hands. Mom whips round.

'Don't – under any circumstances – turn any lights on. And when you come into the lounge, crawl. And Jay? I may need you to reload for me.'

In his bedroom, his head almost completely covered by blankets, John sleeps like the dead. The hand grenade mesh over the window shadows itself on his blanket. In the lounge, framed by an oblong of light from the moon, Mom half lies, half sits beneath the low wall underneath the windows that divide lounge from veranda, her rifle on the inner windowsill, the nose aimed out through the burglar bars, over the front lawn. Swishing sounds and lots of clicks come from beyond the direction of the veranda. Then the sky explodes into a firework display. Tracers of alien green whizzing above the lawn light up the night. I stand and stare.

'Shit! Get on the agric-alert! Jayne! Get on the fucking agric-alert!

I watch at her face. She's never used words like that.

'Snap out of it Jay, for God's sake!'

Another whizzing sound is followed by an explosive thump, followed by a whining sound.

'Shit! I told him to get that bastard fence up!' Mom shouts.

The sounds tear through my chest and I throw myself across the floor to the north side of the lounge where Dad has set up the radio equipment, at the same time catching sight of John wide-eyed in the doorway in his pyjamas. Hanging loosely by his right side is his gun.

'Oh my God! John! Lie on –' Her words are lost in the racket of automatic gunfire going off very, very close.

There are pinging sounds and then the glass around us begins to shatter. Mom starts firing, her shoulders jerking backwards with each round. The weird light makes Mom and the room look like black and white film flickering in the darkness of a cinema.

John dives under the table near me. He points his gun in Mom's direction.

'Don't worry Mom, I've got my gun too,' he calls out.

I'm leaning over the radio trying to figure it out. It feels like ice has been wiped over my brain. A little red light flashes on and off and then I catch on. I put down the uzi and the magazine on the table and pick up the radio.

'Get down! Jay! Get down! Lie on the floor!' Mom screams.

I duck under the table with the radio. In front of me bits of the window explode as the bullets hit. The glass comes down on Mom like jagged rain lit up in the white light. Mom continues to return fire. I put my arm over John's head. The racket of automatic gunfire comes and comes. Another slice of window comes down like a guillotine, landing near Mom's ankle. When the firing stops, John wiggles on his stomach towards Mom, dragging his gun by his side. I drag him back by his ankles.

'Le'me go Jay!'

'No ways man, you're staying here.'

The firing starts again. Crouching, I shuffle my body forwards, holding the radio and the uzi. For a moment, the veranda is all lit up again as if by lightning. The noise is so loud, it's like being sucked into a thunderstorm. Sweat trickles a trail down the inside of my arm. I wipe it on my nightie and start to speak into the radio. A crackling sound follows and then a woman's voice says, "Whisky seven, how do you read?"

My mind is a blank screen. 'They're shooting at us,' I say.

"Small arms fire or mortar? Rocket? Over," the woman replies.

'I dunno. There's lots of different noises – too loud I can't tell.'

'There's lots of men, with guns,' John shouts from behind me.

'There's lots of men with guns. Oh and earlier, I think I heard a rocket.'

'We're under attack from the north-east!' Mom shouts, 'They're raining down on us from the north – small arms fire – rockets and mortar!'

"We'll alert the security forces," the woman says. "Over."

From the other side of the lounge Mom still fires into the darkness. A thud shakes the ground, followed by an explosion, a deep noise wraps around me, followed by an unbearable ringing in my ears. Putting the radio on the table, I grab the magazine and slide back down onto the floor, taking the uzi with me.

'Don't look up Jay! Keep your head on the ground!' Mom yells, glancing round.

I look up again. 'I've told them Mom!' I shout. 'I've told them!' She doesn't seem to hear me as she fires out into the night. Shards of glass fly all around her like spirit dragonflies. Then, like an interval in a film, the noise stops.

A ghost appears in the lounge doorway. It's Granny Rose in her long white nightie, her grey hair wild down her back. She's holding Grandpa Patrick's rifle in her hands. Blasts of automatic gunfire begin again.

'For pity's sake Granny Rose, get down!' Mom shouts, her gun juddering on the windowsill.

Granny Rose ignores Mom and starts walking slowly from the doorway towards the lounge windows. With each step, she fires out into the darkness, straight through the lounge windows and out beyond the veranda. For a while the noise of her gun is lost in the racket. Then the firing from outside stops. Granny Rose doesn't stop firing until she runs out of ammo, then she turns and walks slowly back through the doorway, her bare feet crunching slightly on the broken glass. A thin trail of smoke rises from the end of her gun.

'Bloody cheek,' she says over her shoulder.

'Get over here Jayne!' Mom shouts, loading a magazine into her FN. I snap my eyes from Granny Rose to Mom. 'On your knees!' Mom shouts again.

I crawl over to her, followed by John, belly-crawling. He crouches on the other side of Mom from me, the end of his gun sticking up above the windowsill like a funnel.

'Keep your head below the windowsill,' she says when I get to her. She grabs the uzi and flicks the switch from 's' to 'r.'

'Keep it on single-shot,' Mom says. 'Don't switch to automatic, you won't handle it. Don't open fire unless you actually see them.' She gives the gun back. Her huge eyes, their irises masked by massive pupils, drill into mine.

'Do you understand Jay?' I watch her hands on the FN. They're shaking slightly. 'Only if you see them.'

She hands the gun to me. Dad's shown me how to fire an uzi, so I flick the selector to automatic. My hands are jumping up and down on my lap. I stare at them trying to make them stop. Something cold and hard settles inside me.

'Don't forget to keep squeezing the safety,' Mom says.

'Are they there yet Mom?' John asks.

'No darling,' Mom says.

'They might not come John,' I say. 'Hey Mom?'

'Ja, darling. They might not come,' Mom says looking at me.

For a moment she frightens me. I imagine that she's dead, a zombie. I try not to think of the pictures I think I can see in her eyes.

'I think something moved, Mom,' John says. 'Over there.'

They spill down the kopje, six or seven of them, like the cast of a horror film. When Mom opens fire, they are lit up for a second. They are dressed in suits, trousers and t-shirts. One of them is wearing a long coat and sunglasses with a bobble-hat. Then they scatter like leaves in a storm of gunfire. I'm firing too, the gun juddering in my hands as I try to keep my grip from slipping. Shells are flying from the chamber of the gun, smoking and clinking as they hit the floor. I only stop firing when the noise in my right ear stops and Mom lays her hand on my arm. John puts his gun down.

'I think we shot them Mom.' His eyes are big, glowing out of his pale face.

Then he stares back out of the window. I don't want to see his face, its trickle of blood leaking from his hairline, or hear his voice, so I put my hands over my ringing ears. I can still hear noise. Noises like cupped hands kluping my ears. I huddle, trying to screw myself up in a ball, still hearing the guns though I know no one is firing. Mom's arm on my back feels like sandpaper rubbing on my skin. I wriggle till she takes it away then burrow into the cold floor.

'Shit I need a drink,' Mom's words fire into the silence.

'Shit, I need a drink,' she says again. I cannot bear the noise of her voice. I lift my head.

'Can you stop it Mom? Don't speak. Please don't speak!' I look down again. A dark pool spreads out from under Mom's legs.

'Mom, you're all cut!' Mom straightens her legs. She licks the palm of her hand and swipes at the backs of her legs.

'They're just superficial little cuts,' she says, clicking another magazine into place.

But the blood keeps coming. The noise of her voice hurts. Mom smiles at me with her mouth, her eyes flash and dart around, like torch lights, from me to the garden outside, to John, from left to right. I train my eyes over the lawn. I try to stop forming shapes with my eyes, to just see flat darkness.

'Are they coming again Mom. Will we have to shoot again?'

'I don't think so John-John.'

'But we'll wait and see?'

'We'll wait and see.'

The ticking of the grandfather clock seems to get louder and louder. I concentrate on the ticks to stop myself from hearing other noises that I'm not sure are coming from outside or inside my head. The sky is changing from ink-black to navy-blue and the mountains across the valley are beginning to show their humped backs. We wait. Behind us the house creaks and I count the hours. Each time the clock chimes we jump and snatch up our guns.

'It's only the clock,' Mom says.

The thought of them coming up behind us makes my stomach shudder. I force my eyes out over the lawn again. Every time the flamboyant tree quivers, my finger curls tighter on the trigger.

Mom and John stare over the lawn. A greenish vein flickers like a tiny blind snake in the milky-white of Mom's cold-looking temple. For a minute I think she's dead, so I shift slightly, so that Mom says quietly, 'Steady Jay. We'll get through this.'

And then the noise of the clock seems to be lost in the hum of the bleeding night. John continues to stare out of the window. Now his eyes are glazed and his head tips downwards. He jolts it back and screams, 'What's happening? Mom! What's happening?'

'Please shut him up Mom! Please!'

'Calm down Jay. Stay calm. We can get through this if we stay calm.' Mom has her arm around John. 'It's okay John-John, you fell asleep. Sssh.'

An owl hoots. Mom and I snatch up our guns.

John says, 'Are they coming back?'

'No John-John, I don't think so.'

'They're not coming Jay. They're not coming.'

'Ja. I know. Please be quiet.'

And then for a long time there is a silence that is so loud it threatens to blow my head off. We drift on sleep for seconds then jolt awake to fear over and over, till the birds start to call and the grey dawn comes.

A sound of hammering against the back door makes us grab our guns again.

'Stay there!' Mom says. She walks quickly away on ghost feet, avoiding the scatterings of glass.

We run after her. In the kitchen, Mom flicks on the light. She stands to the side of the back door, her gun raised like something out of a Clint Eastwood movie.

'Who the hell is it?' Mom screams. The banging comes again. John jumps, then grips me like a python around my waist. I feel like I'm made of toilet-paper tubes and I'm going to crumple.

'I can't John – my gun,' I explain. He takes his arms away and I put both hands on the gun and aim at the middle of the door.

'Who the bloody hell are you?' Mom shouts. She raises the gun to her shoulder. 'I'm gonna blow you away!' she says, cocking her gun.

'Ja. Us too!' John shouts. He lifts his gun. We can hear ragged breathing outside the door.

'Mom! Mom! It's Wilson,' I say, pulling at her t shirt.

Mom goes to open the door.

'No! No Mom! Don't open the door,' John shouts. 'It's safe inside! Don't let them in Mom! Mom!' he screams. I hug his head into my ribs with my left arm.

'It's Wilson, John-John. It's Wilson!'

I relax my right arm. The uzi, heavy in my hand, strains at my wrist. I drop it to my side. Mom opens the top part of the door, then the bottom part and Wilson comes in. She slams and bolts the door behind him and switches on the light. John rushes under the table like a freaked-out mouse.

'Switch the lights off Mom!' I say.

'Just stay down and keep hold of your gun.' She goes over to the dresser.

'Thank God you're here Wilson!' Mom says, opening and slamming drawers.

'Where's the key for the lounge door?' she asks him. Wilson reaches into the pocket of his apron and hands Mom a key.

'Get me a drink!' She runs both her hands through her hair quickly. Wilson goes to the dresser, gets down a glass and pours Mom a large measure of Bols brandy.

'Where's Righteous?' Mom asks Wilson.

'He's look for the cattle.'

Mom goes out into the passage.

'Mom!' I say as she brushes past me, but she ignores me. Down the passage I hear her slamming and locking the lounge door. When she comes back in she grabs the drink out of Wilson's hand and downs it, her other hand grips the edge of the kitchen table and her FN swings inwards. She holds out the glass for Wilson to refill it.

'Give the kids some,' she says, downing her second glass. Then the banging starts around the front of the house. Snatching up her gun, Mom puts her face very close to mine.

'Stay here!' she snarls like a lion.

'No Mom!' I move towards her, but Wilson comes between us.

'Look Jay,' Mom says, her hands pressing into my shoulders. 'Terrorists don't knock on doors, they're not polite. Are they Wilson? It'll be Righteous.'

'Aikona Madam. They can not be polite,' Wilson says from where he stands at the sideboard pouring small measures of brandy into two glasses.

'Stay here with John and Wilson, do you understand?' Mom leaves the room.

John emerges from under the table and sits on a chair and begins staring at the hurricane lamp. The moths around the lamp dance and flutter. He wipes at his temple, where a trickle of blood tickles him. His head nods a bit. He's shaking.

'No. They're not bloody polite are they Jay? Where's my gun Jay?' John asks. He starts to get up, but Wilson puts a hand on his shoulder making him sit again.

'I'll get your gun John,' I say. 'Don't worry.'

'Not on your own. Don't go on your own Jay. It's noisy in there. Dangerous.'

Blood is trickling down his head from his cut. Over at the sink, I put the uzi on the windowsill and take a clean tea-towel from the drawer, run it under the cold tap, then squeeze it out. I can hear Mom reopening the lounge door. With cold hands, I take up the uzi from the windowsill. Still holding the gun, I turn round. Wilson is watching me. For a moment, I'm scared that he's going to move towards me to take the gun. I'm scared too that I might shoot him if he does. From the lounge I hear Mom talking, I think to Righteous, so I put the gun back down on the tiles of the windowsill.

111

I place my arms on John's shoulders. His glassy eyes continue to stare at the moths circling the lamp. A vicious looking, long-legged mozzie hovers near his eye level, then moves close to the sticky blood near his temple. He makes no effort to bat it away and allows me to dab the wet end of the tea-towel at the little pink-rimmed eye-shaped cut in his head. When I press away the blood I can see the ivory of his skull.

When Wilson gives John his drink, he swallows it in one as if he's been knocking back the juice his whole life instead of just the dregs of Dad's beer bottles. For a moment I wonder whether to pour brandy on John's cut, but then decide to just let the brandy in him do the business till help comes. Wilson places my drink on the table near me. The brown liquid quivers in the glass.

'Just down it,' John says. He's giggling a bit and his body is beginning to shudder.

The drink sears down my pipes like hot fire. I like it.

'Can I have some more Wilson?' I ask as Mom comes back in with Righteous. Wilson shows my glass to Mom, who nods. He adds another small measure. She sits down next to John and places a hand in the small of his back.

'Don't go back in there Mom, okay? It's dangerous in there,' John says.

'Okay, John-John, I won't go back in there.' Ja right. Only if we don't get any more visitors.

'Sit down!' Mom says to Righteous. Righteous stares at her.

'Sit down!' she orders. Righteous takes off his blue cap and sits down.

'Get him a drink Wilson. And get one for yourself.' Wilson looks at Mom.

'Just do it Wilson. And use the best bloody crystal glasses if you want to.'

John and I start laughing. Mom, me, John, Righteous and Wilson all drinking together. It's funny. My head feels fuzzy, my body warm. When Righteous reaches over for the drink Wilson offers, they look at each other for a moment.

'Tell me what you saw Righteous,' Mom says, her head cupped in her hands.

'The mombies, she's running, running everywhere, medem, some, she's shot,' says Righteous looking down at his hands twisting his cap. He looks at Wilson, 'some –' We stop laughing. We don't know why we were laughing in the first place. Mom adjusts the FN on her shoulder.

'Don't say anymore,' Mom says from behind her hands.

'Why? What's happened?' I ask. 'Can we go and see?'

Then I remember Brandy and Samantha. I look at Mom.

'Mom?' I say. She looks up, greenish colour like bruises beneath her eyes.

I mouth the words at her. She shakes her head willing me to be silent.

'Why did they hurt the cows?' John asks the hurricane lamp.

'I don't know John.' Mom looks at Righteous. 'Because they're evil?'

Wilson is watching Righteous's face. Righteous watches Wilson's long-fingered hands pouring himself a drink.

'Put the brandy on the table and sit down Wilson! Actually no. Please take Mrs Cameron a drink first,' Mom says. 'And take the first-aid kit in please – in case – I'll check on her in a minute.'

'I can do this first-aid Madam.'

Mom looks up at him. 'Go ahead.'

Bringing the edge of the glass to my lower lip, I press it in hard. If my lip split I wouldn't care. Sticking my tongue in I taste the burny-sourness of the brandy and when it tips down my throat, I catch Mom's shadowy eyes. They move quickly to Wilson's retreating back and then she looks at Righteous for a long time. Mom begins rattling questions at Righteous. Her words are like fish hooks flying towards Righteous's slightly opened mouth, his staring eyes.

'Where's Justice?' Mom asks Righteous.

'For this, I am not sure, Madam.' Righteous smiles at Mom with his round eyes open wide.

'I choose to believe you Righteous, don't worry,' Mom says. She rests her forehead on the palm of her blood-smeared hand.

When Wilson comes back, Mom asks him the same questions. Wilson, arms folded, leans against the glass-fronted dark wood sideboard in front of Granny Rose's willow pattern platters and answers more slowly, more carefully than Righteous.

'But he's your grandson Wilson.'

'I have not seen Justice now for two weeks Madam.'

I have.

'Yes he is my grandson. But also he is not my grandson.' He looks at his hands. They are greyish-white around the knuckles.

'Yes Wilson. He is your grandson in body, but not in mind?' Mom says.

'I can mean this.'

'Yes Wilson. You can mean all sorts of things, I'm sure,' says Mom.

Wilson says nothing. Mom doesn't tell Wilson not to worry. For a moment she looks as though she might cry, but then she clenches her back teeth together and forcing another unsmiling smile, she pours some more brandy into her glass. The air comes out from her nostrils in short sharp bursts.

'Can I make breakfast now?' Wilson asks.

'Sure Wilson. Make breakfast. Let's just go on as before,' Mom says glancing at her watch. 'Five o' clock,' she smiles at me, 'they'll be here soon.'

'Why did they hurt our cows Wilson?' John asks.

'Maybe they are angry,' Wilson says from where he crouches, stoking the coals in the stove to life.

'Ja. Maybe they're angry. But this is gonna make the situation a lot angrier.' Mom's eyes burn like charcoal from her white face. Wilson looks back at her. He is not afraid of her anger.

A loud bird screech is followed by the sound of a Land Rover and more banging on the door.

'Must have been a trumpeter hornbill,' Mom jokes as she gets up and peers through the kitchen window. 'Well whada'you know. It's our boys in uniform,' she says.

The kitchen fills up with troopies, loaded up with ammo, their bullet belts hung all around them like hula-hoops, magazines packed around their waists, rifles hanging from their shoulders.

A second later, the sound of propellers jerks John's eyes from the buzzing of insects around the hurricane lamp.

'Helicopter!' he shouts. Then he's up and running as if Santa's coming.

In the front garden, a helicopter emerges over the valley out of the stiff cloud cover and hovers above the front lawn in the mist. John jumps up and down on the dew-soaked lawn in his blue-checked pyjamas.

'It's an Allouette! I wish Dad was here!' he shouts, waving his arms around like helicopter propellers.

The helicopter tilts and the army guys, four of them, wave. They look like they're going to tip out on the lawn. The pilot smiles and touches his fingers to his temple in salute. The troopies jump out before the helicopter lands.

Mom walks up the kopje with the soldiers from the helicopter, her arms explaining how the terrs swooped down on us in their strange clothes. In the kitchen, some of the troops are getting ready to leave in the Land Rover to track the terrs. A blonde-haired medic who looks like an action-man doll smiles at me, then ruffles John's hair and in the process, spots the cut.

'A nice, clean glass-cut,' he says, as he gives John a butterfly stitch, like it's something good to have.

The medic wears shorts and has a tattoo of an eagle on the muscle of his upper arm. The muscle flinches as he sticks tape on John's skull, the wing moves slightly making me smile. The soldier catches my eyes and smiles a response with his blue ones. I look quickly out the window.

'Can I go for a ride in your helicopter?' John asks. 'Are you going to shoot the rest of the terrs? I think we got some of them.'

The smiley medic tells John he'd like to take him but it's against the rules. He'll have to stay here and look after his Mom and sister. Mom comes in and smiles a smile at me that shows she knows we can look after ourselves, but when I think of the firing my legs start to shake. A dark-haired soldier in camouflage trousers and shirt leans up against the sink, watching Wilson stirring porridge at the stove. He takes out a cigarette and offers one to Mom.

'I'll have one of my own thanks,' says Mom, taking a cigarette out of her blue pack. The soldier lights it. He stops watching Wilson and stares at Righteous as he shakes out the flame. As he returns to the sink he sees the uzi and picks it up.

'This yours?' he asks Righteous.

Righteous looks at Mom.

'No,' Mom says, 'my daughter uses that. She's a crack shot.' She smiles at me.

'Proper Rhodesian ladies, aren't you?' the soldier says. He looks at Righteous for a long time trying to pull Righteous's eyes away from the centimetre of drink that's left in his glass.

'What's this hey? A cafe?' His voice cuts through the thick cloud of silence, it makes me jump. John keeps chattering like a parrot to the medic.

'Do you always drink with the workers, Mrs Cameron?' he asks.

The medic looks up and smiles at Mom and me, then he goes back to fixing John.

'Not always,' Mom smiles, taking up her own drink, 'Just today.' They both laugh.

Righteous gets up.

'I must go and see my wife,' he says.

'Yes,' says the soldier. 'Go and see your wife. Check that she's still there. But don't run away okay? Or we'll have to come and find you and that might not be so good.' He laughs. Wilson looks at him from the stove.

'Whada'you looking at?' the soldier asks. 'You got a job to do or what?' He laughs, but it's not funny.

Wilson continues to look at him for a moment and then goes back to stirring the pot.

'Gee,' laughs the soldier. 'Cheeky or what?'

Mom doesn't laugh. She just does that lips-only freaky smile and continues to smoke and watch John yakkedy-yaks to the medic as he gets his butterfly stitch.

'Have you got a Coke or something for this little guy?' the medic asks Wilson. 'He needs one. So does she.' He nods at me.

The dark-haired soldier stops laughing when his radio begins to make crackling sounds. He goes out the back door, his cigarette hanging from his lips. He walks up and down outside the kitchen window speaking on the radio.

'All done. Drink your fizzy Coke.' The medic pats John on the shoulders and smiles up at us.

'Mom's got cuts too,' I say.

'Let's take a look,' the medic says.

'They're just superficial,' Mom says.

She gets up and shows the little cuts on the back of her legs. One of them is deep and guava-pink with little yellow fat spots.

'Come here,' the medic says.

He takes out some gauze and squirts some disinfectant on it. He dabs it all over the backs of Mom's legs. Then he gives Mom a butterfly stitch too.

'Didn't know miniskirts were back in fashion,' he says.

I feel like hitting him even though he came to so-called rescue us. And her. I wish Mom would put something else on. From where I sit I can almost see her pants. Dad's t-shirt doesn't look like a miniskirt. It looks like one of Dad's t-shirts.

The other soldier comes back in and jerks his head.

'Time to say goodbye,' the medic says. 'Hope we don't see you again, at least till after the war!'

'Cheerio,' says Mom.

She's never said that in her life. Neither has she said 'fucking' before but she did earlier.

'Can I come in your helicopter?' John asks. 'I could shoot the gun?'

'Not this time,' the medic says. 'You stay here this time, little guy, hey?'

'Another day?'

'Ja. Maybe another day, hey.'

He tips his fingers to his forehead and salutes Mom. I swear I can see the helicopter propellers reflected in John's eyes even though he's right here at the table staring at the hurricane lamp. And then the sound of the helicopter fades away and the only sound in the kitchen is the sound of Wilson putting porridge on the plates, just like he does every day.

The police anti-terrorist unit arrive about ten minutes later. They do have drinks, even though they're not supposed to. They make Mom laugh too.

'Nice outfit, Mrs Cameron,' says one, winking at me. His moustache seems to grow out of his sideburns.

'Thanks,' Mom says. 'I wore it especially.'

I wish she'd wear something else, and change her tune as well. The PATU men begin firing questions at us.

'When did you become aware that you were under attack, Mrs Cameron?'

'When did you first hear the noises Jayne?'

'Where were you John?'

Da, da, da, da, da,da.

'Under the table.'

'I mean, before you were under the table.'

'In bed.'

'Of course.'

'Hell. What do you think we were doing? Playing charades?' Mom laughs some more and pours herself another drink from the bottle on the table. Then she puts the bottle in front of the Special Branch man, but he shakes his head.

'One enough for you? Well, one's not enough for me. Where's your bloody husband when you need him hey?' Mom laughs.

The three PATU men laugh like they've rehearsed it too, but then they get serious and order Wilson to go to the compound with them. Wilson stops washing the dishes and looks at Mom.

'It's alright Wilson,' Mom says.

'Ja,' says one of the PATU men. 'And now we gonna find out if you know too much, too much.'

Wiping his hands on his apron, Wilson looks at the PATU man. He takes out a rolled up newspaper cigarette from his apron pocket, then moves slowly towards the door, rolling as he goes.

'Don't be too hard on them!' Mom shouts from the dresser where she's getting herself another drink. 'They're loyal, our boys! Bloody loyal.' Then she says quietly, 'most of them.'

Outside the sun has melted away the mist and is busy warming up the morning air. John has passed out on his arms at the table.

'Light me a cigarette, Jay.'

I don't hear her at first. I'm thinking about Justice and the brown parcel he carried under his arm, and what I think those long objects were and about the red VW that looked just like Nessie's and of what Enoch said. Maybe his mother cursed us anyway even though I didn't tell.

'Light me a bloody cigarette Jay!' She makes me jump.

I light her a cigarette, making sure I inhale it too. I hate her when she commands me to do things. Each cigarette puff seems to make the muscles in her face relax. She looked like an angel before, a beautiful avenging angel in a white t-shirt, with porcelain skin and silky black hair, the blood trickling down the backs of her legs. She smiles at me through her smoke. For a moment she looks about the same age as me and I love her again.

Michelle's dad brings Carla back in his car just as the PATU men come back from the compound.

'Hell Irene, it's good to see you,' says Mr Montague.

'Ja. It is good to see me. If the terrs had had their way, you wouldn't have seen me.'

Carla goes running over to Mom, her long hair flying.

'Your workers are nowhere to be found, Mrs Cameron,' the PATU man says.

Mom looks at Wilson and Righteous.

'Where are they?' she asks.

'They are too much scare, Madam,' says Righteous.

Wilson is standing up against the dresser, his arms folded, gazing out through the kitchen window towards the compound.

'Hell, Irene,' Mr Montague says. 'You can hardly blame them. They get the chop if they don't co-operate with the terrs.'

Carla starts crying.

'How could they do this to us Mom? We've looked after them. Their kids were born here.'

Mom drums her cigarette packet on the table, looking up at Wilson.

Wilson begins spooning tea-leaves from our farm into the big metal pot. He glances at Mom but says nothing.

'What did you expect? Civilisation?' Granny Rose appears in the doorway. 'This is Africa. At the heart of Africa pumps a heart of darkness. Am I right Wilson?'

Wilson looks at her, the teapot in his hands.

'You are right Madam,' he says.

'Of course I am,' says Granny Rose. 'Who are you?' she asks Mr Montague, who's sitting next to John at the kitchen table, waiting for a cup of tea and more chat.

'Michelle's Dad,' Carla says, her cheeks shading themselves pink.

'Well they all look the same to me,' Granny Rose says, which would normally be funny because that's what Europeans say about Africans.

'What's that sound Jay?' John asks. The moaning coming from the dairy is like the sound the mombies make when they are about to give birth.

Mom shakes her head at me to be quiet and John goes back to staring.

Granny Rose goes over to the sink and fills a jam-jar with water, screws its lid on, then hands Wilson her paintbrushes wrapped in an old tea towel.

'Put them in the easel-bag with the water-colours. We're going up to Cameron Mount,' she says to Wilson.

Mom smiles and shakes her head.

'You're painting today? On the highest point?'

'Shall I take a flag to mark it?' Granny Rose asks. 'I'll stop painting when I'm dead.'

Wilson disappears into the house to begin the daily work.

The PATU man leans up against the sink.

'The rest of your workers won't be back Mrs C. Your labour force has been well and truly politicised.'

'Terrified, you mean,' says Mr Montague.

'Same thing,' says the PATU man, 'they're getting pretty organised, they have their boy messengers – mujibas – their eyes and ears – all over the place. Some of them are as young as twelve. They'll have warned your workers to get the hell out or face the consequences. They'll have informed the terrs that your husband is away, what your movements are. Hell, if your boys are involved, they'll know what time you had dinner last night.'

Mom blows smoke in the direction of the sink.

'Our boys are loyal,' she says.

'Well, maybe those two are, the two that sleep in the kaya. But I'm telling you Mrs Cameron, those in the compound are running scared. As the chap says. They get the chop if they don't co-operate. I doubt they'll be back.'

'Bloody bastards,' Mom says. She pours herself another drink then downs it.

'Can I have one Mom?' Carla asks tearfully. Mom shoves her the bottle.

The PATU man gets up.

'Your husband will be back soon. We'll have security on your farm until then.'

As he gets to the door, he turns and says, 'I'd seriously consider grenading the periphery of your garden. You can activate from inside.'

'Ja,' says Mom. 'So I can blow up my kids myself?'

'Just a suggestion,' he laughs.

At the doorway he turns. 'It's suicide not to have an electric fence these days Mrs C.'

Mom throws her glass into the sink where it smashes into jagged pieces.

12.

The avo tree has a section of its trunk gouged out like a wound. A crater in the ground the size of a hut, shaped like the inside of a giant bottle top lies in the earth about twenty metres away from the kaya. The noise must have blown their ear drums. John kicks at its ruffled edge. Everyone's amazed that no fires were caused by the rockets and mortars. Bullet-holes pock the white-painted surface of the house, some deep enough to stick your finger into dusty cement and brick. The rockets that went whizzing down from the west slope landed in the trees where we play hide and seek. One of the wattle trees is bent inwards like a man shot, other trees have chunks and branches missing. I think they were meant to go through the roof of the house to set it on fire, or to destroy the compound. Well they didn't aim very well. Unless they meant to aim at the tree trunks. We laugh at their stupidity and it makes us feel better for a minute. The PATU stick collected all the shells and cartridges, but John and I still search. We run our hands in the holes made by the rockets and pull bark from the shredding wounds of the trees, till Mom makes us all go back inside.

We find the dogs at the base of a kopje to the north of the house not far from the dairy. A splatter of lumpy pink vomit crusts in the sun near Brandy. He looks like he's sleeping. Samantha lies near him, her cream and black fur rippling slightly in the breeze. John rushes towards her. His smile vanishes when he realises she's not sleeping and neither is Brandy. He looks at Mom, confused. Mom cuddles him to her side, then crouches down and putting her hands on each of his skinny shoulders, she says, 'they're dead John-John.'

'But why –' he still looks confused. John lies over Brandy like a blanket. His thin shoulders shake with sobs. Nobody says anything. We know what's happened. Everyone knows the terrs give poisoned meat to the dogs before an attack. Bloated cattle corpses lie in the first field like hippos lazing in the sun. Granny Rose pokes at them with the tip of her rifle. They are already beginning to smell. Some have been shot in the head, others have been slashed with pangas.

'Bloody yellow-bellied cowards,' says Granny Rose.

She turns, lifts her rifle and takes aim over the valley. A shot rings out and a mass of birds rises up from the canopy in the valley below.

'Hear that you bloody heathen BASTARDS? Set foot on my property again and I'll turn you to CUSTARD!'

John blinks his long lashes at Granny Rose.

'Ja. And I'll shoot you and put you in the butter churner too!' John yells.

Mom smiles at John. Carla's tears drip all over the front of her cream embroidered gypsy top. My yellow slip-slop slides in something slimy. Toby, a huge black beast, has been bayoneted in the stomach. His innards spill over the grass like coils of raw boerewors in tomato sauce. Molly lies on her side, half-in-half-out of the dairy shed, her legs jut out as stiff as a plastic farmyard animal's. Bessie's head lies in a dark halo of blood, one eye rolled up in confusion to heaven. Mom crouches next to her. The curve of a purple gash rises up from the green grass. Red criss-crosses have been sliced into her lower legs to destroy her tendons, to cause a slow and painful death. Her wounds are encrusted with flies. Carla begins batting at the flies, her arms slicing the air.

'Get away!' she screams. 'Get away!' She starts to sob.

I remember when Bessie first arrived. Carla and I were only little. We asked if we could ride her. So Grandpa Patrick put us on Bessie's back and walked us around in the field. The photos are in the album with the roses on it, us two little girls in shorts on a tan-coloured cow, on a hot-smiley day.

Mom lays her cheek on Bessie's. Bessie moans as if she's labouring.

'Oh Bessie,' she says. 'What have they done to you?'

Righteous stands at a respectful distance from Mom. His usually happy mouth is clamped shut and the muscles on either side of his clenched jaws pulse in and out.

'How could they have done this Righteous?' Mom asks. 'What have cattle got to do with war? With politics?' she asks.

Righteous says, 'I am too much sorry Madam.' He takes off his cap. 'I am too much sorry Madam.' He looks as though he's about to cry.

'It's not your fault Righteous.' She looks up at him as she strokes Bessie. 'It's not your fault Righteous.'

Righteous walks away, wiping the sweat from his head with his blue cap.

'Why did they kill our cows Mom?' John asks.

'I don't know John-John, I don't know why they killed the cows,' Mom smiles up at John.

'Well at least they didn't kill us,' John says.

'Well. Not for want of trying.' Mom laughs a tight laugh.

'Ja. Well they're rubbish at aiming anyway. Bloody stupid terrs,' he says.

'We'll have to shoot them,' Granny Rose says.

'Oh no Mom!' Carla leaves off batting away the flies.

'You got a better idea?' Mom snaps. 'The vet can't come till at least tomorrow. Do you want them to suffer?' Carla looks at the ground.

'Go and get Righteous,' Mom says.

'No Mom! Please don't! Can't we get old Mr Jones to come?' I ask.

'He's in South Africa. Get Righteous back here.'

Carla and I and John run up to the house. As we get to the back door we hear loud cracks, the sound of Granny Rose's rifle killing our cows.

Mom leans the bed frame up against the window in her bedroom, and drags the mattress over to the inner wall, where we all sleep.

John presses into the wall, with me next to him, then Carla, then Mom on the outside with the guns next to her. We are a sweaty mess of bodies and kicked off blankets, with John's arms and legs all over us. A troopie patrols around outside. I listen to the crunch of grass and wish he wasn't there. I have to wrap a pillow around my head to take cover from the clanging and banging in my mind. Sleep is like a shutter opening and closing between being here in this bed and out there in the lounge with the guns and the noise and the shapes and the shadows, and floating pictures of Bessie and Toby with the cuts and the guts all hanging out. I fall asleep remembering Enoch running along a dirt road chasing after a mongoose, and me wetting my pants laughing. In my dream Enoch and the workers have come back and they're hiding in the dawn mist on the lawn, tapping at the window to get in. But then the army guy's radio crackles and I wake to see Mom and Carla rigid as poles, Mom staring at the ceiling. For a moment my heart stops and I think she's dead, but then I see her blink. I watch as a trickle of tears slide out from her right eye and river down into her neck. She lets them flow silently. I don't know whether she is praying or thinking.

13.

Wilson's bare feet swish-swish on the parquet floors as he takes tea into Granny Rose's bedroom or slices the gem-squashes in half for dinner. The slight rattle of the tea-tray or the creak of the knife are the only sounds he makes. I try to trigger him to sarcasm by singing or knocking my feet against the kitchen-chair legs, but he ignores me. When I ask about Enoch he says, *I cannot know where Enoch is.* When I asked whether he meant he cannot know or I cannot know, he said *it can be both.* I feel safer here on the warm veranda than I do in the guts of the house. Every now and again I look out over the quiet green lawn with the huge flamboyant tree stretching over it. Secrets are travelling down to their roots. I pick up the paper that pokes out from under the swing chair. Our farm is splashed all over the front pages of *The Rhodesia Herald* complete with a picture of Granny Rose and Grandpa Patrick planting out the first tea plants back in 1923. They didn't even send a photographer to get a photograph. There wasn't time, so they just hauled these photos out of the newspaper archives. They wanted it in the paper today. A journalist phoned yesterday and spoke to Mom for ages and ages about the attack and here it is, Mom's words exaggerated in black and white. No wonder she hid the newspaper. Mom said she was very proud of John and me and that she was glad that Carla wasn't here because she's delicate. Ja. As highly strung as a racehorse. The journalist called Granny Rose "a brave pioneer of the old order."

'Hey John,' I say. 'They say we're really brave, us kids, for fighting back. They say we deserve a medal.'

John doesn't reply, he just runs a dinky car up and down the veranda steps.

Further down I read, *Second Tragedy for Cameron Family*. I stare at the photograph of my dead Auntie Penny, smiling for all eternity before she died on the Mazoe farm, her hair in a stiff blonde beehive. I don't remember her like that. Further down the page, I read all about the 'mystery' of Auntie Penny's death. It says she was 'friendly with one of the workers,' Prospect, who was accused of her murder. I fix my eyes on the heat shimmering above the rocks at the base of the hill till my eyes begin to sting and water, but still my heart clangs in its bone cage.

I'm poking the scarlet flamboyant tree flowers through the holes in the twisted wire table, while we sit drinking afternoon tea, waiting for Dad's supposed arrival.

'Mom? What happened with Auntie Penny and Prospect?' I don't take my eyes off the flower tablecloth I'm making. 'I saw the newspaper.'

'Ja well. Ask your father. I don't want to talk about his family. Or the bloody Mdisa family,' she snaps.

'Okay. Just asking.' I look up. 'It's my family too you know.'

'You're not related to her. She married your uncle.' Mom jerks her head from staring at the mountains to me.

'Okay, by marriage, jeez.'

'Don't bloody jeez me.' She looks really voos.

We hear the vehicle and us kids jump up. John runs over the lawn and leaps up at him as soon as he appears round the side of the veranda, clinging on like a monkey. Dad takes his beret off, looking at us over John's shoulder. His face looks creased and thin, and sadder. Carla gets up with a sob and I follow, meeting him halfway across the front lawn, hugging him around waist and hips, getting kisses on heads and temples and cheeks. Mom stays sitting as Dad approaches the table, staring at the ashtray, the forefinger of her right hand taps downwards and her cigarette ash floats to the ground between the wire slots of the table.

'Reen?' he says.

Mom doesn't look up, nor does she stand up. There is no make-up on for this arrival. No snazzy top. Her eyes are fixed on the mountains.

'Where were you?' she says, looking over the lawn, and I can see the one with the long coat and bobble hat again, the short uzi firing at us from hip height. Then she stands up and screams at him,

'WHERE WERE YOU? And what took you so bloody LONG?'

Dad doesn't say anything. He just walks round the table and lifts her up by the forearms while she screams and cries and throws herself around and beats his chest with her fists.

'Three days. THREE DAYS IT TOOK YOU!' she screams at him as if he did it deliberately.

John runs away over the lawn. Before he gets to the rockery, where the men came down like characters from a horror comic, he stops and comes running back and climbs the low white wall on the other side of the veranda. He crouches in the corner, his brown scratched legs point above his ears. His eyes when we look at him tell us to look away. He puts his hands over his ears so that he does not hear the strange cries that Mom is making.

In the lounge, Dad sits on the couch with his head in his hands while Mom stands looking out of the windows, her arms folded, telling him what happened.

'I'm so sorry about the fence Reen. I should have got it up after the first attacks in the district,' he laughs, but not happily. 'I felt like it might be tempting fate.'

'Ja. Well fate's been more than tempted,' Mom says.

Dad puts his arm up to the waistband of her jeans, but she turns and walks out of the room. He squeezes his thumb and forefinger between his eyes. When he looks up his eyes are red. I've never seen Dad cry before. He stands and goes over to the windows and lifts his fingers up to the spirals that surround the bullet-holes like he's inspecting a painting in an art gallery, then he crouches and sees the blood stains on the parquet tiles from Mom's leg and John's cut.

'Mom and I both got cut,' John says from the pouf that he's dragged under the table.

'Only superficially,' Mom yells from the veranda.

She keeps saying that.

'Come here,' Dad says holding his arms out to us kids.

'We're in the newspaper Dad, you should see, they said we deserved a medal, hey Jay?' John says.

We sit on one tanned, hairy leg each. It's comforting, our bare legs against Dad's warm bare legs, even though I'm too big to sit here now.

'You're brave little soldiers aren't you. All that shooting practice came in handy Jay, hey?' He smiles and hugs me to his chest.

'I'm proud of you Jay. I'd recommend you for service any day, girls or no girls.'

My cheek presses into his chest as he hugs me. *Ba-boomf, ba-boomf, ba-boomf.* His heart beats powerfully but it's not enough. I slip down onto the floor. Granny Rose walks in wearing a pair of paint-smeared men's jeans, her hair a surprise of unravelling steel wool. She sits down in the armchair, a glass of brandy in her hand. I skid across the floor to lean against her chair. Granny Rose lays a hand on my head, the lightness of her bones judder slightly as she strokes my hair.

'I knew they'd come,' she says, looking at her glass. 'Infidels.'

'I'm gonna be a helicopter pilot,' John says. 'Hey, Dad, you should have seen the helicopter man!' John ducks his head. 'Look at my butterfly stitch, from the glass.'

Dad examines his head. Then he hugs John's head into his chest and makes a gulping sound.

'Hell I'll ask them if they'll take the old girl too, hey Granny Rose? I hear you did some shooting too.' He smiles at his grandmother, then looks at the ground.

'Did I?' Granny Rose asks, as if Dad had reminded her that she'd left her glasses on the veranda. 'They consult the witchdoctors you know, to find out when the best time is to attack.'

'RLI tracked the terrs from the southern ridge to the TTL,' Dad says to Granny Rose. 'One of them was wounded. We got five of them. None of them are Justice. The rest'll be holed up in Mozambique. We'll root them out. He'll have his day in court.'

'Well,' says Granny Rose, 'count your blessings. None of your chickens have been taken by the mambas.'

I find Dad leaning over the gate outside the dairy, having a cigarette and watching the mombies graze after milking.

'Hi Bantam, brought a beer for your old dad? I feel old.' He takes the Castle, sniffs and wipes the back of his hand across his eyes.

'Look at that sky,' Dad says, looking up. 'Huge isn't it? Nothing like the skies out here. Makes you feel small. Insignificant.'

The sky is pale yellow and pink and orange with clouds streaked upwards like in one of Granny Rose's paintings.

'My dad, your grandfather said I'd never make a farmer,' Dad says taking out another cigarette from the pack in the top pocket of his short-sleeved shirt, *You're a city boy. Not like me or your brother Pat. You're soft, too soft for farming.* Dad pushes his arm up as if it's going up a cow and puts on Grandpa Ted's voice. *You gota get your hands dirty to farm. Shit man, sometimes you gota stick your whole arm upa cow's arse, man.'* Dad laughs.

'Don't tell Mom I said that. Dad did all the calving himself. He'd never call the vet. He'd say, *If they're gonna die, it's between me and God. Not between me and that bloody shit-stick Jones.* Dad smiles down at me. 'Seems his prophecy's coming true.'

'But Dad you are a farmer. So it's not true. Will we have to leave the farm?'

'I don't know Jay. It's becoming increasingly difficult to go on. It's been hard enough to run the farm with all my call-ups even with the workers.'

'They'll come back.'

'I don't think so Bantam.'

'We can get new ones. Or we can work the farm, hey Dad?'

'Jay, I'm up to my eyeballs in debt. People have bigger things than tea production to worry about –'

'But you said it helps support the Rhodesian economy.'

'Ja. It does Bantam. But right now the government's more concerned with calling me and the other farmers, and everyone else up, so there won't be much of an economy to be propped up. Let's not think about it hey, little Jay-bird. Let's just enjoy the here and now.' His voice becomes jagged. 'Being together.'

14.

The green shells of the gem squash rock slightly in the china bowl, their yellow centres look sick in the pale light escaping from the glass lampshade high above our heads. Through the doorway we watch Dad yell at Nessie on the phone in the passage.

'How dare you phone me and complain that Justice has been arrested? I hope they put him away for a long time. I hope *justice* gets well and truly done – I didn't put the CIO on your back. If you weren't such a bloody traitor you wouldn't be being watched.'

His paces up and down the dark hallway, his slip-slops making swishing noises on the parquet floors.

'Evidence? Bit of a bloody coincidence, isn't it Nessie? He pitches up and shortly afterwards we get hit.' He kicks the wall with his foot and his slip-slop falls off, which would be funny usually, but right now it's not.

'I'm not looking for someone to blame! Okay I blame you Nessie, for bringing him here. You stupid woman. Wake up Nessie! My family could have been killed. Fuck your stupid liberal fucking ideas! If I see him I'll kill him. Tell him that from me, Nessie, next time you send him a message.' He slams the phone down.

'They've caught the bastard,' Dad says as he sits down again. 'Hope they put him away for a long, long time.' He saws into his steak. The grandfather clock tick-tocks it's doom-gloom sound like it's trying to tell us something apart from the time.

Dad leans against the wall in the hallway, his hand on his forehead, speaking to other farmers about workers.

'I'll be off on call-up again soon, Jack,' he says, running his fingers through his hair. 'They'll send someone else in to look after my family. Stupid isn't it? I'll probably be guarding someone else's farm. But who will run the farm with Reen? There's only so much she can do. She's exhausted.' He laughs, trying to make a joke about it all with the man from the labour department.

'What's happening? Has everyone gone fishing?'

Finally he phones Uncle Pat.

'I didn't wanna have to ask this – I know workers are as scarce as rain when the rainmakers are getting vrot – could you? Just for a couple of weeks?'

After he puts the phone down, he slides his back down the wall and sits on the parquet floor in his shorts with his legs crossed. He looks up and sees me standing underneath the photograph of Granny Rose and Grandpa Patrick leaning on the old Ford when they were young.

'Uncle Pat's sending two of his workers across. He'll drive them here in a few days.'

Then he stares at the ground as if searching for reasons why. But why is a sheep.

We're parked at the kitchen table having lunch when Righteous knocks gently on the kitchen door and comes in. He's dressed in a suit and wearing a hat.

'You look smart, Righteous,' Carla says.

He takes off his hat and looks at the floor.

'Would you like to talk, Righteous?' Dad asks, chewing his sandwich.

Righteous nods, he looks embarrassed.

Five minutes later Dad's back. 'He's leaving.'

Mom lights up a cigarette.

'Shit!' says Carla, folding her arms.

'Don't swear Carla,' Mom says.

'Well it is shit Mom,' I say.

'Ja. It is shit. Seems something pressing came up with his wife's family.' Dad snorts and lifts the left corner of his mouth. 'At least he had the decency to tell me. Not like bloody Moses. Shit man!' he slams down his sandwich.

John begins to cry. Carla gets up and puts her arm round John.

'Don't worry. You'll see Nakai again someday.' Her long hair shrouds him.

'No he won't,' I say.

Carla glares at me.

'Can it Jay,' Mom says, exhaling smoke.

Dad picks up his half-eaten sandwich, looks at it and puts it down again. Now there is only Wilson.

15.

On the back lawn, John and I cut cardboard boxes up and stick them together with parcel tape. We draw body outlines of terrorists in pencil, then colour them in. Laughing, we scribble on curly black hair and draw big sunglasses on one of them, using lots of red wax crayon for bullet holes. Then we prop them on the kitchen chairs but they slide off.

'Ha! Ha! They're dead already,' John says.

We finish putting the sticks in a cross shape so that they stand up against the chairs. John pulls the chairs forward.

'Put them further away man, or it's too easy,' I say, dragging them back.

Our bullets hitting the cardboard making a satisfying popping sound.

'I blew his brains out Jay!'

'Hey, terrs don't have brains!'

I imagine Justice being shot every time we make a hit, but mostly we shoot the trees behind the home-made terrs.

'Jay. Do you think Enoch knew they were coming? And Nakai.'

'No. Not Nakai. Maybe Moses though.'

'I'm glad he's gone, I never want to see him again.'

'Do you want to see Enoch again?' He takes aim.

'Ja.'

'Even if he knew?' He lowers his gun.

'Ja. I'd want to hear him say that he knew.' Or that he didn't.

'Why?'

I take aim at the terrorist. 'So I could blow his brains out.' I shoot at the terr and get him between the eyes.

Uncle Pat arrives in his Land Rover with three of his tobacco pickers. Three African men in dark-blue overalls vault out of the back of the bakkie and wander off down to the gum trees near the kaya to smoke until they're called for.

'Hi kids!' Uncle Pat shouts, a cigarette hanging from his lips.

He has something fat and warm and cute and cuddly under his arm. He crouches down and sets it on the back lawn, and it sniffs the kikuyu grass then topples a little, falls over and gets up again. It's tan and black and looks like a Labrador, spaniel cross. John and I ditch our terrorists and race up the lawn to crouch beside him.

'He's all yours,' Uncle Pat says laughing, his glinty-grey eyes almost disappearing into his tanned face.

He crouches on long, muscly legs and pushes John over so he falls from his haunches onto the lawn and the new puppy jumps all over his tummy. Uncle Pat laughs and ruffles my hair with the hand he's holding his cigarette in, probably sprinkling my hair with grey ash. But I don't mind, we've got a new puppy.

Over sundowners on the veranda, the talk is all about shortages, the shortage of brandy, petrol and manpower due to all the able-bodied men being called-up all the time or people upping and leaving, hundreds taking the gap every month.

'Ja,' says Uncle Pat. 'People weren't short on milking the good life here while they could hey? Now it's hot they're on the chicken-run, slithering off like bush snakes in a veld fire.'

'Ja,' Dad says. 'How we s'posed to run an economy and fight a war, it's beyond me.' He looks at his brother. 'I dunno if we gonna make it Pat. I'm being called-up again soon. Then what? What's gonna happen to the farm man?'

Everyone is quiet.

Uncle Pat offers Dad a cigarette. 'Don't give up boet,' he says leaning over. 'They haven't beaten you yet.'

'Ja,' Dad says, staring out over the valley. On the front lawn, John and Piddle chase each other round and round in circles.

16.

From first light, we're out in the fields with Uncle Pat's workers bringing in the tea harvest. By eleven 'o clock tea break the leather harness straps of the basket attached to my back are grooving red welts over my shoulder blades and rubbing my collarbones raw. I keep trying to switch hands but then I drop the leaves so I shake out my wrists and keep on picking with my achy right hand. Carla keeps on and on like a picking machine. If I stop, she says 'come on Jay', and I come on. I do the same to John who trails away behind me, looking dazed. He wanted to bring Piddle, but Dad said no.

'The sooner you finish picking, the sooner you'll see Piddle,' I say.

The three tobacco workers as well as Wilson are splayed out to the north, south, east and west of the plantations, hand-plucking the tea-bushes, their heads like the rounds of steam-train engines moving through the valley. We'll be here till six, when Dad will drive the tractor and trailer full of green tea leaves to the processing plant, because Moses is not here to do it. We'll be up again at three tomorrow. If the terrs came back they'd probably have a hellava time waking us up.

17.

Our Prime Minister is about to speak to us on the TV. Mom and Dad sit on last-century chairs, their hands gripping the carved arms like they're about to take off in a plane and should be wearing seat belts.

'Never pay attention to a man in a box,' Granny Rose warns us from her spring-chair, a gift from a tea-planter from Assam. *Tell your husband to sit on this. Love Frank,* John found this written on an old yellow tag under one of the springs when he lifted it up to look for one of his marbles. 'Politicians – mark my words,' she warns us, sticking up a finger like a gnawed chicken bone. 'They're only good for dinner parties.' She gets up and wanders out of the room.

'Sssssh!' Mom says as the news music starts. Dad puts his beer down on the coffee table and takes up his Kingsgates.

Ian Smith comes on and begins speaking slowly and firmly. His brow is raised upwards, so that with his nose it forms an arrow straight up to the sky, from where, I think, he must hope his help cometh. He looks like he has the whole weight of Rhodesia on his back. He also looks like he needs a stiff whisky followed by a hug from someone who's already had a few stiff whiskies.

This is not the end. It is not even the beginning of the end but it is perhaps the end of the beginning...

Dad laughs sarcastically and takes a huge toke on his cigarette. 'Churchill, that's bloody depressing, shit, and I thought he said "Not in a thousand years." That he'd never accept African majority rule. Bloody sell-out. Shit man!' Dad slams his bottle down on the table.

'What's gonna happen Mom?' John asks, sitting up.

Mom gets up from her chair. 'Don't raise your voice, please Dave, you're scaring John.'

'Come John-John, off to bed,' Mom leans over and pulls John up from the pouf by his hand.

'Ag, c'mon man, I don't want to go to bed now,' John protests as Mom pulls him up by the hand. 'Come on, you can get into our bed, with the bedside light on.'

'What does he mean Dad? Is the war gonna be over?' Carla shouts from the couch, flicking her feet in ripped legwarmers over the top of the couch.

'It means our Prime Minister is going to negotiate a settlement with the terrorist leaders of this country.' Dad puts his hands to the side of his face, his sideburns ruffle out, then he runs the hand holding his cigarette through his hair, stroking his beard with his other hand. He looks at the floor. For a second I think he's going to cry. But he half raises himself from his chair, his knuckles white from gripping.

'Dammit I need a drink,' he says.

'I'll get you one,' I say.

When I get back with the drink, Dad has his head in his hands.

'Interfering bastards,' Dad says to the floor, as I hand him the Bols and Coke.

'Are the terrs gonna be in government?' I ask.

Mom comes back in from saying goodnight to John and begins to close the wire mesh safety doors that lead out to the veranda. Then she closes the glass doors.

'It'll be the Poms have the final say,' Dad says. 'Hypocrites,' he adds as he takes a sip. 'Americans are just as bad. Bloody Kissinger, trying to further his political career on our backs.' He drops his slip-slop on the floor and runs his bare foot over Piddle's coat who whimpers in his doggy-sleep, unaware of the turmoil that's brewing in the land of the humans.

'I can't believe it,' Dad says, again, his head in his hands. 'He's selling us out Reen. Why would he do that? After all we've fought for?'

'Well, I can't say I'm surprised.'

'What do you mean?'

'Well it was going to happen. Sooner or later.'

'Is that all you've got to say? What does he mean he would accept responsible majority rule? Are bloody communist terrorists responsible? Bloody hell, I've seen what those responsible men can do. Sit down woman,' Dad says to Mom. 'Haven't you got anything to say?'

'Ja,' Mom says, reaching for her Berkeleys and lighting up. 'It's inevitable, Dave. And don't swear in front of the kids.'

'Shit!' he says, slamming his drink down on the table next to him.

Piddle wakes up and starts wagging his tail.

Dad says, 'I hate your attitude.'

'Well what bloody attitude am I supposed to have Dave?' Mom says, sitting back down.

Crossing and uncrossing her blue-jeaned legs, she smokes silently in the blue haze. On the television a woman named Joan complains about a headache for which she is offered Anadin. A pill to fix it.

Granny Rose comes in, wearing her white night gown, her pin-coloured hair a muddle on her shoulders.

'Patrick is trying to get in through my window,' she says. 'I've told him, I'll set the Rottweiler on him.'

Dad gets up and puts his hand under her elbow.

'C'mon, Gran, I'll shut the window, then he won't be able to get in.'

'Nu'night Granny Rose!' everyone chimes like a bunch of clocks. The Rottweiler is Ethel, Granny Rose's mom. She's been dead for years, obviously. Carla catches my eye and I make Rottweiler faces and we start laughing. For a moment, everything seems normal, but it's a pretty funny situation when Granny Rose makes things seem normal.

The phone rings and Mom goes out to answer it.

'Bob says there are no plans for a ceasefire.'

'I could have told you that.'

'Well what the bloody hell are we supposed to believe?' Mom yells. 'Smith's telling us he's accepting majority rule – '

'Ja. So you think we down guns and shake hands then?'

Carla turns up the television.

'Turn that bloody thing down,' Dad shouts. 'Go to bed!'

In her bedroom, Carla and I try to sleep to the soundtrack of our parents arguing.

'Carla? Do you think we'll have to leave?'

'I don't know.' She snuggles up to me. 'Dad'll work it out.' Soon she is sleeping so peacefully that her porridge-scented breath may as well be rose petals. It makes me want to crush her.

'I don't care what your bloody sister Aldie says, Reen. We're not leaving,' Dad yells from the lounge.

'Do you think I want to leave? I've poured years of my life into this farm too you know Dave. I just think we need to face the inevitable. Before the inevitable faces us,' Mom shouts.

'And what is the inevitable?'

'We have no workers. We have no life Dave. How much longer are we going to slave away like this?'

'This farm is my life, Reen. My grandparents built Angel's Peak from the earth with their bare hands. I'm not leaving. John will grow up here and take over from me.'

'John will grow up where it's safe.'

'Is that a threat?' Dad asks. A door slams and there is silence.

18.

At the kitchen table, their words puff out like smoke above me. Carla doesn't look surprised. She looks down at the kitchen table when I catch her eyes. Then she gets up, bends over and twists her hair, tying it into a knot on the top of her head. They must have told her already.

'How can you do your bloody hair at a time like this?' I ask her.

'Geda grip Jay.'

'You geda grip, you stupid cow!' On the table, my hands tighten on the blue glass of the sugar-bowl. I'd like to throw it at her.

'Girls!' Mom says, 'calm down.'

'Calm down?' I press sugar grains into the table with the back of the sugar spoon.

'Why are we leaving Mom?' John asks. 'Can we take Piddle?'

'Of course darling,' Mom says, exhaling smoke.

Of course darling. Like he's just asked if he can take Piddle to the shops.

'We're leaving John,' I say. 'Is that all you've got to say?' I shake my head, my mouth open.

'Catching flies?' Dad asks, trying to make a joke.

'You are joking. Aren't you Dad? You would never leave this farm. Our farm? Would you Dad?' I ask.

'It's not my choice Jay.'

'We've tried to make a go of it Jay,' Mom says. 'We can't run a farm without workers. With Dad being called-up all the time. With the economy being what it is.' She takes another toke on her

141

cigarette. 'With the whole bloody area crawling with terrs.'

'Ja. Do you want us to be attacked again Jay?' Carla asks.

'Shudup! You weren't even here!'

Carla starts crying.

'Did you hear what she said Mom? She's rubbing it in. That I wasn't here. She knows how bad I feel.'

'I'm gonna hit you,' I say. 'I'm gonna hit you so hard that you'll never be a bloody princess in Swan Lake again. Only a bloody ugly duckling.'

Carla flies out of the room.

Dad reaches out to me across the table. I move away from his hand.

He gets up to get a beer, returns to the table and snaps the bottle-top off. It spins over the table and I catch it, digging it into the fleshy part of my palm. It leaves a pretty, lacy imprint on my hand. I dig it in again and again.

'Why are you doing this Dad?' I ask, looking at my hand. `We could make a go of it. Please! Let's just try.'

'We've tried Bantam.'

'No we haven't. Not long enough. Please?'

Dad looks at his beer. 'We're selling the tea business. But not the rest of the farm. A young man from New Zealand is going to part farm, part manage for us. His wife's a nurse, she'll help look after Granny Rose – Godfrey and Patience are coming to work for us.'

'Please Dad?' I'm crying now. 'PLEASE?'

John begins to cry now too.

'Ja please Dad. Let's stay. What about our dead animals? I want to stay with them.'

Mom puts her arm out and John leans against her.

'What about work?'

'I've got a job at the Tribal Trust Land Development Authority. It's arranged.'

'Got a job? You've been organising it behind our backs.' I get up. 'Thanks Dad.'

'Look, you'll like the house in Salisbury. It's the capital of Rhodesia! You can go ice-skating.'

'Bugger ice-skating.'

Dad laughs. 'What?'

'Bugger ice-skating and bugger Salisbury.' I yell it at him over the table as I get up to leave.

'Do you think I feel good about this!' Dad yells after me. 'How do you think I feel? This farm is my life.'

From the doorway I say, 'If this farm is your life you wouldn't leave! Otherwise you'd die!'

19.

Outside Wilson's kaya, the fire is nearly out. Only the palest pinky-red glow, mirroring the sky, is visible beneath the blackened wood and the silken white ash. I knock on the door of Wilson's kaya. There's no response, so I gently push the door open. It smells of Wilson's tobacco mixed with Lifebuoy soap. The iron bed is neatly made up with its cotton cover over the top, carefully tucked in all the way around. Next to the bed is an upturned Mazoe orange box with a candle and some Lion matches on a white doily. On the other side of the room a wooden bar is suspended from two bits of wire fixed to hooks screwed into the corrugated iron ceiling. Wilson's suit is hanging here, encased in plastic. The polished cement floor shines and smells of Cobra wax. John and I have sat here and eaten sadza and nyama and spinach out of enamel bowls many times, even though we were going to have our own supper later.

'Yes, Jayne.' I jump at the familiar voice behind me.

Wilson sees that I have been crying. 'You are not happy. But you will be happy.'

'No, Wilson, I will never be happy again.' I lean against the cement wall.

'Sure, you will be happy, but not in this place. We can sit.' He walks towards the fire.

We sit on the old tyres in front of the fire out front. Wilson pokes the fire with a stick.

'How come you didn't leave Wilson? Even though Righteous did?'

'My place is here. I must look after your grandmother.'

Wilson piles bark and long dry leaves from the gum trees onto the fire. They crackle and give off their eucalyptus smell. He digs at the fire with the stick.

'Please tell me how Enoch is.'

Wilson looks up at me. 'I am not living his life.'

'Please tell him that I also had to leave.'

Mom calls from the kitchen door. I stand up. Wilson stands up too. Metre high cardboard boxes are stacked up all over the back lawn and piled up near the back door. I walk towards the house that is as empty as a corpseless coffin. When I look back, he is standing there watching me walk through the boxes to the house.

20.

There is a stillness when we drive away, like a pause in a film. The birds are quiet in the air that is holding its breath. Granny Rose and Wilson stand side by side, their outer arms raised to wave. Outside my window, the soil blurs red under the wheels as the car picks up speed. As we drive away I think I hear a go-away bird start up: *go-waaay, go-waaay, go-waaay.* On the road to Salisbury, I wonder whether I imagined the go-away bird, because it keeps replaying its mean call in my head. Maybe it just feels like the whole world is against us.

1977

Salisbury,
Rhodesia

1.

In my new classroom, Mr Coetzee's voice soundtracks while I stare over the school wall at the flower bells decorating the jacaranda trees like lilac underwear beneath the curved blue street lamps. *Salisbury Sunshine City* it says on all the t-shirts with the print of the beaming sun wearing sunglasses. Sunshine Shitty. I'm never going to wear the t-shirt. No mahobohobo trees around here, or bush to run around in or mountains to climb. Here the boys keep away from the girls and all the girls talk about is whether they're going to wear boob-tubes to the Standard Five leavers' dance, where they're going to refuse to dance with boys. Everything is neat and tidy and shaped, from the trees to the lawns clipped as short as Gavin's crew cut at the desk in front of me. It makes you want to start a fire or something.

Mr Coetzee interrupts my thoughts, 'Have you travelled far?' he asks.

I look up.

The class laughs.

'Yes you Miss Cameron.'

I look up at him confused.

'You seem to have been very far off.'

I feel myself redden.

'Yes, well do remain on board, Miss Cameron. We don't want to lose you.'

The boy at the desk next to me mouths the word 'freak.' He must have practised it in the mirror. His forehead is about two inches wide and his ears are as big as his cheeks.

The class laughs a bit more as Mr Coetzee begins to walk up and down the classroom between our desks telling us all about swallowing. 'The muscles in your throat clench in such a way that were you to stand on your head, you could still swallow…' Roger rockets his hand up like he always does. Sometimes I wish his hand would just fly up, propeller round the room for a while and then slap itself to the ceiling above his head, peel off slowly and then land on his head like a hat, the fingers feathering over one of his buzzy little eyes.

'I don't think that's possible Mr Coetzee, could you show us?'

Mr Coetzee looks at carrot-cropped Roger for a second, then he spins on his heel and walks over to his desk where he takes out a sandwich wrapped in grease-proof paper, then he walks back to the centre of the classroom, stands in front of the blackboard and looks at us. We look back. He hesitates. Is he going to do it? Someone coughs. Mr Coetzee unwraps the sandwich and takes a bite. We shift in our chairs.

'Wachoo godon your sarnies? Mr Coetzee?' Hulking, spot-ridden, straw-haired Kevin shouts out.

Mr Coetzee looks at him. He chews, but does not reply. He puts down his sandwich on Belinda's desk. She moves her chair backwards, just in case the sandwich tries eating her. Mr Coetzee steps away from Belinda's desk and then kneels down facing the door. Like a Muslim in prayer, he leans his torso forward, elbows bent, hands on the floor, bum pointing at the ceiling, his legs, sticking out of his safari shorts, rise up, their lower halves in knee-high socks and tan polished lace-ups, bend, hover in mid-air and then point upwards towards the strip light. The flaps of his safari jacket flip outwards like a beige tutu. He chews slowly, in the same way that he did when he was upright, only his face looks much redder now and his grey beard points up instead of down. Half the class rushes towards the front of the classroom. Roger stays put in his chair across from mine, and begins to clap slowly, the rest of the class join in. Mr Coetzee swallows.

'He's swallowed it, he's swallowed it!'

The door opens and Mrs Bridge from 5B walks in. 'What is this commotion, Mr Coetzee? What have you swallowed? A sword?'

Mr Coetzee comes down slowly to right himself. 'No Mrs Bridge, but I hope 5A have swallowed the theory of ingestion, because now I would like to move on to digestion.'

At home time, Mr Coetzee calls me back as I try to leave.

'This travelling will have to stop. You might as well live in the present.'

I look down at my shoes and then at the collars of his safari suit; the faint check embroidered into the material brings a feeling of nausea to me.

'Was your farm very beautiful?' he says, stroking his pointy beard.

My words take off and fly around the room, settling on the Geography posters, the tacked up paintings and the silent wooden desks. We are both sailing in a sea of words made by me. When the blizzard stops, I am surprised that it all came from me.

'Ah well. Yes, I can see why you choose to go back there all the time.'

Staring at the tips of my shoes helps me.

'The past is another country,' he says.

Come again? Is he cracked?

'You must move on Jayne.' For a moment I think he's going to put his arms on my shoulders but he just bends and twinkles his leprechaun eyes at me.

'You are here now. The old has gone and the new has come.'

As I turn to leave, he says, 'You do not speak of the other thing that happened.' I pause near the door.

'If you needed to, you could speak to me if you'd like. Or Miss Fielding. She's a good person to speak to.'

My feet run quickly over the deserted quad to the bicycle sheds, faster, faster.

2.

The sprinkler on the front lawn goes tic-tic-tic as the shadows lengthen and the air cools as the doves go *coo-coo-roo, coo-coo-roo* in the guava trees out back. On the veranda, the cerise bougainvillea nods in the breeze from where it clings to the pillar, trying to climb up to the thatched roof. The red cement beneath my bare feet is losing its heat and its lekker smell of cobra wax. Dad, his face as brown as his heavy pottery double-glazed mug, jokes with Carla about her new boyfriend Ian.

'He better come and ask me first before he proposes –' he says, his left foot jiggling above his right knee.

Carla shrieks. 'He's not going to pro –'

'Let me finish! Proposes to take you out.' He slaps his veldskoen, hosing himself at his own joke.

'Oh Dad! Don't be embarrassing!' She tosses her newly-flicked long hair. Some of it gets stuck on her lip gloss, which is as thick as smeared glue.

'Or I'll take him out, one time, on the floor.' Dad punches at the air in front of him.

Across the lawn Godfrey uses his whole body as he crouches and bends near the azaleas encouraging the plants into the soil. Mom hoots as she slows to a halt at the gates and Godfrey goes running. She slams the door of the green Peugeot.

'Mmm secretary bird,' Dad says, reaching out to her. 'How was work with the shrink today?'

'Dr Sheldon is one of the best psychiatrists in this country,'

Mom says, collapsing into a chair. She reaches for her cigarettes. Carla, who's nearest, passes them to her.

'Hey, you making a speech?' Dad says, picking up the newspaper.

'He's the only psychiatrist in this country you mean,' I say. The others have ducked overseas.

'Ja, Jay, that's right,' Dad says, ruffling my hair, as he gets up to go inside to answer the phone.

Carla rolls her eyes.

Dad's still laughing as he disappears into the dark hallway.

'WHAAAAAT!!' Dad shouts from inside. 'SHIT man! Of all the stupid – what? I can't believe it. Well you better bloody find him again.'

Carla and I look at each other as Mom gets up. We follow her inside.

'How could he have escaped? What you fell for that? That's insane! Ja. Make sure it's chop chop.'

Dad slams the phone down. 'Bloody idiots!' He punches the wall really hard with the side of his fist.

'Take it easy Dave,' Mom says. 'What happened?'

'Justice jumped out of the back of a police Land Rover,' Dad says, rubbing his knuckles. 'He's escaped. Him and one of the others.' Dad laughs in disbelief. 'They both lunged at the police sergeant and smacked him over either temple with their cuffs.' Dad has the back of his hand on his forehead. 'They jumped out of the moving vehicle and escaped into the bush. For pity's sake, how did the driver not see them escape? And one guard for two of them? Bloody useless, bloody idiots!' He punches the wall again, then shakes his hand out with the pain.

'I bet that bloody lawyer Patel told him it was the best option. Bloody curry muncher.'

'Well,' says Mom, 'it probably was. Even Patel is powerless against a Rhodesian judge hell bent on hanging.'

'What? He deserved to be bloody hung.'

'Ja, Dave. If he did it. What if we hung him and he didn't?'

Mom puts her arms around him, 'Look the whole country's paranoid about the security situation – they're baying for blood –' Dad shrugs her off and goes into the kitchen to the fridge. We follow. 'Look, all I'm saying is things need to be properly investigated, properly dealt with. We know all about that don't we Dave?'

Grabbing a beer and slamming the fridge door shut he says, 'Bloody Mdisas. I'm sacking Godfrey. I should have got rid of the whole bloody lot of them when we went through this with Prospect.' He uses the cupboard door handle to open his beer.

'Use the opener Dave.'

'Why Reen? Why should I use the bloody opener?'

Mom and I run after him as he heads out the back door.

'You'll do nothing of the sort,' Mom says, grabbing Dad's arm. 'Don't attack him because of his father.'

'Don't tell me how to feel about my family.' He jerks his arm away from her.

'Ja, Dad. It's not Godfrey's fault. You can't sack him.' I grab Dad's other arm.

Dad shrugs me off. 'Bad blood. I'm telling you. Go back inside, all of you. I'm just gonna have a chat.'

'Will it ever end?' Carla says from the kitchen table, her arms folded, curved feet up on one of the green plastic kitchen chairs. 'We should never have brought Godfrey and Patience with us,' she says, 'after what happened. I don't trust any of them either.'

'It's not Godfrey's fault man. He's not his brother's keeper. It's like blaming me for your faults,' I say. 'Wilson and Godfrey. And Enoch,' I have to look at the back of Mom's chair when I say his name, 'are not like Prospect and Justice – are they Mom?'

'We hope,' Carla says.

'They aren't. I know they aren't – hey Mom?'

Mom sighs. 'As far as we know.'

'You can't make people all the same, Carla.' Or can you? Nessie's always telling me to be careful or I'll end up like *them*.

'Enough,' Mom says. 'Let's just let Dad let off a little steam, hey girls? I could do with a drink myself.'

I grab one from the fridge for her.

'Poor Wilson, it's a mercy his poor dead Christian wife didn't live to see what her son and grandson turned out to be,' Mom says holding out her hand to me for the opener.

'What did Prospect do Mom?' I ask, remembering the article about Auntie Penny in *The Rhodesia Herald*.

'We don't talk about it,' Mom snaps off the bottle top, 'Remember?'

'It wasn't an accident was it?'

'Leave it Jay.'

'Why? I want to know.' I fold my arms and lean up against the sink.

'Trust me, you don't,' she says getting up. 'I'm going to rescue poor Godfrey.'

'Ja. I do.'

She turns round. 'There's nothing to know, okay Jayne? Auntie Penny is dead. And for pity's sake don't bring it up with your father.'

Carla's staring at the kitchen table.

'You know don't you?'

'I don't.'

'Ja right. You're as innocent as a cat.'

Out on the veranda, John's still sitting there, staring at his glass, his legs jiggling, in a world all of his own. Over on the lawn Dad is talking to Godfrey, who stands there nodding then shaking his head, not telling Dad what he wants to know as politely as possible; Mom's smiling, her arm on Dad's, trying to get him to come inside.

3.

The trial is all over the newspapers and suddenly I've won the popularity contest at school. *Did you really shoot the terrs? Gee you brave hey? Are you scared they're gonna come back? Hunt you down to Salisbury? Wanna come to my house? We having a braai Saturday. Gee do you think our garden boy might be a terr? My mom thinks so but my dad tells her not to worry her pretty little head about it. But your garden boy was a terr hey? My mom says Africans can't be trusted and we mustn't speak to them. Ja.* 'Unless they're the ice-cream boy...Or the maid...Or the garden boy?' I say. Then they look at me funny again. So I say, *only joking*, and everyone laughs, but when I think of Enoch my laughter goes stale inside.

Dad's not on call-up at the moment, so when he's not at his lawyer's office discussing the trial he reads the newspaper on the veranda. I listen to him on the phone speaking to a journalist from *The Rhodesia Herald.* Yesterday an English lady journalist phoned to speak to Dad about the terrs that attacked us, but Dad wouldn't speak to her, lady or no lady. *The bloody bastard British have too much to answer for.*

'They're dead meat,' Dad said about the terrs. 'I can't wait to see them swing. And you can print that as well.'

The rain sounds like gravel being flung at my window by dream hands. I am painfully aware of my bladder being as full as a melon. Enoch taps on my window and I hop out. I'm so happy to see him even though he has a bandana on and tons of ammo roped round him.

'Are you with us?' He hands me a semi-automatic.

'What do you mean?'

'Choose. Me or your parents.'

'I don't want to choose.'

'My mother says you and your family must die.'

Then he opens fire and the walls of the house become swaying, bullet-pocked flesh and start to fall over. I open my cupboard door to hide and then I scream because Nessie is in there smiling in the dark.

'Jay!'

I'm being shaken awake.

'You were shouting.' Mom smoothes the hair off my forehead.

On Friday evening on the day of the trial, Mom and I and Patience are preparing dinner in the kitchen when Dad comes in through the back door, waving *The Rhodesia Herald*.

'They've hung the other four!' he says cheerfully. 'I can't tell you how happy it made me to see them go down. I looked one of them right in the eyes.'

'Did he stare you out?' I ask.

'No. He just looked down.'

Washing dirt off the spinach at the sink, I find a curly worm and consider how that terr will be looking down through a trapdoor counting the seconds away. Soon worms will crawl out of him. He could have killed us but now we're killing him; it all makes me feel sick.

'And the others?' Mom asks.

'One of them shouted about freedom.' Dad makes a snorting noise and goes to the fridge.

I shove thoughts of Nessie back to the back of my mind.

'Good,' says Mom. She takes a sip of her tea. 'I won't sleep till the other two are caught.'

'Well you're going to be awake for a long time,' Dad says, getting a beer out of the fridge, then attempting to slam the fridge door shut, but he leaves it slightly open, so soon it gapes. 'Bloody bastards are probably in Mozambique right now, plotting to blow up the rest of us. Those that they haven't killed already, they have quite a body count between them. You should have been there Reen.'

'I had to work,' Mom says, slamming the fridge door that Dad has left open with her foot.

'No you didn't. You could have taken time off.' He leans against the sideboard and takes a swig of his beer. 'Priorities Reen.'

Patience stares into the red plastic bowl, into which she's peeling potato rinds. She's become much rounder in her face and body since she came here with Godfrey.

'Sorry Patience,' says Dad. Patience smiles a smile that is not happy, nor sad.

'I believe your husband is going to be interviewed too.'

Patience stares at the potatoes, her rounded cheekbones look as if they have been carved out of oiled wood.

'That is no problem, boss.' She looks down at the long curling peels falling into the bowl.

'We like to work for you,' Patience says, looking up at Dad with her leaf-shaped eyes.

Mom places a hand on Patience's arm.

'We like you working for us. Don't worry.'

Dad smiles at her. 'What a tangled web we've all got ourselves into, hey Patience?' Patience smiles and looks at the potatoes floating in water.

Later, Special Branch turn up in a white Renault. Two men with thick moustaches, suit trousers, short-sleeved white shirts. They go with Dad round to the kaya to interview Godfrey. I try to follow, but Dad sends me packing, so I park off on the veranda with Mom and Carla to wait. They're there ten whole minutes, then they all reappear on the veranda.

'Mrs Cameron.' The one with the darker hair nods at Mom, the balding ginger-haired one nods too, his mouth buried beneath a two-inch pile moustache.

'Any help?' Mom asks.

'We're confident we know where they are and what they're up to,' says the mouthless ginger-haired man.

'Ja,' says Dad, 'so are we. It's getting them out of where they are that's the problem.'

The dark, curly-haired one smiles, his trimmed moustache well under control.

'We have our methods. Don't we Mr Cameron?'

Dad smiles. 'Wanna beer, boys?'

'Not on the job,' they say together, like Tweedle-dum and Tweedle-dee. Everyone laughs and Carla raises her eyes at me as she does so. The Special Branch men jump down the veranda steps and climb into their white Renault. Putting foot hard on the accelerator, they disappear down the driveway in a cloud of red dust.

'Starsky and Hutch,' I say.

'So what did Godfrey say?' Mom asks Dad.

'He said Justice had probably escaped to Mozambique. They said they thought he was probably right. Then they asked him whereabouts.'

'And?' Mom asks.

'He said he didn't know.'

'And?' Mom persists.

'He probably doesn't know. We'll weed him out.'

'That orange moustache was just like a dead animal hanging there,' says Carla.

What a hose, I crack up.

'And who did the Starsky one think he was? *We have our methods.*'

That night I lie awake for a long time, looking at the shadows moving across the ceiling. In the shadows I see people killing people and people trying to kill people. Then I see people being hung, which is still killing people. Then I see more people killing people because they are upset about the hangings and then people killing other people back because they are upset too. I fall asleep thinking about how it's like using people's severed heads to play a twisted tennis game.

4.

In Mom and Dad's room the windows are open wide, the curtains riding on the occasional puff of wind. For a moment I feel panic, as if there's something, a shape behind them. Then I remind myself, we are in Salisbury in the middle of a city, in broad daylight. Dad's FN rifle lies on the counterpane on the pale pink rose pattern. Soon that rifle will be aimed at terrs in the bush. So much for the ceasefire and Dad saying he'd be called-up less. Less is more in this place.

'I know you hate being left, that it reminds you of what happened. Do you think I want to go? Do you think I want to get blown away only to see the leaders of my country chatting round a table with terrorists? People that have murdered my friends, their wives and their children?'

'Stop it Dave!'

They don't notice I'm here.

'Well it's not as bloody simple as "don't go", is it Irene?'

Mom leaps up off the bed.

'I know it's not bloody SIMPLE! Dave! Nothing's bloody simple in this country. It hasn't been for bloody years! I don't know why we're all so bloody SURPRISED!'

'It's the Americans and that bloody Owen – your countrymen and bloody Kissinger who've sold us down the river. Smith's hands are tied. We can't go on without South Africa. Bloody traitors! Once the bridge is closed, there's no more supplies.' He sits down on the bed and takes his beret off, smoothing his hair back with both hands.

'There's nowhere left for us to go, Reen. The whole world is against us. They'd rather believe the savage –' his voice breaks. 'The savage bloody terrs, bloody Robert Mugabe, shit Reen, he's an animal. And Nkomo? What I've seen in this war, I –'

I shift my weight. They finally catch I'm there. Dad turns to look at me.

'Come to say goodbye to your old Dad?'

'Dad? Who's Kissinger?'

'America's ex-foreign minister. Like Van der Byl. The man with the crystal ball.'

'Crystal ball?'

'Ja. The man who's deciding our future for us.'

'Our fate,' says Mom, with an unhappy laugh. She reaches for her cigarettes on the bedside table. 'Say goodbye, then hop it, you're gonna be late for school.'

'Charming,' I say.

'Don't get shot.' My voice quavers as I bend to hug him. Maybe I'll never see him again, like Moira or Patrick, kids from my old school who said goodbye to their fathers when they went on call-up. There was no 'hello' for them, ever again.

Dad laughs a jokey laugh. Mom sniffs and lights her cigarette.

'Bye Dad.'

'Bye Bantam.'

Face down on my bed, hot-wet tears soak the sheets, and the saliva pours out of my open mouth. I hear Dad coming into the room.

'C'mon Bantam,' he pulls me up and hugs me against his stiff camouflage uniform. I press my face into his hard, tanned neck. The dark curls beneath the beret sweep up my tears. I dribble down his neck.

'Nice one Bantam,' he wipes his neck. 'Wanna dribble some more?' He pulls me back by the shoulders to examine me.

'No more crying hey? You've made your pretty little face all red and you look like you've been punched in the mouth.'

I laugh and dribble some more, a thin line of saliva spray lands on his rank badges. He laughs, his brown bicep curves as he lifts his arm to wipe at the spit.

'My little Jay-bird,' he says. 'I know it hurt you to leave, it hurt me to leave too. I know this whole thing hurts. Hey, maybe we can all go back? When the war is over?'

'Those are just words, Dad.'

'Dad?' He turns in the gloom of the passage. 'I'm not going to school today, I'm not sitting with those morons –' I say.

'Don't go,' he says, 'Don't ever hang out with morons unless you have to,' he smiles. 'Today you don't have to. Hang out and talk to Godfrey while he works. Ride your bike, climb trees, talk to the bees, just don't go to school today, whatever you do!'

Godfrey's long fingers turn the rich red topsoil as he prepares the beds at the side of the house for the new plants. His hands are the chocolate colour of the soil. My hands are the opposite colour. Like Top Deck chocolate from South Africa. Dark on the bottom, white on the top. The white is on top of the dark chocolate which is how Nessie would say Rhodesia is. The Europeans living on the top deck, decking themselves out at the expense of the Africans. But that chocolate bar can be turned over, and then the darker heavier side would be on top, and then you might not be able to see the top, white layer anymore. The terrs say that this land belongs to them. Uncle Pat says that we too belong on this land, because we have lived on it and loved the land for generations. He also says that the Shona and Ndebele peoples migrated from up north, so you can argue that they don't own the land either and the land should be shared amongst all the peoples of Rhodesia. Dad just says those who love the land should be allowed to stay on it.

'Godfrey? Do you think us whites should leave Africa?'

He smiles. 'It is not for me to think.'

'What do you mean?'

'You are here, these whites. Now you are here. One time you are not here. But now, you are here.'

'So you don't think we should leave?'

'For me, I cannot say. You must ask your God.'

'And you? Do you ask your ancestors if we must stay or go?'

'They can know.' He smiles down at his planting hands.

'I don't wanna go, I love Rhodesia.'

He smiles. 'This Jayne, she must stay.'

'Okay, Godfrey, don't forget to tell your ancestors that, okay?'

I watch Godfrey's face as he works. The blackish, hollow dip beneath his cheekbone, the long jaw line, are like Enoch's, but his eyes are rounder and less widely spaced and his lips are bigger than Enoch's. *Kaffir lips,* the boys at school say. But African mouths seem so much more generous compared to the thin spiteful lips of the Europeans.

'Anyway,' I say to Godfrey, 'if God didn't want us to move around countries, he shouldn't have given us the ability to make boats and planes and cars and things, then maybe we would have stayed put.'

Smiling, he picks up a trailing plant. Its little leaves form strand upon strand of delicate greyish-green lace. He doesn't look at me as he pokes it into the soil. A wet patch has formed a circle at the base of his shoulders, it clings to the curve of his spine as he bends, his shoulders splaying out like the wings of a bird in flight.

'One time, no one own the land. The land is for everyone. The chiefs, they say, your family you live here. You put your cow here. But no one keep the land.'

'You mean the chief owned the land and gave it out?'

Like Nessie told me about communism. Sharing. Dad says it's against human nature to share.

'Then white men came, making bad contract with chiefs, they take the land, and now black man must pay tax to live on white man's land.'

'But it wasn't their land in the first place?'

'For sure, this is right,' he laughs. At his temple a glistening drop of sweat gathers and begins to roll down the side of his cheek, till it falls and explodes on the grass.

5.

Mom says I should invite a girl from school over. So I invite a girl called Sandra from my class. We climb the mulberry tree in the back garden near the kaya to collect leaves for her little sister's silkworms.

'I used to love silkworm season,' I say from near the top of the tree.

'Ja,' Sandra says, 'I've grown out of it too.'

'Don't mind climbing trees still though,' I say stuffing the leaves in my school dress pocket.

'Well. It's not very lady-like,' she says.

'I'm not really trying to be a lady,' I say putting a mulberry as long as a fat chongololo in my mouth. I squeeze out a fake smile and a bit of red juice trickles down my chin. She looks disgusted. I care rocks.

Godfrey waves when he moves down the path beneath us to go to the kaya.

'Hi Godfrey!' I shout. He looks up and waves. From this angle he looks a lot like Enoch.

'Why you saying hello to the garden boy? He's a munt.'

'What's a munt?' I ask.

'You know, an Af.'

'No. A munt is just a person. It means human being. It's an African word. So you're a munt too.'

'No I'm not.'

'Ja. Maybe you're not.'

She looks ugly with the mulberry juice smearing her big flat face

164

and staining her Abba t-shirt like blood. I have the urge to push her. So I do. In my head. She dies.

'What's funny,' she says, her small blue eyes like pins in my face.

'You, dead in my head,' I say, mostly in my mind.

'What?'

'Nothing,' I say. 'Ssshhh, here comes my boet,' I say as John and his new friend Phillip turn up to collect mulberry leaves for their silkworms. They collect fresh leaves from the lower branches and then sit down in the dirt beneath the tree forming a diamond shape with their outstretched legs, their feet almost touching. Piles of mulberry leaves and two Bata shoeboxes lie between them. Sandra has gone mulberry red from trying not to laugh because they don't know they're being spied on. I consider launching a mulberry missile attack. John's giving Phillip some of his silkworms so that he can start his own silkworm box. They begin layering fresh leaves into the shoe boxes one by one. John takes a silky-grey worm out of the box and lifts it above his head to examine it.

'They're gonna start spinning soon,' John says, placing the worm in Phillip's box.

'Ja,' says Phillip. He uses his forefinger and thumb to tweezer up the worm.

'I feel like squashing it,' Phillip says.

'Ja. Well don't,' John says.

'Who says?' Phillip looks at John.

John laughs, nervously. 'Do you miss your Dad?' he asks.

'Ja. But at least now he won't get killed in the war.'

'Why?'

'He's gone to live down South with his new wife.'

John doesn't say anything. He's concentrating on placing leaves and then silkworms into Phillip's box.

'Your Dad might,' says Phillip.

'Might what?' asks John.

'Get killed in the war.'

John looks down at the box. Something in me explodes. Jumping out of the tree and crashing through the lower branches, I land with a thud on the ground. The boys look up, their faces blank with shock.

'Don't say that you moron!' I shout. 'He won't get killed, you hear? You stupid idiot. How can you say that to him?'

Phillip gets up and runs inside. John begins to cry. I kneel down and pull him close. John sobs against my shoulder, his upper teeth scrape my collar bone and his saliva wets my checked school dress.

'Someone's gonna die!' he howls. 'I know someone's gonna die!'

'Don't say that John. No one's gonna die.'

'They are,' he howls. 'They are.'

Sandra climbs down from the tree. 'Is he alright?'

'Ja. He's fine. I think you better go home though.'

I hug John to my chest. Sandra walks across the back yard and into the kitchen, glancing over her shoulder at us, looking like she's just eaten monkey-poo.

6.

On the veranda steps I'm drawing a moustache on the face of the cover girl on Carla's *Darling* magazine when Uncle Bob and Auntie Aldie zoom in on a cloud of red dust, churned up by the wheels of their jeep being driven too fast up the driveway.

'Howzit Jay,' Uncle Bob shouts as he slams the jeep door, his eyes sparkling at me from his brown face.

'Howzit Jay-Jay,' Auntie Aldie says, going inside, her large, honey-blonde curls bouncing on a waft of Elnett. Chucking his semi-automatic on the lawn in front of him, Uncle Bob stretches his long brown legs, the result of months in the harsh Zambezi Valley. His leg hairs tickle my own legs, only a little less brown than his. He checks out the magazine.

'Ja. She looks better like that. Howzabout a beer man?'

'Okay. And then will you show me your gun?'

'Which one?' he asks. I raise an eyebrow and look at him sideways. He pulls a pistol from inside his shorts. Just then Patience appears to fetch the tea tray. She screams and nearly drops the tray.

'I wasn't gonna shoot you man!' Uncle Bob cracks up. Patience puts the tea-tray down, hands on hips, shaking her head. 'Hau!' she says. 'Why you need gun in the city?' she wags her finger at Uncle Bob.

'Hey Patience, you never know.'

'Did you just get back from call-up?' I ask as he hands me the pistol. I aim out over the lawn at the head of the little statue of an angel holding the birdbath in the rockery down by the front wall.

'Fire!' Uncle Bob says.

So I do. Not at the statue, Mom'd kill me, but at a smudge of white lichen on a rock nearby. A loud cracking sound sends a bunch of birds into flight above the fir trees.

'Cra-zee. You. Eweh,' Patience shrieks running inside, the cups rattling on the tea tray. 'You are too much cra-zee.'

Uncle Bob laughs, takes back his gun and blows at the trail of smoke coiling out of the tip of the gun.

Auntie Aldie comes out.

'Bob! What the bloody hell are you doing?'

'Nothing, just having a little chat with Jay – and showing her my little Russian beauty.' He strokes his revolver.

'Put that gun away!' Aldie yells.

'Hey! You don't usually say that, Aldie.'

'I'm warning you Bob.'

'Hey, don't warn a man with a gun.' He raises the gun.

'Don't even think about it Bob, I'll kill you.'

'Ja, but I'm the one with the gun. You gonna kill me with your bare hands?'

He points the gun out over the lawn. Auntie Adie moves towards him. He points the gun at her. I edge slightly away from him, slightly scared, but tuned in at the same time. This is better than *Shout at the Devil* at the Vistarama.

There's another loud crack in my right ear. For a second I wonder if he's shot Auntie Aldie. And then I hear a loud ping as the bullet hits the post box, down by the gate. Auntie Aldie explodes with blue-smoked words.

'Aldie! How can you speak like that in front of Jayne?'

Mom's in the doorway, hands on hips, wearing the same Edgar's wraparound skirt as Auntie A, only hers is purple. 'Are you completely mad Bob?' She looks like she already knows the answer.

Auntie Aldie shoots Mom a look, and then storms out over the lawn to their jeep. She gets in and slams the door really hard, catching her skirt in the door, she opens it, pulls it back in and then slams it again. Then she tries to start the jeep. Except it won't start. It makes a kind of wheezing noise as if it's laughing.

Auntie Aldie isn't, she looks really voos. I check Uncle Bob. He pulls at his light brown beard, then gives me a sideways look, one pale-blue eye widens. I laugh. He's enjoying the scene. Mom watches too. Auntie Aldie tries the engine again. Her head jerks up and down with the effort, hair bouncing all over the place. She gets out of the jeep and kicks it, then she screams 'GODFREY!'

Godfrey comes running round the side of the house.

'Give me a push Godfrey,' Aldie says.

Godfrey looks confused. He looks towards the veranda. Uncle Bob is laughing.

'Go for it Godfrey!' he shouts.

'The jeep!' says Auntie Aldie, 'give the jeep a push.' She gets in, turns the ignition. It starts straight away.

She leans out of the window, 'It's okay Godfrey, it's started.' She screeches backwards down the driveway, the jeep jolting as she tries to keep it in the right gear. Godfrey runs for the gates.

Uncle Bob's still laughing. 'Howzabout a beer Jay?'

Mom follows me inside.

'What happened?' Mom asks.

I'm at the fridge, getting a Castle out for Uncle Bob.

'We were just sitting there, on the step, talking, and then Uncle Bob got his gun out.'

Mom leans against the orange counter with her arms folded. One of the cupboard doors is loose on its hinges, it hangs open. Mom kicks it shut with her foot.

'I must get Dad to fix that,' she says. 'Pass me one.'

I hand her a beer. The condensation gathers on the brown bottle and then slowly drips down the side. 'And?'

'So he gave me a shot.'

'You shouldn't encourage him,' she says. 'You should not be firing a gun in the city Jay. You're not on the farm now. It's not on.'

'He doesn't need encouraging, Mom. And I know damn well I'm not on the farm.'

Mom looks at her beer, but doesn't drink it.

'Don't say damn. It's about time you came to terms with it.'

'I'll never come to terms with it. We could have got the fence.'

'Don't talk about the bloody fence,' she snarls, her face really close to mine, so that I can smell the honey-sweet beer on her breath.

Leo Sayer looks down at me from his poster from above the couch in Carla's room. He's dressed in a white clown suit, a black tear has been drawn on his face as well as black triangular bits round his eyes. A ginger-haired man crouches near him over a banjo. They both look ridiculous.

'Why're you wearing so much make-up to Debbie's?'

She looks at me through the oval mirror. 'I'm going out.'

'With Ian?'

'You guessed it.'

'Ja, it was hard.' I flip my feet up over the side of the couch. There are piles of clothes all over the floor.

'Gee, this room's a mess.'

'Don't tell Mom.'

'About the room?'

'No man, about me going out.'

'Carls? Are you missing Dad?'

She presses her lipsticked lips onto a square of pink toilet paper, then rolls on lip gloss. Her face looks at me from the mirror. She looks like someone else, much older than sixteen, like a Hot Gossip dancer.

'Sometimes,' she gets up and smoothes down her purple boob-tube, 'but not tonight.' She waggles her shoulders at me.

'I can see your nipples.'

'Nipples! Say that again! Nipples! It's so funny the way you say it.'

Now she's tickle stabbing me.

'Sto'bit! It hurts man! Carla. Dad would freak if he knew you were going out. So would Mom.'

She flings a cushion at me. 'Well, they're not going to find out, are they?'

'How're you getting there?' She looks at me, twists her mouth, and raises an eyebrow.

'They'll hear the car. Piddle will bark.'

'Nope, he always sleeps in John's room. Anyway, Jay, he parks a little way up the road, then comes to my window on foot. Like Romeo. He'll escort me there and back.'

'Don't go into town, Carla – the bombs.'

'Oh ja, there's been two grenade attacks Jay, ages ago, and I'm not going anywhere near those two clubs.'

'Ja, not like Uncle Bob hey?' We both laugh.

On the night of the grenade attacks in town last year, Auntie Aldie went bananas when she found out that Uncle Bob and some of the okes from his unit were going to see strippers at La Boheme in town. *You could have been found dead with a bunny girl, a BUNNY GIRL?* Auntie Aldie screamed. It was a real hose man. Auntie Aldie jumped in her car, drove to Angel's Peak, and moved in with us for a week, giving Uncle Bob the opportunity to go there every night.

'Anyway,' says Carla, 'why would I go into town when I can go to the drive-in.'

I laugh. She laughs. And then we both start singing the drive-in song. Carla sings *Eskimo-paaaaai*, in such a ridiculous way and I use her curtains to make like a comedy Tarzan, until we're laughing too much to sing, so we flop onto the bed.

'Jay? I do miss Dad, but I don't want to think about it. I know how much you're missing Angel's Peak too.'

We're silent for a while, and then I ask, 'Carla? D'you ever think about why we can't mix with the Afs?'

'No. It's always been like this. You mix with the Afs anyway. You're always talking to Godfrey. At the farm, it was always you and John with Enoch and Nakai.'

'Ja, but, does it bug you? That we don't go to school together and stuff?'

'What do you mean *stuff*, Jay? Not really. Well I suppose it's not fair, but we're different Jay. Anyway some schools're mixed, private schools. If us whites hadn't come over, they'd still be running around with their little fur pants on, chucking spears at each other,' she says it in a jokey way.

I laugh. 'Ja, but that would be their choice.'

'Wearing fur pants? Ja I'd wear them too,' says Carla.

'Ja! Show off. But they had the choice back then.'

'What? To wear fur pants? Hell Jay. You think too much. You haven't even been around our commie Auntie Nessie and you're spouting off like her.'

'Ja, to wear fur pants,' I say, ignoring her comment about Nessie.

'In America, black people have their own TV shows,' I say, swallowing the lump down, because of thinking about Enoch.

She turns her face to look at me. 'You need to move on, make some suitable friends.'

There's a knock at the window. We both nearly hit the roof.

'Shit, he's here.'

'Who?' I ask.

'Santa Claus, whada'you think, man? Ian. Why's he come this early,' she says grabbing make-up and putting it into her bag. And then a light appears. And a face. Then another. Hideous to the eye. For a moment we're genuinely scared. And then we realise. It's our brother, and his chommie, Phillip. With their eyelids turned inside out, torches held under their chins.

'I'm gonna donner you!' Carla shouts at their retreating backs through the burglar bars.

Minutes later Ian's face appears briefly.

'Be careful Carls.'

'Tell Mom I've gone to bed when she gets back from the club,' Carls puts her make-up into her gold clutch bag.

'Goodbye you mean.'

She winks a long-lashed, sexy, green-shimmer-smeared eye at me.

After she's gone, I stare at my red face in the mirror. *Suitable friends.* I hate the kids at school. My bottom lip is too fat, one eye is greenish, one eye is brownish. My eyes are swollen from the stupid tears that don't change anything and my hair is all over the place. I pull a few faces. Then I freak myself out thinking about how I'm just lumps of meat and fat and blood and sticks of bones.

7.

It's six-thirty on Dad's first day back at work after call-up and Dad's on his third beer already. He keeps ranting about things in the newspaper, then checking his watch.

'Dad? I'm trying to read.'

'Good for you. I'm trying to stay sane.'

'How was work?'

'Well we drove round the Tribal Trustlands, checking that the irrigation projects were being run properly. They weren't. I tried to convince the chief on the best way to grow sustainable crops to sell. I failed.'

'Good day then hey?' I say, picking up my book again.

Mom comes back at seven, in her tennis whites. She kisses Dad on the forehead.

'Thought you were coming home early?' Dad eyes his newspaper.

'I grabbed a game of tennis on the way home,' Mom strokes his head, 'wanna beer?'

'You said drinks on the veranda at five.'

'No I didn't,' Mom sighs and looks in her handbag for her cigarettes.

'Yes. You did.' I see the muscle in his jaw clenching. 'Am I right Jay?' I look up from my book.

'Don't involve me Dad.' I don't know if they did or not, but Mom could have made the effort to be home on Dad's first day back at work after weeks on call-up.

'I'm going to get a drink,' Mom says.

'What's that smell?' Dad asks.

Near the glass doors, Mom whirls round, her pale cheeks are flushed and her dark eyes spark.

'I'm sick of your childish jibes Dave.'

Dad raises his eyebrows. 'Feeling guilty?'

'No I'm not bloody feeling guilty. Are you accusing me of something? What's that smell? It's disgusting Dave.'

'Oh. Should I do it behind their backs?' he raises his voice, 'like you do.'

Mom goes inside. Dad follows.

'Hey? Carrying on behind our backs?'

'You're paranoid Dave.'

I put the book down on my lap.

'Stop it! Just stop it!' I hear Carla say from inside.

'I'm out there, fighting, and for what? When I come home my wife doesn't even want to see me!'

A minute later we hear the bakkie start up.

In the kitchen Mom leans against the Formica counter biting her lip and running her hands through her hair.

'Is something going on Mom?' I ask.

'How was ballet?' Mom asks Carla, lighting her cigarette and ignoring my question.

'Alright. Who cares?' Carla says as she leaves the room. 'I'm going out.'

'Where are you going?' Mom asks.

'Out,' Carla shouts.

'Out where?' Mom asks.

'Just OUT', Carla shouts. 'Give me a break Mom. To Debbie's! God!'

In the fading light, Mom stands against the kitchen counter staring at the blank wall smoking, her thoughts trapped in her head.

8.

On the wet, black rubber matting, Glen helps me heave the white ice skates on. They feel really heavy, their iron teeth cold to the touch.

'Please have a go with me,' I ask him. 'Please. It's my birthday.'

'No ways man. Ice-skating's for fairies.' He smiles his wide smile up at me as he helps me tug on and then tie a white boot. 'Pretty fairies like you', he says slapping my blue-jeaned leg as he stands up. 'Get out there, Jay, let's see what you're made of.' I watch him walk to the side of the rink in his shorts and velies, then he leans over the barrier to watch me.

As soon as my blades make contact with the ice, I nearly fall on my bum, just grabbing the handrail in time. I'm whizzing round to a song about mountains tumbling and goodbyes; the song works well with the mountains and snow of the painted scenery of the back wall of the ice-rink. I skate round and round, clocking Glen on the benches every time I circle past. He smiles down at me and the world seems perfect even though Dad's away on call-up for my birthday. I clock Glen's eyes scanning another skater. I'm checking her now too. She skates very fast, her body leaning forward, arms slicing through the air, each arm movement seems to make her go faster, as if she has invisible ski-sticks pushing her along. She spins two circuits for every one I make, at one point she is so close to me that I feel her long, dark-brown hair flick into my neck as she whizzes past. Glen's eyes are still following the butterfly-girl. My own wings droop and hang limply by my sides.

I might as well be a moth. I skate slowly to the barrier and watch the clumps of skaters wobble and giggle as they slice through the ice. Then I push myself back onto the ice and just as I gain speed, I nearly skate into a little boy sitting on the rink. The white ice is stained with orange-red blood. The boy holds up his right hand and his coal eyes stare from a face that matches the ice. His fingers hang meatily, dripping more blood into the watery-red pool. A woman comes running, so do two attendants and soon there is an ogling group.

'It's like vultures, isn't it?' says a voice, deep and gravelly, almost like a man's. I look at her. How can this voice come out of her? A butterfly does not have the voice of a lioness. I blink at her, her almost navy-coloured eyes are large, heavily lashed and mascaraed.

'You alright?' she says, 'don't like the sight of blood?' she smiles. 'I don't mind it.'

I laugh, embarrassed. She leans backwards against the barrier, then takes off the blue and red checked shirt that's twisted round her waist and puts it on, over her red halter-neck top, keeping it unbuttoned but knotting it in front. This causes her 32B (I reckon because they're not as big as Carla's boobs) to squeeze forwards a bit. She glances down at them, checking the result with satisfaction. She smiles at me and looks at my own flat chest.

'Don't worry,' she says, 'yours will grow. How old are you?'

I feel my face flush. How does she know I'm worried that I'll always be flat as a pancake? That I too want a training bra in which to stow these weird points away in.

'Thirteen,' I say. 'Today.'

'Happy birthday, I'm fifteen. I know how you feel, because I used to freak that mine'd never grow,' she says. Is this chick a mind reader? I laugh again, a bit embarrassed. We look down at the scene on the ice. The little boy is having a bandage wrapped round his meaty hand. He doesn't make a sound. He just stares at his hand. His mother, too, is white as ice.

'Shouldn't we call an ambulance?' she says.

The second attendant scoops him up. 'No, straight to casualty, it's not far. Shall I drive you?'

'This is nothing compared to some of the accidents I've seen', the butterfly lioness in the tight white trousers says. 'Ever seen a motorbike crash?'

I shake my head.

'My cousin was killed on safari,' she says. 'He stood up in the jeep and leaned out too far, when the jeep was going quite fast. He was decapitated by a msasa tree.'

'God,' I say.

'Ja. He saw him next.'

I laugh. She laughs too.

'It was a long time ago, you've got to laugh sometimes or you go mad.' She flicks her hair back on the right hand side and then tosses her head pony-like.

After they've left, we look down at the blood on the ice, pink on the edges, yellowy-orange, then orange, then red at the centre.

'What does it look like to you?' she asks, licking her dark-red full lips, like Snow-White.

'What? Oh.' I realise she means the blood display.

'Like colour patterns in a kaleidoscope?'

'It's like a Kariba sunset to me,' she says leaning up against the wooden bar near the little exit gap. I see Glen is watching us. She looks up too, I see their eyes lock and feel a stab go through the centre of my chest. He gets up and comes towards us.

'Who's your new friend?' he asks me.

'I don't know,' I laugh.

'I'm Mel,' she says.

'Well hello Mel. Care to join us for a drink?'

After cokes and Willard's salt 'n vinegar chips, my new pal Mel teaches me to skate backwards by holding on to my hands as she skates forwards. She sticks her bum out really far and bends her top half down, her arms outstretched to me. I manage to get the hang of it, forcing the skates out backwards. We end up laughing and screaming and when I do fall on my bum, she pulls me up with power strength. Every now and again, Mel throws hot-sugar looks up at the stalls. Glen catches her sugar in his tanned face, and throws her sweet-eyed looks in return that make her as frisky as Piddle and make me nervous. When we skate together holding hands, she deliberately sticks her bum out when she skates past him. I should hate her for this, but for some reason I don't, maybe because when she turns her attention to me, I feel happy. It feels like I'm part of a triangle that's equal, with us as the three sides.

9.

Mel arranges to meet me at Greenland's Shopping Paradise after school. She's leaning against the red brick wall to the side of the glass doors of Spin City, wearing tight black stovies, black Bata tackies and a pink and white striped shirt with what looks like a man's vest underneath it. And she's smoking. In broad daylight. I wish I'd changed out of my school uniform.

'Howzit,' she says, blowing a plume of smoke straight up to the sky and flicking her hair over her shoulders.

'Want one?' she offers me the red and white box of twenty Madisons.

'No thanks. I don't smoke.'

'No thanks. I don't smoke,' she mocks. 'Yet. Shall we go to the Greek shop for a few snacks? Got your cozzie?'

'Ja,' I say. 'And ja.'

She laughs and flicks the stompie of her cigarette high in the air. It lands in between two parked cars, just as a woman with short brown frosty hair opens her car door.

'That nearly hit me young lady,' the woman says.

'Ja. But fact is it didn't hey?' Mel says.

The woman looks shocked. I try not to laugh. Man Mel's got balls.

'I know who you are,' she says. 'You're Melanie Martin. I'll be having a word with your mother.'

'Ja. And I'll have a word with your husband.' Mel says. 'That hair has to go for starters.' She says the last part to me. I feel part shock and part hysteria myself and am forced to train my eyes on the wall as the giggles come.

'In all my born days, I've never –' the woman looks as though she's going to fall off her heels.

'Yurer, yurer, yurrrer! Gi'me a break.' Mel turns her back on the woman and links arms with me. I take a deck over my shoulder. The woman stares after us from a pinched face. Her raisin eyes glint from behind her winged glasses.

'Stupid cow,' Mel says. 'They're all the bloody same.'

Our laughter floats around us like warm candy-floss clouds. It's like being on a roller-coaster that's beginning to move faster and faster up the first climb and it's too late to get off.

I have a hard time deciding what to get from the huge glass jars of sweets in the Greek Shop. Fuschia Pink and day-glo orange candy peaches? Break your teeth on the outside; cotton-wool-soft sweet white goo in the middle? Yolk-yellow marshmallow crocodiles or pink marshmallow fish? Nigger balls? Black liquorice on the outside, they go brown, then red then orange, then yellow, then white when you suck them. Glen says, *They get more socially acceptable the more you suck them.* Glen always gets his cigarettes and beer and biltong here when he comes to visit. He calls the owner Mr Constantlygreedy, because he's always raising his prices. Mr Constantinedes says, *The war, Mr Glen, the war is raising prices.* Glen says, Ja, I'm fighting in this war – saving arses. They always end up laughing though and Glen always goes there for his Madisons.

Mel grabs a packet of pink sugared peanuts.

'C'mon Jayne, lets go home and get in the pool.'

'Call me Jay,' I say. 'Everyone else does.'

Mr Constantinedes comes over. 'You wan' I help?' He stands very close to us, his fat belly pushing against his blue overcoat.

'No thanks Mr C, we don't need help choosing our sweeties.' Mel smiles up at him and Mr C breaks out into a sweat. He licks his wet lower lip and goes back behind the counter.

'Ag man, I can't decide, I'm just gonna get biltong,' I say.

We wheel our bikes past tall walls and a gate with a sign that says

"Beware of the dog," with a picture of a snarling Alsatian and "This property is protected by Smart Alarms." I'm getting to the bottom of my packet of biltong already.

'Carnivore,' says Mel.

'Ja, nothing like a bit of raw meat hey,' I say putting another piece of the dried raw kudu in my mouth. 'My Uncle Bob says, when he trained, he had to catch a baboon, skin it, leave it to rot and then eat it.'

'Lekker. Bet his wife never kissed him again after that hey?' she says.

'Ja.' I laugh. 'He's totally penga, man. What unit's your dad in?' I ask.

'He's dead.'

'Oh.'

I dump my bike next to the low trimmed hedge near Mel's front door. Bright red berries glisten in the dark green hedge like drops of blood. She hasn't said a word for at least three minutes, the silence between us is like dark smoke. I can't stand it so I say,

'Do you have brothers or sisters?'

'Ja. I've got a boet. He's at rugby today, so you're safe,' she laughs. 'He's a bit of a predator.'

'Meaning?'

'He likes young girls.'

'Oh. How old is he?' I follow her through a side gate to the front of the house. Three levels of lawn give way to a glittering kidney-shaped pool, there is a further quarter of an acre of lawn beyond, laced with trees and flowering bushes.

'Seventeen. He's pretty experienced though,' she laughs. 'It runs in the family.' Mel steps up onto a raised patio. 'We take after our mother.'

'Oh. What's she like?'

'Loose,' Mel says, sitting down on a black wrought iron chair.

'Oh. Is she here?'

'No. She's at work. Probably on the boss.'

I laugh. I don't know how to take her. I'm a fly caught in her web. My wings are buzzing but I can't take off.

'Constance!' Mel yells in the direction of an open door leading off the patio into what looks like a hallway. 'Can you make us some tea?'

'You make youah tea! I'm not your servant.' An African woman's voice travels out to us from somewhere in the house.

'Yes, you are,' Mel says in my direction, then she turns her head towards the door again, leaning back in her chair. 'C'mon Constance man, PL-EEE-ASE!' Mel yells.

'Get youahself, you are lazy.' Constance appears at the door. She wags her finger at Mel. 'You want tea. You make tea.'

'C'mon Constance. You're paid to make tea,' Mel says.

'I'm pay to make tea for Mrs Martin. Not for you.'

'Well. How about you do it as a favour? For our guest?' Mel laughs.

'Huh.' Constance says. 'This one. She can make tea.'

'No ways man,' I laugh, 'I just want Mazoe anyway.'

'You get youahself,' says Constance, adjusting the blue doek on her head. She's so different to Patience, who's powdered-coffee brown. Constance is really tall and thin, with very dark, ebony skin. She sucks at her teeth.

'Eweh, you Mel, you are too much cheeky.'

Mel laughs and follows her inside, muttering, 'Really, Africans these days.'

We sit on the grass below the patio in the sun with beer glasses full of Mazoe orange-juice and heaps of ice. Mel lights another cigarette.

'Sure you don't want one?'

'No thanks.'

Mel laughs and blows smoke rings that grow bigger and bigger as they travel up towards the clouds. She lies down on her back, her legs bent, knees resting together.

'So do you want to hear about what happened to my dad?'

'Ja,' I say, slightly embarrassed. 'If you want to tell me.'

We sit cross-legged facing each other.

'He was Special Forces.'

Like Uncle Bob.

'They were in Zambia. They'd just ambushed a unit of thirty terrs with no loss of life to themselves. Got their ammo too.' She picks at the grass. Her eyes have travelled far away.

'They were sitting down. Laughing and joking. They'd made a

fire for tea. Dad lit a cigarette and checked out their position on the map.' She flicks her ash and tiny silvery fragments float onto the grass. 'Then he radioed in to base in Rhodesia to arrange for a helicopter to pick them up. Base asked him to check their position again. He checked again. Twice. Told them they were near a kopje. North-East of the border. They asked him to check again. He said he was sure. Then my Dad got up to take a pee. One of the African soldiers went with him. Dad was wearing shorts, no top. He was blacked out to make himself look African, because of the attack on the terrorist base they'd just made,' she laughs. 'The African soldier was blacked out too. But then, they always are.'

I laugh. But then I think of Enoch and feel embarrassment and shame floating like oil on cold water.

'Dad took a pee in the direction of the river, towards the Rhodesian border.' Mel looks down. 'Ground force appeared on the other side of the river. When they saw the African soldier, with his ammo and rifle hanging off his body, they opened fire.' She looks up at me. 'They blew Dad away too.'

'Why? How?'

'Dad had given their position as North-East. It was North-West. He'd pinpointed their position by the kopje. There was an identical kopje and identical terrain on the other side. The helicopter had landed North-East and when they didn't find them they had set out to look for them.'

I'm still confused.

'They mistook my dad for a terr. He was killed by friendly fire.'

I don't know what to say. So I say. 'That really sucks Mel.'

Mel laughs. 'Ja. It sucks.'

'How long's it been?' I ask.

'Eleven months and ten days.'

Mel goes inside to get more drinks. I try not to think of Dad, out there in the bush in the terrible heat. Mel comes back with the drinks.

'I used to like going to your school. Mr Hazelwood used to make me laugh. *Now school, it's time you thought about your futures…* Mel makes her gravelly voice slower and deeper, she dips it up and down like Mr Hazelwood does.

She laughs again. 'I quite miss the old bugger,' she says.

I laugh. It's a pretty good impression. Also I'd never dream of calling Mr H an old bugger. Mel does lots of things I wouldn't dream of doing.

'I like Glen,' she says. 'Do you think he'll go out with me?' My stomach takes a big-dipper dip.

'Don't worry,' she smiles a honey smile, 'I like you too.' I feel a surge and settle on her smile like a sticky-legged bee on a pollenous flower.

'I know you do,' I say. As if saying it out loud will make it true.

'Come,' she says, 'let's swim.' She pulls off her stovies and her vest and her shirt then stands in front of me in little yellow and white bikini pants and bra.

'Come on!' she yells as she runs over the lawn to the pool.

As she jumps, she lifts her legs up to her chest. For a moment she is a shrieking body suspended in the air. 'Mr Hazel-WOOOOOD!' she yells. Then she is under, leaving a huge sploshy fountain in her wake. Her bikini top floats on the surface.

I stand with my back to the pool, the front part of my feet balancing on the hot slate, heels dipped towards the water. Time hesitates as I hover, only just balanced, part sky, part earth. For a moment I inhabit the spaces in between. Bending my knees, I hesitate for a moment and then, taking a breath, leap backwards. My back arches as the world tips, toes scraping the sky, fingertips tracing the water before I pierce it with the blade of my body. My body comes full circle, as my chest almost scrapes the bottom of the pool. As my top half comes up towards the light, my body crouches down and I allow my legs to bend. Touching the depths, I push. I'm a bullet tearing through water towards the sky. I break into gleaming light. As I surface, shaking the water from my ears, I feel alive. ALIVE. A-LIVE.

10.

Mom and I drive down the long driveway from the side of the house towards the gate. She's taking me to see Nessie behind Dad's back. Anything, she says to put a smile on my dial again. Godfrey comes running to open the gates.

'Oh for goodness sake, you could have done them Jay,' Mom says.

'Godfrey's doing it – for my sake.' I lean out of the window saluting at Godfrey. Godfrey smiles and salutes me back, then he undoes the lock that doesn't lock, it just looks locked, to scare off those dozies that haven't got the brains to just scale the gate. Mom keeps pushing her hair back off her face, forming a quiff. It looks like it needs a wash. She steers with her right hand, changes gear with her left and draws on her cigarette as it dangles from her lips. She just needs the leather jacket.

'You look like Elvis.'

'Thanks Jay, I'll take that as a compliment.' She blows the smoke straight ahead and runs her left hand through her short black hair.

'Thanks Godfrey!' I bang the side of the car. Mom jumps.

'Do you have to do that?'

Godfrey smiles and lifts his arm in the air as he turns ready to close the gates after us.

'Ja, I do.'

We pass houses set down long driveways, hidden behind light-snatching pine and resplendent trees. On a fence purple granadilla fruit ripen on the snaky vines. Thoughts of Dad, out there in the bush somewhere, curdle feelings for Nessie and a mistrust of Mom's motives flap around in my head. When Nessie phoned on the evening of my birthday I slammed the phone down on her and sat on the step howling. But I looked up her phone number in the telephone book and phoned her the next day. And when I asked Mom, she just said yes, I could go. If she'd said no, I would have got angry with her, but maybe would've felt relieved because I wouldn't have to DEAL with it. On my lap my hands are sweaty and the butterflies gathering in my stomach are not pretty. Mom looks at me and smiles and I almost ask if we can turn back.

We pull up in front of a paved area outside the social sciences building of the University of Rhodesia. Nessie comes towards us down the central path. She's in deep conversation with a young African woman with short close-cropped hair. Nessie looks up, spots us and waves then bows her head back down towards the woman. The woman looks up at us then walks back to the building, her heavy looking leather bag bouncing behind her. Nessie breaks into a barefoot trot, her Indian skirt and bracelets tinkling with the delicate sounds of little bells. She hugs me to her bra-less breast, my nose, buried in her chest, takes in a musky smell. She kisses Mom lightly on the cheek.

'Thanks for bringing her,' Nessie says.

'Well. You were what she asked for. For her birthday.'

No. I asked for a record-player.

Mom click-clacks back down the path in her slip-slops. Nessie hugs me to her side.

'I've missed you. You've grown.'

I smile up at her. She looks beautifully the same.

'How are you? Settling in? School?'

'I hate it.'

'What? School?'

'All of it, school, people, cars, houses, birds, noise, the driveways, the lawns, the rounded hedges. Like they've been blown out of a plastic tube. All of it.'

Nessie laughs. 'Tell it like it is girl.' She raises an arm towards the buildings. 'Welcome to the seedbed of social and political change.'

I sit in Nessie's office, while she argues not so quietly outside the door with a man. Nessie's voice gets louder.

'Oh for goodness sake Peter, what do you mean by 'fraternising?' Yes. I see my students. Here –'

'And outside.'

'What do you mean by 'outside' Peter?'

'Well, you know –'

'No. I don't know. How about you make yourself clear Peter.'

'Okay, well, I've had reports that you have been seen in cars with certain black students –'

'Cars? Plural? What are you suggesting? Am I not allowed to give my black students a lift? Now that would be a tricky situation, wouldn't it Peter? I mean if we couldn't give black people lifts in our vehicles, wouldn't do much for the war effort would it? Or maybe it would? No Sergeant Ndlovu, we can't ride in the same vehicle, so you go up ahead, we'll bring up the rear. Actually yes, that might be handy. Sergeant goes in first vehicle, Sergeant detonates mine first!'

'Ernesta, please. There's no need to go over the top, I'm only –'

'Oh surely there is Peter. I am, after all a woman. How far over the top are we speaking? Is this a warning? Or are the top brass going to deliver that?'

'Ernesta. Please. Try and understand my position. I want to keep the college open. I applaud your efforts. I admire you as a teacher –'

I hear her sigh.

'Okay Peter. I understand your position. I appreciate what you're saying, point taken, now my young niece is in there so –'

'Ernesta. So I can count on you?'

'Oh yes. You can count on me Peter. You always can.'

There's a pause, then I hear the sound of his heels retreating down the echoing hallway.

Nessie and I sit on a bench in front of the fountain on Cecil Square. The fountain spurts up to the sky as if trying to squirt the only cloud that floats fatly above it in the blue. It's lunchtime, and the city has a suspended, slow motion feel. Nessie hands me a steak pie and bobs a straw into my Coke bottle.

'Nessie? Could you pick me up and take me back? I could live with Granny Rose.'

'I'd like to take you back. Really I would, but my dear brother wouldn't sanction it.'

My heart pounds with my thoughts.

'Was Justice behind the attack on our farm? What was he putting in your car that day, when Enoch and I saw you?'

'I don't betray confidences Jay,' she says chewing her pie.

'Weapons?'

'Like I said.'

'Well because you're not denying it, I'll assume they were. I saw your VW, at the farm, just before.'

She throws her crumbs at the gathering pigeons.

'Look Jay,' she says, turning to face me, 'there's things you don't understand, things that are bigger than both of us.'

'Bigger than our family?'

'Ja, bigger than our family. There are things our family get up to that you'd rather not know about. Trust me.'

'Trust you? You mean Dad and Uncle Bob and Glen? They are in a war you know.' I watch a pair of wedged heels and a pair of office shoes walk down the paved path in front of us. 'He's your boyfriend isn't he?'

'He's a student of mine.'

She's not going to tell me anything.

'Why don't you let me take you back to the farm for a visit.'

'No. I'm only going back to live. Not to go and come back.'

'Not even to see Granny Rose?'

'No. What about the terrs they hung?'

'Well they shouldn't have.' She scrumples up her pie paper.

'Why?'

'The evidence was inconclusive. Anyway it was an act of war and hanging is barbaric.'

'What?' My heat rises. I get up and stand in front of her. 'Attacking innocent farm owners?' I wave my Coke bottle around. 'That's an act of war?'

'They're not innocent Jay. They're complicit.'

I scrumple up, then chuck my paper bag on the floor, then pick it up again.

'Why are you on the wrong side?' I ask.

An African man glances up at me from the other side of the path, then goes back to reading his newspaper spread on the grass.

'Am I? Jay this war is about a people's right to freedom. It's been a long time coming.'

'I believe in freedom. But not murder. They've attacked other farms too. People have died.'

'Well then Jay. Maybe it's time you began to examine your people's past. You won't find what you need to know in your history books at school.'

'You're my people. You're my aunt. I was born here – on the farm. This is my country. I have a right to freedom too.'

'You have your freedom.'

'No I don't. None of us do. There's a war on. Where was my freedom to choose when Mom and Dad chose to come here?'

I turn and walk quickly up the path, then break into a run towards Jameson Avenue where the flower sellers are approaching cars stopped at the robots with armfuls of bright, soon to be dead blooms. If I hurry, I'll make it to the avenues and Dr Sheldon's before Mom leaves.

'At least you can run – without worrying about being shot at!'

I run faster.

Dr Sheldon's surgery is in a clump of flat-topped, white-trimmed buildings on Second Avenue.

At the broad, wood-panelled reception desk, a woman asks me to wait.

'Sorry I can't,' I say, rushing past.

'Young lady!' she calls, as I run down the corridor. 'You can't go in there!'

Watch me old lady. I can hear Mom's voice coming from behind the door to Dr Sheldon's surgery and then Dr Sheldon's slow voice.

I open the door. In her pink nylon slacks, Mom jolts and almost drops her cigarette. She's sitting on Dr Sheldon's desk, with her body turned up close towards him. Dr Sheldon glances round her at me, his eyes magnified behind his glasses, his wiry hair standing up from his forehead in surprise.

'Hello Jay. What a lovely surprise. Come in.'

'Like hell.'

I run out again, back up the passage, past the gaping receptionist and out into the glaring sunlight. In the driveway the tears come. Round the side of the building I slide my back slowly down the wall, rough bricks grate over my back. Flowers in the hibiscus hedge dart their yellow stamens from their wrinkled, flame-shaped petals as if trying to speak.

'Get in the car please.' Mom stands with her hand on her hip.

'Stuff you.'

'How dare you speak to me like that!' She scrabbles around in her bag for her cigarettes.

'How dare you fool around behind Dad's back while he's away fighting.'

A group of African nurses in blue-checked dresses and caps that are standing chatting to a couple of African men sitting on a storm drain turn round to look at us.

She grabs my arm, I pull it back. 'Don't touch me.'

'Okay. You can bloody stay here.'

She goes back inside. Probably for advice from Smelldon.

Two minutes later she's back.

'Get in the car Jay.'

A plan edges at my mind. I get up and follow her to the car.

For a long while we are silent. We stop at the robots. An African man wearing a t-shirt with what looks like a roundy-raggedy bullet hole in it, comes hurrying over with a bunch of cream roses. He is momentarily blocked out by a Rixi Taxi coming to a halt next to us.

'I was merely chatting to him you know. I was on a break.'

'So you spend your break-times with Smelldon too?'

'Don't be childish, Jay.'

'What should I be? An adult. Like you? Like Nessie? I hate you,' I say quietly. I hate you all.'

It's getting dark. At the robots near Mel's, I jump out of the car. Mom leans over and tries to grab me, her cigarette drops on her lap and nearly sets her slacks on fire. She slaps at the orange sparks. Which under different circumstances would be a total hose.

'Get back in the car!'

Several of the drivers behind begin to hoot at her as the robots change to green.

'Oh shut up!' she shouts. Then she slams the door and drives off.

At Mel's, the gates haven't been locked. I regret coming when I spot Mel's brother in the driveway sitting on his new 50cc motorbike, chatting to one of his friends from high school.

'Hey look, Rob, girl meat,' Mark calls out.

'Stuff you!' I say, as I walk past.

'No we'll stuff you. Hey Rob?'

Their laughter pelts my back like rotten tomatoes as I get to the front door.

Mel and her mom are on the veranda.

'Howzit,' says Mel. 'I didn't know you were coming.'

'Neither did I.'

Mel laughs. 'Wanna beer?' She waves her bottle at me.

Mel's Mom's face emerges from her nest of yellow hair as she looks up slowly from staring at the table; her lipstick is smeared and her mascara is bruised beneath her eyes. She smiles a silly smile.

'Oh hello. Who are you? Like a beer?' she slurs.

'It's Jay Mom.' Mel points her forefingers in the direction of her ears and spins them round and round, indicating her mother's depth of bombedness.

'She's going out soon,' Mel says, 'aren't you Mom?' she raises her voice. 'Off to The Blue Hart, with Jack, hey Mom?'

Mel's Mom raises her head slightly before dipping her head back onto her chest.

'Let's go to my room,' Mel says. She'll be out soon. I mean in a coma.'

We sit cross-legged on the bed beneath the shelf with all Mel's trophies on it from her show-jumping days. Next to the bed is a photo of Mel in jodhpurs and riding-jacket being hugged by the handsome man that was her father.

'So what happened?' Mel asks.

'Loads. I saw my aunt.'

'The terrorist sympathiser,' Mel says, reaching over me to get her Madisons out of the drawer.

'Ja,' I say. 'My aunt.'

'Okay. Sorry.' She crosses her legs on the bed. 'And?'

'We had an argument. In the park. I ran off.'

'Stormed off in a fit you mean?'

'Ja. Went to my Mom's office.'

She hands me a cigarette. I take it.

'I saw my Mom –'

'You're joking!'

'She was on the desk, facing him. I couldn't really see what was going on. He was blocked by her body.'

Mel lights her cigarette. 'Were they naked?'

'No. But they didn't look like secretary and boss.'

'Oh no Jay. I think they did.' She starts to laugh. I laugh with her, but only to show her I got the joke, even though it feels like it's on me. She holds the lighter to my cigarette and I inhale deeply. Soon I'm the starring part in a coughing production. We roll around the bed, me coughing, her laughing, until the doorbell rings.

'That's my Mom! Quick Mel! Do something!' I thrust the cigarette at her. 'I don't wanna go home.'

'Don't worry I'll take care of it.'

Five minutes later she's back, giggling.

'What happened?'

'I asked Jack to tell your mother we were in the bath and you were staying the night.'

'Why didn't you ask your Mom?'

'She was too bombed.'

I laugh.

'Didn't she ask where your Mom was?'

'Ja. Jack said she was in the bath too.'

'I can't believe she agreed.'

'He's a doctor. People don't say no to him.'

The next afternoon, Mom stands in the kitchen with Auntie Aldie, waving her tea-cup at me. Godfrey's lawnmower drones its monotonous sound from the back lawn.

'Don't ever do that to me again Jay.'

'What?'

'You know what.'

Auntie A leans up against the counter with her arms folded, eyeing me.

'What about what you were doing?'

I walk past them to my room.

'Gee cee em, she needs discipline Reen.'

'Stuff you!' I yell.

'Reeen!' Auntie Aldie shrieks.

Mom comes running down the passage after me. I try to slam my bedroom door, but Mom follows me in.

'Sit down Jayne!' she says. 'Sit down.'

I sit down on the bed. Mom sits down next to me. I move away from her a bit.

'Look Jay, there's no point in you behaving like this. Rol –'

'Roland? You call your boss Roland?'

'Jay. Roland and I are friends. I love your Dad –'

'Not sure Dad'd like you being friends with Roland, Mom.'

Mom laughs. It wasn't meant to be funny. On the wall opposite my bed Granny Rose's four painted flame lilies, trapped in their frame, curl their gold tinged flame petals. They look so fragile, like her delicate painting fingers.

'Look, I know how much you miss the farm. How tough things have been for you.'

I wish there was a tap to switch feelings off, because I'd turn Enoch, Nessie and Mom right off. All I've managed is to change from hot water to cold water, but the water keeps on running.

'Look sweetie. Glen phoned today, he's back from call-up and he wants to see you on the Mazoe farm next weekend. May's gonna drive you.' She puts her arm round my shoulder.

'How about we do something tonight hey? Just the two of us? Carla and John are out tonight. We could go to the drive-in?'

'Ja. I really wanna go to the drive-in with my Mom.' My voice makes a light sarcastic bridge over the dark river in my throat.

She looks a bit hurt, but I care rocks.

'Well how about spaghetti at the Italian?'

'Can I have wine?'

'You can have half a glass.'

I let her hug me as I think of Dr Sheldon's puddle eyes behind his inch-thick glasses.

11.

My Granny May drives very fast out of Salisbury then along Goldenstairs Road to Mazoe. I sit in the front seat watching the landscape change from organised trees and trimmed lawns to blonde bush and camouflaged kopjes. Mel lolls around in the back with a couple of magazines, evidence of my powerlessness to stop her coming. Piddle's in the back, too, panting like he's in the Kalahari. The sun browns my bare legs and sweat gathers in the thin crease between my belly-button and my waist. Outside, African women sit barefoot on mats underneath the msasas, babies tied to their backs with towels, hoping to sell piles of oranges, crocheted table-cloths that hang on string tied from tree to tree, or cooked mealie cobs in pale green leaves.

'Can we have a mealie, May? Want a mealie Mel?'

'No,' May says.

Mel does not reply. She's lying down, her hair tied in a knot on the top of her head, her *Fair Lady* magazine resting on her bare tummy, below her black and white striped boob-tube. Her long legs protruding from red cotton shorts are raised and her largish brown feet, with their funny splayed toes, rest their heels on the lower rubberised window rim. Her feet make me want to laugh. It's as if God stuck them onto the end of her to make her humble. They are the only thing that mess with her perfection.

Mel leans through the gap in the seats. 'Checking me out hey?' she says.

I laugh, embarrassed.

'How much longer? I'm bored.'

'Ages. We're only just out of Salisbury,' I say.

'Can I smoke?' Mel asks.

'Do what you like. Smoke your own though,' May croaks.

'You must have let Dad get away with murder when he was a kid,' I say.

May smiles as she slams the lighter knob into the dashboard with the heel of her palm.

'Live and let live, she says.

As she smokes, pink-cutexed fingernails claw at her face with its hooked nose. She's in a white dress today with a royal-blue paisley pattern, but I prefer her in her BSAP uniform, especially when she displays all her medals for driving through the operational areas, giving two fingers to the terrs, with only her uzi for company to take men over to the PVs and to man the radio stations. She once stopped to blow away a few terrs after they mined a vehicle in her column and then administered life-saving treatment to her African assistant who'd had his arm blown off below the elbow. May's been spending most weekends at the Mazoe farm since Auntie Penny died and she's always been close to her nephew, Glen, even before he lost his mom. The lighter pops out and I pass it to Mel, the smell of her cigarette tip on the lit rings excites my senses. I smile at Mel, feeling like smoking too. She winks at me. Leaning my head back on the seat and putting my feet up on the dashboard, I picture Mom and Dad this morning. Mom pulled out all the stops for Dad's arrival back from call-up last night. She was really looking hot in her tight jeans and high heels, trying so hard that I wonder whether Dad suspects something might be up, but he just lapped it up like Piddle does water on a hot afternoon. Mom sat on his lap for sundowners outside and they went to bed early. She's splashed out a whole heap of money on the Monomotapa hotel to spend the weekend there having a second honeymoon. We hit a pot-hole in the road. I nearly clunk my head on the torn beige ceiling of the car while the engine grinds.

'Can I have a drag?' I ask May.

'No,' May says.

We reach the Mazoe valley. Rows and rows of citrus trees are spread to the left and to the right, planted in plots of orderly rows punctuated every now and again by the blue and green plastic of greenhouses. Irrigation systems keep everything lekker lush. Lychees, avocados, mangoes, macadamias, granadillas, are all farmed here, hey it's Rhodesia's Garden of Eden. From up here, the Mazoe dam looks like a piece of grey slate, glistening in the sun. Through my open window the air is honey-scented and warm on my cheek. A cinnamon smell of saturated earth clings to my nostrils. I look back at Mel and melt in the sunshine of the smile that helps push Enoch to the sides of my mindscape, but soon I forget that she's there and fall into reminiscing with May.

'Who was your best friend when you were a kid at Angel's Peak?' I ask May.

May takes a big suck on her cigarette.

'We didn't know many people, farms were too far apart. Only saw people at Christmas parties or when we took the horse and cart into town to get supplies, which wasn't often. We grew everything on the farm. Only stuff we didn't grow was wheat, so we'd get the flour in.'

'So who'd you play with?'

'Sometimes we played with the Afrikaner kids whose dads were working on the railway.' She puts another cigarette between her lips and slams the cigarette lighter in.

'Granny Rose didn't like that though, she called them Dutch riff-raff,' May hoots. 'Always did like riff-raff.'

'What happened if she caught you playing with them?'

'Mum never caught us, the farm was hundreds of acres – you know that,' she inhales. 'The workers would tell on us sometimes.'

'And then what?'

'We'd get a bloody good hiding.' May cackles and shakes her head, as if the hiding was a good memory.

'Who else did you play with?'

'The kids in the compound.'

'Did you have a best friend?'

'Solomon,' she says, as streams of smoke exhale through her nose and mouth.

'Was Solomon wise?' I ask, remembering Enoch showing me how to climb up the gum-trees to check out the weaverbird eggs, their nests like woven baskets of candied Easter egg chocolates, instructing me on their breeding habits and warning me not to touch the eggs. If I left my scent, the mother bird would reject the eggs.

'Wise enough to keep out of the way of Bessie's legs.'

'Your horse? Why? Did Bessie kick everyone?'

'Ja.'

'Cept you?'

'Ja.' She doesn't take her eyes off the road as she changes gear to slow down and avoid missing a cow that's ambled onto the road. The car grinds then hiccups.

The cow passes, May continues. 'Me and Solomon, we'd get up to mischief, we'd race round the farm on Bessie, play hide and seek, get into the stores. One day Dad caught us in the stores collecting stuff for a campfire –'

'Like what?' Just like us.

'Sausages, eggs, pan,' May glances at me. 'We were gonna take Bessie down to the river, light a fire,' May laughs. 'Dad chased him, I said "Run Solomon! Run!" And he ran man! Boy did he run, fast and round and round in circles like a bloody springbok.'

'Did Great Grandpa Patrick ever catch him?'

'Nah. He was too fast, he ran up a tree. He was a little skellum,' May shakes her head again. 'I got a bloody good hiding that night.'

'Did Granny Rose mind that Solomon was your friend?'

'Hah! She didn't know.'

'What else did you used to do?'

'We'd go swimming in the river. The boys would dare him to go far out, where the crocodiles were. Hah! They didn't realise that the crocs were round the edges. He was safer out there in the middle.' May cranks up the laugh again.

'Did anyone ever get taken by a croc?' I ask, my mind on an image of John, half-drowning, Enoch's long wiry-slim arm reaching out like a branch to save him.

'Ja. One of the worker's children, one of Joseph's little ones – a little girl. One minute she's playing by the river. Next minute she vanished without a trace. At least we think it was a croc.'

'What else could it have been? A python?'

'Ja, there were rumours of pythons on the farm as big as tree trunks. They'd hide in the water sometimes, just below the surface, waiting for prey. They've been known to take the smaller buck by the river: steenbuck – even kudu.'

'Uuurgh, did you ever see any?'

'No, but I did see a huge snake-skin once. One of the workers brought it up to the house for Dad to look at. It had the diamond print.'

'How big was it?'

'Hah! The pile was almost as big as me.'

'How old were you then?'

'About seven.'

'Yuk.' May laughs at me as I pull down my shorts a little and sink back into my seat, shifting my feet on the dashboard and pressing my toes against the windscreen.

'I saw your Solomon not long ago.'

I sit up. 'You mean Enoch?' I say glancing back at Mel, hoping she can't hear. But she has her eyes closed, her hands lightly folded over her midriff as brown and taut as trampoline.

'Who else?' May cackles.

'At the PV? What was he doing?'

'The Highland fling.' Her small blue eyes bore into the road ahead and she coughs again, her mouth smeared with coral Innoxa lipstick puffs.

'Tell me May, man. Did he say anything?'

'Ja. he said "Good afternoon Gogo,"' May says, changing gear.

'He called you grandmother? What was he doing?'

'Planting vegetables. He's a strapping chap now,' she takes a deep toke of her cigarette. 'He was leaving to study,' she exhales.

'Really!' I whip round. 'Where?'

'The Jesuits arranged it. Dunno.'

I settle back against the seat and stare at the little punched holes in the torn roof of the Morris Minor. He called her 'gogo', as if she was his grandmother too. All the workers like May. They call her 'gogo' too. Closing my eyes I try to imagine Enoch at the PV, reading by the light of a candle and writing letters to the Jesuits in a blue-lined exercise book.

The chassis scrapes along the middle part of the driveway as we travel through the orange trees on Uncle Joe's farm. There'd be no Mazoe orange juice and no oranges if it wasn't for the Portuguese who travelled down the Zambezi along the Mazoe River to trade and to settle in this valley. Some of these trees are hundreds of years old. I bet they'd have stories to tell, if they could tell them. I wonder how many hands have been on those trees. African hands, Portuguese hands, English hands? Trees planted in land cleared of msasas and bush. Do those trees know, somehow, in their roots, that they are no longer in Portugal? The car scrapes along a rock or something. Mel sits up, yawning like a panther. 'Are we there?'

'Shit, man,' says May, 'why doesn't George get the stones out of the bloody driveway?'

For a second I consider the possibility of a terr-buried mine waiting to detonate our vehicle, but then, orange trees, green leaves, blue sky, red earth bring me back to a spacious place in my mind. The farm workers are out spraying the trees. I wave at George who stands on my side of the car in his blue overalls and black gum boots, spraying the trees. He waves back, unsmiling, his hair combed out into a thin Afro, a red comb tucked into the back of it, its plastic handle sticking up like a woman's hair slide. Though he's their brother, he looks nothing like Enoch or Justice, with his long, slim nose and toffee-coloured skin. Out of the back window I see him staring at our car. The black tube from the poison canister hanging from his back springs wildly. It should have a sticker on it that says, *Prepare to meet your maker.* May parks up to check out the trees and speak to the workers. *Tic, tic, tic,* go the sprinklers on the baby trees. We drive up to the L-shaped, corrugated iron-roofed, house.

'Piddle!' I shout as his claws scrape and scramble over my bare legs. May grabs her handbag from the floor in front of me, and her gun from under her seat.

The big dogs come running. Mel screams and leaps over the bonnet. Overreaction or what?

'They don't bite, Mel,' I laugh.

'Ja. But they slobber. I hate dog slobber.'

Uncle Joe got the Great Dane 'to scare the munts.' But this dog couldn't scare a chicken. And the Africans are about as scared of him as a puppy. Better to hang a chameleon over the front of the door. Glen says they change colour themselves when they see one.

'Joe!' May calls as we head out back.

In the workshop, Uncle Joe appears from under a bakkie on a little wooden board with wheels on.

'You're growing hey?' he says eyeing me as he wipes his filthy hands on an even filthier rag. 'How 'bout a kiss for your old uncle?'

'No ways man,' I say.

'Who's this pretty lady?' he asks, looking at Mel.

'She's my new friend, Mel,' I say.

'Mighty pleased to meet you, Jay's pal, Mel,' he says, laughing at his own joke. 'I'll go wash up then get you ladies a beer.'

'I don't drink beer!' I shout at his back.

'I do!' Mel yells.

I look at her and laugh. This girl has cheek for Africa.

A huge prickly pear rises out of the dusty ground near the edge of the back stoep. May sits on an upside-down beer crate, her legs crossed, one hand clamped round her beer, the other hand, with its cigarette extended like an extra finger, ruffles Karl's neck. The sun glints off her Elnetted hair, making it look like a silver helmet. Mel leans against the corner pole that rises to meet the asbestos canopy of the stoep on the opposite end to me. A sort of restless hum comes off her body. She's like a prowling cat hungry for Glen-prey.

Uncle Joe comes over and puts his foot up on the stoep.

'How's school? Joined the rugby team yet?' he asks me.

'*No*, I play hockey.'

The rubber of his slip slops is so worn down that the yellow rubber is as thin as card in some places and his blue shorts hang high above his long skinny ostrich legs with bulbous knees.

'I thought we'd braai,' he says running his hand over his bald head. 'Glen will be over later, with his new bird.'

'What's her name?' I ask.

'Sharon,' says Uncle Joe. 'Her dad's the Pork that owns the garage in town.'

'Oh, I know who you mean, Mr Ferreira – what you mean pork?' I picture the fat dark girl that stared out at me from the garage shop as I waited in the bakkie for Dad to pay for the petrol.

'Pork. Like pork 'n beans. Portuguese.'

'Oh. Didn't her mother die?' I ask

'No, ran off with the postman,' says Uncle Joe. 'And then the poor bastard was robbed. By you know who.'

'With a mechanic, you mean,' May laughs, then starts to cough again. Her throat is a phlegm-blender.

'Nother beer?' Uncle Joe asks May. He turns to go the chest freezer at the back of the stoep. May flicks her cigarette stompie out over the yard. It hits the dust and an orange glow sparks into the air. Uncle Joe slams the freezer lid shut.

'Who robbed the garage?'

'I'll give you a clue. David to your Solomon.' May coughs, cranking into a laugh.

'Oh, Prospect and Enoch. You mean Prospect robbed the garage? I never knew that. I thought he went to jail because he was political or something,' I say, digging.

May laughs, 'Ja, his mother didn't call him Prospect for nothing. Hah, hah!' she coughs and cackles at the same time.

No respect for the dead here.

'May? How come George stayed here on the farm after Prospect died?'

She ruffles the fur on Karl's neck. When she stops, he snaps his jaws at a fly that buzzes above his head.

'Penny was fond of him. She was paying for his education. He's always lived here, since he was a little chap – grew up with Glen.'

Uncle Joe opens the bottles on the bottle opener attached to the side of the freezer. He comes over with four beers.

'It's a hot day,' he smiles at May, handing her two.

'You girls wanna Sparletta?' Uncle Joe asks.

'I'll have a beer,' says Mel.

Uncle Joe widens his eyes comedy-style.

'Will you?'

'Ja. Where's the bathroom?' she asks. Uncle Joe and I watch as

Mel disappears indoors, probably to roll more sticky lip-gloss over her pout.

Glen's car crunches into the driveway. I have a funny feeling in my stomach because I haven't seen him for ages, so I escape to the stoep to get a Sparletta orange, listening to the dogs barking and May saying hello. For a moment I don't turn round even though I know they're there. Glen comes up behind me and sinks his hands into my shoulders near my neck. 'Howzit,' he says. I jump, even though Glen has done this kind of thing to me a thousand times before. Glen ruffles my head like I'm about six. I turn around to see a tall, slim girl, with tonged, long dark hair in a white cotton dress with little strawberries all over it.

'She's good enough to eat, hey?' Glen laughs, taking the beer from his dad's offered hand.

'Ag, Glen, man,' says the strawberry girl. 'Aren't you gonna introduce us?'

'May, Sharon – Sharon, May – Sharon, Jay – Jay, Sharon,' Glen, introduces us.

The dogs jump all over Sharon. She screams and May and Uncle Joe laugh.

'Down!' they shout together. Glen just stands there in his blue shorts and khaki t-shirt, holding his beer, his feet planted in his veldskoens without socks, the upper part of him swaying like a big tree, as he laughs to see so much fun. Sharon giggles. A lot. Even though it looks like the dogs have been trying to dig up the strawberries on her dress. When Uncle Joe hands her a beer, she giggles some more and asks for a shandy. *A shandy would be dandy.* I Imagine Uncle Joe, morphing into Fred Astaire, top-hat and tails, spinning a shandy on a silver tray while doing a little dance in his shiny black and white shoes. Glen takes another swig of his beer and winks at me.

'What's a shan-dee?' Uncle Joe says scratching his little pot belly.

Sharon takes the beer that Uncle Joe gives her and the glass half-filled with lemonade.

I wish Sharon'd fly away with Fred Astaire. She looks back at me and smiles a strange smile, as if I've just walked in on her in the bathroom. She moves away from Uncle Joe, who's smiling at her as he smokes and stands near me.

'You're alright girl,' he says.

May, Uncle Joe and Glen have stopped looking Sharon up and down as if she were a prize mombie and are talking amongst themselves as Uncle Joe lights the braai near the workshop. Mel reappears on the stoep, looking like a younger copy of Ava Gardner in *The Night of the Iguana*. She's put loads of eyeliner on.

'Hi Glen,' she says, hand on hip. Glen stares at her like Adam checking Eve for the first time. Sharon is smiling like a contestant in the Miss World competition.

Mel puts her shandy glass down on the edge of the stoep and takes out her Madisons. Then she goes over to where Glen is standing with Sharon and Uncle Joe and May and asks him for a light, before she walks very slowly back to the stoep and sits back down. Glen watches. She smiles as she approaches me. 'Let's go stand with them.'

'No man,' I say. 'I'm happy here.'

'Suit yourself,' Mel says. She gets up and goes over to them. Man, she's forward, and she cares rocks about Sharon who comes over and sits down on the stoep next to me. She smiles. I smile back. 'It's hot hey,' she says.

'Ja.'

'Nice farm.'

'Ja.' I get up. 'I'm going for a walk.' Bye.

'Can I come?'

'Ja sure.' Can't wait.

'Coming for a walk Mel?' I shout. Mel tosses her head.

We set off out back. Sharon must be penga, leaving Mel with Glen. She probably thinks she's too young. Which she is.

'Don't get lost!' says Glen.

'Watch out for the mambas! They like young girls,' Uncle Joe shouts. The last thing I hear is May cackling and wheezing. I glare at Mel from over my shoulder. She waves at me as if nothing's wrong. We walk in silence down the path towards the little river that runs through the back of the property. The land slopes down towards disused outbuildings and the open bush, beyond which lies the compound.

'So. What school do you go to?' Oooh ja, this is going to be an interesting conversation.

'You go to Arundel don't you?' I ask, stopping near a guava tree heavy with golden egg-shaped fruit.

'Ja. I mean I used to. How'd you know?'

A messenger from on high told me. 'Uncle Joe said.' I look up at the sky, mounds of clouds sail by, suspended in their world of angels and air, ignoring the solid, stupid world below.

'Oh.'

I pick some of the leaves from the guava tree and roll them in my hands as Enoch would. 'Did you know that if you boil these leaves and drink the juice, it cures colds.'

'No.'

'It's an African cure.'

'Oh.'

'How'd you meet Glen?' I ask, rolling my foot over some of the rotting yellow guavas that have ripened and fallen.

'He comes to my dad's garage. I work in the shop.'

'Were you there when you had that robbery?' I lean up against the trunk that looks like an extended elephant's leg.

'No. We were in Salisbury,' she says coming round to stand near me. 'One of the workers had the keys. He was tied up.'

'By Prospect?'

'Oh ja. He worked on this farm, didn't he? I dunno if it was him, there were others – a gang. They ran off when the police came.' She reaches down and takes up a bit of fallen branch.

'Did they catch them?'

'Not at first. But they caught that worker that was involved with your aunt.' She snaps a twig off the branch and looks quickly up at me, then down again, her face a bit red. 'Sorry,' she says.

'How?'

'August, our worker, told them he recognised –'

'Prospect,' I say.

'Ja. Prospect. So they came here and arrested him.'

'Oh. Did August know Prospect?'

She shrugs. 'Must have done. My dad says Prospect was a known terrorist, friends with Nkomo.' She looks at the ground.

'And of course there was that thing with your aunt.' She looks up and says, 'Sorry.'

If you say sorry again I'm gonna donner you. The newspaper pictures of Nkomo flash through my mind, how he looked like a fat, smiley baby.

'Okay. What do you know about my Auntie Penny?'

'Same as everyone. It was in all the papers. But there were rumours before.'

'Like?'

'That she was more than a friend to him, that she was giving him money.'

She looks quickly at me.

'I never believed that. It's disgusting.'

'What was?' I flick off my slip-slop and place my barefoot on the cool trunk.

'Your aunt was a nice lady,' Sharon says quickly, 'she was always very nice to me when she came to the shop. When my Mom left my Dad your aunt said I could call her about anything.'

'Did you?'

'Actually I did. It was the night she died.'

'Really?' I push away from the trunk with my foot. 'Why?'

'I needed someone to talk to. Her voice sounded funny. Like she was under water.'

'What do you mean?' I flap my hand at a fly.

'I think she was drunk.'

'Did you tell anyone?'

'No.'

'Why not?' I shout at her.

'Sorry. I just didn't think it was important. There was nothing I could do. I didn't want to be questioned. Please don't tell anyone!'

'It's okay! Sorry I shouted. It's just that Prospect's son was my friend and if there's anything to know, I'd like to know. My family are kind of secretive about it.'

'His son was your friend?'

'We were friends from when I was little.'

Beginning with the first days when he used to come and swing me, I tell her all about me and Enoch. When I finish it's like a river has run through me and taken all the weed and stones and mud with it, washing me clean.

'Wow,' she says. 'Thanks for telling me. I've never had an African friend.'

'Well it's the same. Well no, I mean it is, but obviously it's not. There's no staying the night or going to the same school. My parents stopped letting me play with him when I was eleven.' I fold my arms and aim my words right between her eyes. 'Why did you think it disgusting about my aunt and Prospect?'

'Well,' she looks embarrassed, 'your aunt was married.'

Nice swerve sister.

I smile at her. We both know what she meant, but I let her off. Hell I like her.

'Do you always go out with guys that come into the garage?' I start walking again.

'Ja. Glen's about the sixth or seventh.' I turn round to look at her, eyebrows jumping.

'Just kidding. Glen's the first – I mean, I've never had a boyfriend before.' I look at her, she's gone as red as her strawberries.

Okay, too much information. I don't actually want to hear about it.

'I don't invite people back. My dad drinks,' she says.

We stop near the river. Picking up stones I start to skim.

'Can you skim?' I ask her.

'Of course I can swim.'

'No skim, not SWIM, skim.' I hand her a stone. She looks down at it as if it had just grown out of her hand.

'Go on, skim.' I skim a stone into the river. 'My dad drinks too, especially lately, especially since we moved,' I say. 'He's not usually violent though, he just gets boring.' I raise my eyebrows and smile without opening my mouth.

'I wish my dad was boring,' Sharon says. She throws the stone. It flies high up in an arc and plops into the water, like a jobbie into the toilet.

'Never mind, come on.' I walk towards the dead tree struck by lightning. A huge split in the middle half of it stretches itself up and over the water as if it was trying to escape; it leans so far over that you can just walk right over it to the other side of the river.

The sky has darkened slightly. I think of the little girl being taken by the crocodile as she played on the river-bank in Umtali.

'Wanna climb a tree?' I point to the unlucky tree.

'In this? I'm seventeen.'

'So? There's no age restriction.'

'Okaaay.' She smiles and kicks off her shoes. Black Bata sandals with little wedges. Totally inappropriate. What girls do for boys. And he probably didn't even notice. I tightrope along the damaged trunk out over the water. Sharon follows behind.

'I can tell you've climbed this tree a thousand times.'

'Ja. Why you shaking?'

'I'm scared of heights.'

Enoch cured me of that.

I look up at her. 'Oh. Well you're brave then.'

Our feet are at least a metre above the surface of the water. In the rainy season, the water half swallows the trunk, but now the earth is beginning to get really thirsty for rain.

'It must have been difficult for you, leaving your farm, even after the attack,' she says.

I glance sharply at her. No. I don't want to remember.

'Sorry,' she says. 'I heard you and your mom were pretty brave.' I stare down at where the water swirls around a smooth brown rock.

'Ja.' I say. 'My mom is brave.'

In the water, shadows of the men, looming on the lawn, their weapons pointed at us, appear to me in the dark currents.

'Ja. Well. I don't want to talk about it.'

'Sorry. I didn't mean to upset you,' she says.

'It's okay. I like your dress,' I say, by way of apology.

'Thanks.'

'I wish I had long brown legs like yours,' she says. 'You're so tall and slim. Pretty too. You should wear your hair down.'

'Thanks.' I finger my long hair, tied as usual in a high pony-tail. 'And thanks for telling me about my aunt.' And thanks for listening. I almost say it, but I don't, it's one step too close to the cheddar.

Mel and I hiss at each other in front of the braai. It sends sparks up to the blood-orange sky.

'How could you have done that? You're so forward.'

'Well, I didn't want to go on a boring walk.'

Glen and Uncle Joe are putting the t-bones on the braai.

'You're supposed to be my friend.'

'You're supposed to be *my* friend. And why do you speak about munts so much? Asking your Gran about her friend, Silas – and going on about that one in the PV.'

Embarassed about my earlier conversation, I look at her scornfully. 'Solomon. At least get his name right.' I can't mention Enoch's name.

'Solomon. What's the diffs? Then you creak on about the worker here that's been locked up –'

'Prospect.'

'Who the hell cares? What's your case man?'

'What's your case? Going after Glen like that?'

Sharon comes over. We rein in the barrels, eyes smoking with our unspent ammo.

'Hi,' she says.

'Hi,' Mel says sweetly. If she was a meringue, I'd crush her in my hand.

We do not talk all the way back to Salisbury. May doesn't talk either. She's had too many beers and is using all her concentration on the road and I have to light her cigarettes for her. Enoch would just be another munt to Mel. I slap at the unwelcome hot tears. That's it. I'm never going to speak to her again. Insects zoom into the headlights trained on the gates at Mel's house. Gripping the seat, I stare straight ahead. Then I remember I have to get out to let her out. I look away from her. She gets out. I get back in. Mel sticks her face through my window.

'Thanks for the lift,' she says to May.

'No problem,' May says, 'couldn't have let you walk.'

In my sleep I hear a tapping sound. I wake thinking I'm at Angel's Peak and Enoch is outside trying to tell me something. The tapping sound becomes more insistent. My heart pounding cartoon-style, I sit up and turn to the window. I rip the curtain open to see a face, and almost scream. It takes me a moment to realise it's Mel. I jerk my thumb to indicate she should come through the glass doors that lead into the house from the veranda. Back in my room, we sit on the bed.

'How did you get here?' I stare at her. 'Did you walk?' No white person walks around at night.

'My brother brought me. He's waiting up the road in Mom's car. I came to say sorry. I shouldn't have gone for Glen like that.'

'What did you do?' I ask.

'Nothing.' She raises her eyes up at me. 'Well, I ran a finger down his spine when he was lighting the braai.' She smiles.

I shake my head, my mouth open.

'In front of everyone?' I ask. She nods.

'Did anyone see?' She shakes her head.

'You've got cheek Mel.'

She nods her head up and down slowly. Grabbing a pillow, she begins pounding me with it. Snatching another, I pound her back. Quite hard.

'Wow,' she says, giggling.

'Shouldn't you be getting back?' I ask, thumping her a good one.

'Nah,' she says, 'he's smoking the happy stuff. Friends?'

'Ja,' I say, hitting her hard over the head with my pillow one more time, trying not to think of Sharon.

12.

Mom's decided that I won't get blown up in a bomb blast if she lets me take the bus into town. So here I am, all alone, walking up the pedestrian mall on First Street on a hot Saturday morning, feeling pretty kif in black stove-pipe jeans, black baseball tackies and my denim jacket that Nessie gave me, covered in little tin badges. It's a bit short in the sleeves now, but they're pushed up anyway. My hair hangs straight down like two curtains, but as I pass the round concrete tables and red and white striped umbrellas of the Wimpy Bar, I realise I feel stupid with my hair down, so I scrape it into a ponytail and tie it with the rubber band I have around my wrist. Okes in velies and shorts, men in short safari suits with long socks as well as the suited man type glide past me, as do women in cotton-print dresses or nylon slacks and sleeveless printed cotton tops. An African man comes from the direction of the Kine cinema, dressed in a pink shirt and a brown suit that's about three inches high in the leg above his grey and black diamond patterned socks and scuffed black patent-leather shoes. He wears one of those fifties-style hats, with a bit of a feather sticking out of it. Poor as they are, the Africans are more interesting to look at. Near a bank of cars on the corner of Union Avenue and First Street, a soapstone carving seller dressed in a tight white t-shirt advertising maize-meal is hassling a middle-aged white lady in a dress that'd look better covering a couch in a garage. She stares at him from behind green flick-down sunshades and a bouffant-blonde hair-don't. *Not today thank you. No sorry, too expensive*, she's shaking her head and pursing her lips, as she shuts her handbag with a click. He probably wants about as much for it as she put in the parking meter. At the First Street entrance of Barbour's under the school uniform display, a beggar who isn't even wearing legs is smiling up at me with cracked teeth. He nods, so out of a mixture of guilt and pity, I give him twenty-five cents. As I do so, Sandra and Gail from my new school, walk past me from Truworths.

'Freak,' says Sandra.

I'm not sure whether she means me or the beggar. Hell, maybe the whole scene is freaky to her eyes. I chuck a curled-lip sarky one at her.

'Ja, what are you wearing?' says Gail.

'Shit hey, I dunno, I should have phoned a friend maybe to check myself out first hey, then I could wear a uniform just like you two.' I nod at their dresses, one pale pink, one pale blue, plastic earrings to match, both belted with wide white plastic belts. They could have stepped straight out of the Truworths window display. Sandra's long mousey hair is flicked down the sides, so is Gail's yellowy blonde shoulder length hair. Their faces are as slappable as they always are. They widen their eyes at each other and then burst out laughing.

'You're such a freak Jayne Cameron.'

'Ja. You'll never get a boyfriend.'

'You two look like a pair of shop dummies!' I shout at them. They giggle like the wind-up dolls they are.

Turning to go back up First Street, face burning, I run smack bang into Nessie. She hugs me before I have a chance to escape into the jeweller's in the arcade.

'Jay! How odd. I was just thinking about you.'

Swallowing hard, I say nothing.

'What's up?' She peers into my face.

'Nothing.' I lie. 'Just ran into two cows from school.' And I so don't want to see you now.

'Hey, come.' She turns me round. 'Don't run away again. Let me take you to Barbour's for a drink.'

I allow her to walk me to Barbour's, to hug my shoulders, even though I'm embarrassed because we're in public. I stare at the school uniforms in the ground floor window displays with stinging eyes.

In the grey cool of the terrace restaurant, Nessie finds a corner table, half hidden by a tree in a pot.

'Sit there, I'll get you a Coke float.'

I look down at my jacket, wishing I hadn't worn it. Pressing myself backwards against the wall, I rub my eyes on my sleeve. Nessie comes back.

'What's up? Let's hear.' She puts her hand on my forearm, which makes me start crying again.

'I dunno. I don't care about those cows.'

'Ah. The Rhodesian cow. From school.' Nessie smiles at me. 'A particularly unsightly breed. You shouldn't have to see them at all.'

I laugh. She reminds me of Dad. In some ways they're so alike.

'You miss Enoch.' Nessie says. Hell. Do you have to read me all the time?

'Ja. Well.' I look down at the tiles in the concrete table. 'I stopped mentioning him a long time ago, because everyone thinks I'm cooked if I do. Anyway, I don't know what to think about him anymore. I don't know how to think about anyone,' I say.

Nessie takes my hand. 'I don't think you're cooked,' she says. 'Not even lightly fried,' she smiles.

I pull my hand back quickly, no longer able to look into her eyes. I focus instead on the strings of African beads around her neck above her green t-shirt. The waiter arrives with my Coke float. Good timing. I take a sip, ice-cream and fizz. Nessie smiles up at him and says *tatenda*.

'Why won't you tell me about Justice?'

'Why don't we speak about you Jay?'

'That is about me. About all of us.'

'Good. It is about all of us. *All* of us Jay.'

'You're so weird Nessie! How can you act like you care so much about me, when you seem to care more about protecting a terrorist who tried to murder us?'

People at various tables stir. One or two turn round and look.

'Hi Mrs Jackman!' Nessie calls to a woman she recognises. The woman frowns and then goes back to her conversation.

'See what it's like Jay? This is the heart of it. What you're coming up against at school. Because you're different? Imagine being made to feel different day in day out, sitting on different buses, not being allowed in to the cinemas. In the restaurants? Being made to wear your skin with shame. Well now you're getting an inkling maybe.'

'Well. Maybe I'd be a bit more sympathetic if they didn't try to kill me, Nessie.'

Nessie smiles. 'You could never bring Enoch in here. Have you ever thought about that? Your best friend.'

The tears come again.

She takes my hand. 'They don't want to kill you. They want to kill the system.'

'Oh. And we were just in the way? What's our tea farm got to do with the system?'

Nessie laughs. 'Come on Jay. Don't be naive. It's part of the biggest issue. The land issue. Education's another. Would you like to be denied your education?'

I laugh. 'Yes, actually. I go to school with a bunch of morons.'

Nessie takes my hand, 'I know you love Enoch.'

I laugh.

I wish she wouldn't say things like that out loud. I can hear Mel's voice, *Why do you speak about munts so much?*

'I don't trust Enoch.'

'I hope that's just teenage squirms and not because he's African.'

'Give me a break, Nessie.'

'African girls get married at your age, some even younger. Have you started your periods yet?'

'God Nessie! Can you just be quiet?'

'Well think about it Jay. You can go the same way or you can embrace your difference and be proud of it.' She takes a sip of her coffee then puts her hand on my arm again.

'I want to see more of you Jay.' Her hand is like a brand, searing me.

On the bus home I'm angry with Nessie again. She told me nothing. Women get on the bus, putting their OK bazaars and Bon Marché bags on the maroon seats next to them. A lady on the opposite side of the bus comes over and offers me her magazine.

'Would you like this? I'm finished with it.'

'No thanks,' I say, wishing she'd fly away, realising too late that Carla would've loved the magazine.

At the African bus depot lines and lines of Africans queue for buses. Around me are maroon-coloured empty seats, marooned seats; they seem to accuse me. Why did I have to run into her? I've been happy being friends with Mel, a proper Rhodesian girl who cares about her country.

13.

In the drift of mid-afternoon I doze on the veranda steps, one arm around Piddle's sun-baked back. At first the sound is like mozzies, a low drone, so I ignore it. Then it gets louder and louder. One hand shades my eyes as I sit and look up. The sound is very loud now. They fly low. Dakotas. Masses of them. Mom comes out and runs over the lawn. She stands there, shading her eyes, looking up. There's a lull in the noise. We look at each other. I start to get up. But then there's an even louder noise. Choppers – Allouettes. It feels like they're in the garden. G Cars and Z Cars, as Glen calls them. Z for the troopie carrying ones, G for those mounted with gunners, flying so low we can practically see the pilots.

I look at Mom. 'What's going on?'

'Don't know,' she says without taking her eyes off the sky. 'Let's go phone May.'

May can't tell us anything. Despite the fact that she works at police headquarters and gets all the incoming calls from the security forces about contacts all over the country and beyond. Dad's out in the tribal trust lands. Mom and I sit out on the veranda and drink tea, waiting for something to happen.

'What's going on? At least Dad's not on call-up.'

'I don't know,' Mom says. 'Something big. I can feel it in my bones.'

'Dir. I could see it with my eyes. Are you worried about Bob and Glen?'

'Of course. I worry about all of us. I worry about the whole damn country.'

'Ja Mom. You're such a saint.'

Mom gets up, probably to phone Aldie. I pick up *The Rhodesia Herald*.

Sometime later, I hear the phone ring, once, before it's snatched up. I wait for a minute for Mom to come out and give me information, which doesn't come. In the dark hallway Mom stands with the receiver in her hand.

'What?' I say. Mom stares at me.

'What? What's happened? Mom!'

'It's Glen. He's missing.' Mom drops the receiver on the floor.

Next day, on the veranda, everyone's waiting for the starter gun to fire like at the races, only the trigger-man is taking his time.

'Pass the sugar,' I ask. Carla stares into space. 'Pass the sugar. PLEASE!'

Carla jumps. 'Shit man! Do you have to shout? You scared me.'

'Keep your voice down Jay,' Mom says.

'What? It wasn't turned up. She was in a coma, that's all.'

'Don't say that Jay,' Dad says.

'Hey Dad, lighten up. Nobody's dead you know.'

Dad leaps up. His chair clatters to the floor. He looms over me, his hand raised.

'Dad!' Carla's on her feet too. She places her hand on Dad's left arm.

'Sorry, I didn't mean –' He ignores me, turns and walks towards the French doors. 'Dad!' I shout, 'it's just an expression.'

'Ja well keep your bloody expressions to yourself,' he shouts back.

I look at Mom. 'What?'

'He's right, Jay, you could be a bit more sensitive.' Mom runs her fingers through her hair.

'Well Dad could be a little less sensitive.'

'Leave it Jay. I don't know why you're so cheerful.'

'I just know he's going to be fine. *I feel it in my bones.*'

Mom hasn't been to the club to play tennis. Dad's been hanging around the house a lot more too, instead of going drinking at The Blue Hart. Hell, it's past three o'clock and they aren't even drinking. They have actually been talking to each other and being so much nicer. Carla gets up.

'I'm going to Debbie's.'

'No you're not.' Mom says.

'Mom I'm going crazy in this house. Everyone's cracking up,' she says.

'Well you can just crack up with the rest of us. Dad wants us all together so that's what we'll be doing.'

'Ja, happy families hey,' I smile at Mom and Carla. They glare back, Mom waggling her head at me like a goose.

Mel phones all the time for news. Every time the phone rings it makes me jump. Dad gets really voos, because he thinks it might be news about Glen. The phone rings.

'Tell that girl, if she rings again, I'll strangle her with her own hair!' Dad yells from the veranda.

'Hi Mel. Look. There's no news. I'll ring you when there is. My dad says that if you ring again he'll strangle you with your own hair.'

'Well. At least you've got a dad. I wish my dad was around to strangle me with my own hair.'

'Gimme a break Mel. I'll call when he pitches. And I *know* he'll pitch.'

'Off the phone!' Dad yells from the veranda.

'Mel. I've gota go. My dad won't let me tie up the line.'

I put the phone down. This whole thing with Glen is bringing back memories of her father. She wants me to feel bad though.

'Hey John, d'you wanna play happy families?' I say, grabbing the cards from the shelf underneath the veranda table.

Mom and Carla glare at me. I waggle my head at them. 'I mean cards.'

'Ja, okay.'

'Come over here, it's sunnier.' I say, splaying my legs on the warm veranda floor. 'Let's play mau-mau.'

'No let's play snap.'

'Okay, spread the cards. And don't look.'

John spreads the cards face down on the concrete floor near Piddle. Flies buzz above Piddle's head in a fly halo. He gives a sort of half yelp in his sleep and one of his ears flaps.

'So,' Carla says to Mom, twisting her hair, 'what shall we talk about?'

'Oh Carla, don't take that attitude please. Things are bad enough.'

Dad appears with a couple of Castles. 'What attitude?'

'Nothing,' Mom smiles as she takes her beer.

Dad sits down, knocking back half his beer as he does so.

'Snap!' John shouts.

Mom jumps, then smiles down at John, pleased that he's making a noise. He's been mega quiet since the news about Glen. I turn towards the gate at the sound of a car. John meanwhile quickly peels up a few cards to take a peek.

'Ja, John, you rec I can't see? I can see sideways, like a chameleon.'

He turns over a card. It's a cow.

'It's a cow,' he says.

'Ja, I know. I can see. A big fat cow.'

Auntie Aldie walks across the lawn towards us, wearing a t-shirt and a denim wrap skirt. Her hair is wrapped around big plastic curlers and she's carrying a rifle. Okay, she's not really fat. But she is a cow.

Carla looks down at me from her chair. 'Curb it Jay.'

'What?' I show her John's card. 'It's a cow.'

'Come to shoot us and put us out of our misery?' Dad asks.

'Ja, have you come to put us down?' I ask. Dad and I laugh.

'Howzit,' she says, putting her bag and keys down on the table, then sits down next to Mom. 'Any news?'

Mom shakes her head and smiles, raising her brows as she shakes her head.

'Ja, no news, but we think that's good news,' says Dad. 'Wanna drink?'

'Ja, just a Coke, please.'

Dad gets up to get her drink. He ruffles mine and John's hair as he goes, happier now that he's necked some beer.

Auntie A turns to Carla. 'No ballet today?'

'Well, there is, but Mom and Dad don't want me to go. They're keeping me captive against my will.'

'Like Sleeping Beauty?' Auntie A says. 'Maybe your prince will come and rescue you, hey?'

'Fat chance. He's had marching orders.'

Auntie A raises her eyebrows. 'From Dave?'

'No,' says Carls. 'From the army. He's been called-up, due back any time now though.'

'What? He's a bit young isn't he?'

'Eighteen.' Carla stretches a leg up, twirling her pointed foot near the basket-weave light shade hanging from the veranda ceiling.

'Ja, old enough to go to war,' I say.

'Just play cards hey Jay,' Carla says.

'Ja don't be so twisted, hey,' says Auntie Aldie.

I snort. 'You think I'm twisted? I didn't start the war.'

'Jay,' says Mom.

'Ja, I know. Don't be cheeky.'

'Ja, don't be cheeky,' says Auntie A, like a bloody parrot. She lights a Berkeley and hands it to Mom, then she lights another for herself.

'No word from Bob yet,' she inhales. 'Don't even know if he's in the country.' She takes another drag of her smoke. 'Don't even know if he's alive,' she says as she blows the smoke out through her nostrils. Dad comes back with the Coke.

'What?'

'Bob. I was just saying –'

'Ja, is he dead or alive, I heard.' Dad doesn't sit down. He puts a fresh beer on the table before downing the remainder of the last one.

'Gee, you don't have to take that attitude Dave, Bob's risking his life out there, going into places few men –'

'Ja, ja. He's not the only lunatic running round there in the bush –'

'This time he's gone –' she says.

'Ja, ja. I know. He's prob'ly single-handedly blowing ZANLA to hell in Mozambique right now, anything to get away from you, hey Alds.' He takes another swig.

'Dave!' Mom looks shocked, but sounds as if she's about to laugh. Auntie Aldie takes a sip of her Coke and then puts it down on the table. She flicks off her silver slip-slop and places her foot on Piddle's warm back. Piddle's only response is a slight flick of his ear. He's fast asleep in doggy la-la-land.

'The trouble is Glen always ends up doing his own thing,' Aldie says. 'That leads to danger. When you're in a unit like that you need to stick together.'

'And whada'you bloody know about units?' Dad puts his hands on his hips. He looks like a bossy school boy.

'Well I'm married to –'

'Ja and that makes you an expert?'

Cue the lecture.

'For a start when we're out there, in the middle of it, we sometimes break up,' he swigs his beer, 'so that we won't – all – be – shot – at – once.'

Top marks for Sarky-Marky Dad. What a hose. Auntie Aldie blinks at him. Mom puts her hand on Dad's arm.

'Calm down Dave,' she says.

'Don't tell me to bloody calm down. She doesn't know what she's bloody talking about.'

'I don't have to listen to this –' says Auntie A, her voice scaling upwards.

'Snap!' shouts John. I haven't been concentrating. Dad whips round at the sound of John's voice. John jumps. Auntie Aldie stands up.

'Sit down Alds.' Mom pulls her by the arm. 'C'mon, have a real drink.'

'Ja, sit down and have a real drink. Maybe you'll start talking sense, hey,' Dad says, softer than before, but obviously not soft enough. Auntie Aldie takes a step forward. Mom pulls her back.

'No ways man, not while your husband's here.' She picks up her keys, looking like she's going to cry. Mom lets her go.

'Nice one, Dad,' says Carls, playing with the ends of her hair.

Mom gets up. 'Well done Dave.'

Carla unfolds her long skinny-jeaned legs and gets up too.

'Where you going?'

'To get a drink Dad.' She leans over, puts a hand on his shoulder and says it near his ear.

He touches her arm as she goes past.

'Get me one too.'

'Ja. Us too,' I shout at her back.

John keeps cheating. I don't really care, so I get up to get a drink and grab a packet of Willard's salt 'n vinegar. Mom, Carla and Auntie A are in the kitchen.

Auntie A is crying. 'I wish you'd never married that bloody bastard.'

'Alds, that's my husband you're talking about.' Mom strokes her hair.

'Ja, and our Dad,' says Carla. 'He's freaked out, about Glen. He's just worried, that's all. He's more like a brother than a cousin.'

'C'mon,' says Mom. 'Let's go out, have a gin 'n tonic, that'll sort you out.'

Like hell, a lobotomy wouldn't sort her out.

'What are you looking at?' Auntie A says to me. I ignore her. Mom smiles at me as if Auntie A had just said something nice.

Back on the veranda, Dad says, 'Hey Jay. Put one foot in front of the other and get your old Dad a cold one.'

'Daaad,' I groan, 'I thought Carla was getting you one.'

'Ja, old is right. You're starting to look old Dave, must be all the beer, hey? And it's only twelve o' clock.' Mom's come back from tending to Aldie, her hand on her blue-jeaned hip. She's got her 'just kidding' voice on, but there's poison in there too.

'Nah, it's not the beer. It's the bloody nagging wife.'

Hey, we've had the interval and now it's time for part two, the double act.

'Shit Dave, I was only joking.'

'"Shit Dave, I was only joking"' Dad mocks, 'My arse.' He looks up at her, 'Wha'did you do with your sister?'

'Talking to Carla.' Mom sits back down. 'Okay, I know this is because Glen's gone.'

'Whada'you mean 'gone'. Where'd'you think he's gone, hey, Reen? Hunting?'

Mom takes a sip of her beer. 'I wouldn't be a bloody nagging wife if you were more of a husband.'

Dad takes the last swig out of the brown bottle. 'You're not the woman I married, Irene.' He says it to the floor, quietly.

Mom starts to get up. At the same time John jumps off the low veranda wall. First sign of an argument, he always ducks. She sits back down again. I turn my face away from the veranda and watch John run over the front lawn, straight into the branches of the highest pine-tree. Piddle wakes up and follows him, leaping up at him on the lawn, but John pushes him away.

'And you? Call yourself a man? Sitting on this veranda day after day, night after night. Drinking?'

'Mo-om,' I call out from my position on the veranda steps. 'I'm still here you know.' Why doesn't she just can it? She ignores me, picks up Dad's empty bottle and shakes it at him.

'This isn't how to handle it! It's not gonna bring him back you know, Dave.' Mom gets up.

Dad stands up too. 'Shut up Irene, you look ugly when you're angry, you know, like your sister. Bloody loose mouth like a fish-wife.'

'What?' She moves her face closer to his. 'What did you say? Did you say something about my family?'

'No, your SISTER.' Dad moves his face closer to Mom's. 'I thought you were married to me.' He sits back down again. 'No course not, you're not a Cameron, never were, never will be. When the going gets tough, you'll always be a bloody Pom.' He picks up his beer bottle. It's empty. 'No staying power,' he says, putting it down again. 'Go back to your parents in England.'

Mom turns to go into the house. 'That's it, I've had enough,' she shakes her head. 'That's it.'

'Ja, I had enough a long time ago.' Dad sits back down. 'And take your bloody sister with you.'

Mom turns around, bottle in hand. She flings it at him. It hits him near his right eye.

'You hit me in the temple! I can't believe it, the bloody temple!' For a moment Dad seems stunned. Then he gets up.

'Ja, I hit you in the temple. The holy bloody temple!'

'Mom!' I say. 'I can't believe you did that!'

Mom turns to me. 'Ja, Jay. There's a lot you wouldn't believe.'

'Like what? Hey, Reen. Like what?' Dad follows her into the dining-room.

'You're always bad-mouthing my family.' Mom swings round to face him. 'What about yours?'

'Ja, what about mine? At least they've got some backbone.'

'Don't make me laugh. What about your Aunt having it off with her bloody worker?'

Dad stares at the floor, shaking his head. Then he turns round.

'Ja and her getting shot. An accident? My foot man!' She fires the words at Dad's back. 'He shot her. Because she refused to give him anymore money!'

Dad turns and lunges for her.

'Dad! Dad! Please don't!' I shout. He grabs her wrist. She fights to free herself.

'Leave me alone!' she screams.

'Carla! Carla!' I yell.

Dad lets go of Mom's arm. 'You're not worth it.' He goes back to the veranda. 'I should've known that from the start.'

Carla comes out. 'What happened?'

Mom ignores her as she brushes past her. 'Where's Aldie?' she asks.

'In the guest rondavel.'

Carls and I follow Mom.

'Mom! Whada'you gonna do?' I ask. She keeps walking. 'MOM!'

Mom turns around. 'Get your father another bloody beer.'

'Hey, Mom,' Carls runs after her. 'That's not fair. It's not her fault.' In the archway, Carla puts her arm around me. Mom runs through the kitchen and out through the back door towards the rondavel.

'Yes, it's not fair!' she shouts, from out back. 'Life's not bloody fair! You girls will realise that sooner or later.' As if we haven't. We look at each other and then we hear Mom's car steaming down the driveway. I go to the fridge to get my Dad another beer.

Later Mom summons Dad to The Blue Hart for crisis talks for the rest of the day and then they come back, which sucks. I wanted Mom to go awol for a while. During dinner, I watch Mom and Dad's faces, smiling, *trying*. Mom tries to melt my icy face with a smile. 'Don't be chilly, Jay,' she says catching my expression. 'There's some things you just don't understand, no matter how wise you are in your own eyes.'

Got that right lady. She threw that bottle at Dad on target. I throw a look at her likewise. After dinner, I lie on my bed and try and concentrate on my English composition about freedom. Plot, girl gets lost out in the bush one day, comes across a cave, befriends the folks that live there, doesn't return to so-called civilisation. I've drawn a girl like me with three long-haired dropouts around a fire toasting tuber roots on long sticks. The phone rings. I wait, my hands prickling.

'Shit man, I can't believe it, that's fantastic! Reen! Tell me again. Did he walk? Shit man, must tell Reen! Reen!'

I can hear Mom's slip-slops on the tiles of the hallway. 'Shit man, that's wonderful.'

Imaginative language, as per usual. Dad's just putting the phone on the hook, when I get to him. He has his arm around Mom's waist – shit man I can't believe it. Mom smiles up at him.

'Shit man. Get us a beer Bantam.'

If he says it again, I'll say it too.

'Shit man, I can't believe it,' I say. Nobody notices.

Dad's face is flushed red over purple thread veins that trace their way under the skin on either side of his nose, where beads of sweat rise with his raised temperature. His tawny-brown eyes seem to bulge out of the yellowish-white.

'This calls for a celebration. Get your mother a beer too.' He turns me in the direction of the fridge and slaps me on the bum.

'What's happened. Is he back?' I ask.

He smoothes his hair back with both hands, 'Man! I can't believe it,' he says to Mom, in case she didn't get it the first time. He pulls her in close making her laugh.

'Get the beers first. Then I'll tell you.'

The fridge is just there, he could get the beers himself.

'No man, Dad. Tell me, it's not fair.'

'He's back! At Joe's. Get the beer.'

'Yes! Go Glenda!' I get the beers and grab a big bag of Ripple Chips from the pantry.

When Mom and Dad disappear to The Blue Hart again to celebrate, I call Mel to make her day. Ten minutes later she's on the veranda drinking one of Dad's beers because she's so hyped up. She downs most of the beer in one.

'Easy Mel. You're gonna end up an alcoholic like your mom.'

'No. I'm gonna end up with Glen.'

'What do you mean?'

Mel stands up. She's wearing denim shorts and a white vest, and loads of eyeliner. Dressed for him. Just in case.

I look closer at her. 'Have you cut your fringe?'

'Ja. Like it?' She sits back down and takes one of Dad's Kingsgates out of a box on the table.

'You've got a cheek,' I say, putting my feet up on the table.

She hands me the lit cigarette. I take a drag and give it back to her.

'No coughing today hey? You been practising?' She flicks her hair.

'What do you mean you're gonna be with Glen?'

'Look Jay. If I tell you, promise you won't get angry?' She leans towards me so that I can see the black eyeliner separating along the lower rims of her navy-coloured eyes. She's a 70s Cleopatra in jeans and a red t-shirt.

'No! What?'

'I got off with him. At The Blue Hart.' Her hands fly to her mouth, trying to catch the birds of confession that have just flown out of it.

'What? How?'

'Want me to show you?'

'No! I don't see how –'

'I put my phone number in his cigarette packet at your uncle's farm. He phoned me just before he went on call-up. Stop catching flies, we only frenchied.'

Car headlights light up the driveway.

'Shit. You better go Mel. And stop smoking man!'

Mel stubs out her cigarette, then she giggles and hugs me. 'Be happy for me?'

'Hell. You're not getting married Miss World.'

Her beautiful traitor's legs run over the lawn.

14.

We're all on the veranda waiting for the returning hero. Dad's sparked up the braai and the beers are in a tin bath on ice. May and Uncle Joe are parked at one end of the wide veranda steps chattering and cackling like a pair of old monkeys. 'I can't bloody believe he's home May,' says Uncle Joe. 'I can't bloody believe it man.' May gives a hacking cackle and pours some more Bols from the bottle between her legs into their glasses, her cigarette hanging out of the side of her mouth. Auntie Aldie and Uncle Bob are already here, along with Mom's tennis friend Elaine, as well as Carls and Ian, who Dad's being really nice to. He keeps telling me to get Ian beers.

'No thanks, Mr C. I've had two already.'

'So? You on rations?' Dad asks. 'And who's Mr C? I can't see him,' Dad laughs. 'Ja, and I can't see straight, either.'

Everyone laughs, including Mom, even though Dad is half-bombed.

The headlights of Van's bakkie swing into view. Glen jumps out to open the gates. Everyone gets up and starts clapping and cheering like we're at a rugby match as Glen jogs over the lawn. It would be good if a spotlight were trained on him, and he could run in slow-mo. Dad raises his glass as if Ian Smith has just turned up. 'Where's the beers man?' Glen laughs, jumping onto the veranda.

Van has his thin shoulder-length hair in a ponytail, which makes his horseshoe moustache look like it's going to clip-clop off his face. His name isn't really Van, it's Willem, Van's a nickname, because he's Afrikaans. Lots of Dutchmen have 'Van' in their names. Van

Rensberg, Van der Merwe, Van der Byl. People say, 'Give us a lift Van,' to Van a lot, they think it's a real hose. Van knows all the Van der Merwe jokes. *How do you confuse van der Merwe? Give him two shovels and tell him to take his pick.* For a Dutchman, he doesn't take himself seriously. He tells Van der Merwe jokes himself even. He reaches into the tin bucket for beers.

'Pass a beer Van, no pass two, must be thirsty after that long walk, hey.' Dad clamps his arm around Glen's shoulder. 'You're a true bloody Rhodesian man.'

Glen laughs as the ladies press kisses into his cheeks, and the men slap him on the back. Uncle Bob doesn't get up, he just raises his bottle to him.

'Howzit Bob,' says Glen.

Glen sits on a barstool near to Mom, Aldie and dark haired, button-eyed Elaine, who sit against the wall on the sagging cane couch. Wanting him to know how smashed-in I feel about him and Mel, I try to look uncaring. Glen grabs me round the waist.

'How's my best girl?' All my anger about him and Mel just melts away. 'Better for seeing you,' I say, reddening at my accidentally exposed cheese.

'That's the way. I have something for you.' He pulls a little brown paper package out of his pocket. I tear off the paper and pull out a necklace made of lucky beans.

'Thanks. I love it.' I put the necklace on, trying not to cry.

'Now you'll always be lucky in love. Well that's what the woman who sold it to me said. Mind you, she was on the side of a bush road in the middle of nowhere, plus she needed the bucks.'

Mom laughs, and reaches a questioning hand over from the couch. 'It's lovely Jay.' She hands it back to me and pulls her legs back up.

'Sweet of you, Glen, to think of Jay, after all you've been through.' Mom smiles at me. She's wearing the purple tie-dye t-shirt Nessie made for her.

'She's my little pal. Aren't you Jay?'

My cheeks glow warmer. 'I'll go show Carls.'

Mom smiles and raises her glass at Glen. Elaine smiles a worried smile.

'Welcome back,' she says in a beery voice.

On the other side of the veranda, Carls and Ian are talking to Uncle Bob. Auntie Aldie stares into her glass as if she plans to shrink and dive right into it. She's listening to Uncle Bob's voice on the other side of the veranda. Her eyes mirror the liquid in the glass.

'The terrs hold night-time meetings with the villagers,' Uncle Bob is saying. 'That's when we like to join the party.' Uncle Bob has told me all about this stuff before. He's an expert tracker, only he doesn't track animals; he tracks terrs.

'If we notice suspect things, like say, African villagers preparing lots of food, or making lots of doro we figure the terrs are coming to pol-iti-cise the villagers.'

'To get them on their side? I thought they scared them into it?' laughs Carla.

'Ja, that too. But this is to brainwash the poor buggers. They tell them they'd be better off without the white colonial masters who have taken their land and want to take more. They say they need to join the liberation war, which they call *chimurenga*, so that they can have their country back.'

Ian snorts. 'In Africa it's a matter of the strongest tribe being on top. It'd be brutal without us,' he says.

'Smart boy.' Uncle Bob laughs and takes a swig of his beer, then he looks at Ian for a long time. Ian looks uncomfortable. He smiles at Uncle Bob for a while and then puts his arm round Carla.

'And?' says Carls. 'Carry on.'

'What they don't realise is that if the terrs do get in, they'll turn Rhodesia into a one-party Marxist state, and –' he takes another sip, 'they'll be more controlled than they ever thought possible.

'What else do they do?' asks Carls.

'Who? The terrs?' Uncle Bob asks. 'If the villagers don't go along with the plans of the terrs, the *vakomana*, they round up a family, put them in a hut and set fire to them. This tends to make them agree with them.' Uncle Bob laughs. 'When the Rhodesian forces turn up, asking them whether they've had contact with the terrs, the villagers refuse to say anything. If they do say anything, they get their lips chopped off for speaking, or an ear lopped off for listening to white lies.'

Uncle Bob says 'white lies,' like 'white lice,' in an African accent.

'Really?' says Carls.

'True's fact?' says Ian. 'What do the ous do to make them talk?'

'We have our ways.'

'Give us an example,' says Carls.

'We join the party,' he smiles round at each of us in turn. 'We make sure we follow the dress code right down to the boot polish on our faces and we bring the fireworks. The villagers are very scared of our fireworks.' Uncle Bob nods his head up and down with exaggerated slowness. 'Very scared indeed, when we pull in with those fireworks, they scatter like a herd of bokke near a prowling lion.' Uncle Bob puts his arm round me. 'We make sure the terrs go up with the fireworks,' he smiles up at me. 'Makes for a spectacular display.' He says 'spectacular display' in an upper class British accent. We laugh. He pauses for a moment, then says, 'They never quite forget it. If of course, they can remember at all.'

Ian laughs and shuffles his feet under his chair, holding his beer against his thigh. He's the only guy here wearing jeans. His hair looks freshly washed too, blond and sort of swept back, like a baby's. Carla looks pretty gorgeous as usual, in a red vest top, with matching red plastic earrings and bangles, her hair all flicked out and fluffed up. Uncle Bob gazes at the arched side of her neck. He looks as though he might like to take a bite out of it. Carla looks down, and putting her hand on Ian's leg smiles up at him. Uncle Bob looks at them with his glass-cutting eyes. It's actually quite hard to look Uncle Bob in the turquoise of his eyes, but sooner or later they draw you in like magnets. Mom says he has the *burning eyes of an apostle.*

Everyone's still slapping Glen on the back, like he's a prize mombie, and sort of jostling him around. He's laughing and saying 'thanks man' a lot. Everyone keeps saying, 'Tell us what happened, man.'

'Okay, okay,' Glen says. 'It was a support mission. We'd just crossed the river.' He takes a sip of his beer. 'It'd been raining so there was quite a bit of mud. It was difficult, but we managed to get all three Elands across. And you know how bloody difficult it can be to get those vehicles through the mud, so we decided to stop for a break, it was lekker hot too, we needed some tea, so we built the fire, got the pot on, weapons down, took a load off, sparked up the smokes – and then they just started firing at us through the trees – shit man, we couldn't see where they were shooting from – so we threw ourselves down –'

I think of Mel's dad and feel guilty for not asking her over, because she's been freaking about Glen, but I just wanted to see him without her being here tonight.

'What, on the ground?' asks Van.

'No man, they threw themselves down on each other – whada'you think man – domkop,' Uncle Bob has his arms folded. He's lit up a Texan filter, which is hanging from the side of his mouth.

Van laughs. He doesn't mind that Uncle Bob speaks to him like this. He really looks up to him, because of Uncle Bob's reputation as a crack soldier. He's probably a little bit scared of him too.

'Then Spider – he's called Spider because he can get into anything –' says Glen, 'enemy camps – he scales walls, trees, Spiderman eat your heart out – ja, anyway, he had the sense to throw a grenade, so we saw two of them just flying man, up into the trees –'

'Past Spiderman,' says Uncle Bob, taking a toke on his cigarette.

'We grabbed our weapons and opened fire, for a good few minutes –' he takes another beer from Dad's hands, 'then we ran towards the Elands, there was smoke and branches everywhere, I ran with the rest of them and then I realised I'd left my extra ammo under the tree, where I'd gone to take a dump.'

'Hey, man, you don't dump your ammo when you go dump man, what kind of soldier are you? Bloody shitty soldier man.' Uncle Bob looks round at everyone and laughs loudly.

This time, everyone laughs with Uncle Bob. Glen looks at him and smiles with his mouth but not with his eyes. 'Ja, for a moment I thought I was on a YFC camp, hey, Bob.'

Everyone laughs. 'Anyway I couldn't bloody see a thing man, all the smoke,' Glen says, 'took me a while, I dunno, a coupla minutes maybe, I grab the ammo and then start to run through the smoke in the direction of the vehicles.' He takes a sip of his beer. 'They're moving off, shit, the smoke's still hanging in the air. When the smoke settles I can't see the vehicles – in the direction of the vehicles it's open terrain –'

'Thought you couldn't see them Batman? Or, thought they'd left you behind?' says Uncle Bob.

Glen ignores him.

'Give it a rest, Bob,' says Mom.

'I can't man, she wants it all the time, man.'

Mom glares at him. Auntie Aldie gives him the two fingers. Not sure what that's all about.

'I knew the ous must have thought I was in one of the vehicles,' says Glen, 'or they knew that I'd realised I couldn't follow, because I'd be open target –'

'Ag, they were just trying to get rid of you man,' Uncle Bob inhales with one side of his mouth and exhales with the other, like a comedy pirate.

'I could feel the terrs breathing behind me,' continues Glen, 'I knew they knew I was there.'

'Bloody psychic now hey,' says Uncle Bob. 'Sure it wasn't the wind?'

'Blow it out your arse Bob,' says Glen.

'What the wind?' Uncle Bob opens his mouth wide and gives us a real 'He, he, he,' laugh. Everyone tries not to laugh. I can't help it, though I feel bad. Uncle Bob grins at me. I finger the lucky bean necklace.

'Ja, so,' says Glen, 'I began moving slowly backwards from the direction I thought the terrs were – I knew we'd blown up a couple, and I knew that we'd probably killed a few when we opened fire. It was bloody chaos out there man. But none of us were injured, I was pretty sure that all the ous had made it back to the vehicles. I was on my own without the radio man, and no bloody compass.'

'Ja?' says Uncle Bob. 'What about the men on the other side of the border? Sure they all got out?'

'I can only speak for my lot, not yours Bob. I had to make sure I plotted my direction before the sun went down, but first I had to make sure I stayed alive.'

'Ag ja, wha'da bloody drama man.'

'Give it a rest Bob,' Mom says from the couch.

Change the lingo Mom. Auntie Aldie still stares into her glass. Everyone else stares at Glen, saying 'shit man,' and 'I can't bloody believe it, man.' Dad smiles and shakes his head. Every now and again he makes sort of low whistling noises, which is a bit annoying.

'I belly crawled through the bush, slowly, in those conditions, you don't want to snap a twig – I could hear the bastards in the bush in front of me, so I'm on my belly moving away from Mozambique,' he laughs. 'I didn't bloody want to go back in the direction I'd come from, it was no picnic in there man, we'd had to blow away bloody hundreds, but we got loads of their ammo man, the amount of Soviet shit we picked up in there, man we could start a new war in the bloody Congo.'

'Stick to the bloody plot man.'

'Ja, Glen, one story at a time.'

Everyone cracks up.

'Ja, okay shut up man, bloody peanut gallery.' Glen laughs, so does everyone else. Uncle Bob laughs the loudest.

'So I'm belly-crawling slowly in the opposite direction. I'm expecting a bullet in my back or for someone to pull me by the bloody ankles man.'

'Shit.' Dad gives one of his slow whistles.

'Ja, so eventually I came to a sort of dip, not like a ditch, just a sort of dip in the ground. On the one end, there's sort of a bush, that's hanging over a bit, so I crawl under there to wait it out –'

'Has the sun gone down?' Elaine calls from the couch. Her eyes droop like half-pulled blinds above her red cheeks.

'Ja, see?' Uncle Bob waves his beer at the sky. 'It's dark, man. How many drinks you had Elaine?' Uncle Bob asks her.

Glen laughs.

'No, in the sshtory,' she says.

It's not pretty.

'It's just sinking man, as I crawl under the bush, shit man, seemed bloody ages, moving only inches at a time,' Glen continues, 'I can hear them looking for me, they're so close one of their bloody big toes is practically in my ear. I'm sure they can hear me breathing so I'm playing dead.'

'Ja, you're good at that hey.' Uncle Bob yawns.

Glen snaps and throws his empty bottle at Uncle Bob. It flies past his left ear and lands on the lawn. Auntie Aldie goes inside. Uncle Bob laughs, and standing, takes a knife out of his pocket and holds it up and jumps. He makes a roaring sound and then lands with his knees bent like a Zulu warrior. Everyone laughs, nervously though.

'Just ignore him Glen. He's trying to steal your glory.' Auntie Aldie stands in the doorway holding a glass. Uncle Bob rushes over to her, picks her up and flings her over his shoulder. She spills her drink all over him as she slaps him on the back and screams. Running down the steps and onto the lawn, he dumps Auntie Aldie on the grass, shaking his head and beard, spraying beer everywhere, making a roaring sound like the wild man of Borneo. The audience watch from the veranda.

'That's the way to treat a woman,' says Uncle Bob, coming back up the stairs onto the veranda.

'Bob, you go too far sometimes,' Mom says.

'Ag, she loves it man.'

Auntie Aldie sits on the lawn with her legs out in front of her like a little girl, skirt riding up, blonde curls all over the place, one of the straps of her sundress hanging halfway down her arm. Mom sits down opposite her, placing her jeaned legs over her sister's splayed ones.

'I'm not going home Reen,' she says to the lawn. 'I know he 'spects me to just get up and go home, but I'm not doing it,' Auntie Alds continues to stare at the ground, her voice tearful. 'I'm staying here,' she says. 'I'll bloody sit here till he's ready to leave and then I'll bloody get up and go to a bloody hotel or something.'

'Alds you're not making sense, how many g and t's you had?' Mom asks. 'You stay here tonight.'

'Ja, but I'm not going now. This is my bloody family.'

Mom strokes Auntie Aldie's hair like the older sister she is. 'Don't let him see you cry.'

Over the wall, the dark silhouettes of the jacaranda trees line up like elephant guards along the front fence and on either side of the gates. My eyes catch a movement, John and Phillip landing leopard-footed on the ground, leaping from scoping the scene in the branches of a fir tree. They run along the back fence, hiding behind the large rocks of the rockery, almost tipping over the birdbath, pretending to be soldiers, chuffed at not being seen. A bit later I hear them on the veranda roof, chattering like monkeys. The adults don't notice, they're all bombed, shouting out to Dad about what they want to drink. Glen goes over to Ian and Carls. I get up off the steps and join them.

'Hey, so what weapons did you get?' Ian asks.

He looks so fresh, so eager. I can't believe he's been on call-up, he even has dimples when he smiles. I can't imagine him with a gun. He'd look better on stage, in a play.

'RPG-7, rockets, launchers; AK47s, Russian issue grenades, bazookas.'

Ian laughs. 'No ways man, really?'

'Hey', says Glen, 'You still wet behind the ears? We don't go in for a jol.' They laugh.

'No man, I'm, just, impressed, man.' Ian smiles into his lap. Carla rolls her eyes at me and we laugh. I make like a kid with a gun and she laughs some more.

'Work hard. Go the extra mile. Maybe you'll make the grade.'

'I hope so man.'

Van and Dad start up on Glen, 'Finish the story man.'

'Ja. Finish man Glen, before the sun comes up – hey Elaine?' says Uncle Bob.

'Wha – ?' says Elaine, raising her chin from her chest. Her eyes swim with confusion.

'Ja, I'll finish quickly, so you can tell some of your stories hey, Bob?'

'Ja, you finish everything quickly hey?'

'Don't rise to it Glen,' Mom says. 'We want to hear. We're all bloody proud of you.'

'Ja, we like to hear stories about real heroes,' says Auntie Aldie from where she sits, back on the couch for part two.

'Aaah, you've impressed the ladies, man Glen.' Uncle Bob makes sort of kissy lips at him. This makes Glen laugh.

'Shut up Bob, or no more beers,' Mom says. Uncle Bob bends down from his chair and puts his hand on my shoulder. He whispers, 'No more beers hey Jay, you'll have to belly-crawl me some.'

I laugh.

'Okay so, I just lie there,' Glen says. 'Eventually I figure they've left, and I may as well try to make it to the road. I've still got my weapon, I figure to walk to the main road and then hitch, only problem is, I dunno where the bloody main road is –'

'Shit hey?' says Van.

'I walk south. If I come to any villages before that, I figure I'll pick me up a little guide.'

'Ja, a little lady guide, hey Glen,' Uncle Bob wiggles his hips on his chair.

'Nope, but they will always help with a little persuasion, hey Bob.'

'Ja, anyway, I found the road to Rhodesia before I found anyone. Only person I ran into was an old man walking along to the nearest village store. He put up his hands when he saw me, think he thought I was gonna blow him away.'

'Ja, scaring the madalas now hey?' Dad laughs.

'Ja. Made him come to the store and buy me a Coke.'

'Why?' I ask.

'Well it was either that or use my gun. I had no money and I was bloody thirsty –'

Everyone laughs.

'Then I'm walking along, making for the farm, a truck drives by, and guess who's in it? Van! Man, can you bloody believe it?'

'I gave him the bloody skrik of his life man.'

'I said, Give us a lift Van.'

'He nearly hit the roof – you know what he said? He said, "Shit man, I thought you were dead."'

'Shit man,' everyone says.

'Dad gives a low whistle and puts his arm around Glen's shoulder. 'You're a true bloody Rhodesian man,' he pats Glen on the cheek. Man, he's getting embarrassing, I'm double glad Mel's not here. Over in the corner, where he's been drinking brandy with May, Uncle Joe wipes a tear from his cheek.

Glen looks at me, slaps his bum twice, so I jump on his back, and he gallops me all over the front lawn. Eat your heart out Mel.

'Why don't you tell your story Bob?' he shouts.

'Nah. I didn't get lost. And I keep my bedtime stories to myself,' says Uncle Bob.

15.

It's hotter than an elephant's backside. Near the petrol station, Dad leans up against the car, arms folded, talking to the guy from the car in front. African attendants in red overalls pour petrol into the cars upfront. Mom has gone down south to Kariba with Auntie Aldie to spend money she won in the sweepstakes, John's staying with Phillip and the rest of us are on the way to see Uncle Pat and Auntie Gail in Bindura. Carla's in the front seat putting make-up on in the rear-view mirror, despite the fact that we're headed for the bush and no-one except the monkeys and the snakes are going to see her. *Radio Jac-a-randa! Doo, do-oo, bee, do!* Carla sings, mimicking the tune on the radio. Dad leans in through my window.

'Turn the bloody radio down. You're not at the bloody disco now.'

'I'm never at the bloody disco, I'm too bloody young!' But Dad doesn't hear, luckily, or I'd probably get a klup. Carla laughs.

'I'll take you to a bloody disco soon Jay.'

'Ja? When?'

'When you're fourteen, that's when I first went.'

'So I should go a year earlier then,' I slump back in my seat. 'Second in line, gota shave off time.'

She laughs. 'No way Jose. Next year. You can go with Ian's little boet.'

'Ja really, he's a real Frikkie.'

Carls laughs some more. 'He's cute man.'

'Ja, and so are spaniels, but I don't want them yapping in my ears at the disco.'

'Or licking you with their long wet tongues.' Carla winks at me.

'Sis man, Carls, you're really gross sometimes.'

Carla laughs. 'There'll come a day when you won't mind being licked.' She leans over the seat and runs her tongue all over the lip-gloss on her top lip.

I give her my best Marlon Brando look and turn the radio up, flick my legs over the front seat and settle my upper body on the back seat, almost lying down. Dad leans in again.

'Turn that bloody thing down!' I turn it down. Carla blots her lips on a crumpled up pink tissue. Dad's conversation is louder than the music. Carla sings along to the song about lovers and Liverpool, yuck, liver-in-a-pool, using her fist as a mike. Ian's probably her short-haired lover from Chiredzi.

'Bloody sanctions hey. How long you been waiting?' Dad asks the man in front of him.

'Ag hours man.' He puts his hands in the pockets of his shorts. I notice a comb sticking out from the back of one of his knee-length socks. 'Bloody Poms hey?'

'Ja bloody bastards, but they won't break us.' Dad cups his hands over his cigarette to light it. He always lights up this way, as if there's a wind blowing or something. There hardly ever is. 'Where you off to?' he asks.

'Ag just need petrol man. The wife still needs to shop, even though there's nothing to buy hey.'

'Ja she can still waste your money having tea at Meikles or Barbour's.'

They both laugh and the queue moves forward. The conversation doesn't.

'Where you off to?'

'Bindura.'

'Oh ja, Bindura. D'you know the Pattersons?'

Auntie Gail comes out to greet us accompanied by a pack of dogs of various height style colour and smell. One in particular smells like the chicken house. They leap all over us. The St Bernard dribbles a cup-load of spit all over my carved wood and leather clogs. Gross. I wipe it on the grass.

'That's what you call a spit and a polish.' Auntie Gail laughs.

We are sitting on the veranda drinking tea from heavy brown pottery cups made by Auntie Gail on her pottery wheel. When she's not working as a doctor at the local clinic, Auntie Gail spends hours in her barn studio, throwing clay. Her efforts are displayed all over the house, double glazed plant pots on the veranda, clay ash-trays with curled up edges on the tables, heavy mugs, plates and serving dishes in the kitchen decorated with all the different colour glazes Auntie Gail could get her hands on, then all whacked on together. She often has clay in her wavy, steel-grey hair and little splatters of the stuff on her half-rimmed glasses. The arms and legs that protrude from her sleeveless cotton dress as she pours the tea are a deep tan, so is her face, which still looks young. She doesn't look as if she should have grey hair at all.

Uncle Pat sits down at the table.

'Hello all. Good trip? Stop at the craft stall? There's some lovely little soapstones, local sculptors. Some of our boys sell there.'

'Not this time,' says Dad, 'Irene's the one who likes the sculpture.'

'Ah yes,' he says. He slaps the floppy rolled-up hat he's had in his hands on the table and wipes the sweat from the back of his neck. He looks Carla up and down.

'Who's this?' he jokes. 'Last time I saw you could've sworn you were a little girl.'

Carla smiles and pulls her yellow t-shirt down, squashing for a moment her perfect 34 Bs.

'And you?' he says to me. 'Still a tomboy?'

'Ja,' I say, popping my gum. 'Always.'

'How's the crop?' asks Dad.

'Okay. We'll survive. But we're in debt to our eyeballs. Everything I own belongs to the bloody government. I'm a sitting tenant.'

'A sitting duck hey? We all are,' Dad says.

'No politics today, gentlemen,' says Auntie Gail. The men ignore her. She rolls her eyes at me and Carla.

'You girls can have a turn on the wheel after your walk if you like.'

'Lekker, thanks,' I say.

'What're the farmers round here saying? Matter of time?' asks Dad.

Uncle Pat smiles, 'Us farmers will never leave.'

Dad looks down. As if Uncle Pat can read his thoughts he says, 'Coffee's gonna be the next big thing, you should get your farm manager to clear some land, there's gonna be a whole lot more room for more coffee, you should try it. Maybe it'll be easier for you to sell the farm if you do.'

Over my dead body. If they sell Angel's Peak I'll hitch up there and kill myself on my rock overlooking the mountains with a dagger to my middle Japanese style. I train my gun eyes on Dad but he keeps looking at his hands.

'Maybe I will,' says Dad, he smiles at Auntie Gail as she hands him his tea. 'Ja, maybe I will. When they stop calling me up.'

'How's the young manager getting along?'

'Fine,' says Dad, 'spoke to him this morning. And Granny Rose. She hasn't been well and the New Zealand nurse is getting on her nerves. We're running at a loss,' he says.

'Any news on Justice?'

'CIO are onto him. Apparently he's quite the honcho.'

'The boys are in the macadamia sheds, sorting.' Uncle Pat smiles at me. 'Go say hello.'

From the lawn, acres and acres of pond-green tobacco fields stretch out before me like the Cashel Valley advert. From here on the ridge in front of the house, the tobacco barns look like monopoly pieces on the horizon. A slight breeze makes the hairs on my arm stand up but not because I'm cold. I just feel scared, thinking about Justice. I focus on the tobacco plants but imagine terrs creeping up on us, so run the rest of the way to the barn. Anthony and Neil are standing in front of the wooden tables, framed so the nuts don't roll off. They are taller, browner and lankier than ever. They've got a new kind of angularity about them. Their shoulders have widened, but the flesh hasn't had time to pack itself around the bone. Last time I saw them, Neil's voice was kind of high and Anthony's was deep but would crack every now and again. They're much deeper now. They're running their hands over the nuts.

'Howzit Jay, god iny nut jokes?' Neil asks. He holds a nut up and then flings it into the waste chute.

'No.'

'Wanna hear some?'

'No.'

'Wanna see some?'

'I can see plenty.' I slide the palm of my hand over the nuts. Their surfaces massage my hand.

Anthony grabs his sixteen-year-old crotch. 'I think he wants to show you his nuts.'

I look at him, 'Are you nuts?' I ask, picking up a handful of nuts and walking towards the cracking machine on the huge counter behind Neil. I insert the nuts into the cold metal clamp. A faint whiff of iron comes off it.

'Whez your big sister?' says Anthony.

'Ant wants to show her his nuts,' says Neil.

'Ja, that would really impress her.'

'Why? She seen nuts before?' says Ant.

'Don't you think of anything else?'

'Wha'da you mean Jay? You gota dirty mind.'

I turn back to the machine. I'm having trouble getting it to work. Neil comes up behind me, 'Here, let me help.' He presses in close.

'No thanks.'

He presses in again. 'Can you feel my nuts?'

I tread down on the front of his foot with my clog. As I run from the shed up the sloping lawn, I can hear Neil swearing and Anthony laughing.

Dinner that evening is boerewors and sadza with spinach and carrots, all served with a frown by Jameson. He takes his cooking very seriously and doesn't understand why we want to eat sadza and wors instead of something like roast beef or chicken. But sadza and wors is Dad and Uncle Pat's favourite meal. Granny Rose and Grandpa Patrick started a tradition of making it for the workers after harvest time. When they were kids, Dad and Uncle Pat loved being at their grandparents' for the celebration. There would be huge fires in the metal petrol drums, orange sparks popping against the charcoal sky, flying ants spinning in the smoke, moths as big as bats illuminated under the trees, coils of boerewors like dead bush snakes spitting on the braai, their beery, garlicky smell making everyone's mouths water. The adults are talking about land and what'll happen to it if the terrs get in.

'We have a right to this land,' said Uncle Pat. 'We nurtured it. We don't mind sharing it though.'

'As long as they don't mind us training them up,' Dad laughs. 'We try all the time on the TTLs. They don't wanna be trained. They're throwing government money into the dust. We say to the ones that are trained – to the doctors and nurses and teachers – stay. Teach your people. Treat your people. But they won't. They wanna car. Fine, geda car. But no. They want the city. A house in the suburbs. Their black MPs are wasting their bloody time. And your black farmer? He wants your land. But he doesn't wanna work for it. Or work it. It's his because his ancestors say so. Never mind that his ancestors may have come from the Sahara. No, it'll never work. Culturally we're just too different.'

'Well then,' says Auntie Gail, 'you need to try another approach. You can't just expect people from other cultures to adapt to the ways of the white men. You've got to meet them halfway.'

'And what do you suggest Madam Gail,' Dad says, spearing wors and putting it into his mouth.

'I don't know. Tree planting?' Gail says. Dad laughs.

'You bloody hippie Gail,' he says chewing, 'you and Nessie, one of a kind man.' He swallows and taking up his beer, stares at the bottle.

'We saw Nessie a few weeks ago, Dave. She misses you.'

'Ja. Well. I don't wanna talk about my sister, hey,' he smiles at her. 'You serious about the trees?'

She smiles back. 'I'm serious about the trees, Africans love trees, they're often sacred to their culture –'

Dad laughs.

'Hear me out. They cultivate their trees, the ancestors are appeased, trees yield good crops.'

Dad laughs again.

'I'm serious. You should take this to the TTDA. Look at the baobab for instance. You can make clothes out of it, cream of tartar –'

'Doro – beer,' says Dad, holding up his bottle. 'Why not get them growing the marijuana plant while you're at it? Make clothes out of that and get vrot at the same time.'

Uncle Pat laughs. So does Auntie Gail.

'Look, think of wattle – paper – paper for school books, for education.' She turns her right palm upwards. 'You need to empower them from the grassroots,' she says waving her upturned hand. 'Look at their culture. Not the culture of the west. How would you like it if they tried to foist their culture on you?'

'They're trying. Bloody terrs are anyway.' Dad laughs.

'Don't be so bloody narrow-minded Dave, you work for the TTDA.'

'Ja, that's why I'm so depressed man.'

Uncle Pat smiles and gets up to get more beers.

'Look, we need to look at ways of working together,' says Auntie Gail. 'I'm not moving my family. We're staying. No matter what happens. My children are African.'

I look at her children, two gangly blonde guys born a year apart. They look like twins, splayed on the couch watching the news. Two proper Rhodie boys, even more Rhodie than their parents, happiest in the bush with guns in their hands.

Gail continues, 'My parents are African. I don't care what colour they were. We're born here. We're not leaving this land. Sharing, learning from each other is the way forward. To help set up. It's up to them what they wanna grow,' she smiles. 'I don't know if it's gonna be tobacco though,' she takes a sip of her beer, 'for some, maybe.'

'Shit, Gail, our boys are out there turning into biltong in the heat and you're already defeated. It'll never work. Trust me, if the terrs get in the politicians will lead the way with raping the profits of the land and those in management and administration will follow. The people will end up starving. It'll be a bloody Marxist farce. You're an idealist Gail.'

'And you're a pessimist.'

'No. I'm a realist.' Dad puts his fork down. He looks like he's about to cry. 'I miss the farm man.'

Auntie Gail touches his arm. I can't stand it, him looking like that. A lump bobs in my throat like a marble. Carla gives me a lamie. 'Einah man!' I rub the spot on my upper arm where her knuckles have left a mark.

'C'mon, lets watch Sounds on Saturday.'

16.

Our feet crunch on fallen grey twigs and sticks as our legs move steadily through the pale, dry grass that rises above our knees. Msasas, massed above us, give patchy shade, their leaves small, their branches skinny and thorny. Through the trees we see them, like the rumps of silent grey elephants, balancing rocks. Closer, more and more rocks loom into view, bulging out of the escarpment, some the size of small houses, others, stacked up on the ground, the height of huts, still more the height of cars. Dad and Uncle Pat and the boys are laughing about the name 'Bindura' and how it got its name in the first place.

'It's a meshing of the Shona phrase 'Chi pindura mhuka.''

'I drink chibuku in Bindura,' says Anthony. Neil laughs. 'It means 'turning of the game,' and there's a story attached to that,' says Uncle Pat.

'No jokes Dad.' Neil is mocking because Uncle Pat's a bit of an amateur historian. He's a member of the National Executive of the Rhodesiana Society. He loves European settler history as well as Shona history. Some of the European farmers around here call him a kaffir lover. Even Uncle Joe calls him a kaffir lover, but only as a joke, because he spends a lot of time talking to his workers, finding out about their families.

'Ja. But that's not all it means,' says Dad, winking at Uncle Pat.

Uncle Pat laughs. 'Not in front of the ladies, hey.' He ruffles my hair. If I was a lady, he wouldn't be ruffling my hair.

'Oh ja, bitch in season, that's what it means, hey Dad?' Ant shouts it over his shoulder as he jogs ahead towards something that's moved in the bush. Raising his rifle, he squints through the sights and then lowers it. Whatever it was was quicker than him.

'Or place of fornication.' He looks back at us, the rifle in his hand. His blonde hair and khaki shorts and top are the same colours of the bush. But he doesn't blend in. The animals run away from him.

'Why're they so disgusting?' Carla asks. But Dad and Uncle Pat just laugh. Ous will be ous, hey.

The afternoon is suspended in heat. We begin to move in and out of the rocks while the sun beats down on our backs and the insects nose dive our flesh and screech in the bush. Uncle Pat puts down his rifle on the bush floor and runs his fingers over the rock as if feeling for clues. The rock nearest to me feels like a tarmac road beneath my fingers. It's about three times my size, with a fissure that nearly splits it into two equal halves.

'It looks like a bum,' Neil says.

'Ja, with hair in the middle,' says Anthony, referring to the dried scrub sprouting from the cleft of the rock.

Carla sighs, and takes a running jump to scramble up the rock. Placing her foot inside the cleft, she uses her fingertips to haul herself up, then she scales the rock that balances on top of the other one, till she stands above us, hands on hips, jeans rolled up, pink top, yellow tackies on her feet. She lifts one leg straight up and holds it by the ankle as if it's a spear in her hand, her upper body forming a 'u' shape. Behind her a tree looms above her like a bogey-man. She blows a pink bubble with her bubble-gum. It explodes all over her face. The cousins laugh while she picks it off.

'Nice one Carls,' says Neil.

Neil points his air rifle at her and pretends to shoot.

Carla looks at him as she chews slowly, not blinking. I roll my eyes up at her.

'This looks like a sable,' Uncle Pat says, tracing his finger on the rock over the ochre animal. It has one oblong body, one triangle with a couple of little triangles attached to the sides of the head and four faint dashes for legs. How can he tell it's a sable? It could be a kudu or a roan, or even a cow.

'D'you think it's okay to touch them?' I ask. No answer.

'This one looks like a kudu Dad,' Anthony says. 'Like the one you shot.' I picture the kudu skin on the floor of Uncle Pat and Auntie Gail's lounge. Its beautiful tan skin with its white stripes and the little tail sticking out, flattened on the floor, like we were on the day we thought we might die, its long, spiralled horns hanging on the wall of the veranda.

I scramble up the rock to join Carla.

'Look at the baboons Jay,' she says, gesturing to our cousins.

We laugh. Both are bent over with their hands on their knees.

'All men, Jay, are baboons in a way.' We laugh some more.

'*Eland, Kudu, Sable, Roan, who will take the trophy home,*' I chant at Carla; my fist punches the air, the chant of our old sports house at school. Carla laughs.

'Eland!' she chants back. Uncle Pat and the boys have stopped examining the Bushman paintings and talk about hunting, about how there are not many sable left, not many roan, only smaller buck like duiker. Neil stands with one veldskoened foot up on the rock face. They've all been hunted. By men and boys like them, by the men and the boys in the little rusty rock paintings.

Carla and I turn at the sharp crack of a trodden twig. We look behind us. A teenage African boy appears from behind a tree. A bow is strung round his back and shoulders and he carries a catapult in his hands. He wears only tatty trousers, and I can see the muscles on his back and on his thin arms. For a moment I think I've conjured Enoch up, like a spook. He looks at us for a moment, and then turns and, like a sable, vanishes into the bush.

Moving to another outcrop of rocks, we search long and hard, but don't find any other Bushmen paintings, till Uncle Pat calls us over to some lowish rocks, not much taller than himself.

'Look! Here's a whole row of little figures, kneeling down,'

'They look like they're worshipping or something,' Dad says.

'They're a chorus line,' says Carla.

'Ja really,' Anthony bends over to look. Neil pushes his bum and he falls into Carla.

'Get off me you doos!' Carla yells.

'Actually, Carls, they may be a chorus line, bushmen women are sometimes shown in a chorus line,' says Uncle Pat.

'Naah, man they're just women washing, like they're supposed to,' says Anthony.

'This looks like a monkey,' says Uncle Pat. 'Which reminds me, you know, this area used to be occupied by a chief called Chipadze –'

'Sure that wasn't the monkey,' says Anthony, 'chimp-addzee, chimp-an-zee.'

'Ja, no diffs, anyway,' says Neil. He leans over. 'Can you see any tits?'

'Shut-up, you might learn something,' Uncle Pat says.

'Tell me, Uncle Pat,' I say.

'Tell me Uncle Pat.' Neil's impression of me is actually quite good.

'Voetsak man,' says Uncle Pat. 'Go find a buck or something.' He throws a stick at Neil, he smiles though. Neil and Anthony walk away, rifles in their hands. We hear the 'pings' of their shots as they fire out in the bush. Uncle Pat turns to me.

'Okay, right, there's this chief.'

'Chipadza.'

'No not chipadza, like sadza, Chipadze. He was of the monkey totem tribe –'

I laugh. Uncle Pat does too.

'Ja. But don't tell Ant and Neil. And this chief occupied these lands. One day, a relative of Chipadze's came to settle here, he was of the Nyoni – bird totem – anyway, this relative married one of the chief's daughters. One day, when the chief was resting, he snuck up on him and killed him. The dead man's tribal spirits came to haunt Bindura hill, so Nyoni made a deal with the spirit to keep up the tribe's religious rituals. In exchange, the spirit would supply meat for the people.'

'Is that all?'

'Whada'you mean. Is that all? Not exciting enough for you Jay?'

'No, I just wanna hear more.'

'Okay, so once a year – see that flat rock over there? So once a year, an ox was taken to that flat rock; when the chief raised his hand, the dungwi –'

'Dungweed?'

Uncle Pat laughs, 'The dungwi, a sort of high priest, grabbed the animal by the horns. If the animal died, a message was sent out to the kraals, letting them know that the wild animals could be turned down at the chief's grave.'

'What do you mean turned?'

'Well, like turned towards the village. So that they could be eaten.'

'Urgh, that's gross.'

'Why do you think it's gross, Carla? It's no more gross than piling cattle into a truck and slitting their throats at an abattoir.'

'That's gross too. Anyway, I don't eat meat.'

'Since when?' I ask.

'Since today. Let's go for a walk.'

She hardly eats anything at all, never mind meat.

Carla and I walk in and out of the rocks, running our fingers over the grey and brown lichen-stained surfaces. Near the lip of the drop away into the valley, a huge rock sits heavily between a crop of little rocks that cluster on either side of it. The rock is split into two halves, as if the hand of God had come down from heaven with a massive karate chop. The crevice is narrow, but we walk towards it and slip into its long, cool, opening. A huge shaft of light blocks out the opposite end. My hands are around Carla's waist as she inches slowly forwards in front of me.

'It's like Aladdin's cave. I wonder what we'll find.'

'Rub the walls and see what happens.' I trail my fingers on the rock walls as my eyes adjust to the gloom. A musty, lichen smell pervades my nostrils. And then, like a photograph appearing in the photographer's chemical bath, we see them. Masses of them, sharp and geometric, richly bronzed, as if they were only just painted yesterday.

'Wow.'

It's like a miraculous vision. Miniature ochre men stab at strange looking cows with long necks and triangular heads. Beautifully painted buck leap high above the spears, their horns stretching out from their heads, showers of little arrows litter the sky like needles of rain. To one side, an antelope lies with its legs in the air, a spear sticking out of its oblong body. Further along the cave wall, painted men crouch with bows, taking aim at other, bigger men.

'Do you think they're white men?' I ask Carla.

'Maybe. Uncle Pat would know.'

The light shifts. For a moment we are in gloom as a cloud passes over the sun. We look at each other.

'Let's explore,' Carla presses my hand.

'It feels kind of creepy, like we shouldn't be here or something.'

Godfrey told me that the places where the Bushmen paintings are found are sacred places. The spirits of the painted ones keep watch. If you upset them, they can enter into you and drive you mad, or make all your cattle fall over the cliffs or come down with a deadly disease, like the Rinderpest that killed all of Granny Rose and Grandpa Patrick's cattle when they first settled the farm in Umtali. The gloom makes me shiver.

'Carls, I think we should go!'

As I step backwards into a pile of leaves, a sharp swish makes me scream. Carla grabs me and we turn round and press our bodies to the rock face. A cobra rears up at us from its bed of leaves, its hood spread, its tongue flicking delicately in and out as it sways. We press ourselves into the rock, wanting to be swallowed, to join the Bushmen, to be still. The snake sways some more, and then darts its upper body at us, once, twice, a warning. And then Carla screams. Her scream echoes up to the sky. The snake shoots out of the crevice into the sunlight.

'Oh my God, Carls, lets go.'

Carla says nothing. We don't want to go out the way we came in, we don't want to exit by the same route as the snake. Her pupils dilate like the moon reflected in the night sea as she pulls me towards the entrance and the tide of my blood moves in me. She pulls me deeper into the crevice, towards where the sun shines brightest on the other side. The crevice narrows.

'No! Carls! It's too narrow.'

'No, we can make it. Hell we're only thin.'

I laugh, but only because she has said 'hell' in the way that Dad or Uncle Joe uses it.

She pulls me in further. The crevice gets narrower.

'What if we get stuck?'

'We won't.' Carla's cheeks are red in her pale face. She steps up on a little rock that guards the opening at the other end, her head against blue sky, like a statue. The sun is directly in our faces so that the opening can't be seen clearly. I close my eyes for a moment and when I open them I see black spots.

'Come,' she holds out her hand.

I take it, but before I can step up, Carla steps down. She makes no sound as she disappears. I look down, not hearing anything except the blood pounding in my ears. The valley slopes downward sharply, the landscape is tight dark-green bush with rock showing through here and there. The sky is a cloudless blue dome, trapping the shimmering heat. And then, I see her. She's lying on her side, her legs drawn towards her chest as if she's asleep, obscured slightly by a rocky overhang. The grasses around her look bed-soft, but her head lies amongst scrub on flat grey rock. My chest begins to thud. Turning round, I break into a run. The rocks are everywhere, scattered like my shattered mind. I'm in a rock maze, hearing my voice as it shouts, as if it's coming from somewhere else. Two fingers jab me on either side, causing a scream that doesn't seem to come from me. Swinging round, I look into the face of my cousin, Neil.

'What's your case Jay?'

'Ja, your hair looks really lekker with all those leaves in it.' Anthony leans on a big stick as if he's just finished a long trek.

'It's Carla.' They look at me. 'Carla,' I mentally grope, looking for the words to explain, 'she's fallen.'

'Ja, like vanished? Or off walking?'

'Where's Dad?'

'T'runno,' says Neil.

'What do you mean you don't know!' I kick him hard in the shin.

'Jeez, man.' He stops smiling. 'Back there.'

I run in the direction of Anthony's jabbed thumb. Dad and Uncle Pat are crouching down near a crop of rocks behind Neil.

'Dad!'

It only takes Dad a second to scramble down over the rocks and scrub to get to the clearing where Carla lies. Uncle Pat goes down with him. For a moment they crouch down beside her, looking at her, pressing her. Dad puts his head near her face, against her chest. Uncle Pat is feeling her wrist. I can't bear it. They're taking too long, so I start to come down. Dad waves me back. Uncle Pat gets up and starts climbing back up to the lip of the escarpment. He runs past me towards the Land Rover. The boys run too. They hop in and drive off, bumping over the rocky dirt track, the engine grinding and protesting.

I slide down the kopje on my heels and bum till I'm down there too. Dad's FN lies on the floor next to him. Carla appears to be asleep, she looks so peaceful.

'Dad?'

'She's not dead.'

'Why isn't she moving?'

'She's unconscious.' Dad lays his hand lightly on Carla's chest. I think I can see it going up and down, but I'm not sure.

'What's going to happen?'

'Uncle Pat's going to radio for help from the farm.'

Dad doesn't ask me what's happened, nor does he take his eyes off Carla. He begins to stroke her hair, pulling some of it up through his fingers. Tears slide slowly down his face and drip onto Carla's chest. Dad looks at his wristwatch occasionally. Apart from that he stares at Carla. The sun stings my shoulders, Christmas beetles sing loudly in the bush and Dad's neck in his army issue cap turns a deeper reddish brown. When help finally arrives, it's not an ambulance, nor a helicopter. It's Auntie Gail in the Land Rover, with two African men, and a stretcher, with a khaki bag on top.

'Where's the bloody ambulance?'

'Couldn't come over the bush. It's waiting on the main road.'

'The helicopter then.'

'All in service. War remember?'

'No, I bloody forgot.'

Auntie Gail touches Dad's arm.

'Let's check her and get her onto the stretcher.' Auntie Gail feels her pulse and listens to her chest.

'We've done that.'

Then she goes behind Carla's head and gently puts her fingers under her neck.

'The splints.'

One of the men hands her a splint wrapped in bandage that she slides under Carla's neck. He hands her another two, she places them on either side of Carla's neck and quickly bandages around Carla's neck and chest.

'Right, plank.' Auntie Gail slides the large plank under Carla's body.

'Shouldn't you correct her legs first?'

'I've done this before, Dave.'

Auntie Gail and the boys slide the plank under Carla's torso. The men from the hospital help her.

'Shit man, she's not a sack of bloody potatoes,' says Dad. Auntie Gail looks up at Dad through her half-rimmed glasses, Carla's legs in her arms. It takes a long time for them to get her onto the stretcher. Auntie Gail spends ages straightening her legs.

'This one's broken.'

'Shit.'

It's like slow motion, with Carla as the bionic woman. They strap her onto the stretcher till she's rigid, like a mummy, her face no longer flushed, but the same colour as the bandage.

Dad drives. I sit in the back with Auntie Gail and one of the men from the hospital, who looks out of his window. The back of the bakkie is piled with sacks – another bed for Carla to lie on. Auntie Gail looks at me from the other side of Carla. 'You okay?'

'Ja.'

'I'll get you a cup of tea with lots of sugar in it when we get to the clinic.' She has Carla's wrist in her hand. Dad seems to be going quite slowly. Auntie Gail bangs on the back window. 'Go faster!'

'I don't want to bloody kill her!' Dad shouts into the wind.

'You won't! Go faster!' He speeds up. We bump up and down, so does Carla. I imagine the broken bones in Carla's leg, a big white bone split into three white bone hyphens, suspended in warm red blood. We get to the end of the bush track and then turn onto the dirt road towards the main road where the white ambulance waits.

'Keep driving.'

'What?'

'Keep driving.' She gestures at the ambulance-men who are

leaning up against the ambulance, signalling her arm in the direction of the clinic. The men jump into the ambulance and put the siren on.

'What's the point of that?' I ask.

'They'll go before us, we'll follow directly behind, clinic will be on standby.'

When we get to the clinic, it's the ambulance men that lift Carla out of the Land Rover and take her through the glass doors into the low red brick building with purple bougainvillea climbing up the one side. I don't want to go inside just yet, so I sit outside on the burnt yellow grass, picking at it, the sun burning through my back. People going in and out of the building turn to look at me as they pass. An African lady in a white uniform brings me a cup of tea. There's lots of sugar in it. When I've drunk it, I get up and go inside. For a moment, I cannot see, it was so bright outside and it's too dark in here. When my eyes adjust, I see the African nurse who brought me the tea sitting at the reception desk and am about to ask her where my Dad is when I notice him at the far end of the corridor speaking on the phone. Mom. She's going to kill him. Bet he's glad she's in Kariba. I sit down on one of the grey plastic chairs against the wall, diagonally across from him. The ammonia-pine smell of disinfectant makes me feel sick again. Suddenly Dad starts shouting.

'It's not my bloody fault! She's bloody lying there! You bloody blaming me? Shit man!' Dad keeps running his hand through his hair. 'I don't bloody know if she'll DANCE again, Irene! I don't bloody know if she'll WALK again!' I swing my feet and look at the white bits in the grey lino on the floor. The lino bits begin to drift. I see little white boats on a stormy grey sea. Auntie Gail comes out of the room from across the hall where they have Carla. She sits down next to me. Dad slams the phone down when he sees her and comes and sits down on the other side of her.

'Well?'

'Well, we're moving her to the Andrew Fleming.'

'Why? When?'

'She needs to be scanned. We don't have the equipment here.'

'Is she still unconscious?'

'Yes, she's had a nasty fall. They'd keep her under anyway.'

'Why?'

'For the trip.'

'I want to see her.'

She pats Dad's hand. 'It's looking better than I thought.'

'You can travel with her, if you like.' She turns to me. 'And you Jay, how about staying with me and the boys for a few days?

Good. I don't want to go home. No one has asked me what happened and I don't want them to. It feels like somehow it was my fault. Dad gets up with Auntie Gail.

'Stay there,' she says, 'I'll be right back, and then we'll go and get a cool drink and some magazines or something, okay?'

Dad starts walking off down the corridor. He doesn't even say goodbye to me. Maybe he's forgotten? Halfway down the corridor he turns back and looks at me.

'What happened? Why did you go off on your own? What were you playing at?'

Looking at Dad I don't know what to say, so I say, 'I don't know.'

'Whada'you mean, you don't know? You were there weren't you?'

Auntie Gail takes his arm, 'Come on Dave, now, you know it's not her fault, can't you see the child's in shock?'

The white bits in the lino are no longer swimming. They are fixed hard into the grey. Kicking my heels against the chair legs till they hurt, I stare at them, squinting my eyes at the little white boats that seem to be sinking.

17.

Leaves large as elephant ears kiss my bare arms. There's no sound but the faint rustle of the tobacco leaves as I walk, my open palms stroking the leaves, my wandering fingers dewy with their moisture. There's no breath to the warm air, just a whiff of earthy vanilla, dry, sweet and heady. These leaves are born to die, born to be smoked, not even to be eaten, to give life. I think it was the Red Indians who thought of doing it in the first place. Maybe that was their revenge on the white races that stole their land. I'm going to walk and walk as far as I can before turning back when the sun sets. Maybe I won't go back at all. I'll just vanish into the tobacco plants like smoke. And then I'll haunt this land forever. A tobacco flower girl drifting on hot air.

The tobacco sheds are cool. They smell like rooibos tea and honey mixed with smoky earth. The furnaces on either side of the barn pump hot air into the interior. The wives of the workers sit on the floor on mats, tying the tobacco into bunches and tossing them onto piles. They sing and chat, rocking their babies on their backs, working steadily, as if generated by the furnace. Above, suspended on lateral poles, the tobacco hangs drying like hundreds of vast withered brown bats. The hot air causes them to move like lazy fans, slowly twisting this way and that in the steady drone of the furnaces and the hypnotic beat of the heat. Outside, the men are bundling and pressing the tobacco into huge square bales, ready to take to the floors in Salisbury. Here the men shout and sing loudly, slap their gumboots, whistle, laugh, the trickling sweat pouring down their backs. A worker stands on the back of the lorry, positioning bales. Uncle Pat stands near the large wheels, smoking, one foot in the interior groove of the wheel. Tonight there'll be a party in the compound, lots of doro for the workers to get drunk on, dancing and smoking, because each worker is worth his weight in tobacco.

The sun has formed a shadow grid across my legs as it hits them from in between the wire mesh of the table. The tiles near the wall of the veranda are hot, hot, hot. Two little black beetles scurry along the baking grooves of the top step of the veranda, pushing a bit of toast or something from this morning's breakfast. The phone rings. I jump. The sound echoes down the passage to me from the kitchen sideboard, ominous rings from a heavy old Bakelite phone, like something from a Hitchcock film. It rings again, four short bursts and then a long one, the trills of the party line. The phone rings again. I almost get up, but then I hear Auntie Gail's voice.

'That's fantastic news!'

I slump back in the wire chair too heavily and hurt my back between my shoulder blades. It feels good, like a reminder of being alive. 'Do you want to speak to her?' I hear Auntie Gail say. I rub black lead all over the background of my drawing of a rose bush.

'Okay. Tomorrow then.'

Auntie Gail's footsteps echo down the dark hall. She comes out in a denim apron smeared with clay, a pen in her hair. She smiles.

'Great news.'

Leaning forward, her hands on the wire chair opposite me, she says, 'Your sister's awake and asking for food.'

I don't know which is weirder. The fact that she's awake or the fact that she's asking for food. As I watch, the two beetles drop over the edge of the step at the far point from where they started.

Back home, Mel phones as I'm dumping the art stuff Auntie Gail gave me in my room. She thinks I'm an artist like Granny Rose.

'I've got something to tell you.'

My stomach folds in half. I sit down on the hallway step, bags on the floor and let Piddle jump on my lap.

'What?' I ask, wiping away Piddle's face licks.

'I'm going out with Glen.'

'How? When?' I peel the nail varnish from my big toenail.

'When you were away. I hitched to Mazoe to see him.'

'You hitched to Mazoe?'

Patience clatters around in the kitchen making tea. The sounds annoy me and I almost ask her to be quiet, even though I know it'd be cheeky, but then she smiles at me and I almost slam the phone down on Mel because I'd rather shoot the breeze with her than listen to Mel's twisted tale.

'Ja. It was my birthday and I wanted a present.'

'What did he say?'

'He was surprised. But dare I say pleased.'

'Dare I say? Are you penga Mel?'

Mel laughs.

'So how did it happen?'

From their wedding picture on the hall wall, Mom smiles up at Dad looking about sixteen in her medieval-looking dress with white flowers pinned to her lace veil.

'He gave me a lift back home.'

'And?'

'I kissed him at the gate.'

'He kissed you back?' From the photo, Dad beams at me from a mutton-chop sideburned face. He seems so happy.

My sister nearly died and all this time she was plotting to get off with our uncle.

'Dir.'

'Mel you're fifteen.'

'Not anymore. I told you. You missed my birthday. I'm sixteen.'

Slapping my palm on the wall, I let it slide. It leaves a ghostly imprint. Patience looks down at me and smiles, a mug of tea in her hands. I feel like hugging her doughy brown knees where they protrude from her blue house dress but obviously I don't.

'Thanks, Pashe,' I say reaching up for the mug.

'Welcome home,' she says, her smile as wide as a couch.

Ja. Welcome home. Thanks Mel.

18.

Carla's been moved from intensive care at the Andrew Fleming hospital in town. She doesn't remember a thing, not the cave, not the snake, niks. When we get to her room at the hospital, Mom and Dad pretend they haven't argued all the way here in the car, they're all big smiles and extra politeness, like a pair of politicians on the make. The first thing Carls says is, 'Have you guys been arguing?' This really makes me laugh, because Mom and Dad are so bloody predictable. Mom and Dad laugh too, but in a fake slow way, like John's toy machine gun on low battery. Carla's laugh is also a bit weird, *uh, uh, uh*, but this is because her neck's in a big white brace. Her head sort of hovers above it, dark hair splayed up over the white pillows. I'm afraid to touch her.

'Careful,' Dad says. What does he think I'm gonna do? Give her a friendly punch? We stand around the bed as if it's a casket with a body in it. He clutches Carls's foot.

'Ow!' Carla yells.

Nice one, Dad.

'Shit sorry chicken, did I hurt you?'

'Just a bit. Sit down, Dad.'

'What's your case, Jay? You're staring at me as if I'm an exhibit in a museum,' Carla says.

My smile is pasted on. She's like a stranger.

Mom stands with her hands folded in front of her with her own smile stamped on her face like an air-hostess welcoming people on board her aircraft.

'You can sit down you know,' Carls says. 'Just be normal for

Pete's sake, I feel bad enough as it is, without you guys behaving as if this is a funeral parlour.'

There's nervous laughter as Mom and Dad shuffle off to the blue plastic chairs near the window. The curtain near the bed gapes, shrouding Carla for a moment. Mom rushes to close the window.

'No! Leave it open. I need the air. And I like listening to the cars going past.'

Mom sits down on one of the chairs near the window while Dad picks up *Scope* magazine and sits on the other side of the room near the door. Just the thing to read in hospitals – murder, mayhem, cars and nudity, that's about the scope of it. Carla holds out her hand to me. I move closer.

'This place is full of troopies,' she whispers.

'Really? In the war?'

'Ha, ha! No in wards.'

'Ha, ha. Nice one Carls.'

'Oh hello.'

I turn at the sound of Mom's voice. A dark bearded man has appeared at the door in a wheelchair. What's left of his left leg is bandaged just above the knee, his other leg is a mess of scratches and bruises. He seems perfectly happy in spite of his injuries.

'Shit! Spike! What happened to you man!' says Dad.

Turns out Spike's a friend of Uncle Bob's.

'Had my leg shot off.'

'Hell. That was silly.' The men laugh.

'Ja, I'm totally legless now.' Dad and Spike crack up. Mom does her wooden dolly impression.

'I think I'll just nip down to the cafe for a few things – Carls –'

'I've got everything I need Mom.'

'Well, I'll just see if I can get a copy of *Fair Lady* –'

Spike moves the wheelchair over a bit so that Carla's gaze can rest on him, smiling up at Mom as she passes. Mom smiles back, then she escapes with a clickety-clack down the corridor.

'Just came in again so you could look down on me some more,' he says to Carla.

Carla smiles. Dad pulls his chair closer to Spike. He lowers his voice.

'What happened?'

'Mozambique. We hit a disused hospital where the gooks went to catch zees during the day.'

Dad laughs and takes his Kingsgates out of his pocket without taking his eyes off Spike's face.

'Nursey won't let you smoke in here,' says Spike.

Dad smiles. 'I'll let her tell me that herself.' He hands one to Spike and lights it, the blue flame hisses and a salty sulphuric smell rushes at me. Spike keeps taking glances at Carla, who looks like a pretty fairy made of white cardboard.

'Ja so?' says Dad.

'Shit man,' says Spike, looking at Carla, 'I've been in the bush too long.'

'Well you won't be going back,' says Dad.

'I will. But not for a while.'

Dad laughs. 'Scout's honour,' says Spike, 'they'll make me a prosthetic.'

'Really?'

'Ja man, everything else works fine.' He continues to look at Carls. 'I'll still be able to get my leg over.' Dad and Spike laugh. Dad doesn't seem to notice that he's drooling all over Carla. Carla minds even less.

'Ja, so what happened man?' Dad asks.

'Okay. So we're in the hospital. There's four of us including Bob.'

'I didn't know he was in Mozambique.'

'Who said we were in Mozambique?'

'You did.'

'Ja, well it's not something we broadcast, attention pleez, attention pleez, we're going to make a hit in Mozambique, don't worry, no fine, should be back for the evening news.' Dad and Spike laugh.

He's as penga as Uncle Bob. He winks at me. Carla's pupils look huge. Like a kudu.

'He's weird,' I say.

'Ja. But good-looking hey,' Carls says.

'Ja. But have you noticed there's something missing?'

Carls starts to crack up. 'Ja, but I don't think he has – I mean, he's not letting it get in the way,' she says.

I'm crying with laughter.

'Sssh, he can hear man.' Carla smiles and half raises her hand at Spike. Spike smiles and salutes her. Even in the bloody hospital, her in a neck brace and traction and him with his leg off. Some things don't change.

'Have they been fighting again?' Carla asks.

'Ja. It's getting unbearable. Mom's staying at Auntie Aldie's a lot. Dad's always down at The Blue Hart. Has Ian been in to see you?'

'Ja really. I want him to see me like this,' she says sarcastically. Anyway, he's on call-up.'

'I won't dance again,' she says. 'No,' she says when I try to protest, 'the doctor told me, I've got three pins in my leg and my back's a wreck. I'll be in a neck brace for quite a while.'

'Like one of those paper dolls with the fold-out pins to bend the arms and legs.'

'Ja, like one of those.' We laugh together, but not with happiness.

Dad's head to head with Spike.

'Ja so. We blast the hospital,' says Spike. 'Then Bob and I and two others move in to pop the rest. We reckoned there were two in there. Bob went in first. Disabled two. I moved ahead of him. I'm edging up the hallway, moving past a doorway on my left when I'm sprayed. I go down. Bob pulls in and blasts him. I see him go down. He looked me right in the eye from the floor, he had a kind of smile on his face. And no shirt on, a big lumpy pink scar on the side of his chest. The two others move up to the second floor. They both took hits. Big hits.'

'Shit hey,' says Dad.

'Ja,' Spike laughs. 'I can't think about them.' He looks down at his hands, 'My china's man – two of them dead.' For a moment I wonder if he's gonna cry.

Then he looks up, 'But life goes on, hey?' he bellows. Dad flinches and smiles.

'So Bob's the last man walking,' Spike looks up and smiles, showing two wide rows of perfect teeth. 'I can hear him radioing for fire force cover. I musta passed out, woke up, I'm being dragged backwards along the floor, it's all warm and slimy man, I ask if I'm dead,' he laughs again. 'Bob says, "Ja and I'm St Peter."' Spike laughs again. 'Then I pass out again. I'm out but I can hear the helicopter. Next thing I'm airborne, looking out the open doors. As the 'copter tips, I see fire force go in. The 'Z' hovers, the ous are jumping out, the place is crawling man, they're just flying in from the woods man, our boys are going down as soon as they drop in man, shit it's like hell man, I can hear the bullets pinging off the base of the 'C,' man. Then I hear the hawks. Shit man, I know it's serious, the hawks don't come in, unless –' He laughs again. 'The retreat was a mess man. I thought we were never coming out.' He drags on his cigarette with his thumb and forefinger. 'One of us was left behind,' he exhales laughing. We all stare at him. My stomach churns. He was there, on the same mission as Glen with Uncle Bob. We all stare at him. My stomach churns. Spike's moustache blurs, as the dawn rises in my mind, then it hits me like a punch in the head.

'What? You've gone white.' Carla says.

'Justice. Remember his scar. On his chest?'

'No. I never saw him with his shirt off. Did you?'

'Ag don't be stupid man. He had this big pink knotted scar on his chest.'

'So?'

'So? Weren't you listening? He was *there*.'

19.

It's Christmas in Rhodesia and Christmas beetles sing... plays from the nurses station down the corridor. It's Christmas night and Carla and I are reminiscing about Christmas past, while lightning streaks the sky and the thunder booms like distant bombs. The earth gives up a rich cocoa smell and then the rain falls hot and heavy. The nurses have been in and sung Silent Night by candle-light, which made us cry. They left the candles on the windowsill, so the room is bathed in pale golden light. We laugh about how I sussed when I was little that there was no way Santa could stuff bicycles and guitars and stuff down the chimney and that it was Dad that drank the beer and ate the biltong that we put out for Father Christmas. We laugh about when Auntie Aldie took us to Greaterman's one year to have our picture taken with Father Christmas. John refused to sit on his knee and said, "You're just a man in a suit." Then he looked down at Father Christmas gum boots and said, "and you're wearing the garden boy's boots." Carla and I laughed so much we peed ourselves. Auntie Aldie was so cross that she gave him a smack on the arm right there in front of everyone. She threatened to give us a smack too, which made us laugh even more. Auntie Aldie told Mom all about it, but Mom also thought it was funny, so Auntie Aldie left really voos that night after dropping us off, speeding off down the driveway in a cloud of huffs.

I stay with Carls during her physio. It's painful to watch. One of the nurses comes in dressed in flared white trousers and tunic. She has a straight page-boy haircut, sharp brown eyes and a wide, narrow-lipped mouth that she purses together as she works on Carla. She begins by carefully taking off her neck-brace, then she holds Carla's neck and moves it gently from side to side, then gets Carla to do the same. Carla cries quietly as the nurse exercises her leg with her strong, brown muscular arms. Her hand in mine is as bony and crumpled as a dead bird's wing.

Spike hauls himself in on crutches just as the nurse is leaving.

'You're out of your wheelchair!' Carla squeals.

Spike comes slowly towards the bed. He's wearing jeans, one leg tucked under the stump, and a pale-blue t-shirt, his longish hair wet and combed back off his high forehead. He kisses Carla on the cheek, we all laugh as one crutch clatters to the floor. Carla makes room for him on the bed on the opposite side to me, which isn't difficult. Her reed-like form is mummied beneath the sheet.

'You remember my sis, Jayne?' Carla asks.

'How could I forget, she's almost as pretty as you,' Spike says.

'Ja,' I say, 'she was a hard act to follow.'

'Well, you followed her quite nicely,' Spike says. Then slapping his cheek lightly, he says, 'Christmas kiss?'

I kiss his left cheek which is zingy with aftershave.

'Cheeky chap,' Carla says.

'An ous got to take his chances where he can.' Spike jokes. He leans back and takes out a tiny wrapped box from the inside pocket of his jeans and places it on the top of the folded-up sheet near the centre of Carla's chest. Carla breathes in sharply and opens the little box. A tiny silver heart-locket slips from her hand onto my side of the bed. I pick it up for her. It has 'Spike' engraved on one side and 'Carla' engraved on the other. Carla flings her arms around Spike's neck. My heart sinks for him.

20.

At The Blue Hart, the bar area is choka, loud and steamy with boozy breath and reeking of peppery sweat. Uncle Bob monkeys around to get attention. The bar manager smiles and lifts up the glass he's filling for another customer. I ask him about the shooting at the hotel.

'What hotel? I don't go round shooting up hotels, who told you that?'

'I heard Dad tell Spike at the hospital,' I yell in his ear above the noise. Uncle Bob half turns round, keeping an elbow on the bar.

'Ja. I hear he has a soft spot for your big sister.'

'Uncle Bob, I know who the guy with the scar is.'

'What guy?' Uncle Bob puts his arm around my shoulder.

'The guy who shot Spike.'

'Which one. There were at least six of them.'

He eyes a blonde woman in a black-belted red dress. He wiggles his eyebrows at her when her eyes meet his for a moment, before she flicks her hair and turns her back on him.

I shake my head. No wonder Alds is as jiminy as a cricket.

'Oh. I thought you weren't there.'

He grabs me and squeezes me, 'Hey, you got me there Jay.'

'It was Justice.'

'Nooo! Jay you're joking me, hey!'

'Uncle Bob, I'm serious.'

He looks at me, mock serious. 'Jay, I'll let you into a secret, those terrs that attack us on the farms? They couldn't attack us if our

Godfreys, our Wilsons, our Enochs and our Justices weren't helping them. We can't blitz them all though hey? But we do try.'

'C'mon, Wilson? He's been with Granny Rose from the start. She delivered his daughter.

'Justice is a terrorist leader, isn't he? He tried to kill us, or at least organised it?'

'Well Jay, if I see him again, I'll be sure to shoot him properly next time. Okay?'

'Oh so you meant to shoot him?'

He raises his eyebrows and pulls a tight smile at me which tells me he probably did and leans over to the bar manager, 'Hey, when are we gonna get our table, I'm bloody starving, I could eat a baboon man.'

The men at the bar laugh and raise their glasses. Bob has this effect on people.

'Just tell me man Uncle Bob, about Enoch and Justice.' I pull at his shirt.

'So. Nancy Drew, howz about a t-bone? You need some meat on your bones, the ous like it man.'

I don't know whether he didn't hear or doesn't want to answer and I'm too gutless to ask again, partly because I don't want to know the answer, so I decide to ignore the words in my mind too. *They're getting pretty organised, they have their boy messengers – mujibas – their eyes and ears – all over the place. Some of them are as young as twelve.*

Outside, at the tables under the trees, Dad's getting bombed. I feel scooped out inside. Every request from Enoch, every act of friendship on either side mocks me like a lie. Eventually, I ask Uncle Bob to drive me home. The clear eye of the moon stares down at us and hot night pours through the open windows of the jeep. Insects splatter against the windscreen. Every time one does, Uncle Bob makes noises like a fighter plane crashing, 'Meeeeaaaauuuu, pewww, pwwwah, there goes another one –' The jeep rattles and bounces. When we hit a bump, Uncle Bob makes himself jump up and nearly hit the roof, then he lets his body come down with limbs flailing all over the place. For some reason, I find this a total hose and join in, laughing so much that my throat hurts and I think I'm going to kotch. And then we stop and calm down. Uncle Bob sticks his head forward and pulls his beard with his left hand, with his right hand he steers the jeep. His forearm rests on his lean, tan and muscular right leg. He looks straight ahead, pulling his beard, still being funny – sort of. He looks quickly at me. 'Wha'da you looking at!'

He makes me jump sky high. And then he lets out a whoop of laughter.

'Hell you're easy to scare Jay.'

Through my window, rocks, bushy shapes, and the sporadic lights of houses beyond glide by in the darkness. A thorn tree, white bark gleaming like bone, reminds me of the thorn tree that night in the compound with Enoch. He seemed as surprised as I was to see Justice carrying the package that night. So I decide it can't be true about Enoch. Uncle Bob concentrates on the road. The smooth, taut skin at his temple and around the cheekbone above the curls of light brown beard, look exposed and boyish somehow. We are skin and bone, as vulnerable as brain beneath the pulsating skin of a baby's fontanel. How do we live in this flesh as easy to crush as fruit? For now though, I feel warm and safe with Uncle Bob, my body clattering around in the hard body of the jeep.

'Uncle Bob?'

'Ja, my little Rapunzel.' He lights a cigarette.

'Where've you been?'

'At The Blue Hart, with you.'

'No. Really. This call-up.'

'In Mozambique. Trying to get Justice.'

'You mean justice. Or Justice? Did you get him?'

'No,' he laughs. 'We got some others instead.' He laughs again, and switches to a cut-glass British accent. 'It was one big, bloody balls up, and I tell you what, I'd like to cut off the balls of the bloke responsible, and bloody feed them to him – sorry to speak like this in front of you Jay, my princess, but this country is about to die – of stupidity.'

'Uncle Bob, you're scaring me.'

'Shit hey, I'm scaring me, no one knows what's what anymore – it's the monkeys up top, don't know what they're bloody doing, meantime we're bloody dying like flies – well not us – most of the poor bloody RLI – their stupid bloody comaaanders – bloody balls-up.'

'We're not gonna win the war are we?'

'Jusss, you're sharp – no – lost that a while ago, to politics – we're just fighting to bargain now – but don't tell anyone hey – but we could've – if we'd moved faster – if we'd blown the heads off some of the bloody idiots up top – if we'd had one or two men I know allowed to implement one or two things – if they'd let us into Mozambique just after the Porks moved out to smash bases, shit we could've blitzed them from the start, but because of the stupid-arses up top, we couldn't do that.' He sucks his cigarette hard. 'So we just keep throwing more of our boys into the fire –' he exhales. 'And ZANLA and ZIPRA, they can build a mighty big fire, all along our borders, and there are only so many of us and we can't do anything bloody sensible without their bloody say so, and when we do there's some bloody idiot in communications that gets it all fucked up, excuse my French, my little lay-dee.'

'I think I'm in the picture now, Uncle Bob.'

'Ja. You can see the corner, I'd never show you the whole picture. It'd hurt your eyes hey, shit, mine hurt when I close them.'

1978

Salisbury

1.

Our country floats on a sea of suspense and confusion. We have an interim government of 'black moderates,' or 'puppets,' as Nessie calls them. Men the government has handpicked to begin the transitional process to black rule. Meanwhile the war goes on. Nessie says it's only a matter of time before Mugabe, 'the man of the people' takes power. He's still out there, along with Nkomo fighting our whacked out, hacked off army.

School is kif, because Mel's there and even though she's in form four, I get to hang out with her at break times, when she bothers to turn up for school. Whenever Glen's around, she bunks off to spend time with him. It's a bit like eating raw chilli on your food, but Glen has tried to make the pain easier to swallow. At first they make you cry, then your tongue burns, then you deal with it, then hell, hopefully you even begin to like the buzz. Sometimes he surprises me by picking me up at the school gates and taking me to the drive-in, or for take-away at Gremlin's. It's been months since Carla's accident. Her leg cast came off six weeks ago, but she's still not dancing. Madame insists that she goes to classes to watch, telling Carla that she must continue to observe, and to keep dancing in her mind. Oh ja. Carla has officially dumped Ian and is now seeing Spike, who's stunned the doctors by managing to walk on crutches from time to time. When he comes to visit Carla, he hauls his way onto her couch with the crutches and then just stays there for a few hours, firing 'O' level biology questions at her, before hauling off down the driveway where he gets picked up by his African driver.

Mom thinks it's their shared accidents that are keeping them together, a mutual cripple-club thing. At least they're bringing a little extra love into this house, because there's plenty being lost between Mom and Dad.

Nessie picks me up from school on Friday. It's my fourteenth birthday on Sunday and she's taking me out tonight. Nessie's flat is really mush. The hallway is just a typical parquet floor, like in any other flat, except there's no furniture in here, no hall table or anything, just the phone stretched out on its cord on the floor. Nessie's bedroom has a double mattress on the floor and a pile of books either side. The curtain is a Kenyan kikuyu sarong on a wooden rail. It doesn't really stretch across, but she doesn't like closing the curtain anyway. She likes to let the night come in.

Nessie scopes my outfit. 'Nice jeans. You're gonna need a jersey or something.'

'I didn't bring. Where we going?'

'Wait and see. Here.' She chucks me a red tracksuit top.

We're driving through Salisbury. I rec she's going to sneak me into one of her notorious college parties, or maybe even a disco. So when we leave the city behind, I get suspicious.

'Where we going Nessie?'

'Wait and see,' she smiles.

We travel for a while along the main road out of Salisbury, then cut onto a dirt road. The car shudders as bits of stone are thrown up under the chassis and insects blitz themselves on the windscreen. Nessie lights up one of her dagga smokes, and puts the radio on, it's reggae, we laugh at the appropriateness of it. Shacks and small tin-rooved, brick African houses appear on the edge of the bush. Now and again an African walks or cycles along the side of the road, groups of mostly young African men stare or whistle at the car as the headlights catch the wolfish gleam in their eyes.

'I can't believe you're taking me to a township Nessie.'

Nessie laughs.

'Well we could just go to the movies, but I thought you might prefer to live one for yourself.'

I giggle. Maybe the dagga's getting me high too, maybe I'm just scared.

Nessie pulls up in front of a cluster of corrugated iron shacks. Tinny African music floats in the cool smoky air. Nessie gets out of the car and bending, twists her hair into a knot on her head. I pull the hood of my tracksuit up.

'Don't feel you need to disguise yourself Jay.'

My laughter is high and hollow. I'm bricking it.

We weave between the shacks towards a largish cement building.

Inside, African men and women are seated at tables in a blue-smoke haze, drinking vomity-smelling chibuku from cartons and Lion lager. A band at the back of the hall is playing the African jazz we could hear from the car. The singer wears a purple crocheted bobble hat over his dreadlocks. Sweat soaks his thin t-shirt, and rivers over his wiry arms and down his temples as he blows into a saxophone and the crowd whistles and cheers. Several women get up and begin dancing near the band, bobbing their full round bottoms up and down as if trying to get them to float on imaginary water. The air is so smoky, my eyes begin to stream. We're the only Europeans here and people are looking at us. I follow Nessie to the back of the hall where a woman is selling beer at a table.

'Coke or birthday beer?' Nessie yells at me.

'Birthday beer!' I shout back.

She smiles as she hands me a Lion. I down half of it in one and begin to chill out almost immediately. Nessie turns as a man clamps his hand on her shoulder. She gives him a hug. He whispers something in her ear. I've never seen a white person hug a black person before.

'This is my niece Jayne,' Nessie says, 'she's fourteen tomorrow. Nessie this is Patrick.'

Patrick is dressed in checked tan and brown trousers and purple t-shirt with peaked cap.

'Ah. Old enough to be married,' Patrick says. 'Do you like our chimurenga music?'

'Ja, I think so, I've never heard it before.' I smile at Patrick. He looks nothing like his red-hair-and-freckles European name.

'Come, let us sit. Let us drink!' he says.

We squeeze our way through sweaty people and tables to the other side of the room, where men and teenage boys sit with a few women. I recognise the woman from University College that was chatting to Nessie when Mom dropped me off last year. Her hair is no longer close-cropped. She has allowed it to turn into an Afro. Bright red lipstick and gold hooped earrings make her look like an American singer. She's magnetic.

'Nessie!' she waves. 'Raised Fist was just telling me about some very interesting developments,' she says, her graceful hands conducting the air around her. Nessie leans over the table to talk to her. Some of the men and teenage boys look at me and make comments. A tall young man has his back to me. His back, triangular and muscled under its red t-shirt looks vaguely familiar. He takes a final sip of Coke and then turns to put his empty bottle on the table. As he does so, I see the side of his face, the unmistakable rounded sweep of cheekbone, the curved wing of the nostril. A flash of black eye catches mine. Looking down, I touch Nessie's arm to get her attention as my legs begin to shake. She turns for a second and then goes back to her conversation. I want to run, but where would I run to? I pull her by the leather belt of her jeans.

'Just a sec Jay. This is important.'

Anger pours through me like molten lava. Finishing the rest of my beer quickly, I put the bottle on the table. I feel him coming towards me and I don't know what to do. Man! Anything could happen to me here. I even consider ducking under the table. When I turn and look up, he's standing right beside me.

'Jayne,' he says.

My heart does the rubber-ball. He's wearing black suit trousers with a Coca-Cola t-shirt and sandals made out of rubber. He's so good looking that I can't keep my eyes on him and my gaze keeps sliding to the ground.

'Hi Enoch. I never thought I'd see you again.' The words come from a tin-can body. He looks the same, only wider, taller, *deeper*.

'Why do you say this?' He looks amused, as if he's laughing at me, which strengthens my anger.

'Why do you think?' We have to lean in close, to make ourselves heard above the music. My face is heating up, I'm glad it's dark in here.

'When did you leave the PV?' I shoot the words out and I'm glad I have, otherwise I might never have said them.

He laughs and I lean in to hear his reply, my cheek touching his for a second

'As soon as I was able.'

'What do you mean by that?' A quick look in his eye, there is no guilt there, only softness, even kindness. But the softness makes my inner metal harden.

'Sometimes, Jayne, something happens and then you are not on your own terms.'

Riddles. For a moment I focus on his long-fingered hands taking out a Madison from the red and white packet and putting it between his lips.

'Well whose terms are you on? Justice's? I thought you were better than that?'

'How can one be better than another?' He folds his arm and cocks his head slightly as he looks me up and down.

'By making the right decisions,' I take a step backwards and he smiles. The friends that he had been chatting to a little while ago glance in our direction.

'Have you made the right decisions?' He leans his head forwards slightly.

'I can't. I'm too young.'

He puts his hands on my shoulders. It's a shock because he always avoided touching me in the past.

'You are never too young to make the right choices if you can think. If you cannot think, then you must stay with another's choices.'

His face is very close to mine and the warmth of his hands is distracting me.

'Must I betray my own people?' he slides his hands down my upper arms.

'When you betrayed me I had to deal with your choices,' I say, jerking my arms free. I thump Nessie on the back. 'I want to go.'

He puts his cigarette back in his mouth. 'What is it like to no longer be in the mountains?' he asks.

'It's hell, thanks.'

'Yes,' he says, tipping his head back and exhaling his cigarette smoke straight upwards, 'we are on even ground in that case. Now we must all find a way out of this hell.'

'You take everything I say and use it to make a point. It's quite annoying you know,' I say, snatching his cigarette from his hands and putting it between my own lips.

He laughs, and as he does, he catches the eye of one of his friends who calls him with a movement of his head.

Nessie breaks away from her conversation and straightens back up, 'Hi Enoch,' she says, as if she saw him yesterday, which maybe she did.

The music is screaming in my head. Nessie's friend comes over.

'Oh, Grace, this is my niece Jayne. She loves the music.'

Watching the edges of her hair gleam in the bluish light, I say nothing. She's like a more beautiful version of Donna Summer.

'He's singing about the government,' Grace yells at me, her warm breath musky in my ear. 'He says Ian Smith is like a hyena searching in the bush for dead meat.'

I wish she wouldn't bloody speak. She's so much better just to watch. She whispers something in Enoch's ear and they both laugh.

'A drink?' Grace asks us.

'A beer would be great,' Nessie says. 'Jay?'

'A beer would be great,' I say sarcastically. Feeling Enoch's eyes on me, I put the hood of my tracksuit up.

He laughs. 'And now you are a child again. When did you begin drinking beer?'

'When did you become a terrorist?' I say looking past him at a woman dancing with her back to a man who is bending over her shoulders, his head hovering over her bouncing chest.

'I am not a terrorist,' he says.

'A moriba? I mean a *mujiba* then?'

He laughs at my mispronunciation.

'I want to bring freedom.'

I laugh sarcastically.

'You think it's funny. Do you think it is only for whites to be politicians?'

I feel bad. Everything I say is the wrong thing or means something else to him.

'How you gonna do that?' I ask, folding my arms, feeling stupid. But he does look more like a footballer than a would-be politician.

He folds his arms in a mocking way. 'Just like a white madam,' he laughs.

'I'm not a white madam.' I glare at him, but then look away. His eyes are too dark and full of movement. In them are negatives of all that he has seen and done.

'You want to hit me,' he smiles. 'Come, here.' He bends down so that his face is near mine and taps his jaw with his fingers. 'Hit me and then we can be friends again.'

'How did you know I wanted to hit you?'

'I know you. For a long time we were friends.'

'But we're not friends now are we?'

'Why? I am your friend. I like you. You are pretty now.'

Embarassed, I scan the room. Man. Where's Nessie disappeared to? At a table not far from us, a man is watching me with a lion's stare. The men who Enoch was talking to earlier, train their eyes on me; they are dressed in t-shirts and trench coats; one of them has sunglasses halfway down his nose, another wears a trilby hat. Enoch raises an arm at them and they nod, continuing to look.

'Who are they?'

'Friends. Maybe they are friends.'

'Ja. Maybe not.' Do they all dress like that? Arms folded, I shift my body sideways to him.

Enoch laughs. 'I like this new Jayne.'

Nessie and Grace arrive back with the drinks. In the time it takes for Grace to hand me my beer, Enoch disappears. Grace goes back to her seat between a couple of other men and a woman wearing a grey jumpsuit and a black cap.

'Can I smoke?' I ask Nessie.

'If it'll put a smile on your dial,' she digs in her bag for her smokes, then lights a couple of Madisons and places one in my lips. 'What do you think?'

'That you're crazy.'

'Aren't you pleased to have seen him?'

'*No.*'

'He's good-looking isn't he?' she smiles.

'No.' Yes. Crowding for room in my mind, conflicting thoughts about him, bite each other's butts.

She puts her arm around me, 'Come, let's go get into the music.'

We make our way through the crowd towards the band. I notice that the three scary-looking men have vanished too. I look for Enoch amongst the group he was standing with, but can't see him. The crowd around the band has thickened, and the air is cloudy with dagga smoke and the sharp oniony smell of sweat. Mel would say it smells like munts. The thought of the shock if Mel or anyone else I know found out about me being here make me almost laugh out loud.

'That's better,' Nessie shouts, pulling my hood back. 'You're beautiful when you smile.'

He said I was pretty, and he acknowledged our friendship, these thoughts make me feel high, but then I think back to the farm and I come back down with a thud. Pulling my hair around my cheeks even though it's too dark to see their redness, I search the crowd for him.

Patrick comes over.

'Let's dance Nesta! Can your Jayne dance?' He smiles at me. 'If she can drink, she must dance!'

Nesta?

Nessie pulls me by the shoulders into the crowd. Bodies and music swirl together, making me move from side to side, pressing against me. My head is warm and fuzzy. Nessie takes my hands and moving her hips, and gesturing with her eyes, shows me her moves.

'That's the way!' Patrick encourages. He swivels his hips up to Nessie's, they raise their arms and make hip movements together. Above the crowd, I keep looking but don't see him. Hating myself for it, I try to stop looking. We dance till the band take a break. Nessie laughs and puts her arm around me.

'You're quite a mover Jay,' she shouts above the whistling and the feet stamping.

'For sure, you can dance,' Patrick laughs. 'And now let us drink, let us smoke.'

'I don't think so Patrick. I must get Jayne home.'

'Oh I am too much disappointed,' he jokes. 'But I understand discipline is the way.'

We laugh, though I don't find him funny. Nessie grabs his hand and they do the two-way grasp of African friendship. Then he does the same to me.

'Nice to meet you Jayne. You have a very good and clever aunt.'

Outside, between the shacks, ours is the only car. A grizzled African man sits on an old tyre near a fire; he laughs when he sees us, lifting up his hand, then he goes back to chatting to the fire. As Nessie gets in to the car, I lift my hood up, wondering if I'll ever see Enoch again. As my hand squeezes the cold metal of the car door handle, I hear footsteps running up behind me. His hand grasps my forearm. As I turn, he places his hands on my upper arms, he presses them slightly.

My eyes are level with his wide collar bones.

His Adams apple bobs as he swallows.

'I will see you again Jayne.' I feel his hand lifting my wrist. He turns it over and licking his finger he draws a line, then he licks his finger and draws another parallel line, part way around my wrist, till they almost touch. He smiles.

'Why did you not make them meet? Like a bracelet?'

I can't take the heat of his eyes so close to mine, so I look away.

'They cannot meet now. But one day they can meet.'

He turns round and walks away without looking back.

Then I'm in the car unable to look out at him, trying not to cry.

'See you soon Enoch,' Nessie calls out the window as she backs out.

Finally I look out at him walking away, but he doesn't look back. He never looks back. And now I wish I'd looked at him hard in the eyes. Laying my cheek against the cool seat, I watch the shacks and the people standing round oil drum fires till they are obscured by dust and exhaust fumes. Nessie squeezes my leg knowing I do not want to talk. The music fades away till only the sound of the VW can be heard. On either side of the road the bush crouches like the misshapen humps of animals beneath the yellow eye of the moon. I trace the place where he traced the lines, stopping short where he left them, incomplete circles, his taste branded into my skin. My head judders against the back seat. I have become an accidental traitor.

2.

On Sunday morning Mom and Carla and John come into my room in a big squawking happy birthday procession.

'Happy birthday beautiful,' Mom says.

'Happy birthday ugly,' John says, giving me his pressie, which turns out to be a shell necklace that he got Phillip's mom to get me down south.

'Aah. I love it John-John, you must really love me.' I try to hug him, but he goes 'ugh' and runs away. Carla gives me an envelope of gift vouchers from Spin City and Mom gives me an outfit I wanted from Next Century Boutique. As I open it, I begin to cry, tears splashing onto my sheet.

'It's not that bad,' Carla laughs. 'Hell I'll have it if you don't want it.'

'It's not that,' I laugh and cry. 'I just miss Dad.' I feel like I've murdered someone and stashed them in the cupboard.

'We all do,' Mom says, lapping up the half-truth. 'Hey cheer up, Patience has made a special breakfast.'

Through the window I can see Godfrey wheeling the wheelbarrow full of soil across the lawn then dumping it to create a new rockery bed. High up in the pine tree the weaver birds are busy and the dense jacarandas block out the light on the road. What happened on Friday is what I imagine an LSD experience to be. Unreal wrapped in real. Maybe I need to spend less time with Nessie and never see him again, just go back to being Mel's pal and

Dad's daughter and Bob and Glen's niece. If Enoch and I had never been friends in the first place none of this would have happened. *She's the one who can't resist Pandora's box,* Mom used to say about me.

Later, Dad calls from Mt Darwin, near where he's stationed.

'Happy Birthday Bantam. There's a surprise for you in the desk drawer.'

Hope I never surprise you Dad.

'Come home Dad.'

'I will.'

But he won't. He won't for ages. The call-ups last longer and longer and then when he's home he's hardly around, or he drinks too much and annoys everyone, even me. I've betrayed him. More secrets pile onto the others like tar over clean pink lungs. That afternoon the blood appears like the stain of accusing guilt.

'That's why you're so tearful,' Mom says.

Her words make me cringe. *Old enough to be married,* Patrick said. I finger the silver studs Dad left in the drawer in the little brown envelope, just wanting to curl up on his lap. Tears drop all over the hard little butterflies in my palms.

3.

Mel and I are lying on two towels on the sizzling stoep in Mazoe over the long weekend waiting for Glen to pitch up. Mel's checking her cleavage, two perfect halves that curve out of her red bikini top. Next to her I look like a long, brown skinny boy. She ties her dark hair into a knot at the nape of her neck and lowers her sunglasses to their proper place. The pressure cooker inside me is singing.

'Mel? Do you think Godfrey's good-looking?' I say, trying to build up to telling all.

'Why, do you?' she glances at me. 'You into garden boys now? Get a grip Jay. First Bruce Lee and now Godfrey. How about our garden boy? Nelson? Or Sixpence?'

'What a hose Mel. It's okay to say whether an African man is good-looking you know,' I say sitting up.

'Well I can't say he gets me in a spin. How far have you gone?' Mel says raising herself on her elbows.

'Typical,' I narrow my eyes at her and shake my head. 'I've known him and his brother since I was little. He tells me about what it was like growing up in his village. About life in the TTLs, stuff like that.'

'Well, Jay that sounds really nice. But I don't think there's much future in it.'

I throw a bottle-top at her. 'I didn't say I liked him in that way, you doos.'

I just can't spill all the beans.

'Charming. You're the one who asked me if I think he's good-looking. I don't by the way. I do however, think Glen's totally kif.'

'Ja, I know that.'

'Whez he anyway?' Mel says.

'Out with George. They'll be back soon.'

'Come let's do your hair – turn.'

I turn my back on her. She takes my hair and twists it, then pulls it into a knot and stabs a wire hair-pin from her own head into it.

'I can't believe how quick your hair's grown.'

'Mel? Godfrey has a brother.'

'No kidding, how unusual for an Af, he probably has ten.'

'Mel, that's racialist. You'll have to stop all of that soon, you know.'

'S'not. Just realistic.'

'Mel? Back at Angel's Peak I was friends with Godfrey and George's brother.'

'Lucky you,' she pulls up my hair, then she stops. 'George? African George? From here? Slow down chick, I can't keep up. You hung around with an African boy?' She laughs. 'No friends at school, hey Jay?'

Don't they all sing the same tune?

'Well. Not many. We were good friends. I liked him. A lot.'

'Look Jay. I don't know what you're trying to say. Lots of farm kids play with the workers' kids. They grow out of it.'

I lie back on the hot cement of the stoep floor, the sweat from my back wetting the towel, my eyes prickling. Go their way and I feel a traitor to him. Go his way and I lose them.

Karl comes over and licks my face. 'Urgh, yuck, go way Karl.' I shield my liquid eyes from the sun with my arm. Mel leans back on her elbows next to me, tipping her head back to soak her face with sun, her hair falls out of its knot and brushes my naked shoulder.

'Uh that tickles!' I say, forcing my voice over the lump. She nudges my hip with hers, bone knocks against bone, then she sits up again and holds her Kodak instamatic over us in her outstretched arms. I can see us reflected in the lens, two girls, one in a red bikini, one in a green one, a wedge of sky above and a sliver of stoep roof behind us. She clicks and as she does so, I scream as two hairy legs in veldskoens plant themselves on either side of me. Glen looms above me, his gun slung over his shoulder.

'Shit Glen you gave me a fright!'

Glen laughs. George stands not far off, looking out towards the bush. Mel just lies there beneath her sunglasses.

'Don't you say hello?' Glen asks her.

'Sometimes,' she says. 'But not today.'

George walks off up the drive, flicking the end of his cigarette high over the mopani trees.

'Hey George –' George looks back over his shoulder. 'Don't forget the beers,' Glen shouts. 'The bottle store closes soon. And the da-gg-a!' He drags out the word as he reaches down and tickles my stomach – the gun practically dings me on the nose.

'Hey, get your gun outa my face man. I need it – my face, that is.'

'Ja, it's quite pretty. You girls wanna swim?' Glen asks.

'In the reservoir? Ugh, you kidding man? It's all slimy, and there was a water snake in there last time I checked,' I say.

Mel rolls over and grabs the suntan oil. Handing it to him, she undoes her bikini-top and lies flat on her front. Glen squeezes the runny brown oil into his palm, rubs his hands together and begins smoothing it all over Mel's back, running his hands up between her shoulder blades, out to her arms and down her spine to her coccyx, finishing with a gentle slap. Mel re-clasps her bikini top and sits up. Glen sits down next to her, lights a cigarette and offers her one. She takes it.

'Thanks, but no thanks,' I say.

'Didn't offer you.'

'I know.'

Mel takes a few drags, blows straight up into the air, then hands the cigarette to me. I take a couple of drags, blow three wobbly smoke rings, one of which frames a flying bird against the sky. The last time this happened I was with Wilson and Granny Rose. I hand the cigarette back, deciding it's a sign.

'Hey good, Jay. Soon you'll be blowing castles in the sky,' Glen stands up. 'Speaking of castles – drink anyone?'

'Ja beer please,' Mel says.

'Does your mom know you drink?'

'Don't make me laugh, she's too drunk to notice. Does your mom know you get the garden boy to buy you drugs?' Mel sits up and flashes a beamer at Glen.

'Ja, well you don't wanna join her.'

'Look, spare the lecture, grab the beer.'

'Yes, mam.' Glen goes to the kitchen to get the beer.

Mel slaps my thigh and laughs.

Glen leads the way down the path that I walked down not long ago with Sharon. He's shirtless, and the muscles of his brown back are like polished driftwood. Sticking his bum out, he wiggles it from side to side, which is quite a hose. Mel doesn't laugh though. She walks behind him, concentrating on his back. He looks back at her to see if she's cracked a smile. She hasn't. She doesn't get his humour, only his body. Suddenly Glen stops. Mel bumps into him and steadies herself by grabbing onto his waist. Mel and I are both barefoot, me carrying my beer glass of Mazoe orange. It's only a matter of time before one of us steps on a patch of paper thorns.

'Uuugh!'

Yip, it's Mel. She sits down. Glen crouches down in front of her and begins flicking away the thorns and pulling out bits with his nails. Mel makes squealy noises like a piglet that's got wind of slaughter. I stand waiting with my arms folded wishing she'd shut her cake-hole. We continue, single file, Mel in the lead, Glen following with the towels over his shoulder, me trailing behind. Each time he has his hand raised as if he's about to pat her on the bum or run a finger down her back, she turns round and he pulls his hand up, pretending to smooth back his hair or rub his chin. The grey cement reservoir looms up ahead of us in the long grass. I'm watching where I tread, mindful that mambas like to bask against the sun-baked heat of the cement. Glancing over the lip of the reservoir, I see it's filthy. No little brown water-snakes though. Glen comes up behind me and lifts me by the waist.

'No! Glen! Put me down!' I slap at his back. Mel watches Glen out of the corner of her eye as she knots her hair onto the top of her head. I don't blame her. He's Rhodesian army fit, all six pack and brawn. Glen puts me down and runs a little distance into the bush.

Then he turns quickly and starts running towards us. We both take off like springbokke. Glen chases after us, rushing at me and then at Mel, his intended prey. We take off again in different directions. Glen's footsteps fall silent. We know he's sneaking up on us, but from which side? Mel and I meet in the middle, we're both laughing, though trying to do it silently. Mel's face is flushed, her stomach moves quickly in and out, she screams as Glen rounds the corner. I don't bother to move. It's her he's after. She takes off, the pants of her red bikini slip inwards slightly on either side revealing wedges of pale untanned flesh. Glen catches her easily, slinging her over his shoulder. She should have 'Glen' stamped on her bum, like a pocket of Mazoe oranges. I just catch sight of her slapping Glen's back as she screams 'no Glen no!' which means 'yes Glen yes,' then there's a splash and her scream is blocked out as she hits the water. My back against the reservoir, I slide down onto my haunches. There's another, bigger splash as Glen jumps in. I don't need to turn round. He would have tipped her in, run some distance away and then vaulted in with one arm and one leg as leverage. I know, because he used to do it to me.

The sun's getting lower. It must be about five. The shadow of the reservoir creeps up the ground. Where the longer grass gives way to bush, the compound with its seven huts is deserted. The squealing and splashing has stopped, now there's just the gentle lap of water beneath the wide sky. Standing up I see they are on the other side of the reservoir, the water a clear grey disc. Glen has his back to me. At first I cannot see her, she is blocked out by his body, but then her head moves slightly behind his and her arms move up behind his back. He has her pinned to the wall of the reservoir. I feel like a hyena watching a pair of frolicking lion cubs. Cubs I didn't really want to see born, so I wander back to the house to get another drink.

Inside it is still and silent, except for the gentle click, click of the clock above the mantelpiece in the lounge. Part of the way down the passage to the bathroom, I'm distracted by the open door of Uncle Joe's study. This room is usually locked. I push it open. The desk chair is in the middle of the room, slanted slightly towards me like an invitation. A grey metal desk runs almost the full length of the barred window. Both sides of the windowless walls are lined with shelves packed with rows and rows of *Farmers Weekly* magazines and loads of files about orange and lemon sales. A calendar from Ferreira's Motors hangs by the window. The July girl wears denim shorts and a cheesy smile, her hair is all flicked at the sides, like Auntie Aldie's, except hers is red and two black stars block out the nipples on her otherwise naked breasts. The top drawer is unlocked. A black foolscap journal lies on the top of a pile, red taped along the spine, like the ones Dad uses for work, stuffed underneath with receipts and bills. Loads for The Blue Hart in town, where Uncle Joe does lots of drinking with May. I pull these forward and looking deeper into the drawer. I pull out several cut-out newspaper articles.

A headline reads, *Mazoe Woman Murdered, Prominent Mazoe Farmer Denies Wife's Affair, Farm Worker Jailed.* There's a picture of Uncle Joe, in overalls, with his arms folded. Distracted by the wind blowing the curtains inwards, I pull them across. Then I realise this might look odd so I pull them back out again, but not completely. I sit down in the desk-chair and pushing the door to slightly, check out the first article.

It is alleged, that on the 5 January, 1972, Mrs Penelope Cameron, wife of Mazoe farmer Joseph Cameron, was murdered by Mr Cameron's farm manager, Prospect Mdisa, sometime during the night. Mdisa's lawyer, the alleged Communist Nadim Patel, argued that it was well known that Mrs Cameron was on warm terms with the worker. He went on to say that Mrs Cameron had given Mr Mdisa money, outside of his wage packet, on several occasions. Mrs Cameron's lawyers stated that Mr Mdisa had terrorist links. It is believed that Mr Mdisa made several trips to Mozambique in the months leading up to Mrs Cameron's death. Mr Patel argued that he had family there and that this was perfectly natural behaviour. Counsel for Mrs Cameron countered that this was perfectly natural behaviour for a terrorist.

I read the second article. *Mazoe Farmer Joseph Cameron denies that his wife was having an affair with the defendant, Mr Prospect Mdisa. He said that his wife was a friendly woman, who was on good terms with all the workers, and no more friendly with Prospect Mdisa than with anyone else. He maintained his wife was depressed, he stated that depression ran in her family and that her father had shot himself after losing his farm in Centenary some years previously. He did not think that she had been murdered, and referred to those that did as idle gossipmongers. Mrs Cameron sustained a single gunshot wound to the head. Her injuries were significant, so much so that the coroner found it difficult to judge the distance of the shot fired. Mr Van den Bergh believed the shot was fired at very close range. There was difficulty in establishing whether gunshot residue found on parts of Mrs Cameron indicated whether the shot was fired by her own hand or not.*

In another article, I read: *Coroner Records Suicide Verdict in Cameron Case,* and in yet another:

Mazoe Farm Worker Jailed For Theft. The farm worker accused of murder in the Cameron case has been jailed for ten years for the break in of Ferreira's garage. I look at the caption, October 1972.

Someone's walked into the house. Whitening with fear, I'm figuring on diving under the desk John-style when a figure appears outside the window. It's George. He looks at me without smiling and then nods. Then he walks off. How long's he been standing there? Putting the newspaper cuttings away, and slamming the drawer shut, I hurry out of the room and back outside.

Back at the reservoir, where Mel and Glen are frolicking noisily now, George is sitting leaning against a tree almost opposite to the place I was at before. I sit down near him, leaning against the cool cement wall of the reservoir.

'Hi,' I say. George nods and then goes back to staring out over the bush, chewing slowly on a long piece of elephant grass.

Freaked that he saw me in Uncle Joe's office, I don't know what else to say. He takes out some newspaper and begins measuring out some tobacco into it, just like Wilson used to. Feeling that he's telling me telepathically that he's not going to say anything, I smile at him. He nods but doesn't smile. Then he lights his smoke and looks out over the bush. You'd never think his father was Prospect, villain in our very own family death scandal. On another day I would like to be friends.

In the hallway at home, Carla and I both lunge for the phone. Carla grabs it first.

'Hi Mel,' she says in a high sarcastic tone.

Carla doesn't approve of Mel's relationship with our uncle. She doesn't like Mel being around full stop. They're like two beautiful alley-cats vying for territory. One day they'll come to scratches, but meantime they just prowl around each other, sizing each other up, dressing each other down.

'It's Me-e-lll,' she trills. She holds the phone out to me, then she leans against the hallway wall, tapping her walking-stick.

'What's your case man? You need to get back to ballet,' I say.

She whacks me with her stick. I grab it and she nearly topples over. From the receiver Mel goes, *Hello? Hello? What's cutting man? Jay!*

Shoving Carla out the way, I get on with the yak. Mel's in mortar-attack mode. She says her brother saw Glen and Sharon together at Mabelreign Drive-In.

'I'm gonna kill him!'

'No you're not.'

'Well, he's my boyfriend! What's he doing with her?'

'Hold on,' I say, putting my hand over the receiver.

'Carla. Hobble the hell out of here. I don't stand around listening to you when you're cooing at Spike.'

Carla laughs and shuffles off into the kitchen like the beautiful cripple she still wants to be. Madame recs she doesn't need the stick, she could probably pirouette along with the rest of them.

'Nothing,' I say to Mel, 'as far as we know. Can we trust your brother?'

'Can we trust Glen?'

'Can we trust anyone? You stole Glen from Sharon.'

'I can't believe you said that.'

I can't believe it either. She slams the phone down. I click our own receiver into place and slump down on the step between the hallway and the dining room, rocking myself on the loose clicking parquet tiles, waiting the two or three minutes I know it'll take before she calls back.

'Sorry. Still coming to Lisa's party?' she asks.

'No. I changed my mind because of your bad behaviour.'

'Good. See you at mine to get ready.'

She slams the phone down again. Bet she's got some witch plan.

4.

We're sitting on the veranda waiting for Mom so we can all go out to the Italian for supper to celebrate Dad's return from call-up after nearly three months.

'She cutting her hair or what?' Dad says.

'She wants to look nice Dad.' I say.

'Ja, well I appreciate the effort but how long does it take?' Dad replies.

Carla comes through the French doors onto the veranda. She checks out my faded yellow *Rhodesia is Super* t-shirt and old jeans.

'You changing? Wanna borrow some of my makeup?' she asks me.

'No thanks.'

'That's right, all you need is a smile Bantam,' he smiles at me. 'I could eat an Italian now, hey boy,' Dad says to John.

'Well maybe not a whole one hey?' John says, pushing a spring of dark hair out of one green eye.

John has grown so much since Dad's been away. *Hey you been eating ladders?* Dad joked about me too. *Been eating beanpoles? You could be the high jump with those legs.* Dad looks different too, thinner, his brown skin more leathery. His beard has flecks of grey in it and there is grey on the sides of his hair too.

Mom comes out. Dad gives a low whistle. She looks pretty mush in her green halter neck top, black trousers and long dangly gold earrings. Carla looks pretty good too, in stovies and white t-shirt. Hold the white plastic earrings though.

'Shall we stay here? Send the kids out?' Dad says.

Mom laughs.

'We are here you know, Dad,' I say.

We park up outside the shopping arcade and before you can say chop-chop, a smiling Italian man with a handlebar moustache is saying 'welcome back Mr Cameron,' and taking us to our table.

'I want spaghetti,' John says.

'Can we have Portuguese Rosé Dad?' Carla asks.

A couple of men drinking beer at a nearby table check her bum out as she slides herself into her chair.

'For you chicken, anything,' Dad says.

'Oh look,' Mom says, 'it's the Nelsons. Poor woman.'

'Why poor woman?' John asks.

'Don't you remember?' I say. 'Their only son was killed two years ago, near the farm. Shot out of his helicopter.'

'Sssh,' says Mom. Mr Nelson is coming over.

'Have you heard the news?' asks Mr Nelson. 'About the British missionaries up in Vumba?'

'Oh God. No. What Bill?' Mom says.

'In the Vumba. Not far from your place. Three couples including the minister. Three women, three kids. A three-week-old baby.

'My God Mom,' says Carla.

'Bloody savages.' Dad says as he calls the waiter for wine and beer.

'Have a drink Bill?'

Frank Sinatra grins over Dad's shoulder from the black and white framed photograph on the wall behind him.

'Better get back to the wife.'

Man he looks miserable.

'Get her over here man,' Dad says.

'No she's better on her own, not up to talking much, these days.'

'I'll go chat to her,' Mom half gets up.

'Better you don't Reen,' Bill says.

'Ja Reen, you heard what the man said. Park,' Dad jokes, but Mom glares at him.

'They were all bludgeoned, including the baby. The women –' Bill rubs his bald head.

'Not in front of the kids please Bill,' Mom says reaching for her cigarettes.

'Ja. We don't like horror stories,' I say, 'we've had a really sheltered life.'

'Don't be cheeky Jay,' Mom says.

Bill rubs his head again, before staring down at his sausage fingers.

John stares at the red and white tablecloth. The waiter brings the wine.

'All of us,' Dad says pushing his wine glass over. 'Kids too.'

The waiter smiles and pours.

'The baby had her little hand curled around her mother's finger man.' Bill has tears in his eyes.

'Have a drink man,' Dad says.

'Ja Bill. Have a drink,' Carla and Mom say.

'No must get back. We're going down South next week. Permanent.'

Dad looks at the tablecloth.

'I'm sorry to hear that. Very sorry to hear that,' Dad says.

'You're a good bloke Dave,' Bill says. 'Well. I'll be off then.'

Mom watches Bill's retreating back.

'You didn't have to say it like that Dave.'

'Like what Reen?'

'You know, *very sorry to hear that,*' she says sarcastically.

'Well I am very sorry Reen. I'm very sorry about this bloody war and what it does. I'm sorry he's taking the chicken-run.'

'He's been through a lot Dave.'

'Ja, Dad.' Carla says flicking her hair away from the back of her top.

'Be quiet Carla,' Dad says.

'Do you think others haven't been through a lot? Aren't still going through a lot Reen?' He leans over at Mom. Mom presses her lips together and taps her forefinger on the table.

'Dad? Come on,' I say.

'You keep quiet too my girl.' He raises his voice even more.

Carla gets up and storms out.

'Hey! Where do you think you're going?' Dad yells.

He sits down and slams his hand on the table.

Bald Luigi comes running over, his face dragging his moustache.

'What is the problem Mr Cameron? Please sit down. I get you something.'

'Bloody family support group hey? I come back from months on the border and look what bloody happens.'

'A drink on the house.' Luigi rushes off to the bar to get the cure.

A couple of men at a nearby table raise their glasses at Dad. Dad raises his.

'Hey, I should be sitting with you,' Dad shouts over to them. 'What does a man have to do to get some solidarity round here?'

'That's it!' Mom grabs her bag and follows Carla out.

'No way man,' Dad says. He grabs Mom by the wrist.

'Get off me Dave!' She twists her wrist out of Dad's grasp.

Bill comes over.

'Dave, hey, Dave.' He puts a hand on Dad's shoulder.

Dad shrugs him off and follows Mom out.

John and I look at each other and smile as we pick up our wineglasses.

'What shall we do?' John says.

'Let's order,' I say.

We laugh and pick up the menu.

'Mom swore like you can't believe that night,' I say.

'Ja,' John says. 'Remember my cut?'

I pick up my glass. 'Ja. Remember the brandy?'

'Ja,' he says.

We clink glasses, and then in our silence, we see reflections of what happened that night flickering in each other's eyes.

5.

In the salmon-pink tiled bathroom of her mother's sunken bedroom bathroom area, Mel and I are getting ready for Mel's friend Lisa's party. We're wearing satin boob tubes bought by Mel's mother out of guilt money extracted by Mel for having suffered the trauma of catching her mother at it. Mine's purple, Mel's is pink. Compared to Mel, I feel really green, but being around her, our eyelids caked in glitter shadow, blue for her and green for me, and wearing really dangerous boob tubes is enough to make me imagine I'm on a level with her, though not chest-wise.

'You should have seen the fight my parents had at the Italian.'

'Tell me about it.'

'Dad went ape when Mom told him off for being upset about this bloke taking the gap down south.'

'Well I don't blame him. Our troopies aren't risking their lives so people can duck.'

'Ja well. It was a big scene. Carla stormed out, then Mom, then Dad.'

'Lucky you were in an Italian restaurant then, they would have understood.'

I laugh. 'Well John and I sat there and ordered spaghetti and pizza and drank two glasses of wine each. We felt quite bombed by the time everyone came back.'

'Ja well everyone's always getting bombed around here too.'

'I'm still as flat as a pancake,' I say to Mel pulling my boob tube up in the mirror. We stare at ourselves.

'No you're not!' Mel laughs pulling down my top.

'Yours are so much bigger than mine. Like the buns versus the coconut macaroons.' I tug Mel's dress down. She shrieks and tugs mine down too. We're on the floor laughing, buns and macaroons flying all over the place.

'Watch my hair man,' Mel says.

Our hair has been carefully flicked with Mel's mom's hot tongs. As I try to stand up again, she shoves me back down on the pink fluffy bath mat.

'It won't take much for Glen to whip that off you,' I laugh. We stand up again and adjust our dresses in the mirror.

'Well, he's not gonna get the opportunity,' Mel says.

'Have you spoken to him yet?'

'No. I don't answer his calls. I want him to suffer.' She lunges at me and grabs at the top of my dress. 'Shall we stick some socks in?'

'Ja, just one though, rolled into a tube.' We open the bathroom door, laughing. Mel's dark, thick-set, cow-eyed, rugger-bugger brother Mark is there.

'I'm as flat as a pancake,' he sings.

'Put a sock in it man,' Mel says.

'I'd be glad to. Jay?' He gestures towards his bedroom.

'Very funny. Where's Mom?'

'I'm driving.'

'Ja, right, in your dreams. Mo – om!' Mel shouts as we walk up the white-painted passage hung with studio portraits of Mark and Mel as gorgeous big-eyed babies. Maggie Martin is on the veranda, drinking a G and T and smoking. She looks like an older, more tanned version of Mel except her long bouncy hair is dyed blonde.

'Can we go Mom?'

'Ja. In a minute.' Maggie's head tips forward slightly towards her glass.

'Please, Mom. Now.' Mel is scared that Maggie will be too bombed to drive.

'Okay, man.' Maggie says. 'It's not the bloody races. Hi Jay.'

'It bloody is,' Mel says to me. 'A race against time.'

Maggie is already half bombed. We pile into her car, Mark in the front seat, me and Mel in the back.

'Turn the radio on Mom,' Mel asks Maggie. Mark switches it on.

'It's *Rumble in the Jungle*,' says Mel.

'It's not called *Rumble in the Jungle*, it's called '*In Zai-in-Zaire.*'

'It's just called *Zaire*, kiddies,' says Mark, looking at us in the rear view mirror. Maggie slaps his right ear to get him to move his head out of the way.

'Klup him harder next time,' says Mel.

'It's about Muhammad Ali's fight in Zaire,' says Mark, still leering at us in the rear view mirror.

'Thanks for the education', says Mel, smearing purple lipstick on her lips, leaning forward to look in the mirror.

'It's not helping,' says Mark.

Mel pulls a finger at him. Mark laughs and reaches for Maggie's Berkeleys and offers them to us in the back.

'Ja, Mark. For sure.'

'Mom knows you poke.'

'Don't be gross Mark. Did you hear that Mom?'

'Yes, darling. I know you smoke.'

'That's not what he said. Anyway, I don't smoke. I've only tried it now and again.' She whispers to me,' like on a daily basis.'

'Ja, like fifty times a day,' says Mark.

Mel's mom is not fazed by anything. I wonder what Mom's reaction would be if she saw me sitting here with all this make-up on, feeling all these weird thoughts, with my hands all sweaty, starting to feel like a doos this dress. Approaching the big gates to Lisa's house I want to duck. I want to look cool not hot. I wish I was in my jeans and my denim jacket with my new Boomtown Rats badge. I smear some of my pink lipstick onto a tissue. Imagine us walking in and everyone bursting out laughing. And that moment of entry is now only moments away. Mel doesn't look worried at all.

'Don't forget to stuff your bra!' Mark yells as we get out the car.

'Stuff you!' yells Mel.

'Mel!' Maggie calls.

Mel ignores her, so she hoots, and then shouts, 'I'll be here at eleven. Be ready.'

'I thought she was going to tell you off for saying stuff you,' I laugh.

'Nah, she doesn't give a stuff,' says Mel. 'Let's party!'

Everyone's around the pool in the huge spot-lit, lush-foliaged garden. Large French doors leading from the dining-room to the pool patio area are wide open and the dining-room table is laden with food. These people have bucks man. I notice some of the guys from the boys' high school. Toby is splashing around in the kidney-shaped pool with a girl. He flings her in the air, her scream cuts off as she sploshes into the water. Mel flicks her hair and eyes up Toby. He's just her type, dark, lean and muscular, with pretty green eyes and strong planes in his face, a bit like Glen, lankier though. Mel turns round and goes inside. The girl surfaces and laughingly adjusts her bikini top, shaking her orange corkscrew hair.

Mel's eating chips 'n dip in the dining-room, ignoring the couple holding hands and whispering to each other.

'Lets get a drink,' I say.

Lisa and Joe, Toby's blonder, older brother, are in the kitchen. Lisa's getting a cream soda out of the fridge, Joe is leaning against the sideboard, looking sexy in jeans and t-shirt.

'Hi Lis,' we both say together.

'Hi Mel, Jay. Do you know Joe?'

'We know Joe,' we say in unison. He's in form six, captain of the high school boys' rugby team and most of the girls except me, think he's kif.

'Hi, Joe. Where are your parents, Lis?' Mel asks.

'Next door at a braai. Joe's in charge.'

'In charge of what?' asks Mel, sitting down at the kitchen table.

'The boys and girls,' says Joe, taking a swig from his beer bottle.

'Oh really? says Mel. 'So, what are we drinking?'

'Well, I'm drinking beer and you're drinking cool-drinks.'

'I'll have a beer, thanks,' says Mel.

'How old are you?' asks Joe leaning up against the kitchen counter, his blue-jeaned legs crossed at the ankles.

'Sweet sixteen,' says Mel, 'and needing a kiss.'

'You're so forward,' says Lisa.

'Better than being backward,' Mel says.

'Beer for you,' says Joe, passing Mel one out of the fridge.

'Castle or Lion?' he asks me.

'Okay, Castle,' I say, a giggle travelling up my back. Mel kicks me on the ankle, while she smiles at Joe.

'You girls always have to push it, don't you?' says Lisa. 'Make sure my parents don't see. I'm going swimming.'

'So, you chicks in Lisa's class?' asks Joe. I've never been called a 'chick' before, so I giggle. Is this what happens when you wear make-up? Feeling like I've suddenly walked into someone else's life, I take another big swig, the beer's already making me feel fizzy. Mel is asking Joe about rugby, as if she gives a flying paw-paw. For some reason this makes me laugh, and I spit some of my beer in a spray as I do so. This makes me laugh even more.

'Get a grip, Jay,' says Mel.

I laugh some more.

'On what?' I ask.

'Who feels like swimming?' asks Joe.

He says who, but he means Mel.

'I'll go,' she says.

'You haven't got a cozzie,' I remind her.

'I'll borrow one of Lisa's. Coming?'

'No thanks.' They leave the kitchen and I finish the beer. It feels good, like suddenly seeing a rainbow after grey skies. I wonder whether to tell Mel about Enoch tonight. I'm beginning to feel a bit better about my dof dress too. I go over to the fridge and reach for another Castle. The sound of a man's 'hello,' makes me hit my head on the edge of the fridge. It's Lisa's father.

'Sorry, I was just –'

'No, please help yourself. And pass me a beer while you're at it.'

Feeling nervous, in a giggly sort of way, I don't know whether he means 'help myself to a beer,' or just help myself to a soft-drink. Deciding not to take the risk, I grab a Coke and turn round. Lisa's father is smiling at me. He has very twinkly blue eyes, grey hair and a tan, a bit like Paul Newman, though I feel sure Mr Nash was just an ordinary man before, a 'Lisa's dad' kind of man. He smiles at me, then, realising that I've been smiling at him for longer than necessary, I turn away.

'Pretty dress,' he says.

I feel all warm inside, picturing 'warm' moving through me, an orange glow, spreading from my feet upwards to my head where it tingles and floods.

'Ja. I'll just go swimming,' I say.

'Don't forget to take your dress off,' he says. For some reason I don't mind that he has said this. As I walk away, I trip over a bit of loose lino on the floor. Mr Nash grabs my arm and looks right into my eyes.

'Careful,' he says.

I laugh and leave the kitchen to look for Lisa to ask to borrow a cozzie. Glancing over my shoulder, I almost feel like Mr Nash is going to follow me. The thought scares and excites me at the same time. Down the passage heading for Lisa's room, I am distracted by the sight of albums scattered over the deep-white pile of the carpet in the sunken lounge. Kneeling in front of the stereo, near huge wood-framed picture windows overlooking the south side of the garden, I check out The Carpenters. Karen Carpenter could definitely use a snack. She reminds me of a lighter-shaded, less pretty version of Carla. Looking at her makes me feel gloomy. Dad's probably still sitting on the veranda at home, getting bombed, or sozzling at The Blue Hart. My mind-frame switches from Dad to Enoch. But Dad keeps coming back. Dad on the veranda, night after night, when he's home from call-up, going on about 'the situation,' not caring who he's talking to. These days he speaks the same way to Mom, Carla, me, Godfrey, his mates, the dogs. I picture Mom in Dr Sheldon's office, draped over his desk, possibly as Dad imagines her, a paranoid projection, as Mom calls it. I force myself to think of something else. Mr Nash smelt of tobacco, like the Texan Cigarette man. Enoch had a clean, strong smell, and his breath has a kind of fermented sweetness to it. White boys have a marshmallow whiff to them or disguise themselves with Brut. If any of these people came near me, I mean properly near me, I'd freak right out. Joe and Toby are good looking. I could lie awake in the dark and think about them, imagine what it might be like to kiss them, but they're not exciting. Maybe because they are not dangerous. I pick up *Super Trouper.* I still love ABBA. I'll always love ABBA.

The party seems to be all over the place. Walking past Lisa's room, I see Mel is half-sitting half-lying on Lisa's bed. Joe is half-lying on her. They remind me of the marble statues I've seen in books on Rome, though Mel and Joe have their clothes on still. My feet feel like they have been cast in cement, like I'm on my own little marble mound, set in silent stone. My eyes sweep over them, they do not see me. Peter Frampton looks down at them from the wall, as do the members of Led Zeppelin. Mel and Joe are beginning to heat up. Joe's hand keeps sliding up Mel's leg. Mel keeps slapping it, as her tongue flicks in and out of Joe's mouth. Every now and again she pauses from this flicking to giggle and then she flicks again, flick, flick, flick, she's the snake and Eve at the same time.

I snap out of it and stop staring. As I turn to leave, I notice that Joe has pulled Mel's boob tube down slightly. Underneath the ruching I can see his fingers working like a seamstress.

'They're not udders, you know,' says Mel.

'Shut up, you cow,' says Joe, giggling.

'Only waist up,' says Mel.

They make me want to kotch.

'Yes, Mam,' says Joe. They both laugh.

Out by the pool area, the floodlights are on and the huge lawn is lit up. Down by the tennis courts, I notice Gavin and Wayne and Sandra and Gail. Kevin is speaking to swotty Claire, who's wearing blue make-up and has flicked the fringes of her short, mousy hair. I bet Kevin can't wait to get his big bear paws all over her. Kevin puts a hand on her thigh and I wonder if I have the power to control people with my thoughts. Must try mentally drowning Joe later. Claire places Kevin's hand firmly on the grass. I wander off.

The grass and palm, fern and elephant ear leaves bunched around the garden glow green under the security lights. I take off my sandals to enjoy the thick, coarse blades of the kikuyu lawn underfoot, prickly and soft at the same time, with just a faint suggestion of moisture. The moonflowers smell like Carla's *Charlie* perfume mixed with honey and heat.

And then the sound of footsteps over the grass. I wait. One, two, three seconds before turning around. Would be good if Bruce Lee came flying out of it with a mighty leap, but it is Mel who shatters the night.

'Come and play spin the bottle.'

We sit in a large circle on the lawn, the Bee Gee's singing night feverishly from the portable record player on the lawn.

Sandra holds the bottle. 'Are we gonna strip?' she asks, as if it were cards.

'I hope so,' say Toby and Joe at the same time, clinking their beer bottles together. Mel looks at me, I turn my bottom lip down in mock horror, eyes bulging. Then, remembering my annoyance, I look away.

'I'm up for it,' Mel says.

You're up for anything.

'Ja. I saw,' I say. Mel glares at me. I look at Joe, his pool-clear eyes focus on Mel. In this light, he looks about twelve, his brother looks similar, like two over-grown, naughty foundlings from one of my childhood books.

'I'm not,' says Lis.

'Chicken,' says Morag, leaning against Toby.

'My parents,' says Lis.

'They're next door,' says Joe, 'and the last time I checked, they were all vrot and having a real hose, man.'

We all laugh at this description of fully-grown parents drunk and killing themselves laughing.

'Kif, let's do it,' says Kevin, his arm around Claire who looks stiff. Well, she was a prefect at school. Most of the girls are smiling like zombies and the boys are giggling like girls.

'Okay, if the spin hits you, one piece of clothing off,' says Sandra bossily.

'I'm glad I'm wearing my glasses,' says Claire, putting them on.

'Ja, but are you wearing any brookies?' asks Mel.

'You're a cow, Mel,' says Claire.

'Moo,' says Mel. Joe slaps her leg and laughs.

'Okay, that's enough. Let's play,' says Sandra, and she gives the big, glass Coke bottle a whacking spin.

The bottle is pointing at me.

I am only wearing my boob-tube dress. I wipe the smile from my face with my hand.

Everyone looks expectantly at me. 'What?' I say. 'I've taken off my smile.'

'That doesn't count.'

'Why not? You have to take something off. If I had my shoes on I'd take those off.'

'C'mon. That's not fair.'

'Life isn't fair. I'm not taking anything else off.' I walk off leaving them staring and laughing in disbelief. 'Except myself,' I say over my shoulder.

Back in the kitchen, my face feels like I have been sitting in front of a fire for two hours. As I open the fridge I feel someone's hand on my shoulder. I turn around, and he puts his hand under my chin.

'You're going to be nice when you're older,' he says. Inside I throw daggers at him, but my face is frozen. I stand there for a minute and then walk away, very quickly to Lisa's room. Leaning against the rumpled bed on the floor in her room, I hug my legs up to my chest, wishing I could see Enoch again, feeling as if someone has sucked out my body and only left the skin. Through the window I can hear the shrieks of the girls, and the boys shouting, 'Get them off! Get them off!' I can still feel Mr Nash's hand on my chin.

At home on the veranda, the hanging cane chair squeaks as I twist it round and round till the rope hanging from the ceiling is all knotted up and I'm cocooned in it. Mel, just arrived, plonks down on the saggy couch. I haven't seen her since the party. Meantime she's made up with Glen. She chucks a Crunchie and some biltong at me.

'I bought you presents.'

'Bribes you mean. I can't believe you did that to Glen. You knew you were gonna make up with him.'

'No. I hadn't decided.' She kicks off her clogs and crosses her jeaned legs on the couch.

'And Joe?'

'Joe's got a girlfriend,' she says taking out a Madison from her battered leather bag.

'Oh. So it's all evens Stevens.'

'Look, Jay, when you've had a boyfriend –'

'Suck my toe.'

'Well if you'd like me to –' she flutters her eyelashes.

'Don't be gross, Mel.' I twist the chair so that my back is to her.

'Please don't tell Glen.' She fixes her navy eyes on me.

I lift my feet off the floor and the chair spins faster and faster, blending Mel, the veranda, the cerise bougainvillea and the secrets searing my brain.

6.

As we walk in her flat door I'm arguing loudly with Nessie about whether the Bee Gees use effects on their voices.

'Nah. They just wear very tight trousers,' Nessie says.

She flings the door open wide.

'Surprise!'

On the old car seat couch beneath a framed picture of Ghandi is Enoch. He gets up, smoothing down his khaki trousers, and pulling down his faded pink vest. He reminds me of pictures I've seen in John's photo-book of young Brooklyn boxers.

'I'm just popping to the Greek shop for some cigarettes, be right back.' Nessie winks at me as she goes out the door. Enoch smiles at her. Man. I wish she wouldn't leave.

Not knowing what to say, I end up saying 'Howzit,' as if he's a white guy.

'It is good,' he smiles, coming towards me.

'What?' I laugh.

He takes me by the shoulders and comes to kiss me. I turn my cheek so his lips graze my cheek.

He laughs too. 'You say, "howzit." I say "it is good."' He leaves his hands on my shoulders.

Uncomfortable, I try focussing on the bright coloured cushions made by the women workers at Angel's Peak.

'I said I would see you again,' when he takes his arms away I am aware of a faint smell of not unpleasant perspiration masked by Lifebuoy soap.

'Ja. You did,' I fold my arms.

'Come,' he says, reaching a hand towards me, 'we can sit.'

I sit right over on the other side. He smiles, because of the gap that divides us.

'Let's just sit and pretend nothing's happened, hey?'

He laughs, and picking up his packet of cigarettes, offers me one, which I take.

'Where have you been?' I ask. Leaning in for the lit match that he offers. 'Spying out other farms for attack?' I finger the black and white mattress ticking covering the faded red seat.

He stops smiling. I don't like what seems to be his disappointment in me, but I don't like thinking about what he may have been up to either.

'I have been far,' he says.

My cheeks burn. 'Mozambique far?'

'If I can get an education in my country, Jayne, I will have an education in my country,' he exhales straight up towards the ceiling. Our smoke hovers around the picture of Ghandi.

'I know it's not fair, you know Enoch. I'm not stupid.'

'Many others are stupid.'

'You mean the Europeans.'

He opens his mouth wide and laughs, slapping his thigh as he does so.

'Not just the Europeans,' he takes another inhalation of smoke, then keeps his eyes fixed on mine as he holds it in as if it's dagga smoke and not Madison.

'What do you mean by education?' My eyes flicker up at him, but fall back to the couch. I think of what Nessie has told me about young clever Africans going to Mozambique and Zambia for training. 'You went to Mozambique after John nearly drowned didn't you? Is that when you began your education?'

'Some things are necessary.'

'Was it necessary to attack our farm?' I become conscious of my knee jiggling up and down.

'Many farms have been attacked,' he settles back on the sofa, his legs relaxed and slightly apart.

'Does that make it alright?' I can't relax.

'Nothing is alright Jayne. I do not think it is alright,' he leans forward and crushes his cigarette in the beaten copper ashtray.

'So why did you say nothing? Why didn't you warn me?' I look up at him. 'You made me keep that secret, when we followed Justice.'

'I saw too with you. That day we saw together,' he shifts forwards on the sofa and leans his elbows on his knees, distracting me with the contours of his arms.

'You mean you didn't know till that day?'

He nods as he looks up at me and I want to believe him.

'You were a mujiba weren't you?' I crush my cigarette butt into the blackened copper of the ashtray.

He looks down at the woven rug on the floor. 'When you have a cage built for you, you must escape it. And help another to escape also.'

'You mean the PV? Is that why? Did that make you do it?'

'All I wanted was to live in peace and learn.' He stands up and putting his hands in his pockets, begins to pace in front of the window. 'But then they took my father. And now I cannot rest. We must have change,' he looks out at the jacaranda tree that shakes slightly in the breeze that is coming in from the open window.

Looking down at my hands, I bite at the inside of my lip, welcoming the breeze that cools my hot face.

He turns to face me. 'Sometimes you are trapped on a bridge and there are lions on one side and snakes on the other.'

'Well I know who the snakes are,' I say getting up. 'You are not who I thought you were. You made me keep secrets, but now you won't give me straight answers. You betrayed me. We could have been killed.'

He takes his hands out of his pockets. 'You, you, you. It is not all *you, you, you*.' He slices the air with his hands, just like he used to when I used to follow him hunting, 'but *you* are alive. And yes maybe I have become someone else,' he says, taking me by the shoulders again. I wish he wouldn't because the physical presence of him becomes too distracting when he touches me and makes me more confused about what is right and what is wrong and whether there are any rights or any wrongs anymore.

'Oh. You mean, because of the war. Because of white Rhodesia.'

'Yes and yes,' he puts his hands back in his pockets and looks at me. His eyes look so sad, that for a moment I wonder if he is going to cry.

'What about me. About my family?' I say, trying not to cry myself. 'We too have had to become someone else.'

'No.' He shakes his head. 'It is not the same. You have choices. We have none.'

'No,' I say. 'I do not have – I did not have any choice. You made me into a traitor.'

'To who, to what are you traitor?' He sits down next to me again and his long fingers cover my hand.

I whip my hand away, and immediately feel bad because he still looks pained. We sit in silence for a moment. Our feelings piled up heavily on the seat between us. He is the first to look up. I look directly back at him as he lifts his hand and strokes the side of my face with the back of his fingers, sweeping down from my right temple slowly over my cheekbone, then his knuckles gently graze the right hand corner of my mouth. I jerk my head away.

He takes his hand away. 'You are angry, Jayne. Sometimes anger is the beginning of a new thing.'

'I'm sick of the way you speak!' I say jumping up, surprising even myself. I have no idea what is going on inside me anymore. I feel like jack-in-the-box. 'Why did you and Justice do this to us? Where is he? He ruined our lives!'

I wave my hands around.

He stands up and grabs my wrists. 'It was not Justice – not me that did this to you.'

His wide mouth is level with my eyes. The hollow in his neck pulsates. It looks so fragile, I feel like stabbing my fingers there and ripping.

'I wish you no harm Jayne. Only good.' He pulls my face towards his with both of his hands. As he comes to kiss me I bite down hard on his lower lip. Shocked, I run for the door.

'I wish I'd never seen you again! Tell Nessie I took the bus home.'

Running through the hall, I trip over a loose bit of parquet flooring, stubbing my toe and losing my slip-slop.

'Must I betray my own people?' he shouts to me as I crouch for the slop.

When I glance back, he is touching his lips with the tips of his fingers. He is not angry.

'Like you made me do?' I yell.

'My father was shot.'

I stand up slowly. 'It was an accident,' I say, turning round to see him standing, his hands at his sides. He looks like the boy I knew. My throat hurts with the emotion that is threatening to explode.

'No there are no accidents in Rhodesia. Only coincidences,' Enoch says. 'They say he was trying to escape from the police vehicle.'

I stand there for a moment while his words sink in, before beginning to walk away.

Enoch follows me into the hallway. 'He was shot when he was escaping. But why should he try to escape when he was soon to be released is a big why.'

I stop at the other end of the corridor, staring at the red cement wall in front of me, my back to him. I feel him waiting. But I cannot turn round. I want to run up to him but I don't. And then another burning thought comes up.

'You told your mother didn't you – about when Dad was going on call-up – she ordered the attack didn't she?' I hear Granny Rose's words again. *They consult the witchdoctors about attacks.* The silence between us gives me the answers I need as it always has. Taking off my slip-slops, I run down the cool of the polished cement corridor into the traffic and noise of people and birds outside in the clear air. The tears come, I slap at them, keeping my face down so no one will ask me if I am alright.

'Hey! Jay!' In the street, Nessie comes running from the direction of the Greek shop. 'Where are you off to? Hey, are you okay?' she puts an arm around me.

I move away from her arm. 'Home.'

'Without your stuff?' she asks, putting her arm around me.

Her long hair, her jasmine perfume feels suffocating.

'Go for a walk and cool off. I'll ask Enoch to leave.

'Good idea. And this time make sure it's for good.'

'You don't mean that.'

'I bloody do,' I say heading for the park. 'Don't tell me what I mean.'

In the deserted park, I sit on a bench and allow myself to weep until the pain in my throat and chest goes away. After a while I sit up, dry-eyed. Dad said it was an accident. I thought he meant a car accident.

That evening Nessie takes out a huge black pot from under the sink.

'Wanna chop the tomatoes? I'll do the onions.'

'Why was that man at the shebeen called Raised Fist? Sounds like an Indian chief,' I ask.

'That's his chimurenga name. His freedom name.'

'You mean he's a terrorist?'

'I mean he's a freedom fighter.'

I slide the tomatoes into the clear plastic bowl with the knife. My hand shakes, I was in a place with terrorists. Maybe even the terrs who attacked us were there. Maybe one I tried to shoot. The sharp steel in my hand catches the light from the overhead strip and reflects for a moment the image of Nessie. Dad'd kill her for sure if he knew, hell maybe he'd participate in her disappearance. She pours the sadza into the boiling water, brushing the residue off her white hands.

'Aren't you worried I might tell Dad where you took me for my birthday?'

'No,' Nessie smiles. Man. I might tell Dad just to shock her. To show her I'm not as predictable as she thinks.

'When are you going to make up with Dad?' I ask.

'I haven't broken up with him.'

I chop the tomatoes in half and then into quarters and then into eighths and then into twelfths. They make me think of cut-open hearts.

'Do you care about what happened at the farm?'

'Look Jay, you're all alive and well. This country was taken by violence and enslaved. Violence gives birth to violence. Slavery gives birth to anger and hostility. Zimbabwe's people were tricked into giving power to the pioneers. You know the story of Lobengula, the sanitised version at least. Imagine living in your country, according to your customs, and having some foreigners come and take your land, tell you where you can live and make you pay them for the privilege!'

'I'm sure it wasn't that simple.'

'Well that's basically how it was.'

'Why? Were you there?'

'C'mon Jay.'

'Well that's not what I've heard.'

'Well obviously not Jay. In this country you have to dig a little deeper to find the dirt. It's been pretty on the outside for a long time.'

'Well it's not pretty now. Nearly getting killed is not pretty. What about all those missionaries they've murdered? Man! Babies. People who are here to help them?'

'Yes. People have a lot to answer for.'

'Oh ja, which people, right? Are you talking about what happened to Prospect?'

'Oh Jay. That is one incident amongst so many.'

'Just an incident? Justice – Enoch's father?'

'I mean just one of the many atrocities.'

'So he was killed?'

'What do you think?'

I don't bloody know what to think. He must have been a terrorist or they wouldn't have killed him.

She wipes her onion-streaming eyes with a tea-towel. 'There's a much bigger picture of cause and effect.'

'You must be kidding Nessie. You can't blame us for the murders of the missionaries. You didn't see what happened to John, to Dad, to all of us – at the farm. How can you say that?'

She's looking at me patiently, sympathetically.

'Don't look at me like that. It makes me want to scream. You could have got me killed the other night.'

She smiles. 'No. We were with friends.'

The knife in my hand slams into the board.

Nessie puts her sadza smeared hand on my arm.

'I took you to see your best friend. He was the one who could have been killed for being there. For being here. I took those risks for you.'

'Huh. My best friend was a mujiba.'

Nessie says nothing.

'Right?' I eye her.

'Do you consider your father, your uncle, a murderer?' She stares back at me.

'No. Answer my question.'

'I just have.'

I slam down my knife. 'Man. Do you all go to the same cryptic college? Can you just give straight answers for once? I need to go Nessie. Dad thinks I'm at staying the night at Mel's.'

She takes me by the shoulders.

'Let's eat, and then I'll take you.'

'Whatever you say Nessie.' I cut the tomatoes smaller and smaller.

We're just finishing eating when there's a knock at the door. Nessie gets up quickly, her chair screeching behind her. The phone starts to ring, making me jump. Nessie laughs as she brushes past me. 'Ooops, the flat's taking over –'

She trips over the phone wire as she makes for the door. One of her leather sandals spins on the floor as she opens it.

'Patrick!' Nessie giggles, 'Welcome! There's food in the pot,' says Nessie. I sit there staring at the sadza, remembering standing on the edge of a granite cliff in Inyanga years ago. Creeping towards the edge of the mountain, moving closer and closer to the edge, inch by inch, my brown dusty feet in my old white five-year-old sandals, the pink nail polish patched in the centre of my toe-nails. *What you doing, silly, don't stand so close to the edge.* Dad's big strong arms, closing in on me like gates.

'Ah my young dancer friend.' Patrick comes in wearing a flat cap with a black suit and pink shirt.

Grace comes in next, wearing a red beret with sticky matching lipstick, Communist fashion statement.

'Any trouble coming up?' Nessie asks as Grace flings her beret on the couch and runs a hand over her shorn head. Zero afro now.

'Well, we did see the caretaker, who asked us where we were going at this time of night. Just like being at school,' Grace says, plonking herself down on the carseat-couch.

'What did you say?' Nessie asks.

'I said we had to wait for the baas to come home from after dinner drinks before he could pay me. I said that I was the cook.'

Patrick sits on the beanbag on the floor. He smiles at me.

Nessie laughs at me. 'I don't think I've ever seen you look lost for words Jay.'

Nessie takes the pot of sadza off the table and puts it on the floor in the middle of the room; she does the same with the frying pan of wors and the little white enamel pot with the tomato and onion gravy in it.

As I get up to take my plate to the kitchen, Nessie looks up from where she's crouching on the floor in front of Patrick and the pots.

'Jay, could you grab another plate?' She smiles. 'And some knives and forks. Thanks.'

Sure. And should I polish the ammo as well?

In the kitchen I lean against the kitchen cupboards, running my fingers behind me on the metal ridges of their tops. Outside, I can hear the high-pitched sound of a woman arguing with a man. The traffic moves slowly up and down. African jazz comes from the lounge. I open the drawer, staring at the stainless steel. My vision blurs. Maybe Nessie and I will be locked up together. Nessie will shout. Nessie will be sarcastic. Nessie will go over the top. But we won't be able to get out. The steel cutlery is cold in my warm glistening hands.

Patrick lies on the floor propped up on an elbow eating sadza with his hands. Grace perches on the edge of the couch delicately holding a piece of wors between her thumb and forefinger. They didn't need knives and forks. I hand them over anyway.

'Come and join us Jay.'

Ja we could discuss manoeuvres.

'I think I'll go to bed if that's okay.'

'Okay,' Nessie smiles, 'I'll come and tuck you in.'

On Nessie's bed, pooled in the square of light cast by the streetlamp, I want to think of something other than Enoch, Nessie and the *freedom fighters* in the other room. Back home, at Angel's Peak, lying upside down on my bed with my feet on the wall, I could see the edge of the huge flamboyant tree curving itself over the lawn and watch the frangipani outside my window. I used to love lying there in the afternoons, reading, listening to the louries or watching the dust float like fairies in the shaft of sunlight streaming in from the window onto the floor. Sometimes the light would disappear suddenly as if it were afraid of the rain that it knew was coming; the sky would darken and the sky would split with cracks and whips of lightning and bellows of thunder. The earth could do nothing about it, just strain beneath it, the rain soaking into the earth. A most delicious smell came after the rain, dry, spicy, dampened, soil heat smell. Afterwards the earth would feel good, after this forced drink, and the green would glow on the rows of the tea plantations and the earth would turn a richer, darker brown. Bugs and worms and snakes would churn up this soil and slime in and out of it, wallowing and slithering and swallowing and regurgitating and shitting. And then the earth would be still, until that dry smell came again. And then the tremble in the earth would rise and the rain would come, because that is what is good for the earth. The swikiros would come down from the hills after praying to the rain spirits. And the worker in his gumboots and blue overalls in the field would dig his spade into the earth and look up and sniff the air. And the woman with the long pestle would stop pounding the last of the maize from the store-house and look up and smile at the sky, pleased at the order of things. The maize would grow. And the people would be pleased. I drift off to sleep.

I wake because I'm still on top of the African print fabric cover and it's cold. Nessie didn't come to tuck me in. I listen to the voices coming from the next room. Now it seems there's more than four. I can hear other male, African voices. One, in particular, sounds cold.

'This act will make their bones crumble.'

'We will strike them in their hearts,' Grace says.

'One decisive act. This is what we need.' The rumble of Patrick's boomy, friendly voice.

The phone rings and I listen to Nessie's voice outside the door. 'It's good to hear you. We've just been speaking about it. I understand – I do understand correctly don't I?'

There's a pause and then I hear, 'We will be together again – yes, I know there are more important things.'

From the lounge I hear, 'So. Who's for tea?' Followed by the laughter.

I need the toilet, but I'm too scared to leave the room, so instead get under the covers, burrowing deep down into the bed, trying and failing to make a warm nest, my feet are so cold.

7.

The avocado-green walls glow in the dining-room. We Camerons
are cocooned in this light, on this night in 1978. The water in my
glass shivers. John's kicking the dining-room table. Dad looks up
from *The Rhodesia Herald*.

'Will you stop that bloody kicking boy!'

Mom leaves off staring into space and puts her hand on John,
smiling at him.

'Bloody bastards! I can't bloody believe it! Can you believe it
Irene?'

'What? What can't I believe?'

'Mom?' I say.

'What?'

'Have you gone penga? You're behaving like a robot. You can't
say, "What can't I believe," as if Dad's got access to your headspace?'

'Ja,' says Dad, from behind the paper, 'someone else got access
to your headspace, hey Reen?'

'How was your Women's Institute meeting?' I ask Mom.

'It was stimulating. Made me think.' She flaps her hand at a
hovering mozzie.

'About what?'

'Well. It was about the future role of women in African society.'
Mom sighs and spoons some more mash onto her plate even though
she hasn't finished the last mound. She looks at her watch.

'Sounds optimistic.'

'Hmm. Where is she?' She means Carla. Carla is late back from her first proper ballet prac since the accident.

'Bloody interfering bloody American UN bastard.' Dad breaks off to shovel some mash and wors into his mouth. Bloody terrorist supporter. He thinks Mugabe is a gentleman! What kind of man must he be? If Mugabe is a gentleman? Is he a cannibal axe-murderer?'

John's potato explodes from his mouth as he laughs. It settles on the tablecloth and partly Mom's forearm.

Mom brushes her arm, hardly noticing. Has Sheldon been giving her drugs or what?

'Don't shout Dave,' she says staring at her food.

'Would you bloody look at me woman!'

Mom looks at Dad, pretty reluctantly.

'Can you BELIEVE it? They'd put that bastard on the throne.'

John is laughing into the rest of his food, spikes of dark hair bobbing in the circle of light from the glass-shaded bulb above.

Mom slams down her fork.

'Ja, I can bloody believe it Dave! I'd bloody believe anything!' She gets up, her chair clatters to the floor behind her. John and I stare up at her; her skin seems thinner and whiter than ever, as if the blood has shrunk inside her. Her purple t-shirt looks grubby. There's a pale arc of gravy from her plate just under the band at the top of her pink wrap-around skirt. Her hair, which lately reaches past her shoulders, is wrapped around green plastic rollers. She picks up her plate and heads for the kitchen. John looks at me, eyebrows raised, front teeth over bottom lip. Dad looks up from his paper. 'Wha'did I say?'

'I dunno, but Mom believes it,' I say.

Dad doesn't look much better. His hair is going greyer around the temples and he's got a little pot-belly despite his frequent call-ups.

The front door slams and Carla walks in, her long hair wild around her winged shoulder blades. 'Hi!'

'HI!' shout John and me.

'Has everyone gone bloody mad?' asks Dad. 'Why are you all shouting?'

'Ja,' say John and me, like the two old men from the muppets.

320

We crack up. 'We are quite, quite mad – Dad,' I add.

'Bit late aren't you?' Dad asks Carla, but she's already out the room.

'BIT LATE AREN'T YOU!' Dad yells.

Carla keeps walking.

'Hey!' Dad gets up. 'Hey where d'you think you're going?'

Ja. Come back for the inquisition. He follows her down the passage.

'To drop off my stuff –' Carla's voice tails off, like her ballet career.

Mom comes back in. 'Is that Carla?' she says, all perky as if she hadn't come over all weird.

'No. It was the second coming of Christ.'

'There's no need for that Dave.'

'There bloody is. Someone's got to bail us out of this mess and I believe it's only the Messiah that's able to do it.'

'Don't blaspheme Dave.'

'Ja, ja. Every Sunday. You're in the cathedral, doek on your head, hey Reen?'

Carla's come back into the room. She sits down next to John, ruffling his hair as she does so. John squirms out of the way.

'How was ballet? Good to be back? Will you be on track for December?' Mom asks, still perky, but showing the strain in her rapid-fire questioning. Carla's supposed to be in The Nutcracker in December.

'I didn't go,' Carla says.

Surprise!

Mom smiles. 'Pardon?' she says. Mom never says 'pardon'.

'WHAT?' Dad slams the paper down on the table.

'There's no need to shout Dad,' says Carla, curling her hands over the back of my chair.

'Oh there isn't? Well give me a good reason not to. Okay?'

Mom looks at him. 'Dave, just –' she looks back at Carla. 'What happened?'

'Nothing, I just didn't go.'

'You just didn't go?' Dad says. 'Get me another beer Jay.'

'Ja, that's your answer to everything Dad,' says Carla.

Dad gets up.

'You better give me an answer, my girl. And watch your mouth.'

John sticks his lower lip out, while lowering his eyes, he's trying to watch his mouth. He's so stupid that I laugh. Mom is staring at the gravy-splattered tablecloth.

'You had no intention of going. Did you Carla?'

Ding! Lights on Mom!

'Nooo. And if people were a bit more reasonable around here maybe I'd have told you sooner. Sorry,' she says quickly, glancing up. 'Sorry Mom. I don't mean it like that. It's just – difficult – all your expectations. I can't explain it Mom. I feel like I've been rewired.' She lifts her palms upwards. 'And it's wrong. I've been rewired all wrong.'

She looks down at her hands, then up at Mom.

'Hey, we're reasonable,' says John, snapping out of his face routine.

'Ja, we are,' I smile at John. Carla smiles at us. Our parents look confused. Dad gets up and goes out of the room.

Carla looks at Mom, she takes her hand. It's like a scene from some soapie.

'Pass the tissues,' says John. That does it, I crack up, I laugh so much that my stomach hurts. John falls off his chair, all I can see are his tackies waving in the air. Carla and Mom ignore us.

'Mom, since the accident, I've just lost my desire to dance. I can't explain it. It's just not in me anymore. The will to dance. It's gone.'

Mom cries quietly, her tears dripping on the tablecloth. We stop laughing.

'I mean. It's not just because I don't have the same strength anymore. It's – I just don't have the hunger for it anymore – Mom, if I'm gonna dance, I want the juicy parts. I'm not content with being on the sidelines. And if you're going to be a principal you have to be really hungry for it.'

'Oh Carla, you've always been so talented,' Mom says, wiping her eyes with the back of her hand.

'I know,' she laughs. 'I mean, there are lots of talented dancers Mom, I just don't want it enough anymore.'

'Waah, ha, haaaah!' John falls on the floor and mock sobs, which makes everyone laugh.

Mom sighs. 'Well Carls, whatever makes you happy.'

'Thanks Mom,' Carla goes over and gives Mom a big fat hug. Dad stands in the doorway ankles crossed, one slip-slop hanging off, a beer in his hand. Carla goes over and gives him a hug too. 'I'm sorry Dad,' she says.

'Waste of bloody money.' Dad looks down at his brown beer bottle as if he's speaking to it and not to Carla.

'It wasn't Dad. It made me happy – for a long time. Just not anymore.' She turns back to look at Mom, 'Mom, Dad, I'm gonna be an air-hostess, I got the papers from Air Rhodesia today.'

The girl is a star in her own show. Even if it is a low budget soapie.

Carla's begun her air-hostess training and has got us tickets on the viscount flight for Kariba this Friday. So we'll be ducking from the suburbs and seeing some of *Rhodesia is Super*. Glen might come too if he gets leave from call-up, and if he does, he's promised to bring Mel. And mushy-sterek and I'd kiss you if your name was Derek, we're going to stay at Caribbea Bay, pools and nightclubs and all. Carls says she's going to dress me up and try to sneak me into one of the nightclubs for the first time. I'm lying on Carla's bed watching her pack.

'Mmmm, very sexy,' Mom holds up a pair of red pants. 'Oooh and a bra to match.' She looks at Carls. 'I hope you're being careful.'

'Ja, like you were, hey Mom?' Carla says.

Mom puts a hand on her hip and looks at Carls.

'Ja well, don't try tell me I was conceived after the white wedding Mom,' Carla persists despite Mom's mock-horror expression.

'Carla!' I say.

'Well it's true Jay,' Carla snatches the pants from Mom's hands and flings them on the top of the pile of clothes in her case.

'I'm just saying be careful Carls, I'm not judging you,' Mom says, slapping her on the bum. 'You are my daughter, I have a right to worry.'

'Okay, worry, but I'd prefer if you didn't think about it as such. Okay Mom?'

'And I'd prefer it if you didn't discuss it,' I say.

When Mom leaves, Carla tries on her new bikini.

'I don't think my boobs are big enough for the cups. Look there's a little crease here.' She shows me a slight puckering on the left side of her bikini top.

'So? You can't notice it. Anyway people won't be looking over there.'

Carla pulls a face and chucks the cushion from the dressing-table stool at me. I catch it, but don't throw it back. Instead, I settle it over my stomach.

'Do you ever worry about Dad's drinking?' I ask.

'No not really. Mom drinks just as much, so does everyone. How else are they meant to cope with this bloody war? People dying all over the place? Anyway, why worry, I wanna party.' She does a little sixties dance, jiggling and waving her arms up and down.

Carla flops down on the bed next to me.

'I can't wait to get to Kariba.' I say. 'I'm sick of this town. At Angel's Peak, the msasa leaves will be fiery red and the mahobohobo trees will be full of fruit now.'

'You're quite the poet Jay. But time to get over it though hey?'

'I'll never get over it. Why should I?'

Flicking through her albums on the floor I say, 'Donna Summer, urgh, I hate disco. What is she wearing?'

'Why don't you like modern music? You're so weird Jay.'

I like chimurenga music too. The thought of dancing at the township makes me well up. Why do I have to like what is complicated?

'Jay? Are you crying? Why so sensitive? You can keep loving the old stuff.' She looks into my face. 'It's okay, I won't tell anyone!'

Imagine marrying Enoch. Our children would be classed as coloureds. When I was little, I kept trying to spot these rainbow-coloured people I had heard about, but not seen. Seen and not heard.

She digs me in the ribs. I scream. Then laugh.

'I'll say.' She puts her head on my shoulder. She gets off the couch.

'Want your nails painted?' she asks.

'Ja, for sure. Can I have that glittery Miners stuff Granny sent from England?'

'You ca-aan. Come sit on the bed.'

'Thanks Carls.'

Carla opens the little white cupboard by the bed and takes out a pale blue yoghurt tub, opening it up to reveal bottles of nail-polish and multi-coloured eye-shadows. She sits cross-legged on the bed, the faded red stool-cushion on her lap. I sit cross-legged in front of her as she selects a little square bottle of pink glittery nail polish. She unscrews the top and the smell of the polish hits my nose. I inhale deeply.

'Jay! You freak.'

I laugh. 'I love the smell of nail polish.'

Carla wiggles her bottom into a more comfortable position. 'Okay, hands. You're a beautiful freak, Jay.'

I extend my right hand onto the cushion. Carla bends over it and begins to slick my nails with polish. It feels cold and wonderful. I love its hard, glittery, fake beauty and its chemical smell. Carla's so beautiful, with her tanned skin and red bikini, her dark curls hanging over her face. She looks like she did in an old picture of her at the sea-side, concentrating on building a sandcastle, not noticing Mom or Dad, or whoever it was that was taking the picture. She looks up at me and smiles. I smile back. Carla finishes my pinkie nail. 'Other hand.'

'So, how's it going with Spike?' I say.

'Ag, I don't know, he's good-looking and everything. But he's, I dunno, he's got psychological problems – because of the war – and he's so bloody jealous.'

'And you haven't?'

She glances at me, knowing I'm talking about her eating.

'You know nothing about my life. About what's happened to me – how I feel.'

I try to shift the atmosphere by joking around. 'You never give your boyfriends cause for jealousy hey?' I shove a cushion at her with my foot.

'Going out tonight?' I ask. 'Who're you going with?'

She doesn't say anything.

'Is it a secret?'

'I'll give you a clue' she says, concentrating on painting my index fingernail, 'he flies.'

'Superman?' I laugh, willing a warmer response. 'Obviously not Spike.'

'Spike's in England, with his aunt, getting treatment.'

'Carls. How could you?' I sit down on the bed.

She glances up at me. 'We've broken up. Well, I told him I couldn't marry him.'

'You mean you were going to marry him?' I say shaking my hands to dry my nails.

'Well I was thinking about it. Everything changed after the accident.'

'Ja. I remember. You dumped Ian for Spike.'

'Don't try to be clever Jay.'

'What? So you said you wouldn't marry him, but not that you were gonna break up with him – Carls – that's dishonest. You're two timing him. With someone who flies? A pilot? You know what pilot's are like.'

'Well, yes actually. I do.'

'You're disgusting Carla.'

She looks at me, both eyebrows raised. 'What about you?'

My hands begin to sweat.

'What about me?'

'Well. Let's talk about honesty Jay. You like African men, don't you?'

'Whada'you mean? I'm fourteen years old? How can you say that?'

'You always preferred blacks to normal friends.'

My blood heats. I stand up. 'You mean Enoch? He's not normal? You're the one who says girls need guys who are older.'

'You're such a cow, Carla,' I shake my head. 'I can't believe this.'

'Well it's time you took a long hard look at yourself and moved on.' She gets up, turning her back as she screws the lid on the nail polish and puts it back in the tub.

'Meaning?'

She turns around. 'This is Rhodesia 1978. Not cloud cuckoo-land.'

'Huh, this is cloud cuckoo-land.'

'How can you expect me to go out with Rhodie boys? I have nothing in common with them.'

She laughs, 'How about your skin colour? Do you know what people will call you?' she laughs.

I think about Courtenay back in junior school. 'Yes I do.'

'You need to stop feeding the toilet your food.' The words fly out like bats as I walk out and I wish I hadn't said them. *Beautiful freak* she said.

My fingers knot and unknot the twists in the telephone wire, heels rocking back and forth on the loose parquet tiles of the hall floor, *click, click, click, click.*

'Would you like to come to the farm with me this weekend? To see Granny Rose? I think it's time Jay. It's been nearly two years.'

'When? No I'll be in Kariba. Besides, I've seen her, here and at Uncle Joe's since we left. See? You don't know everything.'

There is a pause.

'Kariba? What day are you going on? What time are you leaving? Are you sure? And coming back? Give me your flight details and I'll pick you up.'

'Oh ja. Dad'd love that.'

'Give me your flight details anyway.'

'Why?' The receiver is heavy in my palm.

'Just tell me Jay.'

'I'll check the time with Carla.'

I pull out another twist in the telephone wire as Carla comes out of the bedroom.

'Bye Mel!' I say clicking the receiver into place. Its black arm rocks slightly in its cradle.

Their arguing cuts into the night like a panga fight. Mom's voice is high, accusing. Dad's bellows back. I cover my head with my pillow. My bedroom door opens and Carla stands in a wedge of light.

'Can I come in?'

'You're in already.'

She sits down on the bed.

'Jay? I'm sorry. For the way I spoke to you. Look. I don't understand you, but I love you anyway.'

I hug her. 'I'm sorry about what I said too,' it was low.

'Low,' Carla says in a low voice and we both laugh.

After she leaves, I realise she probably thinks I have as big a psychological disorder as hers. So would most people around here. Maybe I do, or maybe they do. Is it catching? Can a whole country get it?

8.

Dad drops us off at the airport. I give him a big hug, and he gets a pink lip-glossed cheek from Carla, before we head through the glass doors. Huge photographs of Victoria Falls, Zimbabwe Ruins and Lake Kariba hang from the high walls that extend to the open plan second floor. People are streaming in from recently landed flights below the *Welcome to Salisbury Sunshine City* sign. Walking past the little gift shop that sells copper ashtrays, *Rhodesia is Super* t-shirts, biltong and soapstone carvings, we check the bags in and then head up the stairs to the bar and park off on stools at the central bar watching the South African Airways and Air Rhodesia planes landing and taking off through glass windows in front of us. The doors to the viewing area are locked and the balcony is closed now because of the war. Outside, a patch of black birds, small as coffee grinds appear from the pale blue above an aircraft. Heat rises from the gleaming silver bodywork of the plane in undulating ripples.

'Look,' I say.

'Ja. Mike says it only takes one bird in an engine to bring down a plane,' says Carla.

'Great, thanks for sharing that with me.' I take a swig of my lemonade, laced with some of Carla's Castle. She said it would steady my nerves, even though I don't feel nervous, just excited.

'Even a jumbo jet?'

'Ja,' she takes a pull on her cigarette. 'Apparently,' she exhales.

'Shit hey.'

'Ja. Shit hey, and shit happens.' She takes a sip of her drink.

A little girl presses her face to the window, her left hand wrapped around her Coke bottle, right hand resting on the glass.

'Remember when we could just go out on the balcony and watch the planes,' Carla says.

'Remember when we used to come here in our pyjamas and wait for Auntie Aldie to arrive from South Africa.'

'Ja, she'd have South African sweets for us.'

'Ja, fizz-pops. We were only after the loot.' I throw some pink sugared-peanuts into my mouth.

'You're such an oke Jay.'

Enoch doesn't think I'm an oke.

Carla stands up as Mike approaches in his Air Rhodesia uniform, looking like a blend of James Dean, Clint Eastwood and someone else good, who I can't put my finger on, basically, the Good, the God and no Ugly. He's greyish-blonde-haired with a tanned face and steel blue eyes.

'You're quite the lady,' he says smiling at me. 'You must be Jay.'

And you're quite the man, handsome pants, I smile back. He bends slightly to kiss Carls. Carla puts both her hands round his neck to kiss him and as he draws away, she strokes one red-finger-nailed hand down his cheek.

'See you girls soon,' Mike says as he turns and walks off towards a couple of air-hostesses in pale blue Air Rhodesia skirt suits standing a little way off. They smile at him as he approaches, one of them pulls her tight skirt down a little, both flutter at him like butterflies as Carla and I watch.

'They better watch it,' she says.

'No, I think you better watch it,' I say.

As we walk across the hot tarmac, the smell of plane fuel mixed with excitement gives me a high. I feel like leaping in the air and clicking my ankles together, or just racing across the tarmac spinning and jumping with my arms flung out, like Julie Andrews in the Sound of Music. I'm lugging my shoulder bag so I just kick at my bum with my heels instead.

'Bloody lunatic, Jay.' Carla laughs.

The screaming of the engines jacks me up even higher. Carla hugs me round the waist as we reach the top of the steps where our smiles plant straight into the faces of the air-hostesses who were talking to Mike. Carls immediately stops smiling.

'Hello,' they say together.

'Are you Mike's friends?' The one with the blonde pony-tail says.

Carls says nothing. 'Ja,' I say.

'Mike said for us to take you to the cockpit,' the one with the dark bun, says. I'm sure she emphasized the 'cock' bit.

'Oh, ja, we'd love to go to the cock-pit,' I say.

Mike is sitting in his high-backed, black-leather pilot's seat without his cap on. His straight grey hair is spiky and shiny. He introduces us to the co-pilot, a dark-haired, freckly-faced guy also called Mike.

'Just as well we use our surnames, hey, or one of us Mikes would've had to get on our bike, hey,' says dark-haired Mike.

Dark-haired Mike is about as original as salted chips. Carla runs her hand up the back of her Mike's hair. His spiky grey hair ripples through her fingers. 'Hey,' he says moving forwards a bit, he seems a bit embarrassed.

'What do all those do?' I ask, gesturing to all the dials.

'That tells us how high we are,' he says. He points to another instrument.

'And that tells us which direction we're going in so we don't get lost!'

'Oh, great, I say.'

He laughs again, 'Don't worry, we have everything under control.'

Carla's giving her Mike a sort of shoulder massage.

'Apart from Carla,' I say. Everyone laughs and then the radio crackles. Carla's Mike starts speaking into the radio. *Roger, ten minutes and you can clear us for take off.* The person in the control tower says something else that I don't quite catch. Mike laughs.

'Who's Roger?' says Carls.

'Ha ha,' I say.

'You lovely ladies will have to leave now,' Carla's Mike says, 'we've got a plane to fly.'

Carla takes her hands off his shoulders, he pats her left hand.

'See you when we land. Shereen and Sandra will take care of you.'

We walk out through the little door. I bang my head on the top as we do.

'Oops,' says Sandra, the dark-haired air-hostess. 'Take your seats please.' She indicates the middle area of the plane.

Shereen smiles up at us from the service area, where she crouches, pulling out metal drawers with miniature bottles of booze and tins of mixers.

'Shereen and Sandra – lekker names hey Carls?'

'Bitches,' says Carls.

As our plane moves slowly down the runway, Carla lights up. Shereen comes over.

'Could you extinguish that 'til after take-off please,' she says. Carls smiles stiffly at her, but she puts out her cigarette in the ashtray in the arm of her seat. 'Go wipe up some vomit Shereen,' she says to her retreating back.

I laugh. 'Ja, go serve drinks, sky-waitress.'

Carls puts her head on my shoulder and we look out the window over the wing together. The plane is slowly turning.

"*Ladies and Gentlemen* (everyone laughs), *this is your captain Mike Tanner speaking, I'd like to welcome you aboard this Viscount 307, flight 23, to Kariba, hold on to your hats* (everyone laughs), *we'll be taking off in two minutes. I'd like to take this opportunity to introduce you to Mike – yes Mike* (everyone laughs) *Viljoen, my co-pilot, and to wish you a very enjoyable fright* (more laughter) – *I mean flight.*"

People laugh a bit more nervously.

At Kariba airport, we hop in our taxi and our driver puts his foot down flat. The car jolts forward, the beads hanging off the rear view mirror swinging.

'Eh he, where you going ledes?' The driver smiles at us, zero teeth in front.

Carla and I try not to crack up. Every now and again the driver looks at us through the rear-view mirror and smiles some more. The movement of his lower jaw causes his grizzled beard to point horizontally forward. He has a bit of what looks like porcupine quill through his nose as well as two round wooden plugs about the size of buttons through his upper and lower lips. And then, remembering something Uncle Pat said I twig, he must be Batonka – one of the oldest of the tribes of Rhodesia. They have the best huts with solid wood carved doors and raised sleeping levels. Other tribes laugh at them because they let their goats sleep below them. They bury all the belongings of their dead with the deceased not far from the front door and then dance on the person's grave until their spirit returns to the family. Uncle Pat said Batonka girls get their first six teeth knocked out by the tribal dentist. She needs to be held down, her head gripped in the vice of her mother's thighs and hands, her brothers and father holding down her legs as the blade of an axe head is inserted between two teeth, while another axe head knocks them out, bloody roots and all. Hot porridge is smeared over her gaping gums to dull the pain. We wind around hills dense with sun-bleached bush. The dam wall looms above us in the distance, holding back the waters of the biggest man-made lake in the world.

'Shit hey that's incredible,' I say.

'Ja, amazing view, hey,' Carla says.

The driver nods and smiles. Buried in that dam wall are the bodies of eighty-six Italian workers who fell into liquid cement while constructing the wall after the valley was flooded and the wildlife rescued and herded onto the islands. We descend the hills at the base of the Matusadona Mountains that cradle the lake, which is as big as Wales. Closer and closer, we edge towards the island-studded water. A speedboat cuts up the lake, its wake like a plane unzipping the sky. Branches and butterfly-shaped pods from the high mopani trees litter the sun-baked road.

'Ele-phant,' the driver says; he slows down even more than he has so far and takes his hands off the wheel, extending them outwards. 'Ele-phant.' Then he points to the road and puts his right hand to his lips.

'Oh, elephants break off the branches to eat the leaves,' I say.

Our driver nods, smiling, pleased to have got his point across. The lake gets closer and closer, until we can see the white branches of the drowned trees of Kariba clutching towards the sky like the skeleton hands of drowned sailors.

In our hotel room, I flop down on the cream bedspread and wave my legs in the air.

'I 'spose I'll be sleeping alone in this bed,' I say.

'Come check the view,' Carla says.

I lean over the balcony with her. It looks like the sun has exploded, the clouds are whipped up and smeared over a blood-red sky into various shades of pink and orange. The dead trees of the lake stick up blackly now towards the sky as if they've been burnt by the sun. It's beyond words.

'If I never see another sight again, I could die knowing I've seen the best sight on earth,' says Carls.

I bash Carla's hip with mine.

'Don't say that Carls, you give me the freaks.'

'Well, you know what I mean,' she says.

'Hey, nice pair of bums,' says a voice.

We swing round to look into the room. It's Glen, in shorts, slip-slops, and sporting a huge furry beard. I run over and hug him. He lifts me up and I swing my legs up round his waist.

'If you leave door open, you don't know who's gonna wander in hey.'

'What's this, fur?' I ask, grabbing his beard.

Glen laughs. Carls comes over and gives him a kiss on the side of the cheek.

'Like the beard. I'm going to shower.'

Glen takes the chair in front of the mirror and desk combo, while I fling myself on the bed.

'Where's Mel? How'd you get here?' I ask.

'I was dropped off, hey.'

'Uh huh, working in the area? Gisa'slug.' He hands me the bottle.

He raises his eyebrows up and down. 'I phoned her mother, and asked her to put her sixteen-year-old sugar-baby on a plane. I'm fetching her from the airport later.'

'I'll see you and your sister in the downstairs bar. The pilots're down there, 'he walks towards the door, sticks his bum out, and wiggling it, he looks over his shoulders and makes his voice go higher, 'with some air hostesses.' He pats an invisible mound of coiffed hair and goes out the door. He's quite a hose.

Everyone is getting bombed around the bar. Carla's draped across Mike who sits on a barstool drinking brandy and cokes. He keeps slapping her on the bum. Shereen sits on the other Mike, who keeps nearly falling off his barstool every time she lunges at him. He musses her hair so that it looks like a yellow pantomime wig. Orangey-red lipstick kisses are smeared all over her face. She's part pretty, part road accident victim. Sandra went back to Salisbury on the late flight. I'm sitting in between this lot drinking cokes, although I did have a beer earlier and then the Mikes presented a united front and refused to buy me anymore. Mel comes up behind me and tickles me, I turn round quickly and almost fall off my chair. Glen follows, ruffling my hair as if I'm still six years old, even though he's brought my best friend with him.

'How was your flight?'

'Delayed. And then your uncle was late.' She grabs at Glen's beard.

'A Castle, a Coke and a brandy and Coke,' Glen calls over to the barman. The barman brings the drinks over.

'Did you hear about the attack at the hotel up the road?' the barman asks, folding his arms over his beer-bop, which is as big as a hippo's.

'Ja, the ous got there just as the guys were flying out through the back. We floored two of them,' says Glen, sliding a tall glass of brandy and Coke towards Mel.

'Can I have a straw please?' asks Mel. The barman stops wiping the bar top and flaps down the rubber mats with Castle and Black Label printed on them.

'A straw? You drink brandy and Coke with a straw? How old are you?' asks the barman.

'Give her a straw,' says Glen. The barman hands her a red and white stripy one. He's totally bald apart from a huge shaggy moustache. Smoke hangs in the dull orange light behind him and a cigarette dangles from his mouth.

'Ja, but we're not flooring enough, hey,' says the barman.

'Ja, but we're trying our best hey,' says Glen.

'Ja, but maybe not hard enough,' says the barman.

Glen slams down his beer.

'So our lives aren't hard enough for you?' Glen says.

Mel strokes Glen's back. Dark Mike stands up, knocking over his barstool. He picks it back up and steadies it, looking up at me as he does so. I smile, he stretches out his lips and widens his eyes at me, then follows Shereen out towards the exit door. She's weaving slightly; as I watch her right ankle caves in, so she stops, wobbles, and slowly takes off her right shoe and then her left.

'I'm not saying that,' the barman says to Glen. Holding his cigarette between his thumb and his index finger, he takes a hit. 'My brother's RLI.'

'Well I can see why you've got a problem then, hey,' says Glen.

'Hey you gota problem with RLI?'

Glen turns to the guy standing next to him, a young blonde guy, tall and skinny in his khaki shorts and yellow t-shirt.

'No,' Glen says. 'Not today. Have you?'

'I'm RLI,' says the blonde guy.

'Ja, I'm sorry about that, hey, you'll get over it,' Glen jokes. 'Wanna beer?' Glen turns back to the barman, who's still eyeing them.

'Two beers,' he glances at the blonde guy's drink. 'Lions.'

The barman takes two beers and slides them over. 'On the house,' he says. Glen looks him in the eye, but doesn't say anything, then he slides one over to the blonde guy. The blonde guy looks confused. He still doesn't know whether Glen was apologising because he felt sorry for him being in the Rhodesian Light Infantry, or because he was sorry for being sarcastic about them. Glen says the RLI sometimes come in after missions and mess up the operation, losing them valuable terrorist prisoners, who they need for information. He complains they're only interested in kills, rather than the long-term outcome of the war. Dad says all the army units squabble and think they know best. Glen opens a fresh packet of Madisons and offers a cigarette to the barman, who takes one, another to the blonde guy who shakes his head, but raises his beer and says cheers. I sit down next to Mel.

'That was like an episode of High Chaparelle,' I say.

'Ja, I didn't know who was gonna blow whose head off,' she says.

Glen passes Mel a stool. She smoothes her long white cheesecloth dress under her bum and sits down.

'You can sleep in my room tonight if you want. I'm pretty sure Carls won't be in our bed.' I cast my eyes in Carla and Mike's direction, Carla has Mike's face in her hands.

'That's okay. I'm staying at Glen's friend's place.'

'Oh. Whose?'

'Don't know, some oke who lent him the car. He's on call-up.' She raises her eyes up at me, her mouth remains on her straw. She starts chewing it, trying not to smile. Glen asks for another brandy and Coke for her, even though she's only had two slugs out of the one in front of her. Carls has already disappeared, she didn't even say goodnight.

'How come your mom let you come?'

'Glen charmed her. Anyway, she's gone away this weekend with her new boyfriend,'

'The Pom?' I ask.

'Ja, the red-faced, pink-skinned Pom, let's not talk about him, I might kotch all over the bar.'

'Don't do that, Glen already has, in a manner of speaking,' I say.

We clink our glasses together and I remember the day I first met her, at the ice-rink, how she skated in smooth elegant circles around the ice, and came to a halt in a perfect arc, how Glen and I were caught like moths to her flame. Glen is back into his war convo with the RLI guy at the bar. Mel gets up and whispers in his ear and Glen calls the barman over then continues his conversation till the barman returns with two cokes. She hands one to me.

'Come, let's go check the moon.'

We sit on the patio outside. The moon hangs like a huge butter-coloured boulder over the lake and the lawn glistens wetly under the garden lights. Mel takes a huge sip from her glass and then, taking a half bottle of Bols out of her bag she empties a glug into her glass.

'C'mon,' she says, gesturing to me to do the same.

After I've taken a huge sip of Coke, she pours a glug into my glass.

'Ugh! It's disgusting!'

'You'll get used to it. Here have a bit more.'

'No!'

And now we're both warm and fuzzy and I'm telling Mel about John and I drinking brandy after the attack. And then I tell her about the attack and Mel tells me about how happy life was when her Dad was alive and before her mom was a drunk and then, carried along by the caramel sweet river of brandy-love between us, I tell her all about Enoch, the beginning, middle and end.

'Shit man, Jay. That's so romantic,' she smiles at me, 'I just wish it wasn't with an Af man.'

It's like a punch in the stomach. Winded inside, I look up at her.

'I'm only joking, man! Can't you take a joke?'

Mel puts the cokes down on the grass.

'Come, let's dance by the light of the moon.'

She starts waltzing me over the dewy grass until we both trip over her dress and I land on her in a giggling heap.

9.

Next day I'm feeling pretty queasy and panicky about having told Mel. We've got one day left and I've hardly seen Carla, so much for our Kariba jol. For the last two nights she's slept in Mike's room, but he's leaving this morning. Glen's gone down to the harbour to arrange a boat for tiger fishing. Mel and I are sitting having breakfast on the patio overlooking the lake, which is as calm as a looking glass reflecting the sky. Well, Mel is eating like there's no tomorrow. I could no more eat than swim butterfly stroke across the lake.

'Hungover?'

She clocks my face.

'You're so white man. Hope you're not sweating over last night. I'm sorry you didn't tell me earlier. Shit man, you gonna work for the CIO when you older?' She forks up some scrambled egg which makes me want to kotch, so I duck for the ladies. When I get back, Carla and Mike are canoodling near the furry base of a palm tree, a few tables away.

'Why's she not going with him?' Mel asks, 'Jeez, look she's glued to him.'

'She's gonna fly back with me day after tomorrow,' I say. 'What time you going tomorrow again?'

'In the morning. You?'

'Next day. At five.'

'D'you think she'll switch with me, then we can have an extra day together?' Mel asks.

'I dunno, I said I'd go with Carls, I've hardly seen her. She's been with lover boy all this time.'

'Well, what's the diffs. If we swap tickets, you get to stay an extra day with me,' she smiles, her glass of orange juice cocked in my direction. 'And if we don't catch any tiger fish today, we can have another go tomorrow, hey?'

'I'm sure you'll charm the tigers out of the water. I'll see what Carls says.'

Glen comes over the grass. 'Hey you girls ready? The boat's waiting.'

'Coming,' I say swallowing the rest of my orange juice, which I instantly regret, it makes me feel like kotching. 'I'll just say goodbye to Mike.'

Carls is standing in her long flowery halter neck, brown back glistening, giving Mike a huge hug. They spot me eyeing them and come over.

'Off to catch tigers?' Mike says. 'Catch one for me.'

'Ja, see you Mike,' I say.

'See you Jay,' he pats Carla on the bum. 'Look after your sexy sister.'

'Uh uh, I'm gonna feed her to the tigers,' I say.

My hand ripples through the cold, navy-coloured water of the lake. On the bank on my left, crocs slide silently into the water. I estimate one croc for every ten seconds.

'I wouldn't do that if you wanna keep your fingers, Jay,' says Glen, smiling at me from where he stands, holding the wheel of the boat.

'They're too far away man,' I reply.

'Depends how hungry they are, hey? We're not far enough to the middle yet. When we get to the middle you can jump in if you want – crocs won't get you there – weed might though – Kariba weed is killer.'

'I'll jump in after you then.'

He laughs, 'Gooi me a cold one.' I throw him a beer from the ice-box. The sun sparks off the water, making its deeps look like the night sky with stars. Inky masses of weed wave beneath the surface as the sunlight ripples through them. I catch sight of a tiny gelatinous shape.

'I think I just saw a jelly-fish thing.'

'Ja, tigers aren't the only fish in the lake, you can catch bream, barbel, eel – and huge vundu, bigger than your arses,' Glen looks funny in his army issue floppy hat and ladies round black plastic sunglasses.

'Hey you,' Carla flicks her bottle-top at him, 'leave our arses out of it,' she smiles.

'What?' he shouts back, but the wind and the noise of the motor drown her out.

Carla's taken off her red plastic-framed sunglasses and put them on her lap. Something's making her smile.

'What?' I smile. 'What?'

'Nothing.' She smiles again and squeezes the sun cream.

'Come on Carls. Spill the beans,' Mel looks up from where she's stretched out on a towel in her bikini, reading *Scope* magazine; she looks back down and sighs when the info doesn't come. Feeling a rush of love towards her for not judging me and for still wanting to be my friend despite all she's said in the past about Afs and the jokes she's made about blacks, I almost fling myself at her, but reel myself in. Maybe that stuff was just jokes, throwaway stuff she's worn like an old jersey just because it was around and she was cold. *You have to think for yourself or you'll become conditioned*. Nessie's voice plays in my head.

'Come on. You're keeping something from me,' I say when Carls keeps up the smiling.

'No! Nothing!' Carla says.

'You mean something!' I jab her in the side with my finger as she pulls off her t-shirt to reveal her red bikini top.

'Einah! I'll tell you later.' She takes off her shorts and lies down on her back on her towel, extending her neck backwards, her hair splaying out behind her. She wriggles her red-painted toenails. This is one satisfied cat. Mel shoots a glance at her and then puts down her magazine and moves up behind Glen. Standing behind him, she places her arms around his waist. He moves her in front of him, placing her hands on the wheel of the boat, then he moves behind her gently guiding the boat with his left hand as she steers, his beer bottle in his right hand. She squeals as he nuzzles her neck.

'Come on Carls, tell me now, I'm not gonna be able to concentrate on the fishing.' Carla looks up at Glen and Mel, then whispers to me.

'Okay. We're getting engaged. Mike asked me this morning.'

'This morning? I thought something was going on.' I try to muster up some excitement, because I just can't see it happening. I shift closer to her and say, 'Carls, that's so exciting!' trying not to sound false. She sits up and we hug.

'Am I bridesmaid? I'm not wearing pink okay?'

Carla laughs, 'Let's have another beer, let's celebrate!'

'Okay. Can I tell Mel?'

'Tell Mel.'

'Mel?'

'I heard. Congratulations.' Mel sounds genuinely unhappy for her. I shake my head at Mel indicating my disapproval at her lack of enthusiasm. Mel raises her eyebrows in a 'what?' expression. And then I remember Spike. How's he gonna take it? I hope she really does get married this time. Third time lucky.

Mel is whispering into Glen's ear. 'Hey, coz,' he shouts at Carls through the wind, 'congratulations! Who is he? Oh ja, the pilot, I can't keep up.'

Carls flicks the dregs of her last beer at him but he moves his waist quickly to the left and the liquid cascades over the deck.

Glen and I thread fat pink worms onto the rods. Carls is still in her bikini stretched out on a towel on the floor of the boat. She's never liked fishing. She opens her book.

'Come on, fish today. Do something different. You'll be married soon,' I say.

'What and then I can't fish?'

'No and then you'll cook fish.'

'Aikona, the cook boy will,' she says.

'Not when the war's over,' I laugh. 'You'll have to learn to cook.'

Glen has his legs bent, Mel's in front of him. He pulls the rod back and with her hands on top of his, flings the line high over the dark water, the line wheezes and whizzes, followed by the plop of the buoy.

'Are you two always joined at the knees?' Carls asks.

'Ja, if I can help it. Get fishing, I'll show you how to gut and cook it later,' Glen says.

'No chance.'

The afternoon sun moves lazily over the sky and the water laps at the boat. Carla sits with her book between her legs, right arm pressing her fishing-rod onto her right leg. On the other side of the boat, Mel and Glen have their backs to us, Mel's head on Glen's shoulder. A slow drone of a motor in the distance cuts through the lull of the afternoon. Glen gets up, clipping his rod to the side of the boat, then moving to the middle of the boat, he stands with his legs akimbo, and begins to rock the boat, then he makes little darting movements from one side of the boat to the other.

'What are you doing?'

'Waking up the fish, they're all sleeping.' He grabs another beer from the cold-box and then sits down on the side of the boat.

'It's not working, Glenda,' says Carla.

Glen gets up again, pulls off t-shirt, glasses and hat and stands by the side of the boat.

'I'm going to wake them up!' He dives off the side.

'Bloody lunatic!'

'Shit, those tigers are gonna eat him!'

'The weed is gonna strangle him!'

'Ja, you laugh, but if he doesn't come back up again, none of us will be able to get this tub back to shore,' says Mel.

Carla and I look at each other. She widens her eyes at me. This makes me crack up again. Mel stands up. 'Glen!' She looks back at us. He is taking a while to surface. I look at Carla.

'Shit.' Carla and I sink back down. Then the boat tips backwards on our side. Carla and I scream as something wet and slimy hits the backs of our necks. Now it's Mel's turn to laugh. It's Glen. We turn round.

'You bastard!' Carla leans over and shoves his forehead back into the water. 'I hope the tigers nibble your nose!'

Glen climbs back into the boat dripping. He shakes himself like a dog.

'Eeugh, stop it Glen man, the water stinks,' I say. He goes up to Mel and gives her a hug, she doesn't seem to mind, even though she's in her bikini and the water is freezing. Then Carla yells again, her fishing rod bolts, but she just manages to grab it.

'Glen! Help!' The rod is a bucking bronco, arching and extending and pulling Carla with it. I hold on to her arms. Glen comes up behind her and begins helping her reel in. Still the rod arches and pulls, even with Glen helping. He wheels in, the reel unwinds, he reels in again. Mel comes over.

'It's like the fish is doing the fishing.'

'Ja the humaning. Hope it's not a croc.'

We laugh, but they're really battling. The line is only out a metre or so now. They both pull and then Glen begins to heave.

'Just don't let the bloody thing snap,' he says.

'You don't let the bloody thing snap! Shit I can't go for much longer,' Carla says.

'Don't stop now Carls!' I say.

'Ja, hang in there, Carla,' says Mel.

The fish explodes out of the water. Long as legs, flashing silver, it leaps into the air and then crashes back down onto the surface of the water. Mel and I move backwards towards the other side of the boat.

'It's so fat. And long!'

'Don't let it get away Glen!'

'What is it? It's massive.'

'Vundu – it's a bloody vundu! Big bugger!'

Carla steps out of the way and Glen gives one more jerk and it's in, flopping and flipping on the bottom of the boat, its glassy eyes reflecting the dying sun, its whiskers moving round like antennae searching for life.

Glen gives Carla a hug, 'Clever girl.' I hug her too.

'Ja, well done,' says Mel, 'it almost looks like a shark.'

'Shit hey, I'm quite chuffed,' says Carls.

'Ja, not bad for a ballerina,' says Glen, 'he's a big bugger,' Glen lifts the fish by the mouth, then slops him down near the back of the boat. 'Ladies, this calls for another beer.'

'Shame,' I say, taking a look at him. 'He doesn't look happy does he?'

'No,' says Glen handing me a beer. 'He's not meant to look happy, he's meant to look dead. He's an ugly bugger isn't he?'

I take a swig of the beer. A few minutes ago this fish was the king of the lake, swimming around happily, eating smaller fish, weaving in and around the weed. Next thing he's dead, shocked eye gaping at the sun, jelly blood around the mouth. We crouch and sit around him, drinking, toasting.

'Right,' Glen says, getting up. He hands Mel her rod. 'You too, Jay, we came here to catch tigers.' I take up position on my side of the boat. Carls lies back on her towel with her book and her beer. She's earnt her rest. The tiger fish come in thick and fast, as if the vundu had Rhodesia Heralded the catch, small ones, medium ones, they lie on the bottom of the boat, gills flapping, bodies arching, their razor teeth bared as they gasp for air. I catch my own little pile of tilapia and bream.

'Those will be lekker on the braai,' Glen says, 'bit of lemon is all you need.'

The sky is turning orange as Glen puts down his rod and crouches down to examine the catch. He picks up a tiger and growls like a dog as he thrusts it at Mel, its two rows of teeth look fit to eat her.

'Go away, Glen,' she laughs. Glen begins chucking the tigers back into the lake. These are the lucky ones that swim away, the vundu and the bream are coming with us. They will be gutted, filleted and braaied. Glen puts on his t-shirt, hat and sunglasses and starts up the motor. We're chugging away from the death scene under a kaleidoscopic sky. Dark silk-like undulations of water pleat by us as we move towards the shore, past the dead, accusing trees that used to stand on land before the lake was flooded.

I look down at the vundu fish.

'I'm sorry,' my eyes say. Its dead eye stares back at me.

The sky is a blood-red canopy over the black mountains, the gigantic fireball of the sun has sunk behind the lake. Carla and I sit out on our balcony getting fizzy-warm on beer and listening to the insects orchestrating the night. Our cigarette tips punctuate the navy sky. There's no furniture on our balcony, so we sit on the still-warm red tiles, our backs leaning against the knobbly stucco balcony wall. A Cape-eagle swoops and lands on one of the dead trees, I can see his head and feather collar silhouetted against the red sky, the king of the lake. I blow out puffs of smoke rings.

'I just hooped a star with my smoke ring – try it.'

Carla starts blowing rings, but she's crap at it, and soon starts laughing. I do too.

'Ja, but I was better at blowing soap bubbles than you,' she says.

'Remember how we used to sit in the bath back home for ages, blowing soap bubbles and pulling faces in the mirror behind the taps?'

'Ja, you just hogged the soap, so you got more practice,' I say.

'Jay? I've had the best few days I've ever had.' I look at her. 'No really, and not just because of being with Mike. I really love him you know, but being with you too.' She stares at the sky.

'Ah. I wish you were staying now.' I often feel torn between her and Mel.

She stares at the sky.

'Jay? I admire you. The way you question everything, you're not afraid to feel differently to other people. I wish I was more like you.'

But I am afraid. Of my own thoughts and feelings – of what I might do – or not do.

'I'm sorry about not trying to understand more – with your eating.'

'It's okay. I've kind of dealt with it. I think. It was fear.'

'What kind of fear?'

'I've been afraid of death – the war – losing people. Afraid of life too.'

'Shit. I didn't realise it was that bad,' I say.

I put my arm around her. 'Do you miss life at Angel's Peak?' I ask.

'Not really. I never slept through the night! I wanted the city anyway. I thought I wanted culture.'

'I miss Umtali, my old dance classes. That feeling of anything being possible. I wanted to move to Salisbury, even overseas, because

346

of opportunities. Now I don't care. All I ever wanted to do was dance, and after the accident, I sort of lost that energy in my body; it wasn't just my leg, I lost the hunger. Giving it up was a release. Now family is all that matters.'

'I put my head on her shoulder. Her hair smells of shampoo. 'I can't face going back to Angel's Peak,' I inhale. Unless it's to stay,' I say exhaling.

'You'll meet someone and move on. All I want now is to be a stay-at-home wife and mum,' she takes a sip of beer, 'to be honest, I've always been a bit jealous of you and Mel.'

'Jealous of Mel? I didn't realise.'

'We just haven't been as close since she came on the scene.'

'Carls?'

'No. It's okay,' she says putting her hand on my leg. 'We go through phases don't we? But we'll always be close.'

'Carls? Do you think I'd have grown out of my friendship with Enoch if we'd stayed?'

'No. I don't think so. You've always been an unbridled horse, like Nessie.'

We laugh. She puts her hand on my leg. 'I am sorry about not being more supportive of how you felt about Enoch.'

'That's okay. I know it's been hard for you to understand. It's often hard for anyone to understand anything outside of what they have experienced. But we have to try. My English teacher was speaking about empathy recently. It made me realise that there seems to be a lack of it in this country and I don't really understand why. Maybe it's human nature to be selfish, but it's human nature to be in relationship with others too, it's just that it sometimes seems to me that people even get into relationships for selfish reasons. Anyway, I'm sorry I haven't always been understanding enough about what you were going through Carls.'

'I'm different to you that's all. You let everyone know how you feel. Partly because you are so in touch with how you feel. Others aren't always.'

'Or they don't want to look at how they feel,' I say.

'I suppose so. We're not all as brave as you, Jay.'

She gets up. 'C'mon, let me show you some moves. I feel like dancing.'

'I thought you were over ballet?' I say flicking my cigarette butt over the balcony

'You oke,' Carla says referring to my cigarette flicking. I'll never be over it. I'll always want to dance. Only from now on I'll be mistress of the dance,' she holds her hands out to me, 'just mirror my movements.'

'Wow Carla, very insightful.'

And then I mirror her moves on our balcony until Glen comes to pick us up for the braai. After we have eaten the braaied fish that we caught earlier and that we all agree is the best we have ever tasted, Carla and I lie on the lawn of Glen's friend's house and don't say very much at all, because we don't need to. Head to head, we blow smoke rings and look at the constellations in the sky, bright as diamonds on black velvet.

10.

The bloody car won't start. It's an old Renault 4 and it's wheezing.

'You girls are gonna have to get out and push or we'll never get Carla to the airport,' Glen says.

Mel hops out of the front and we push the front seat forward to get out. The seat is so old and frayed at the base that it practically flattens as it goes down. The three of us pack a bit of horsepower at the back and Glen takes off down the hill, cracking fallen branches as he goes. He stops quite a way down, so we have to run to catch up to where he's waiting, engine idling. Running down the hill is a bit of a hose, and when Mel falls over in her white dress, legs in the air, like some fallen angel, we nearly wet ourselves.

'Put foot Glenda,' says Carls, puffed out as she gets back into the car next to me, 'I don't wanna miss my plane.' She looks at me and squeezes my leg.

We have to run straight up to the check-in desk. Once we're there Carla has an argument with the ground hostess who doesn't want to change her ticket.

Eventually, Glen says, 'Look, we've just had a death in the family and she has to get back early okay?'

'Okay, you're lucky the flight's not completely full, we've got two planes going out one after the other. I can't put anything in the hold. Is that all you're taking?'

'Yes, thanks,' says Carla, flashing a golden one at the woman.

Carla hugs Glen, then Mel, finally she hugs me and kisses me on the lips.

'See you soon,' she says.

I hold on to her hand as she goes. Looking back, I see the hostess walk with her towards two long queues. She directs Carla to the queue on the left. In front of her, two little blonde girls in orange flowery dresses hold onto their father's hands. Carla turns and blows a kiss at me and I feel a tug in my stomach.

Outside the car window, the thorn trees are grey and brittle, their white thorns pointing at the sky. Mel and Glen coo and canoodle in the front of the car. Wishing Carls had stayed now, I feel a strange sense of loneliness, like I'm losing her. I feel angry with Mike for pulling her away. A stay-at-home wife and mom? She'll be like a caged bird. There'll be a wedding photo of her snapped looking beautiful, like Mom and Dad's and then she'll begin to fade as she grows weary with marriage, with children.

'Look Jay,' Mel says, 'wave goodbye to your sister. 'She points out of her window to the plane that has just banked and is turning left over Kariba towards Salisbury.

After a trip to the market to buy curios, we walk into reception to get our keys. Glen approaches the widely curved desk, while Mel and I wait in the main hall area. At one end of the reception desk a man and a woman are yelling at the woman on duty, who's just put down the telephone receiver. The woman Glen is approaching at the other end of the desk looks really freaked out.

'Is that all you can tell us? Are you sure that's all?' The woman's voice is hysterical. The man pulls her away, she's crying. Other people come up to the desk as Glen leans over to speak to the woman. Glen turns and comes towards us; he looks white, like he's going to be sick. Something clutches at my stomach. My blood begins to throb in my head and my hands become slippery. As I walk towards Glen, my foot slides in my slop.

'Jay.'

'What?' His hands grip my upper arms. 'What?' My legs feel like they're loosening around the knees.

'Jay, the plane – the plane that Carls –'

'What?' I scream. 'What?' My hands push at his chest.

'Jay the plane's gone – disappeared.'

'What? Don't be stupid, they don't – you mean it's crashed?'

'It's crashed?' My voice tears out, screaming from far away. Mel puts her arm around me. I push her shoulders.

'Get away! Get away! You should be on that plane.' I punch Mel, pulling her hair, kicking at her. Glen holds me, as I buckle over. The woman on the desk is calling for a doctor. People in the room are screaming and crying, holding on to each other, swearing, others mill about in the lobby with their hands over their mouths, holding their heads, standing around looking stupid, swallowing, their eyes staring. A woman slumps on the floor against the reception desk, her child lies across the legs of his mother, looking up at her, 'God help us,' she says over and over.

A man in a suit lies on the floor sobbing, his legs curled up. It's like an asylum. Glen half pulls, half carries me to our room, he flops me on the bed, the unmade bed where I slept with Carla.

'Oh no. No! Oh, no. I choke on the words, moving my body on the bed to try and get it out of my head. Glen tries to hold me but I kick and push him away.

'Oh please God, no, please no.' My head pounds and screams. A man walks in and sticks a needle in my arm. Mel is crying.

'Why are you crying?' I scream at her, 'why are you crying?'

The world turns black as all the voices are sucked through a dark tunnel.

11.

The cathedral is hot and packed. Angry crowds spill out into the street outside; a man holds a placard that reads "Go to hell you murdering bastard," a suggestion to Ian Smith about what to say to the terrorist leader when he next sees him. The Dean's voice sounds like the condemning voice of God. *But are we deafened with the voice of protest from nations which call themselves 'civilised'? We are not! Like men, in the story of the Good Samaritan, they 'pass by on the other side'. One listens for loud condemnation by Dr. David Owen, himself a medical doctor, trained to extend mercy and help to all in need. One listens and the silence is deafening.* Unable to sit, Mom is sobbing loudly and falling all over the place. Dad and Auntie Aldie sit on either side of her and try to keep her upright. Mom runs her hands through her hair over and over again, moaning and crying.

'How can I live without Carla? My baby?'

John is curled up on the floor. Women all over the cathedral are screaming and crying. Dad too is crying, around us many men weep too. My head feels like it's going to split in two, like a ripe pomegranate. I vomit on the floor between my legs. Nobody notices. *One listens for loud condemnation by the President of the United States, himself a man from the Bible Baptist belt and again the silence is deafening. One listens for loud condemnation by the Pope, by the Chief Rabbi, by the Archbishop of Canterbury, by all who love the name of God. Again the silence is deafening,* the Dean continues.

People in the cathedral keep shouting things out. The shouts echo up through the arches and get trapped in the beams.

'Murdering bastards!'

'Damn them all to hell.'

There is booing from the peacemakers. Mom's head lolls back, for a moment she looks at me. She hasn't tried to hug me since I came back. Auntie Gail sits next to me, rubbing my back. But it annoys me. I don't want anyone to touch me. I'm like a brittle, empty shell, ready to crack at any moment, with vomit on my lips. John stares up at me from the floor. I pull him up onto the pew and put my arm around him. But he sinks back onto the floor.

I do not believe in white supremacy. I do not believe in black supremacy either. I do not believe that anyone is better than another, until he has proved himself to be so. I believe that those who govern or who seek to govern must prove themselves worthy of the trust that will be placed in them. One looks for real leadership: one finds little in the Western world; how much less in Africa! Mom is wailing, 'Oh no, oh no, no – please, no, don't say it, please don't say it.' She looks crazy. She has a right to her craziness. Nessie comes in. At first Dad doesn't see her, but then he gets up and goes over to her before she has a chance to sit down.

'Are you happy now? Are you fucking happy? Your niece is dead. Your friends killed her.'

'My friends didn't kill her Dave. The war killed her. She was my niece, I need to be here. Please Dave.' They haven't seen each other for over two years.

Uncle Pat goes over and kisses Nessie and puts his arm around Dad. Dad puts his head in his hands and begins sobbing.

'I don't think I can get through this Pat,' he crumples onto the bench in the brown suit he got married in before Carla was born.

Pat sits down next to him. He takes a little silver flask from the inside of his suit jacket and gives it to Dad. Nessie comes and sits with me and Auntie Gail. She pulls John off the floor next to her, then she hugs me by the shoulders. John has the same stare that he had in Angel's Peak when they came. It happened again, as he thought. Only worse.

The ghastliness of this ill fated Flight from Kariba will be burned upon our memories for years to come. For others, far from our borders it is an intellectual matter, not one which affects them deeply. Here is the tragedy! The

especial danger of Marxism is its teaching that human life is cheap, expendable,
of less importance than the well being of the State.

John slithers to the floor as a man's voice echoes through the cathedral.

"I'll kill every one of them, I'll take up arms myself, root them out and kill every last one of them," an old man says. Some people cheer. Some boo. Nessie looks at me and shakes her head, she squeezes my waist tighter.

The voice continues. "If Smith is too much of a coward to carry on fighting, we'll fight to the death…" Again the boos, the cheers. My mind can't contain it, it's seeping out through cracks in my skull. Carla, beautiful Carla, how could they? I clasp my hands behind my neck to try to drown it all out, then realising I'm in a brace position, I start to collapse on the floor. Nessie takes my arms down gently, pulls me up and hugs me, mouthfuls of her hair getting in my mouth, my tears and spit wetting her hair.

On a cloudless day in mid-September our small party of close friends and relations gather beneath an acacia tree as Carla is buried. The sky domes above us, a rich mauve. No planes haunt this empty sky. Her sleek white coffin snugly protected from the umber-coloured soil dazzles my eyes as the sun hits it. How appropriate for an almost star like Carla. I look up and catch Mike's eye, he looks dignified in his uniform. I can't work out whether he's been crying or not. Auntie Aldie is wailing. Auntie Gail and May look calm in their uniforms, both accustomed to staring death in the face. Ant and Neil look uncomfortable in their suit trousers and shirts. Spike, recently returned from the UK, supports himself on crutches, the tears rivering down his face. I wonder if he's caught wind of Mike. Carla probably never told him. Reverend White is speaking about love, about how it is kind and forgiving and holds no records of wrongs. Mom begins to howl and then slumps to her knees; the flame-lilies clenched in her fist, she bangs her forearm on the coffin. It's unbearable to watch. Dad goes over and gently tries to help her up, but she wrenches away from his grasp. Dry-eyed and empty, I'm thinking about when we went to Matopos when we were little and I got tired climbing all the way to the top of the balancing rocks.

Carla kept pulling me by the hand *Come on Jay, just a little further...* and then I feel desperate, not knowing how to see a world without her in it. My eyes scan wildly. Beneath the msasas a little way up the hill, Nessie stands in a long black dress, her hair up, sensitive that her brother may not want her there. I leave the gathering and go up to my aunt. Taking her by the arm, I lead her to back to where I was standing. Dad, supported by Uncle Pat, and possibly his flask, sees but makes no objection. Near the car park a group of journalists have gathered looking for scraps. This funeral is not just about our family. It's about all of us.

12.

Weeks later, I'm numb, alone with the pain that sits heavily on my chest. In the still heat of the night, I lie on my bed in my bra and undies looking at the ceiling, willing my mind to go blank. I have left the curtains open because I want to see the moon. It hangs, fat and golden and pocked in a sky spread with stars. Ragged blankets of opaque cloud veil the moon then travel quickly across the expanse. We looked at the moon, Carla and I, many times, from cars, travelling through Rhodesia at night, *Mom, how come the moon is going so fast? It's not, it's the clouds that are moving, not the moon.* A gust of wind causes the curtain to billow, then knocking at the window causes me to jump.

'Shit, Mel. Go round to the back door, I'll let you in.'

We sit down on the bed facing each other, me in my pants and bra. Mel in a blue tracksuit, her hair tucked into the hood. She touches my leg.

'How do you feel?'

'I don't know – weird – I still can't believe it. I expect her to –' my voice breaks, 'walk in. Mel I can't talk about it. I'm sorry I screamed at you – at the hotel.' I take a deep shuddery breath. I stare at a freckle on my leg, blinking, but the tears splash anyway. For a long time there is silence.

'It's okay Jay, you were in shock.' Mel continues to look at her hands.

I swallow.

'I keep thinking of how she must have felt, having survived the crash, and then them coming – and – shooting her – while she was trying to bandage the wounded – at least, we think that's all they did.'

The lump in my throat gathers and becomes painful.

'Not just her. But the children. I can't stand thinking of how frightened they must have been.'

Mel puts her hand on my leg.

'I know.'

'It's just so savage. Why murder tourists in a plane? Mel? Did it feel real when your Dad died?' God. I can hear Nessie explaining it rationally in my head.

'Not at first. My Gran told us. She said our Dad had gone to heaven,' she smiles. 'I didn't see Mom for days, she was at her sister's place crying, freaking out – drinking – well drinking more than usual.'

Mel snorts a bit. 'She hasn't stopped since.'

'But how did you feel?'

'It was afterwards. I remember sitting up in bed after I'd had a bad dream – I had quite a lot of nightmares after he died – and just calling him, and there was no response, and then I knew that he was dead – that he would never come, no matter how hard I called.'

I look up at her through my fringe. The bedside light is shining behind her, lighting the back of her head like a halo.

'Mel?'

She wipes her eyes with the back of her hand.

'I miss him. It never goes away.'

I want to hug her but I can't.

'Mel? It hasn't been easy for you, has it? Your mom and everything – and your brother –'

Mel laughs, 'Ja, he's a doos.' We both laugh, and Mel slaps my leg.

'I better voetsak outa here before my mother comes stumbling in.'

'Thanks for coming Mel.'

In the tomb-like quiet of the house, I dream. I'm wandering through the rooms of Angel's Peak. The sun is shining very brightly, but inside the house it's dark. The furniture is all different. In the library, the butterfly display cases are still on the walls, but they seem bigger. There are no longer butterflies inside them, but weapons, revolvers, pistols and sub-machine guns. Out on the veranda, the pillars are crumbling. When I lean my hand up against one it crumbles away. Carla is lying on the lawn. As I approach she sits up and smiles. Her middle section is half blown-away. I hear screaming and the sound of my mother's footsteps running.

'Jay?' Mom sobs, 'are you alright?'

After a moment I recognise her and sit up, touching my face that is as wet as hers.

I sleep again and my dreamscape shifts. Now I am in the bush, the heat is burning me, I can smell petrol and smoke. In the distance the woman from the hotel is weeping *Oh God no, oh my God no…* Walking towards a clearing in the bush, I can see something sticking up. It looks like the top of a sail. Closer, I see it's made of metal, the tail of an aeroplane. I keep walking and begin to see seats all over the bush. It's dusty. People are still strapped into the seats, some upside down, some of the seats are empty. A little boy asks me *Can you give me a drink? My mommy won't wake up.* An old couple wave to me from their seats. The man raises his glass to me and the lady smiles, she has blood coming out of a crack near her mouth. I continue to walk towards the clearing. An air hostess stands in the bush, near to the wing tail; she holds up her white-gloved hand, her hair is a mess and she keeps smoothing down her uniform. She smiles at me. *I'm afraid you can't go in there,* she says, *everyone's dead.* I can hear screaming.

'Carla! Carla!' I sit up in bed and realise it's me screaming. I can still hear the sobbing in the distance, from down the hall. It's Mom.

I sleep, then wake up. This time it's a man sobbing. For a while I think I'm just going crazy, then I realise it's Dad, out on the veranda, outside my bedroom window. The sound is unbearable. I walk down the passage. Carla's bedroom door is closed. I hear a voice from inside. It chills me. Then I realise.

'John? Is that you?' The broken voice. She's in there.

'Mom?'

'Go back to bed. Leave us alone.'

I don't know where to go. I run out the back door and lie down on the cold concrete of the stoep. She was talking to her in there as if she was still alive.

1979

Salisbury,
Zimbabwe-Rhodesia

1.

The ghost of Christmas is past and so is a New Year spent clustered around the TV with Mom, May and Auntie Aldie watching depressing news reports and cast-off UK and USA programmes and everyone talking about Carla more and more as they get bombed. Mom decided not to put up the Christmas tree because she couldn't face doing it without Carla, but then she and Auntie Aldie did it with John. Collecting lots of pine cones helped me to not freak out crying. I painted little funny figures on them and then gave them to John to hang on the tree, crying as he did. Everyone cried some more when Dad and Uncle Bob and Glen phoned from wherever they were on call-up, for them not being here, but most of all for Carla. And now it's nearly my birthday and Dad is going to be home this year. Maybe we can go out, just the two of us, hell we could have a beer, that'd be mush.

Mom comes out onto the veranda with the tray.

'Where's Patience?' I say, annoyed at my doodlings being interrupted.

'I gave her the afternoon off,' she says dribbling tea over the tea cosy and onto the tray as she pours it into a cup.

'Why?' I put down my pen and shut my book lest Mom see what I've written about her, resplendent with illustrations.

'Felt like it. She's gone home to see her family. Besides we should get used to coping on our own.' She picks up my notebook. 'Done any more cartoons?'

'No,' I say snatching back my book. 'Making tea for ourselves you mean? Man it's gonna be tough now that the tables have turned. Patience is the madam these days and you're the house girl.'

Mom laughs. 'I think you should see Dr Sheldon.' She slops some tea into the saucer as she passes it to me.

'Nervous Mom? Why should I? Are you tired of him?'

She gapes at me.

'Joke. Will he give me happy pills?'

'I just think it'd be good for you to let it out. You're so emotionless, inward – angry.'

I think she'd prefer it if I wept and freaked out all the time.

'Sorry Mom. That I'm not emotional, outward, mouthy.' I mimic her tones.

'You're impossible Jay.' She picks up her *Fair Lady* magazine and begins flicking through it, trying to read me.

She wants to conduct our grief so it fits into her orchestra.

Mom looks at her watch. 'Where's your father? Hung over I suppose. He's going to be late.' She slaps the magazine shut and chucks it on the cup-ringed knobbled-glass of the table. In my head I hear their argument from last night. *You think we bloody fought for nothing? I'm away fighting and my wife's away at bloody women's meetings talking about accepting change? Spare rib, bloody crap man!*

Don't be so bloody sexist Dave. Change is coming – it's here. You might as well accept it.

You going through the change of life? Bloody crazy man.

In my notebook, I finish drawing Mom click-clacking in high heels through a turnstile marked 'change.' In the distance is a sign advertising an African women's meeting. Since Bishop Abel Muzorewa has been voted in, *The Puppet* as Nessie calls him, we can all officially mix without curdling. Hell Enoch could come and take tea with me right here on the veranda in full view of everyone, if he wanted to that is.

'Oh bugger off to The Blue Hart and drink another crate of beer,' Mom says as I get to the kitchen.

'Do you have to speak to Dad like that Mom?' I say leaning up against the door frame. 'You're so disrespectful.'

'Don't speak to me about respect. I was just *trying* to explain to him about Mrs Emery.'

Dad walks in through the back door. 'And I was trying to explain to her about Mr Emery, who she left, for a coloured man and now she wants to take his kids and his house.'

He sounds exhausted as if he's had to repeat himself over and over again.

'I didn't say –' Mom takes a step towards him and raises her voice.

'Can you stop it? Please,' I say, picking at the bits of loose dry paint in the door frame. 'It's awful.'

'Hurry up and get dressed Jay, we've got a long drive ahead of us,' Dad says, feeling for his cigarettes in his top pocket then walking out the back door.

Mom lights up and stares out the kitchen window.

'Bloody waste of time,' she says smoothing back her hair. 'Bloody waste of life! The terrs'll be coming home soon,' she says waving her cigarette above her head at the open window so that Godfrey comes running up thinking he's being summoned. 'All victorious!'

'It's okay Godfrey! Just chatting about the terrorists – I mean the freedom fighters coming home!' she raises her voice.

I roll my eyes.

Godfrey smiles slightly, nods and says, 'Yes, Madam,' and goes back to work.

'He thinks you're mad Mom. Pretty twisted don't you think? Sending our guys off to war, to be sacrificed, when our government's given up anyway.'

Mom straightens up, stubs out her half-smoked cigarette and tightens the cord of her stained yellow towelling dressing-gown.

'It's not that simple Jay. He can't just hand over to terrs straight from the bush. He's had to make sure the African leader who got in was moderate. That white interests are protected.'

'Like we've protected black interests?'

'Wooah there young lady. You been speaking to Nessie?' she smiles. 'One liberal in this family is quite enough thank you.'

'I was only playing devil's advocate.'

2.

Dad and I drive in silence for about twenty minutes. I can tell from Dad's face that he doesn't want to talk. He drives fast, pushing the gearstick hard with the heel of his hand. I open the window to smell the dust, and sense the crackle of energy in the air. The muscle at the base of Dad's jaw moves in and out like a pulse as he stares hard through the windscreen where the insects splat and die, gathering above the windscreen-wipers in a mass grave. The car tips slightly on my side, then bumps.

'Shit!' says Dad. 'A bloody flat.'

We pull up in the dust on the side of the road. Dad gets out and slams the door shut. The sound, after the hypnotic engine and dull, deafening wind, crashes through my head. He goes off into the bush to take a leak. Getting out of the car, hand raised to shade my eyes, I look up the endless grey tarmac road into the shimmering heat of the horizon. Nothing but grey. Not even a tree. I lean against the bakkie. Dad's taking a long leak. Getting back into the bakkie I try to tune the radio. Nothing doing. I put my bare feet up on the dashboard, then restless, put my feet down again. I look out of Dad's window. He's standing staring into the bush. For a moment I think he's moving, but it's only the heat, the light, playing tricks on me. I try the radio again. I look up. He is moving. I get out. The red dust is warm beneath my feet, but I leave its silken comfort and move into the bush myself.

'Dad? Dad!' He doesn't turn round. 'Dad!' I begin to run. 'Dad!' The word tears at my throat. Dad keeps walking deeper into the bush. I run after him. The bush scratches me as I race through it. The sun stings the back of my neck. Dad keeps walking. I look back at the car, it seems far away. Dad too seems far away, like I'm swimming and I've not felt like I've swum far, but the tide has pulled me out. Dad keeps walking away from me. Then I remember the flat, and begin to run, away from Dad, towards the bakkie and jump into the driver's seat. I'm gonna drive this thing to Chiredzi with or without a flat. With or without Dad. Bastard. I check under his seat. He has his gun with him. I feel around for the ignition keys. They're not there. I bang my head against the steering wheel.

'Shit! Shit! Shit!' My head hits the hooter.

I hear my sounds dimly through dry sobs. Then, the sharp sound of the door being opened. I look up, breath sweeping up from the end points of my lungs. He has an odd look on his face. Wiping the tears, I look up at him, my mouth open. I taste dust and saline as I get out to walk to the other side of the car. Putting my hands over my ears, I slide down the bakkie and sink to the ground, as the tears flow over my open mouth and splash in the dirt. Dad's still in the car. He's not getting out to change the wheel. I get up and open the door and sit in the passenger seat. Dad stares straight ahead. I wait. From the corner of my eye I see his FN on the dashboard.

'I nearly did something stupid.' He looks at me. 'But then I remembered you were in the car.'

God help me, he's finally cracked.

We drive on through the endless bush in silence. The car judders and crunches on my side. In this way we finally get to Chiredzi. At the garage, the petrol attendant shakes his head when he looks at the tyre.

'This one baas, cannot be change, you must have new taia.'

'So put a new taia then hey, chop-chop.'

Dad goes over to the garage shop to buy Kingsgates. Halfway there he turns round. 'Want anything?'

'No.'

'I'll get you a Coke.'

In the tribal trust land area we drive through a haze of russet dust past a scrubby dry mealie field with a black-stocking-faced scarecrow with dried mealie cob hands. Little stones ping beneath the chassis of the car. Dad pulls up in front of some low, tin-roofed buildings. In the dusty yard, three skinny dogs fight over a bone, one of them yelps and moves off in the direction of a large thorn tree. On the stoep, in front of the stores, an old African man with long grizzled dreadlocks sits drinking beer. He looks up at us from red and yellow eyes. My eyes adjust slowly, as I follow Dad into the general store. Dark shapes hanging from the ceiling turn out to be bundles of bicycle tyres. Behind the counter are rusty black Raleighs and the place smells of sweat and old fires. An African man comes in and nods at us before taking a glowing green Sparletta cream-soda out of an old chest freezer, covered in an ad that says *Three-in-one-super-duper, Lyon's Maid Ice-Cream* on it. Candles, Lifebuoy and Lux soap, Lion matches and hair products clutter up the space below the counter behind the grimy glass. Through the back door African music rises sharp as the bashing of tin cans and a few mangy chickens scatter as if in a dance. The man scratches his head and walks slowly past us towards the counter like the man from the land that time forgot.

'Yes baas?' he says as he passes Dad.

'I'm looking for Mr Pamberi.'

'Pamberi is there by the irrigation project.'

'Ja, but where is the irrigation project?'

The man gestures out towards the door through which we came. 'That way.'

'That way? Just follow the road? That way?'

The man cracks a smile. He doesn't have many teeth left and the few that are left are yellow as old newspapers.

'For sure, baas, that way, one time.'

Back on the road I wonder if anyone in front of us could see us for dust. It's like driving through a dust storm. Then, like Eden, there is green. Row upon row of green. Sprinkled by the tic-tic-tic of sprinklers flicking sun flashing silver H_2O against the blue sky.

A broad, round-faced smiley African man comes towards us from the cement buildings.

'Mr Cameron! You are late! Come for tea.'

His face is plump and smiley, like a Buddha's. He puts out his hand to shake Dad's and claps him hard on the shoulder as he does so. Dad laughs and returns the greeting.

'And who is this daughter? Is this eh Cameron princess?'

'Ja princess number two.'

I wish he wouldn't do that. It's like an arrow in the chest every time.

'For sure. This one, she's a true princess.'

Then he laughs. His laughter echoes across the dry ground and disappears into the soaked earth of the green irrigation system.

'This is Mr Pamberi, our project manager.'

'Hello,' I say.

Inside, there's a small wooden table with a file and a notebook on it; at the back, a bench with a kettle, a packet of Katiyo tea, some mugs and a bottle of milk. Mr Pamberi gestures to the two plastic chairs on the near side of the table.

'Please. Sit! Sit!'

Dad and I sit down.

'So how are the three trainees coming along?' Dad asks.

'Aah! I will tell you everything, everything! But-e-first –' he shakes tea into a metal tea-pot – 'the tea.' He smiles over at me. 'I am of the opinion, Princess Jayne, that-e tea is good for the thinking process.'

'I don't know hey. It hasn't worked for my wife.'

They laugh heartily at Dad's little joke. I stare at Dad, seeing him walking out into the bush. The look on his face when he reappeared. The thought of the homeward journey makes me feel sick. Mr Pamberi puts the tea down on the table and sits down opposite us, smiling away like a young chap who's just made the tea for the first time. I load up on the sugar.

'The project? How's it going?' Dad asks.

'The project,' he pauses and examines his fingertips, 'is good. The workers. Not so good.'

'Why? What's up?'

'One worker is good. He is still here. The others,' he smiles and nods, 'they have gone.'

What's he like when he delivers good news? Does he sing it out opera-style?

'Gone? Where?' asks Dad, king of the two word question.

'One worker, he has gone to pay lobola in Manicaland, he cannot come back for three months,' he smiles, 'at-e least.'

Dad nods encouragingly. 'And the other?'

'The other. He has gone back-eh, to England.'

Dad sits forward. 'Back to England? How?'

'He take the plane.'

Dad sighs, 'No not how he got there. I mean how, how did he afford it? And the visa?'

Mr Pamberi leans forward, 'It seems,' he pauses for effect, 'that this other worker too, he has a wife.'

'What? A wife in England?'

'Yes. A white wife. In England. There by the agricultural college, in Wales.' Mr Pamberi belly laughs, 'Maiwee! Young people these days,' he shakes his head and smiles. Dad looks less amused. He's wearing his patient face. He raises his eyebrows, looks at the ceiling and sighs again.

'I can't believe it. We pay for a young man to go to agricultural college in England –'

'Wales,' corrects Mr Pamberi.

'Okay. Wales,' says Dad, 'and the bloke studies, lives there, at our expense.' Dad jerks his head up and down every few words for impact.

Mr Pamberi continues to smile.

'And after he has finished studying – at our expense. He flies back,' Dad tilts his head sideways, 'again at our expense –'

Mr Pamberi raises his eyebrows and smiles, waiting for Dad's punch line.

'And then? He flies straight back?' Dad tilts his head the other way.

'Eh he, but eh not, Mr Cameron, at our expense! At the expense of the new wife!' Mr Pamberi cracks up, he slaps the table in glee, which makes me jump and makes him laugh even more. And then Dad cracks up too. He laughs more than he's laughed in months, he too slaps the table. He laughs till tears appear in his eyes. He laughs like he's just been released from Ingutsheni. I wouldn't be surprised if Dad and Mr Pamberi leapt up, linked arms and followed the yellow brick road all the way through the irrigation system. Mr

Pamberi leans back in his chair as their laughter subsides, his chubby arms stretched around a belly the width of a small child.

'So!' Dad slaps the table. 'Mr Pamberi, what are we going to do about this – this little problem?'

'Find more workers?'

Dad sighs again. 'And where, Mr Pamberi are we to find these workers? And –' Dad does the raised eyebrows bit again, 'I don't think I'll be able to persuade TTDA to sponsor another romantic break to the UK.'

Mr Pamberi is off again. 'No problem Mr Cameron. I have a nephew – he is very clever. He was educated by the Catholic priests in the missionary school not far from here –'

'Good,' says Dad, 'I hope he took a vow of celibacy.'

Tune in for the laughter, it's like the bloody Goon show.

'No! No! Mr Cameron!' Mr Pamberi clasps the table to help him speak through the tears of his laughter, 'My nephew,' he wheezes, 'my nephew – this one, aaih, maiwee, he's already married.'

'Okay,' says Dad, 'let's hope he sticks to just the one wife hey?' They crack up again.

When the adults finally calm down, we go for a walk through the irrigation project. Mr Pamberi shows us the pump room that looks like some weird engine house and makes strange noises too. This he explains, is the latest in 'clean technology.' He calls out to the young worker Simeon, who, Mr Pamberi explains, has an engineering degree from Manchester University in England and helped in the design of the pump and irrigation system which the development authority are hoping will supply the TTL with constant water for their crops.

'It is so much better here Mr Cameron, at home there is too much torture for the African farmer. Many, many have been brutalised by the terrorist, the burning, the beating the chopping. The children taken away. Too many, even the mother, the grandmother, have died. Here we can be safe.'

We walk back to the bakkie as the sun spreads across the sky like blood in water.

3.

Granny Rose's death comes like a whisper compared to the scream of Carla's. Mom is out at John's school rugby game when Uncle Joe calls. Dad stands in the hallway in the fading light, staring at the wall.

'When?' he says. 'I should have been there. One of us should have been there.'

We all should have been there.

'Wilson? He's a good old boy. Faithful to the end. She was probably happiest with just him.'

'It's Granny Rose isn't it?'

Dad raises an arm and flattens his palm against the cold wall. He pats the wall a few times.

'Ja. This time it's Granny Rose.' He takes a deep rattling breath in and smiles at me with liquid eyes.

Dad and I sit on the couch in the lounge reflected in the curved jade-coloured glass of the TV screen.

'She used to give quite wild parties you know. When we used to stay there, Nessie and I used to climb out the window onto the veranda roof, lie on our tummies and spy on them. One new year we saw Grandpa Patrick dressed as Granny Rose and Granny Rose dressed as Grandpa Patrick. Them and their cross-dressing guests all played cricket on the front lawn. Wilson and Righteous were watching round the side of the house, holding on to each other with laughter, tears were rolling down Righteous's cheeks. At midnight they fired their guns at the moon. In the morning all the flowers from the flamboyant were scattered over the lawn like dead red birds.'

'That's very poetic of you Dad.'

'It's a poetic place though isn't it Bantam?'

'Ja.' I snuggle in close and he kisses me on the ear, and I catch a waft of sweet yeasty beer breath. We sit there, coasting, while the evening slips into night and Dad tells me things I never knew about him and Nessie and Pat when they were kids. He and Nessie were always down at the compound playing with the workers' children, but at about eleven, Dad got embarrassed about his friends at school finding out, so he stopped going.

'I tried to stop Nessie from going too. One night she sneaked out and Dad caught her, so she got sjambokked. The next morning she just sat on her burning rump, eating breakfast as if nothing had happened, calmly asking Dad for the sugar. He thought she'd stop going there after that. But she never did.'

'That's so Nessie. Don't you miss her Dad?'

'Ja,' he sighs out his cigarette smoke.

I want to say more, but then I figure, best I don't. The glow of Dad's cigarette studs the dark with luminous orange and the bottles start to clutter the coffee table.

'She always had a thing for blacks. Defending her students. As far as I know she always stayed in touch with – what was her name. Oh ja. Grace.'

'Grace?'

'Ja. Her childhood friend. One of the labourer's daughters, Lovemore I think his name was. She joined her sociology class. They all joined her class, Justice too. They knew she was sympathetic.' He tips his ash into the mini-tractor wheel and porcelain ashtray on the arm of the couch. 'She's a brilliant teacher. Or so I hear.'

'How did she first meet Justice?'

'We were visiting Granny Rose and Grandpa Patrick one weekend. He pitched up with his mother. They had some complaint or another. She was never happy with her husband working for Grandpa Patrick. Grandpa Patrick sent them packing but Justice came back that night. I woke up – and went to Nessie's room – your room. She was watching out the window. Justice was bleeding –'

'Where?'

'From the chest. He was just holding his hand to his chest and saying something to Grandpa Patrick. When she turned from the window and I looked at her face – her expression – I can't describe it.'

'What were they arguing about? Don't know. He had cheek that boy. There was something disturbing about him. After that, when we were there, she used to go and try to find him. He was studying with the Jesuits so I'm not sure how often she saw him. She became quite – secretive.' He laughs in a regretful sort of way and stares at the ceiling. His face in the twilight looks young and smooth again and I cannot see the grey at his temple. It is not difficult to see him, on the corrugated-iron roof of the veranda, giggling, spying with Nessie, like John and Nakai used to do before their chain was broken, like Dad's was, but not through choice. I wonder how John would have chosen and why some of us choose and some of us don't.

In my room, I stare at Granny Rose's four painted flame lilies on the wall opposite my bed. The flame-like petals seem to me to hold secrets in their cupped interiors. I notice a green bud rising off the stem that I'd always considered a leaf. Drifting off, I envision Justice in her class, watching her walking up and down barefoot, waving her hands in the air, ideas being batted back and forth. Ideas developing later like a scar darkening from pink to purple on a chest.

4.

Mom decides to stay behind in Salisbury with John, so Dad and I travel back to Angel's Peak without them. Dad and I, and Mom and John are like two separate pieces of bread with nothing to fill the space in between now that we've lost Carla. Mom escapes, to Aldie's, to the club, to her meetings even when Dad's around. He too escapes, usually to The Blue Hart. The bleeding heart, the place where soldiers and other men's wives go to forget.

The undercarriage of the car sinks as we clatter onto Birchenough Bridge, her huge steel girders arching gracefully over us. Below, the Sabi River is the colour of chocolate milkshake. My hands sweat as the car carries us closer and closer to Angel's Peak. The urge to run becomes overwhelming. I cannot be there without Carla, without Granny Rose.

'Dad, I think I'm gonna be sick.'

'No wonder. Keep your head up. Unwind the window further – get some air.'

'No, no. I can't.'

Help me, don't make me do it, please.

'We can't stop, Bantam, if you need to be sick, wind down the window.'

'Okay.'

I look down, my stomach churns. 'Dad, can I have a tape on?'

Dad turns the knob. We pass over the bridge, to Clem Tholett's *Because we're all Rhodesians*. I feel a painful tearing at my throat. Laying my head back on the juddering seat, I watch the grey-tinged clouds pile up out the back window while the tears trickle into my ears.

At Christmas Pass we see Umtali cradled in the valley below us, the Vumba Mountains and home rise in the south-east. As we climb the mountains the mist drops like an eagle and the sweet air cools. A dryish tea smell rises in the crisp air. I keep my eyes fixed on Dad's hand on the gearstick. Bumping along the dark dirt road that leads to the farm-house, I look neither to the left nor to the right, I know every tree, every rock on this road and I cannot bear to look at them. Approaching the first gate, I hear the distant sound of a baboon barking and the scattering sound of wings in the trees. I stare at the palms of my upturned hands.

The back door is open. I watch my leg take the final step over the threshold. The smell of old pictures, paint, dog-coat, covers me like a familiar blanket as we walk into the kitchen. I catch sight of Granny Rose's framed roses on the kitchen wall, John's gun in the hallway that he wasn't allowed to bring, part of the poinsettia tree glimpsed through the window and the trees across the back lawn that are now a broken bridge across a gaping hole to a graveyard I don't want to visit.

Wilson stands there like a greying statue at the stove, as if we left him there amongst the ashes of the oven, two years ago.

'Hi Wilson.' I want to throw my arms around him, but obviously I don't.

'You are back. For sure you are back. And you are grown.' He wipes his hands on his fraying apron, they shake slightly. Dad claps his hand on Wilson's shoulder.

May and Nessie stand up from where they have been sitting at the kitchen table smoking, looking at the paper.

Nessie wipes her hands down the front of her jeans several times as if she has just washed her hands then comes over and hugs me, then she goes to hug Dad. But Dad sees her coming and bends down to kiss May on the cheek.

'Hi May. Hello Nessie.'

'Home at last,' Nessie says, lifting her hands in the air then settling them on her waist. She looks at Dad like a child hoping for sweets.

But Dad chills the air. 'I'm off to see Stephen,' he says.

'Better hurry. He's packing his bags,' May says, 'He's going back to New Zealand. Father's died.'

Dad heads out the back door. Nessie follows.

'She's in the library,' May says.

'Who?'

'Mum,' May cackles when I look confused, 'in her coffin, in the library.'

Of course Granny Rose is 'Mum' to her. Even now I find that impossible.

Granny Rose lies in the library in an open ebony-wood coffin with silver handles. She's dressed in her cotton nightie, buttoned up to the neck, her knitted lavender cardigan over the top. Her skin is thin as tracing paper, fine lines river across it under the pinkish-white Max Factor powder. Pale pink blusher and bright pink lipstick over blue lips make her look like a strange doll, not like her at all. Her hands lie over her chest. They look like they have been moulded out of white wax. The rings have been taken off. She wouldn't have liked that. Her eyelids are like pale blue, delicately cut butterfly wings. I touch her cold hands, trying to communicate my feelings for her through my own warm blood. A living Granny Rose moves through my head like a silent black and white film… Granny Rose on her horse, galloping over the fields, the dogs scampering after her…Granny Rose going after May's first boyfriend, with a riding whip after she ran away for the weekend to Salisbury with him. The boy's mother blocked Granny Rose from getting near her son when she stormed their veranda looking for him, so instead she cantered all over the flower beds on their farm. And when she calmed down she asked May, *Why on earth didn't you go to Beira for a weekend's adventure?*

I've decided not to go to the funeral. Instead I walk through the trees where we used to play and summon up the voices of Enoch, Nakai and John so well in my imagination that I scare myself and break in to a run until I find myself at the base of the lucky-bean tree. No flowers carpet the ground. The tree is as bare and lifeless as a sculpture of itself. The books are still there in the crook of the tree that is like a shelf, their pages yellowy and drowned and bloated from the rains. Long John Silver and the ship are unrecognisable. I do not enter the compound, but walk out into the bush. From a smooth, round rock that emerges from the high grasses like an elephant's rump, I weep without noise, tears dripping over my arms onto my jeans and splashing into the rock. Near the base of the mountain tall cabbage trees raise their fuzzy microphone-shaped heads beyond the river. I do not sense Carla with me, like people say about loved ones and I cannot bear to think of her voice so I try not to. Her spirit is not here. She must be somewhere else. Across the valley I see an eagle, circling high above the granite peaks. It flies high up and vanishes into the white hot sun.

After the funeral, the house is swamped and it's hotter than blazes, even with all the fans turning. It feels as if the vultures have swooped in. May and a whole bunch of yabbering ladies from neighbouring farms and from town are crammed into the kitchen, ordering Wilson around and preparing food for everyone to stuff their faces with. Mrs Roberts from Staple Farm Supplies pushes her wing-framed glasses up her nose, and smiles sympathetically at me while holding a butter-knife mid-air, then continues to cut bread with a reddish, farm-wifey hand. I haven't seen her since before she lost her son when her husband's bakkie detonated a land mine. Granny Rose would hate having all these people here. *There's too many flies in this kitchen. Buzz off!* she'd say. Imagining Granny Rose pulling into the kitchen with a big can of Killem and spraying them all dead makes me smile. In the lounge, the guests are eating Willard's ripple chips and bits of pineapple and cheese on cocktail sticks with cherries on the end. They part like the red sea as I walk through them. Their thoughts are transmitted to me loud and clear, *poor girl losing her sister like that... she must be thinking about her... I heard they raped her first...they were bayoneted...*Stuff yourself folks, for you too may die at any moment.

'Hello Jayne,' says Mrs Viljoen through her thick-red-lipsticked mouth, 'you must be desperately sad at the moment.'

'Thanks,' I say, thinking, I'm desperately sorry that you're here and why the frikus are you? Mom's not even here.

'You're such a pretty young woman now,' she says, lifting a leg and adjusting a red strappy high heel. She looks like a woman keen to squeeze every drop of action out of any occasion, disco, farmers' fair, funeral, whatever. Outside, in the blaze of afternoon, I sit on my rock, my back to the house and veranda full of guests, hugging my knees and looking out over the tree canopy towards the hazy blue mountains that push into Mozambique.

Dad walks onto the lawn with Uncle Pat and Auntie Gail. Nessie comes down the veranda steps and hugs Uncle Pat who puts one arm around his brother and another round his sister. Auntie Gail puts her arm around Dad and they walk towards me. I wonder what Nessie and Dad spoke about when they disappeared after Dad went to speak to the no longer farm manager Stephen.

'It feels like the end of an era,' Auntie Gail says, as they get closer to me; her shoulder length steel-grey hair and brown kaftan stir in the breeze. The sun shines.

'It is,' says Nessie.

'Like hell,' says Dad, reaching out for me, 'I'm holding on.'

'Hope you've got strong teeth and nails then,' says Nessie.

'You don't change do you Nessie,' Dad says, unsmiling.

'I try not to.'

'This family could blow up in your face and you'd remain committed to your bloody cause wouldn't you?'

Auntie Gail puts her hand on Dad's arm. For once Nessie doesn't say anything. She turns and walks away, the little bells on her black gypsy skirt jingling.

'Have I finally broken her?' Dad asks.

Auntie Gail follows Nessie, but Nessie raises her arm when she sees her coming, so Auntie Gail turns back. I get up and put my arms around Dad's waist, watching Nessie's back as she walks towards the dairy.

'Can we not have this Dave? Today?' Auntie Gail says. 'She's trying so hard.'

'Her guilt will not bring back my daughter.'

'Neither will your hate,' Gail says.

Dad stares at the ground for a moment, flicks his cigarette high into the valley and then walks away.

'Don't speak to him like that! How can you know how he feels?' The words shock me. I wasn't expecting to say them.

Auntie Gail holds out her hand to me, but I turn and run back down to my rock and fix my eyes on the aloes and yellow and black striped cacti below me in the valley and at the red-hot pokers that seem to scrape at the sky. Out of the corner of my eye I can see where Nessie has dug out an oblong of earth to plant a new rose-bush in memory of Granny Rose. I try not to look at the young willow tree that Nessie planted for Carla sweeping down towards the valley like a green waterfall reflecting her beautiful, gone grace.

5.

Granny Rose's room smells of Yardley and mothballs. I cannot sleep in my old room, so I'm sleeping in here, with Nessie, in the king-size teak bed from Burma that Carla and I used to pretend was a ship when we were little.

Nessie comes back from the bathroom in one of Grandpa Patrick's shirts. She sits down on the bed.

'Do you think it's a bit morbid? Sleeping in here?' she laughs.

'No. It makes me feel close to her,' I say, moving slightly in the hope that she'll take her arm off my leg. I shift and Nessie gets up and goes round the other side of the bed and leans up against the headboard, one leg raised. The curtains bloom behind us, the faint wind carries with it the scent of roses. 'Okay Jay. Let me tell you a story. Once Granny Rose told me how Wilson rescued her from certain death in the old pantry that used to be attached to the kitchen. Remember? I think she was putting the eggs into the water glass. Maybe it was the fumes from the sulphur that she had lit to cure the ham haunches she'd hung, or the lure of the sausages strung up from the rafters, who knows? Granny Rose said that when she pulled out the huge tin box of eggs, a cobra darted out from his hiding place behind the tin box and bit her on the forearm. She must have screamed, because Wilson came running in from the kitchen. He took her arm and began sucking and spitting, sucking and spitting, where the two red fang marks were. He didn't even look around to check where the snake was, though Granny Rose said it "vanished into the sunlight".'

Nessie pauses to knot her hair at the nape of her neck. Her musky perfume masks the faint fragrance of Yardley.

'There was no chance of getting a doctor, it would have taken hours by horse and cart to get to the nearest doctor in Umtali. Granny Rose would have died on the journey and anyway Grandpa Patrick was away on business. So Wilson sucked all the poison out of Granny Rose's arm, and then Granny Rose fainted. Wilson carried her to her bedroom and laid her out, covered her with the quilt and then sat next to her, waiting for her to wake up. This was as much as Granny Rose ever told me, but Mum filled me in. May said that on that day, she and Uncle Joe were down at the river –' Nessie turns onto her side to face me, plumping up her pillows. 'When they came in at six and found the house all quiet they guessed something was up. In Granny Rose's bedroom, they found Wilson leaning over her. Later, when Uncle Joe asked why Granny Rose was hugging Wilson, she said that he was just adjusting the bed covers, but they shouldn't tell Grandpa Patrick in case he got cross, and if anyone told him, she'd make sure she got old Mr Van Rensburg to sjambok them. But May says she saw Granny Rose's arm around Wilson's shoulders and from where she was standing, she was sure she saw their faces touching. Anyway, they were really scared of old Mr Van and his sjambok, so no-one ever told Grandpa Patrick about Wilson being in Granny Rose's room, though of course Granny Rose had to tell him about the snake, the marks were there plain to see, on the inside of her arm.'

'I never saw them,' I say, remembering Wilson taking the first-aid kit into Granny Rose's room after the attack.

'Well you would have had to have looked.'

'Why are you telling me this now? To upset me?'

'Would it upset you that Granny Rose may have had feelings for Wilson?'

'Like you've got feelings for Justice?'

'Or you for Enoch.'

'That's not true Nessie, he was my friend.'

'Was?'

'Yes. Was. Did he help kill my sister?'

Nessie sits up and folds her long brown legs.

'I don't think so Jay.'

'You don't think so? How about a straight answer?'

'Okay. I don't believe so.' I remember what Justice said. *Inside she is warm.*

'I heard you and Justice, together, in their mother's house just before the attack.'

'So many things you've kept silent about,' she says.

I turn to her shaking my head. 'Rich or what?'

'So young, so cynical.'

'Made to be.'

'Dad told me about you and Justice as kids – and about Grace. She's an old friend of yours isn't she? Did Grandpa Patrick attack him?'

Nessie smiles. 'In a manner of speaking.' She reaches a hand out towards me. I don't take it.

'Can you just give me straight answers? What happened to him?'

'That's his story.'

I sigh and shake my head. 'You all went to the same school didn't you? The Cryptic School. What about Auntie Penny?'

'That was an accident. She was drunk at the time, she'd been taking money from the business and giving it to Prospect. They were involved with each other Jay. When Joe found out, there was a row between them and – well she shot herself – I don't know whether she intended to or not. It was pinned on Prospect. They went for him after the Ferreira garage robbery. He wasn't even there, they made the worker *confess* that he was. They picked him up and stuck him in Chikarubi.'

'Poor Glen. Where's Enoch's mom – Prospect's wife?'

'In Mozambique. She's very revered you know.' She twists a silver and turquoise ring on her hand. Hands that have touched Justice.

'Ja. I'm sure she threw the bones and told them when the best time to attack would be.'

'Jay. It doesn't have to be like this. We have to build together. We can't take old mindsets with us.'

Her elves' eyes are sparkling, her long black hair is all sheeny in the glow of the bedside lamp.

'I've always loved you Jay.'

I laugh. 'I don't think love for you is the same as for other people.'

'You're cruel Jay.'

'Maybe I've been made cruel by what's happened to me. What was it you said? Violence gives birth to violence? Well cruelty gives birth to cruelty.'

She shifts closer to me on the bed. Her face is flushed, her pupils blocking out the green of her irises. The black tendrils of the hair on her temples are damp.

'Birth is violent. This country is giving birth to another. But after the violence of birth comes growth.'

'Oh. I thought it was enslavement that came next. Let's just forgive and forget hey?'

She puts her hands down, sighs and gets into bed.

'Yes. Let's.' She gets under the blankets. 'You'll come round.'

The room glows in the pinkish glow of the dawn. My head feels full and heavy, my thoughts like soldiers marching this way and that. Skeletons rattle in the wardrobe in front of us and voices haunt me, Enoch's, Carla's, Granny Rose's, Dad's, till I'm convinced I've gone penga. I imagine Granny Rose rising from her coffin in the library and wandering around the house. When the birds get louder and the room floods with light, I slip out of the house and glide through the dense mist hovering above the lawn like dry ice and sit shivering, hugging my legs on my rock. The tips of the mauve mountains are just visible above the swirling cloud. I talk to Carla till the mist lifts over the canopy of the trees in the valley and the voices stop.

6.

At three 'o clock what is real tugs away like a balloon from a child's hand and what is unreal settles like dust. This is how it feels as the remainder of my family sit in a block of sunshine on the veranda listening to the sound of Godfrey mowing the lawn and the oblivious doves cooing *coo-coo-roo, coo-coo-roo*.

'You know why we're all here, Jay?'

'Ja. Mom, I think we all know.'

'Your Dad and I have decided to separate.'

My mother scissors her legs and tugs her hands through her hair. She takes a drag of her cigarette, then looks at her hands that shake slightly to the hum of her inner chaos.

'No kidding? You've been sep-a-rate, for a long time.'

John starts to cry. Mom hugs him to her.

'We're going to live in South Africa, Auntie Aldie is coming too. I'd like you to come with us.'

'So it's a double act? Hey, let's leave our husbands for the bright lights.'

I look at Dad on the other side of the table. He takes a deep breath, when he breathes out his breath shudders, like an old machine gun that can no longer fire. He looks down at his empty glass.

'Jayne. Do you want to live in a country run by Marxist terrorists?'

'Changing your tune again Mom? Well, I've lived in a country run by hypocrites and half-wits,' I say hooking my toes over the cane edging of the veranda table.

'I'm not leaving. I won't go and live in a country run by racialist redneck Afrikaners,' I say folding my arms. 'I'm staying. With Dad.'

'That's a bit of a generalisation Jayne.'

'Ja. I learnt that stuff here.'

She sighs.

'Well that's it then,' She waves her cigarette in the air, conducting her final tune.

The axe comes down from on high and splits the table in two, leaving two halves, Mom and John on one side, me and Dad on the other. John cries silently.

'Dave? Did you know about this?' Mom asks, putting her arm around John.

Dad looks up from lighting his cigarette. He's leaning forward, his elbows just above his knees. 'First I've heard about it.'

The words seem heavy and hard to get out.

'Jayne. You'll have the chance of a decent education in South Africa, you need your mother.'

'Ja. I need my father too. My country. I'm not going. I've decided. This is where I belong.'

Dad gives me a watery smile through his cigarette smoke. When he inhales he takes in a quarter of the cigarette.

'So. I must lose both my daughters,' she says getting up.

'Your choice Mom,' I say.

We watch as John runs across the lawn towards the pine tree near the gate, its branches like a climbing frame reaching to the sky.

In my room, John leans against me on the bed and cries and cries.

'I don't know what I'll do without you Jay.'

'Hey John, I'll come and visit you.'

'No you won't. You hate Mom.'

'No I don't. I love her really. I'm cross with her, that's all.'

John's face brightens. His dark hair is wavy and the flecks of hazel in his green eyes make them look like semi-precious stones in his tanned face.

'Ja. We shot terrs together didn't we Jay?' His eyes glisten.

The dusting of freckles around his nose look so vulnerable, they make me want to cry. I force the lump back down, but like a cork in water, it keeps bobbing up again.

'Ja, John. We'll always be joined. I promise I'll write lots and visit, okay?'

'And phone?' he says hopefully.

'And phone,' I smile.

After he's left I lie face-down on my bed soaking the pillow, wondering whether she ever thought of asking Sheldon to counsel her on her crumbling marriage. My mother's face as she fired out over the black lawn, comes back to haunt me, the glass shattering behind her like jagged halos. I loved her so much during that time; she was prepared to kill for us. And now she's ready to leave her husband without a fight. Divorce too, is like death. It'll rot John inside. Like it's fermented my love for her.

1980

Harare,
Zimbabwe

25.

After the rains have cleared, I walk from the bus stop towards First Street to meet Nessie at Barbour's cafe. All Nessie's predictions came true. Salisbury is now Harare, the freedom fighters are in power with Mugabe on the throne. The lift doors open and I walk towards Lord Kitchener. I'll buy Mel a pressie from here for her engagement, maybe Glen too, as if he'd ever wear Kitchener clothes. Mel was worried I'd be upset about the engagement because of Carls, even though I tell everyone they can talk about her. I talk about her now. I have to. I want Mel to be happy, hell, I want to be a bridesmaid. Besides, Dad is moving back to Angel's Peak and May is going with him. They're going to clear land for coffee planting. So we're going to farm tea and coffee. I'll live with Nessie while I finish school here and go home for all my holidays. Wilson will still do the cooking, and Patience is coming to help in the house along with Godfrey who'll take care of the garden and help with the coffee too.

Nessie's sitting at our usual concrete table in the corner. With her is Grace who lifts her hand and waves. Her hair has changed again, short at the sides and swept up geometrically. Red plastic earrings I've seen before. She wears a ZANU PF t-shirt. Opposite her, with his back to me is an African man in a suit. When he swivels in his chair to face me, my heart thrashes around my chest like a hooked fish. His hair is shaved off so that his cheekbones rise up out of the planes of his face like shelves below those wide apart, long-lashed eyes as deep as ink-wells. He smiles at me as if I had arranged to meet him.

Nessie eases herself out from where she is sitting next to Grace with her back to the wall.

'Want a Coke float?' Nessie asks.

'No. I don't want a Coke float,' I say rolling my eyes as I turn to leave.

'I'll just get you a Coke,' Nessie says into my ear, her hand on my arm. 'They have something they want to say. Please sit down, just for a minute.'

Enoch gets up and indicates the chair next to him. He puts a Madison in his mouth and offers me one.

'No thanks,' I say, sitting down and folding my arms around my canvas shoulder bag. No one speaks. These are not people that comment on the weather, the drinks, the service.

'I'm sorry about your sister,' says Grace eventually.

'Really? Why?'

I listen to the sound of pedestrian feet in the concourse below, and to the traffic getting heavier in the avenues.

'Yes really.'

'How are you sorry? Whose side were you on?'

'I am a freedom fighter. I was, I am, on the side of freedom.'

'Ja, but whose side were you on?'

'Comrade Mugabe is my commander.'

I turn to Enoch. 'And you?'

'I was in Tanzania. I went there after I left Mozambique.'

'Ja and we all know what you learnt there.'

'I learnt many things. How to move forward.'

'Really? I think I will have a Madison.' I take up the red and white packet off the table and take out a cigarette hoping he can't see that my hand is shaking.

He lights my cigarette.

'Who were you with?' I exhale.

'We are all comrades together.'

'Did your commander teach you how to shoot down aircraft?' I laugh sarcastically and take another drag.

He touches my hand, with his long gentle fingers. I snatch mine away, remembering the news footage, how Nkomo supposedly laughed and said, *it was a military aircraft.*

'I did not kill your sister.'

'No. But your friends did. Didn't they Grace?' Grace is leaning towards me, trying to draw me in with her eyes. I think of Carla, how she turned to me and smiled as she walked to her death. I start to get up.

Enoch stands up. His chest is close to mine, my eyes level with his neck so that I smell his clean soap smell mixed with something else, the smell of him. He puts a hand on my arm. Nessie is coming through the patio doors. With her is a tall African man, his hair no longer in little twists, but grown out into dreadlocks; he too is wearing a suit, but I recognise him straight away even though he walks with a limp. With him is another man.

'This is Morgan,' Nessie says, introducing a smallish African man in a suit wearing round, metal-framed glasses.

'I ordered you a toasted cheese and tomato in case you're hungry.'

I laugh. 'You've ordered me a cheese and tomato sandwich? You think I feel like eating?'

Nessie smiles her determined smile. 'Jay, please sit down.'

Justice sits down opposite me, he takes an Everest out of his top pocket, taps it on the table and lights it without taking his eyes off me. I start to turn away again.

'Wait, please,' says Grace. 'I lost three brothers and a sister, two of my brothers were killed by Rhodesian soldiers, another was killed accidentally in Mozambique. The Rhodesian army said, 'Sorry, wrong place, wrong time.'

I look at Grace. Her face betrays no emotion.

A smiling waiter puts my sandwich and Coke down on the table.

I say tatenda, but push the sandwich away as soon as he leaves. 'You're a commander aren't you?' I ask Justice. 'That's why my Uncle Bob's unit tracked you. That's why they came into Mozambique to find you –'

He keeps his gaze steady on my face as he smokes, showing no emotion.

'Morgan lost his whole family, burnt to death in their village.

The hut burnt down with four generations of the family in it.'

I stare at Grace.

'No this time it wasn't the Rhodesians, it was comrades,' she smiles at Morgan, and then at me. 'He was accused of informing the Rhodesians – it was a mistake – Morgan's family are loyal comrades.' Breath snorts through my nose. Bloody idiots. More mistakes. *Comrades.* It sounds so stupid.

I sit down. Nessie sits down next to Justice opposite me. I drink my Coke, jabbing my straw up and down between sips.

'You paralysed my sister's boyfriend, my uncle dragged him out of that hotel,' I say to Justice.

'I have looked your uncle in the eyes and he is a man of boldness. He is welcome to join us on the same side in our new Zimbabwe.'

'Thanks, I'm sure he'd love to,' I say scornfully.

'There are many turncoats in your uncle's special unit. Your uncle will understand the new conditions.'

'Like hell.'

'White Rhodesia killed my father, my friends.' He places his hands on the table and moves his upper body towards me. 'I could not attend my father's funeral.'

'There are, were African soldiers in the Rhodesian army you know. Not all the Africans are on your side.' I move my chair back, it screeches like nails on a blackboard. I look round. 'You all knew about it. Should I be grateful that you checked my flight?' I ask Nessie. 'That you warned me?' I glare at Enoch, then snatch another cigarette from his packet.

Justice continues to smoke and look at me as if what I am saying is of no consequence whatsoever.

'Why did you do it?' I ask Justice.

'When I looked inside my father's body. I found the answers there,' Justice says.

'It was an act of war,' Enoch says quietly. 'It was not my want that anyone should suffer.'

His eyes lock with his brother's. I grip the table with my hands.

'When your forces shot us in our camps and buried us in ditches – that was an act of war – hundreds of women – elsewhere many children died too. Just because they were not on holiday – is this a problem?' Justice says looking me in the eye. 'White Rhodesia killed your sister.'

Nessie puts her hand on his arm. The blood in my face drains. Pale white heat takes its place.

'You attacked our farm.'

'All the farms were to be attacked.' He grinds his cigarette in the ashtray.

'I saw you that night, loading weapons into Nessie's car. Were those the weapons you used to attack our farm?'

'They were for an operation.' He takes another cigarette out of his packet and taps the cigarette on the table.

'A farm I suppose?' I look him in the eye.

'Do you think we could not have killed you all that night? It was our intention to get you off our land.'

Getting up I say, 'Thanks for the education Nessie.'

'Please sit down Jay,' Nessie pleads.

The light shifts and rain begins to fall on the concourse outside.

'No,' says Justice, 'she won't sit down with terrorists, she's a white Rhodesian.'

'I can't help the colour of my skin.' I watch the rain dripping off the concrete walls.

'But you can help the colour of your thoughts – your actions,' he says. 'Until you can sit down with us, how can we have a future?' He crosses his legs and watches me as if I'm on stage.

Enoch takes my hand. I watch as it squeezes mine and I think of the day Wilson squeezed my hand before I left. I sit back down, folding my arms. The distant traffic slashes across the wet roads.

'Let me tell you a story,' Justice says, leaning forwards and clasping his hands on the table. 'One day there was a wise woman who lived on some land. The same land on which her ancestors had lived, land the chiefs had apportioned her family to live on for many generations. A day came when a white man came to the village and said that he owned the land and the people must leave, or alternatively they could work for him.'

He folds his arms and sits back slightly in his chair, enjoying the way he says 'alternatively' and the attention of his audience.

'The people were angry and consulted the chief. But the chief said there was nothing he could do. Since the days when the Europeans had come with guns and defeated their leaders and made them pay hut tax for their huts built by their own hands their old way of living was taken from them. Now they had to pay one way or another for living on the land of their fathers.'

I raise my eyebrows. 'And?'

'That man was your grandfather and that woman –'

'Your grandmother?' I widen my eyes sarcastically at him and jab at the Coke with my straw.

He nods his head slowly a few times too many. 'Correct.'

'I know what you're trying to *say* Justice, that your family owned the land before us, so it belongs to them. But we built up that land, made it fertile, farmed it –'

'And we did not farm? Our pumpkins, our beans?'

'Okay. The houses and the business – the tea are ours. Our lives have been spent on that land for three generations. We've loved the land. You can't blame us for what happened with our grandparents.'

'So who must take account?'

'Do you expect us just to hand over all we've worked for?' I stare at the cold, hard concrete of the table.

'You are alive here.'

'No I'm not.' I snort. 'Leaving our farm – being forced off our land destroyed us.'

'Yes. It has destroyed all of us. Maybe now you can understand,' Justice says. Morgan kisses out his lips and nods his head. He reminds me of a reverend.

'So what is the solution?' Enoch says.

'To share the land,' I say to the table.

Justice claps his hands in the air like a flamenco dancer. 'That is the solution.'

Oh ja. Really simple.

'Well people would have to be trained, to prove themselves, or else be given a small section for them and their families –' I say.

'Colleges can be built to train people –' Grace says.

'Ja. Well let's hope so hey.' I turn to Justice. 'Are you going to train people first before you divide up the land? It's not easy running a tobacco farm. It's hard graft, but it's what floats the economy.'

'You sound just like your father Jay,' Nessie laughs.

'Where there is only one fruit, it needs to be shared and its seeds must be planted in the ground,' Enoch says.

'Ja but who's going to plant them in the ground? Things don't just grow by themselves.' Apart from hatred. I get up again.

'We have a bright future Jay.' Nessie gets up and comes over to hug me.

How bloody annoying it is when she says that. Lovely Nessie, what a beautiful traitor she is.

'Can't I give you a lift?'

'No thanks, I'll take the bus,' I swing my canvas bag onto my shoulder, with its picture of Lord Kitchener on it, his finger pointing, "*We want you.*"

Justice gets up and I glimpse the edge of his scar through his open shirt. I can't imagine him planting anything.

'How did you get that scar?' I ask.

'An old man tried to whip me with a sjambok, so I took my own knife and opened my chest so that my blood would drip into the ground of my people. During the war it was there – like the mark in the ground a white farmer makes to plant –'

'A furrow,' Nessie says, gazing up at him like a chick at a rugby match.

'You mean my grandfather. Did he still whip you?'

'No. He did not.'

And then he laughs a deep rumbling belly-laugh like Moses'. And everyone else laughs too, except me, because I'm convinced he's mad even though he speaks some truth in riddles like the joker. Grace stands and says goodbye. Morgan stands and puts out his hand, I put my hand on his and he puts his other hand on top, moving it up and down.

'Fambai zvkanaka,' he says.

'Ja, you go well too,' I say.

Justice gets up, nods at me, then brushes flecks of ash off his suit.

'I will be coming to see you,' Enoch whispers in my ear as he gets up. I smell his sweet warm porridge-scented breath and feel his warm hand between my shoulder blades. I raise my eyebrow at him and without looking back, head towards the lift and down into Robert Mugabe Avenue.

Author's Note

After the Rains was inspired by events that took place in the 1970s, during the Rhodesia/Zimbabwe civil war. Some of those events appear in this book, though I have used artistic license in my portrayal of them. Though the families and characters are fictitious, you may recognise the names and occasional comments made by some of the key political figures of the time.

During my research, I read a variety of historical publications and personal accounts of those who fought in a variety of ways, on both sides of the war. I am grateful that these accounts are widely available. However, I would like to acknowledge *Selous Scouts, Top Secret War* by Lt.Col Ron Reid Daly as told to Peter Stiff. I hope that former Scouts and other members of the fighting units will tolerate my fictional accounts if they happen upon this book. I have tried to remain true to those that have inspired me in various ways, and there are many, on both sides. *Rhodesians Never Die: The Impact of War and Political Change on White Rhodesia c 1970-1980* by Peter Godwin and Ian Hancock, is, in my view, essential reading for anyone wishing to write about this period of Zimbabwe's history. *A Short Thousand Years* by Paul Moorcroft, was helpful too. In the cathedral scene in the third section of the book, the words of the sermon belong to the Right Reverend J.R da Costa, Dean of Salisbury, given in the Cathedral of St. Mary and All Saints in Salisbury, Rhodesia, on 8 September, 1978, at the memorial service following the Kariba air disaster.

Amongst many others, I would particularly like to thank Laetitia for her editorial input over the years and for her support of my work.

Special thanks to Richard and Luellen for their kindness, and to Vimbai for her help with Shona terms. Also thanks to my parents - Johanne, for her keen eyes and wisdom, and Paul, for sharing his stories. Finally, deepest thanks to Simon, for his unfailing encouragement and belief in me.

www.emilybarroso.co.uk

Glossary

Af: African

Ag: see/look; said for emphasis, as in 'Ag, no man,' or to imply weariness, woe or sympathy (Afrikaans)

Aikona: means no (Shona)

Arvie: afternoon

Avo: avocado

Bakkie: small pickup

Bobotie: dish made from mince, egg and curry (Afrikaans)

Boet: brother (Afrikaans)

Biltong: dried meat, South-African/Zimbabwean snack

Blek: black (Afrikaans)

Boerewors/wors: farmers sausage (Afrikaans)

Bok/ke: buck/s (Afrikaans)

Bols: brand of brandy

Bombed: drunk

Braai/braai vleis: barbeque/barbeque meat (Afrikaans)

Brookies: girls underwear

Chimurenga: revolution/war of liberation (Shona)

Chibuku: African brand of beer sold in cartons in Rhodesia/Zimbabwe

Chikarubi: maximum security prison Rhodesia/Zimbabwe

China: friend

Choka: full

Chommie: buddy

Chongololo: black centipede found in Zimbabwe (from the Shona chongororo)

Christmas Beetles: noisy bush beetles

Cook boy: African home cook

Curry muncher: derogatory term for an Asian Indian

Dagga: Marijuana (Afrikaans)

Dassie: guinea-pig like animal

Doek: head scarf (Afrikaans)

Dof: thick/stupid (Afrikaans)

Dop: drink (Afrikaans)

Doos: vulgar term with various meanings: idiot, in this case (Afrikaans)

Domkop: thickhead/dumbhead (Afrikaans)

Donner: hit/beat up

Doro: beer (Shona)

Dozies: sleepy types/dozy twits

Einah: expression of pain (from the Afrikaans eina)

Ek se: I say (Afrikaans)

Eweh: you (from the Shona iwe)

Frekked: dead/killed (Afrikaans)

Frik/us: mild form of the 'F' word

Frikkie: nerd (Afrikaans boys name)

Gee cee em: mild expletive

Gooi: throw (Afrikaans)

Gogo: grandmother (Ndebele)

Granadilla: passion fruit

Hau: expression of surprise, as in 'How can this be?'

Hoik: pull up

Hondo: war (Shona)

Hose: laugh

Howzit: 'How are you?'

Hurling: vomiting

Hwai: sheep (Shona)

Ingutsheni: mental hospital in Bulawayo/Zimbabwe

Ja: yes (Afrikaans)

Jeez: mild expletive/expression of shock or surprise

Jobbie: poo

Kaffir: derogatory term for a black person

Kak: shit (Afrikaans)

Kaya: servants quarters

Kif: cool or nice

Klup/kluping: hit or smack/hitting

Kotching: vomiting

Lamie: punch

Lekker: delicious, nice, something good (Afrikaans)

Madala: old man (from the Shona word, mudhara)

Maiwee: from amai/mother, expression of shock, surprise or pain (Shona)

Mazoe: orange juice/orange-growing region of Rhodesia/Zimbabwe

Mealie: corn on the cob

Miggies: little flies/insects (Afrikaans)

Moff/moffie: gay guy

Mombie: cow (from the Shona mombe)

Mujiba: look out/informer for the freedom fighters, during the chimurenga war (Shona)

Munt: person; can be used in a derogatory way by whites towards blacks (from the Shona munhu)

Mush/Mushie sterek: nice/very nice

Muti: medicine (Shona)

Neos: felt tip pens

Niks: nothing (Afrikaans)

Nganga: witchdoctor (from the Shona n'anga)

Nyama: meat (Shona)

Ous: blokes, guys

Okes: as above

Omo: washing powder

Owie: expression of pain used by kids

Panga: machete; sometimes used as a weapon

Pawpaw: papaya

Penga: mad (Shona)

Pom: British person, derogatory

Porks: Portuguese people, derogatory

Rondavel: round, thatched hut (from the Afrikaans rondawel)

Rooibos: red bush tea (Afrikaans)

Sadza: a thickened porridge eaten with the hands (Shona)

Shebeen: illegal drinking den

Sis: expression of disgust (from the Afrikaans word sies)

Sjambok: whip (Afrikaans)

Skellum: scoundrel or rascal; often used in an affectionate way towards kids (Afrikaans)

Skrik: fright (Afrikaans)

Slops/slip-slops: flip-flops

Soapie: soap opera

Sozzling: drinking to get drunk

Stoep: outside area, similar to veranda, but often uncovered and at the back of the house

Stompies: cigarette butts

Stovies/stovepipes: skinny jeans

Swikiro: rainmaker (from the Shona, svikiro)

Tackies: sports shoes or trainers

Terrs: terrorists

Toke: a hit (inhalation) of a cigarette or joint

Troopies: soldiers

Vakomana: boys, freedom fighters (Shona)

Veld: African grassland/plain (Afrikaans)

Veldskoens/velies: suede bush shoes (Afrikaans)

Voetsak: bugger off (Afrikaans)

Voos: angry (Afrikaans)

Vrot: rotten, drunk (Afrikaans)